The Sp
Summer Seduction

KIM LAWRENCE
CATHY WILLIAMS
MAGGIE COX

Published in Great Britain 2013
by Mills & Boon, an imprint of Harlequin (UK) Limited,
Eton House, 18-24 Paradise Road, Richmond, Surrey TW9 1SR

ISBN: 978 0 263 90557 1
ebook ISBN: 978 1 472 00130 6

05-0613

Harlequin (UK) policy is to use papers that are natural, renewable and recyclable products and made from wood grown in sustainable forests. The logging and manufacturing processes conform to the legal environmental regulations of the country of origin.

Printed and bound in Spain
by Blackprint CPI, Barcelona

UNDER THE SPANIARD'S LOCK AND KEY

BY
KIM LAWRENCE

Kim Lawrence lives on a farm in rural Anglesey. She runs two miles daily and finds this an excellent opportunity to unwind and seek inspiration for her writing! It also helps her keep up with her husband, two active sons, and the various stray animals which have adopted them. Always a fanatical consumer of fiction, she is now equally enthusiastic about writing. She loves a happy ending!

CHAPTER ONE

SUSAN Ward manoeuvred herself down the ramp into the kitchen, her daughter and husband protectively shadowing her progress.

Propping her crutches against the chair her husband pulled out, Susan lowered herself into her seat, ignoring her nearest and dearest as they hovered anxiously.

Maggie, watching the procedure apprehensively, released a relieved sigh when her mum was safely seated. 'You're getting pretty good on those things, Mum,' she observed, privately concerned that she was also far too ambitious. It was lucky her dad was now retired from his job on the oil rigs so was around to keep an eye on things when she wasn't.

It had been three months since the experimental surgery, but to see her mum, who had been confined to a wheelchair for the last eighteen years, on her feet even for short periods still gave Maggie a thrill.

And now, if things went according to plan, in a couple of months she would no longer need the chair or even the crutches.

Susan dismissed the comment and turned her frowning regard on her daughter, who took a seat opposite. 'Never mind that, how are *you* feeling? *Really* feeling,' she added, holding up her hand in anticipation of her daughter's reply.

'She looks exhausted, doesn't she, John?' She appealed to her husband for support.

John Ward's warm glance swept his daughter's pale face, touching the warm dark ebony curls that clustered around her heart-shaped face. 'She looks beautiful.'

Oh, well, Maggie reflected, at least I have got one fan even if he is my dad. 'Thank you, though according to you I was beautiful when I was twenty pounds too heavy, had teenage acne and braces,' she reminded him.

'Don't change the subject, Maggie,' her mother said sternly.

'I told you, I'm fine, Mum,' she replied, pasting a determinedly cheerful smile on her face to illustrate the level of her fineness.

She had perfected the 'I'm fine' smile a long time ago, because no matter how bad her day had been Maggie had always been pretty sure growing up that her mum's had been worse.

This conviction dated from the day when her dad had returned home from the hospital with her baby brother and no Mum—she had been four at the time.

Her other brother Ben, at the noisy toddler stage, had run around the room while John Ward sat with baby Sam in his arms and explained to Maggie that Mum would not be coming home yet and when she did Maggie would have to be a big girl and help her because Mum was not well.

Maggie had only vaguely understood the explanation of what was wrong with her mother, but she had known it was bad because her big strong dad didn't cry.

The tears had scared her and made her feel sick inside. She had begged him to stop crying, and promised that if he did she would never *ever* be a bad girl.

Of course she had not been able to keep that promise, but

the determination that had been born that day to protect her mum and stop her dad crying had never left her.

Compared with what her mum had coped with, a broken engagement and a cancelled wedding faded into insignificance.

'Seriously, I am fine,' Maggie promised in response to the sceptical looks directed her way as she anchored her heavy dark hair at the nape of her neck with one hand and accepted the mug of coffee her father passed her. 'I'm just sorry about messing everyone about this way,' she added, her brow furrowing as she tried to calculate how much her parents had already laid out on the wedding.

It was easier to address the practicalities of the situation than think about what an idiot she had been. 'All that money,' she fretted.

'Forget the money,' her father said firmly. 'That's not important—' He broke off mid sentence as the door opened to let in a cold gust of air and two young men in muddy rugby kit.

They ignored their sister, grunted in the direction of their father and mother before heading for the fridge.

'Glass, Sam,' Susan said out of habit as her younger son raised a carton of milk to his lips.

He lowered the carton and said, 'We lost, if anyone's interested.'

His older and slightly more intuitive brother nudged him with his elbow and removed the pad he was holding to his own cut lip. 'They're not interested, Sam. So what's up, guys?'

Maggie got to her feet. Telling her parents had been bad enough—they at least, bless them, had not asked any awkward questions even though she knew they were dying to. She could not, however, rely on her brothers to be similarly restrained. 'Nothing. That lip could do with a stitch,' she added, casting an expert eye over her brother's mouth.

Ben rolled his eyes and, taking the carton from his brother, took a swig of milk before subjecting his sister to an equally critical narrow eyed stare. 'Sure. You *always* look like death warmed up.'

'I've just worked a ten-night stretch in a busy casualty department,' Maggie reminded him.

'So?' Ben retorted, looking unimpressed. 'Nothing new there—you always work crazy hours. You have to be certifiably insane to be a nurse.'

'Thanks.' Maggie's mouth twisted into a grim little smile.

Simon had called her the *perfect nurse.* The recollection sent her stomach muscles into tight unpleasant spasm, though, to be totally accurate, apparently Simon had been quoting his mother, the possessive Mrs Greer, whom Maggie had found to be manipulative and very overprotective of her only child, when he said this.

She resisted the temptation to cover her ears as snippets of that conversation drifted through her mind.

'Obviously you won't work when we are married. You can help out with my constituency work, and the social engagements.'

'I like my work,' she had replied, wondering how Simon would take the news she had no intention of giving up work.

'Of course you do, darling. Mother has always said you are the perfect nurse and when she moves in—'

Maggie had been unable to hide her horror. 'Your mother is going to live with us?'

Simon had looked annoyed by the interruption, giving a thin lipped smile. 'Of course.'

He had made it sound as if it were a done deal, and why not? she thought with a grimace of self-disgust. She had always gone along meekly with what he said.

'Did you get any injuries from the train derailment I saw on the telly, Mags?'

Maggie dragged her wandering thoughts back to the present and responded to the ghoulish enquiry from Sam with an absent nod of her head.

'That explains why she looks so wrecked,' Sam observed.

Ben shook his head. 'No, it's not work…' His eyes widened. 'Are you pregnant?'

The colour flew to Maggie's cheeks, and Susan Ward looked uncomfortable, making it obvious that this had been her first thought too.

'Ben!' his father warned.

'No, it's OK, Dad,' Maggie said, placing her hand on her dad's shoulder. 'It's not a secret.' She took a deep breath. 'If you must know the wedding is off.'

Sam closed the fridge with his elbow and let out a silent whistle. 'So no more slimy Simon!'

'Simon is not…' Maggie stopped. Actually he was. She suddenly felt pretty stupid that her little brother had recognised the characteristic and she hadn't.

She had wasted four years of her life on Simon, which might have been acceptable if she had been desperately in love with him, but Maggie now knew she hadn't been.

Maybe she was one of those people that couldn't fall in love? A depressing thought but a definite possibility; she had certainly never experienced the sort of blind, intense passion her friends spoke of.

'Do you have to send back the presents? There's a coffee maker that's much better than the one we have—'

Sam's brother cut across him. 'Did he dump you? Or…God, had he been cheating on you?' The idea drew a chortle of laughter from his brother. 'I didn't think he had it in him.'

'Simon did not sleep with anyone.' Not even with me, Maggie thought, swallowing the bubble of hysteria in her throat.

'Well, what did he do, then?'

Maggie's eyes fell as she hesitated. For the first time in her life she felt awkward bringing up the topic of her adoption.

She had never had any hang-ups at all about being adopted, no yearning secret or otherwise to find her natural mother—it had never even occurred to her that Simon had any concerns.

Though concern was clearly an understatement considering the lengths he had gone to to trace her birth mother. Thinking ahead, he had called it; anticipating future problems, he had explained with a self-congratulatory smile.

Maggie closed her eyes and could hear him calling her birth mother's identity 'a potential skeleton-jumping-out-of-the-cupboard situation' before going on to explain in the same pompous manner that a politician in his position—one with a future—could not be too careful.

'He had a problem with…' She looked at the expectant faces and hesitated again.

Mum and Dad had told her years ago that they would understand if she wanted to contact her birth mother, but Maggie had never believed they could be as all right with the idea as they appeared.

Maggie, who had always been keenly conscious of the crazy guilt thing Mum had about not being able to do the things with her children that able-bodied mums took for granted, had no intention of searching out a mother who was able to enter the mums' race on sports day.

To her mind even thinking about her birth mother felt like a betrayal of the parents who had loved and cared for her, and why contact a stranger who had given her away and risk rejection for a second time?

Would they believe that Simon had made the unilateral decision to search for her birth mother? Or would they think that she had decided they were not enough family for her? Maggie decided there was no point taking a risk.

'It was a lot of little things. We simply decided that we didn't suit. It was all very amicable,' she lied, absently touching the bruised area on her wrist.

'Maggie will talk about it when she's good and ready and you two,' John Ward said sternly, 'have all the sensitivity of a pair of bricks. Your poor sister—'

'Had a lucky escape,' Ben interrupted. 'And don't look at me like that—I'm only saying what everyone else is thinking. Sorry, Maggie, but it's true.'

Susan broke the awkward silence that followed this pronouncement.

'What you need is a holiday.'

Maggie laughed. 'You think I should go on the honeymoon cruise?'

Maggie had no desire to go on the cruise that had been a cause of friction. Though Simon had reluctantly agreed that it might not be proper to take his mother on their Mediterranean honeymoon, he had assured her that next time of course she would go with them; Mother apparently loved cruises.

He hadn't asked Maggie if she enjoyed them.

'Oh, goodness, no, there'd be too many middle-aged people on a cruise,' Susan exclaimed, adding, 'Where did I put those brochures you brought home the other day, John? I think they're on the piano stool. Go get them, Ben.'

'Mum, I can't go on holiday. There's so much to do. I need to cancel the—'

'Your father and I will do that.'

John nodded. 'Of course, and you might as well say yes, Maggie, because your mum will wear you down eventually. She always does,' he added, dropping a kiss on the top of his wife's fair head.

He wasn't wrong. By the time the weekend was over Maggie found she had booked herself on a European coach tour.

Her mum had mixed feelings about her choice.

'But, Maggie, there will be nobody under forty on a coach tour.'

'Mum, I'm not looking for romance.'

'What about fun?'

It was a question that Maggie considered on more than one occasion over the next few weeks.

Maybe, she mused, she ought to put sensible on hold and try spontaneous, though not as spontaneous as her friend Millie had suggested when she heard the news of the broken engagement. Fun was one thing but, as she told Millie, the idea of a casual fling with a stranger did not appeal to her.

She had responded with a mystified shake of her head to Millie's suggestion that she might not have met the right stranger yet.

What Millie didn't get was that she simply wasn't a very *sexual* person.

CHAPTER TWO

RAFAEL worked his way across the room crowded with members of two of the most ancient and powerful families in Spain, brought together to celebrate the baptism of the twin boys who were the result of the marriage that had joined the two dynasties.

His cousin Alfonso, a frown on his face, approached.

Rafael arched a dark brow. 'A problem?'

'I've just been speaking with the manager, Rafe.'

Rafael nodded encouragingly.

His cousin shook his head and said quietly. 'I can't let you pay for this, Rafael.'

'You don't think I'm good for it?'

His cousin laughed. The extent of Rafael's fortune was something that was debated in financial pages and gossip columns alike, but even the most conservative estimates involved a number of noughts that Alfonso, who was not a poor man himself, struggled to get his head around.

Like all the Castenadas family members present, Alfonso was *old* money, though like many of the old families, including his wife's, the Castenadas family were not the power they once had been.

Except Rafael, the family maverick whose massive fortune was not down to inherited wealth.

When Rafael's father died in a sailing accident he did leave his son an ancestral pile and several thousands of acres, but the land that hadn't been sold off had been mortgaged to the hilt and the ancestral pile had been sadly neglected.

The estancia had needed a massive investment of, not just cash, but enthusiasm and expertise to bring it into the twenty-first century.

Rafael had both.

In the last year Rafael-Luis Castenadas had added a newspaper and a hotel chain to his already wide-ranging holdings. It was a long way from the disgrace Alfonso's uncle had always predicted his son would bring to the family name.

'If he was still with us Uncle Felipe would have been proud of all you've achieved.'

Rafael raised a dark slanted brow to a satirical angle. 'You think so?'

Alfonso looked surprised by the question. 'Of course!'

Rafael shrugged, recalling his father describing his career choice as a 'passing phase.'

'All things are, I suppose possible.' All things except his ability to please his father, Rafael mused, unable to recall the *exact* moment he had realised this, but able to recall the sense of release he had got when he'd finally stopped trying.

Following this revelation there had been a short interval when out of sheer perversity he had adopted a lifestyle guaranteed to embarrass his father.

He had rapidly outgrown the rebellion, but he was still paying the price for this youthful self-indulgence, those early colourful bad-boy antics had attracted the attention of the press at the time, and Rafael had never totally shaken that youthful reputation or the interest of the media.

'But surely…' Alfonso protested.

Rafael's lips curved into a sardonic smile.

'My father was an elitist snob—being a Castenadas was his

religion.' How anyone could think an accident of birth made him somehow better than his fellow man had always seemed bizarre to Rafael.

The lack of emotion in the dry delivery, as much as the sentiment, made his cousin stare.

Reading the shock and disapproval Alfonso struggled to hide reminded Rafael that, though he had always got on well with his cousin, who was the epitome of a decent guy, when it came to family pride they were not reading from the same page.

'You will allow me to give my godsons this gift.'

Responding to the charm in Rafael's smile—very few did not—Alfonso grinned back. 'Gift? What were the cases of vintage wine?'

Rafael's arm moved in a dismissive gesture. 'Wine is a good investment and I managed to locate some rare vintages.'

'I'll say, and I'm grateful on the boys' behalf but that's not the point, Rafael.'

'The point is I wish to do this for my godsons. They are, after all, my heirs.'

Alfonso laughed. 'I won't raise their hopes. You're thirty-two, Rafael—I think you might manage an heir or two of your own,' he observed drily.

'I have no interest in marriage.' Why perpetuate a flawed formula?

He was surrounded by failed marriages, unhappy marriages and expensive divorces. If marriage were a horse it would have been put down years ago on compassionate grounds, but it was a product of wishful thinking and people, it seemed, needed dreams.

Rafael was content with reality.

He rarely had a relationship that lasted more than a couple of months, which was as a rule about the time when he started hearing '*we*' a lot. It was also generally around this time he began to find the qualities that had first attracted him to a woman irritating.

He was not waiting to find his soulmate.

'I will leave the domestic bliss to you and Angelina. I do not buy a restaurant if I want a meal and I do not intend to take a wife in order to have sex.'

Alfonso winced and said, 'Nice analogy.'

'I do not have a reputation for niceness,' Rafael reminded him. He did, however, have a reputation for being utterly ruthless and single-minded when he pursued a goal. It was debated whether it was this ruthlessness, his sharp analytical mind or a combination of the two that accounted for his success.

Rafael, not given to introspection, had never attempted to analyse the formula; he did what he did because he liked the challenge—when he stopped enjoying it he would walk away.

An hour later all was still going smoothly—so far, at least. In the days when he'd had to attend every last family event, Rafael had seen far too many that had gone sour to rule out the possibility totally.

It might at least liven the proceedings, he mused, and almost immediately felt ashamed of the selfish sentiment. This day meant a great deal to the proud parents so for their sake he hoped the day stayed boring.

With luck he would not be obliged to see his family until next Christmas.

He put down the drink he had been nursing since he arrived, glanced at his watch and wondered when he could leave without causing offence.

'Have I thanked you for all this?'

He turned at the sound of the voice behind him, the hard light of cynicism that made several of his relatives uncomfortable absent from his eyes as he smiled at Angelina.

It was hard not to smile, not just because his cousin's wife was a beautiful woman—it was more than that. Angelina was the most genuine person he had ever met, she had a warmth that made people around her feel good.

A tall woman, and one blessed with symmetrical features set in a perfectly oval face, a slim, elegant figure and an aura of serenity, his cousin's wife was probably many men's idea of a perfect woman.

Rafael had wondered more than once why he wasn't attracted to her in a sexual way, but he never had been.

'Alfonso has already thanked me.'

She watched the uncomfortable look cross his face and gave him a hug. 'Why do you hate people to know you can be nice?' she wondered.

'I am not nice. I always have an ulterior motive—ask anyone.'

'Yes, you're totally selfish. I can see how much you're enjoying yourself.' She angled a quizzical look at his dark face. 'Wondering when to make your escape?'

There was an answering smile in Rafael's eyes as he asked, 'Should I mention you have baby vomit on your shoulder?'

Angelina carried on smiling, displaying a perfect set of white teeth as the dimple in her chin deepened. 'No, Rafael, you should not.'

The first time he had seen Angelina and Alfonso together it had been obvious even to a cynic like him that they were crazy about each other, and as far as he could see the honeymoon was still on.

Ten years down the line, who knew?

'Motherhood suits you.' He saw the flicker cross her face and knew he had inadvertently dredged up a memory.

'Thank you, Rafael. The twins, it's hard not to think about… It was all so different this time.'

Rafael had no trouble interpreting the disjointed sentence. He watched her swallow and wished he had kept his mouth shut.

He saw her lips quiver and hoped she was not going to start crying. He put a lid on his empathy, a sympathetic word or gesture now would no doubt open the floodgates and he had a major dislike of female tears. 'Why think about it?' he said brusquely.

Rafael's philosophy was if you made a mistake you lived with it. Beating yourself up over it was to his way of thinking a pointless exercise, and an indulgence.

'You're right.'

'If only more people realised that.'

Generally appreciative of his ironic sense of humour, Angelina did not smile.

Her shadowed eyes were trained on the far end of the vaulted hall where her husband, a son balanced expertly on each arm, paused to allow admiring relations to kiss the cherubic cheeks.

'He is such a good father.'

'And you are a good mother, Angelina.'

She shook her head. 'It makes me think…did I do…?' She lifted her troubled brown eyes to Rafael. 'Was it the right thing?'

Rafael had no doubt. 'You did the right thing.'

Rafael had strong feelings about advice: he never requested it and he never gave it.

It was a sound position, it was just a pity that he had forgotten and made an exception for Angelina.

'But I hate lying…'

'Confessing might have made you feel better, but what would it have achieved other than—?'

'Make Alfonso call off the wedding. He would never risk a scandal.'

'Maybe,' Rafael lied. In his mind there was no maybe.

He actually had no doubt at all what the outcome would have been had Angelina found Alfonso and not himself at home the day she had arrived at his cousin's city apartment to confess all.

Would Alfonso have felt sympathy for Angelina, forced to give birth at sixteen to her married lover's child? Yes.

Would he have married her after she had confessed? No.

'You did the right thing, Angelina. Why should you suffer now for a mistake you made when you were little more than a child? You were the victim then—is it fair you be the victim now? Everyone makes mistakes…'

'Alfonso doesn't,' she said wistfully.

Rafael might have said that Alfonso wasn't perfect, but he knew it would be a waste of breath. To his wife he was.

'It doesn't seem right I'm this happy. I wonder if she's happy, my little girl. I wonder sometimes…'

'Better not to,' Rafael advised tersely. 'Why think about what you can't have?' He had wasted many nights wanting his mother back, but he was no longer ten and he knew better.

CHAPTER THREE

MAGGIE WANDERED THROUGH the winding streets just soaking up the atmosphere. She had a whole afternoon to do her own thing before she needed to be back at the hotel for what the tour guide had enthusiastically described as an '*authentic* paella experience.'

Attendance was optional but he'd told her it was highly recommended.

Having paused for a glass of wine at a pavement café, she pulled the map from her shoulder bag. The tour guide had declared the street market a *must* for any visitor to the city in search of authentic Spain and, according to her map, it was really close.

Half an hour later and totally lost in a maze of alleys Maggie decided to admit defeat. With the clock ticking and the tour guide's instruction to be back at the hotel by seven if she planned to join the group for dinner, she finally decided to head straight for the cathedral.

Maggie was just beginning to think that she would miss out on seeing that too when she spotted the distinctive spire of the cathedral directly ahead.

Standing on the pavement, sweat trickling down her back—the day had been hot; the evening was sultry without a breath of breeze to offer relief—she waited for a lull in the steady stream of traffic. It quickly became clear there was none. Not that this seemed to bother other people, who just stepped confidently into the road weaving their way through the traffic to an accompaniment of horns, yells from drivers and rude gestures to the opposite side of the congested road.

Before she could think better of the idea she stepped out.

The security outside the hotel was tight; the media had been kept away, only a couple of approved photographers had been permitted access, though unfortunately Rafael's departure coincided with their arrival.

'Since when were *you* camera shy, Rafael? I'd heard you are *very* photogenic. I think your face and reputation keep half the scandal rags in business.'

Rafael reacted to his elderly uncle's cackle of laughter with a sardonic smile.

'I suppose I was slightly naive to think that my family at least would give me the benefit of the doubt.' Rafael liked women, he liked sex, but if he had bedded as many beautiful women as the press liked to suggest he doubted he would have the strength to get out of bed.

'You were never naive, Rafael—not even when you were a baby like those two… I remember your baptism like it was yesterday,' his uncle reminisced. 'You bawled your head off all through and your father kept saying, "Elena, do something," and she did, though I doubt if Felipe had an affair in mind.' He angled a look that held more curiosity than apology at his tall great-nephew's face as he added, 'No offence intended.'

The muscles along Rafael's strong jaw tightened, but his expression did not change as he promised, 'None taken.'

'Her mistake was confessing. Honesty is not the best policy, especially when dealing with people like your father. How old were you when he…?'

'Threw her out? Ten.'

Old enough to feel angry and betrayed. An image flashed into his head and he felt nothing as he watched his ten-year-old self begging his mother to take him with her and shouting when she tearfully sobbed she couldn't.

'It was a tragedy she died so young.'

Before he ever had a chance to retract the things he had yelled at her as she left.

Not insensible to the sensitivity of the subject, Fernando slid a glance at Rafael's stony profile before observing, 'There are worse things in life than being considered a sex god.'

'A hard reputation to live up to.'

The comment drew a laugh from the older man. 'Modesty,' he mocked. 'That's not like you, Rafael.'

'You think I need a lesson in humility?' Meekness was to his mind an overrated virtue, he had never turned the other cheek in his life and he wasn't about to start any time soon. In his world displaying any weakness was fatal.

'You care what I think?' Fernando stopped dead, his attention straying across the road. 'Now that is what I call a remarkably good-looking woman…she reminds me of someone…Rafael…?'

It was not hard to identify the object of his relative's admiration. She stood poised uncertainly on the edge of the pavement watching for a gap in the heavy traffic that moved through the congested street.

A little above medium height, she had a natural poise and elegance that made her stand out from the crowd even wearing standard-issue faded denims and a loose cotton tee shirt that hinted at the lush curves of her breasts, the natural attribute he suspected had first drawn his reprobate great uncle's attention.

As his glance moved upwards to her face she stepped backwards as a scooter mounted the pavement. As she lifted a hand to throw the ponytail that had flopped forward over her shoulder her head turned and he saw her face for the first time.

The breath left his body as Rafael froze, feeling as if someone had just landed a punch in his solar plexus.

'Over there…I think she's trying to cross the road. You see her?'

'I see her.'

'Now that is what this party lacked—a few pretty faces to look at.'

'Not pretty,' Rafael contradicted.

His elderly relative looked outraged. 'Not pretty? What is wrong with you? Don't tell me you like your women like sticks. A woman should be soft and—'

'Beautiful,' Rafael corrected, cutting across his great-uncle's list of womanly attributes.

As his brain emerged from its temporary paralysis his eyes remained trained on the slim figure, but it was not the brunette's face or her indisputably womanly figure that held his stunned gaze.

He glanced briefly at his great-uncle, who played the forgetful old man card when it suited him but was anything but; the last thing Rafael needed at this moment was Fernando to realise why the girl looked familiar to him.

He was surprised he hadn't already.

The sooner he got him safely away from this potentially explosive scene, the better.

Rafael dragged his eyes off the brunette. Still aware of her in the periphery of his vision, and aware he was not the only one aware of her—this was a woman accustomed to male attention—he offered his great-uncle a supportive arm, nodding to the driver who held the door open as Fernando took his place in the car.

The car moved off and Rafael was able to focus all his attention on the brunette.

She was obviously heading for the hotel. If she walked in now he could imagine the reaction and there were photographers to record the moment for posterity and every tabloid on the planet!

An illegitimate love child reunited with her mother while the unsuspecting husband and social elite looked on. My God, the girl had to have engineered the moment for maximum embarrassment—not that her motivation or her feelings were what he needed to concentrate on now, he told himself, blocking out this line of speculation.

This was about damage limitation. Let Angelina have this day at least before disaster in the shape of this girl arrived.

He couldn't let her go into the hotel.

So how did he stop her?

He found himself wistfully contemplating a less civilised and much simpler age when he could have simply slung her over his shoulder.

This not being an option, he had to repress his natural instincts and opt for more subtle methods. As he sifted through the possibilities he was very aware that no matter what action he chose, he could not give this situation a happy outcome.

The story had everything: sex, money and a beautiful woman—or in this case two!

If she walked through those doors now he could imagine the reaction to that face and tomorrow's headlines. He couldn't allow it to happen.

Rafael tried to narrow his focus to the here and now. It was a struggle: he had a mind wired to asking why…where; a question mark was a challenge to him.

As he walked towards the road his mind was working fast as he sifted through the possibilities. What was she doing here?

Coincidence did not even make it to the list.

Rafael did not believe in coincidence any more than he

believed in the Easter bunny or the general decency of his fellow man…or in this case woman. He did believe in protecting the people he cared about.

His silver grey eyes narrowed. The brunette, her hair and other things bouncing gently, had begun crossing the road towards the hotel entrance, confirming all his worst suspicions.

He felt something kick low in his stomach—anger, he told himself—as he watched the gentle sway of her hips in the tight jeans she wore.

Of course there were decent and genuinely *good* people—people like Angelina. He liked to think he was not without the odd scruple, but this woman was not one of life's innocents.

It always amazed Rafael how that vulnerable minority managed to get through life with their ideals and their lives intact while most people were out for what they could get regardless of the people they trampled over in their pursuit of whatever ambition drove them.

What was driving Angelina's daughter?

Greed, revenge…possibly a combination?

A child genuinely wishing to discover a parent would hardly choose a public occasion to do so.

Then as he watched she stepped off the pavement. *Dios,* he might not have to worry about scandal—the girl was a traffic statistic waiting to happen!

It was pure luck that she reached his side of the road before disaster struck—or almost. He watched as she jumped in response to the blast of a scooter horn as it whizzed past her, lost her footing and began to fall back into the moving traffic.

CHAPTER FOUR

MAGGIE lifted her head, a smile of gratitude ready to thank the person who had leant a steadying hand and pulled her onto the safety of the pavement.

'Thank you…' The words and the smile died a death as she found herself looking into the lean face of her saviour.

The sound of the traffic retreated somewhere into the recesses of her shell-shocked brain. She was looking into the dark face of the most beautiful man she had ever seen or even imagined.

She was too startled to disguise her reaction. Maggie's gaze travelled in wide-eyed appreciation over his strongly sculpted features.

This was not a face anyone would forget in a hurry.

As a child Maggie remembered wondering what her mum had meant when she spoke of someone's 'beautiful bones.'

He was what she meant.

The genetic gene pool had been very generous to this tall Spaniard, who had been gifted cheekbones sharp enough to cut yourself on, a strong aquiline nose and a firm, angular jaw.

His unlined brow was broad and intelligent and he possessed the most striking eyes she had ever seen—pale icy grey, almost silver, the striking colour intensified by the dark ring around the iris, they were fringed by incredibly long spiky lashes that were as dark as his strongly delineated ebony brows.

But it was his mouth that Maggie couldn't take her eyes off. Was it the hint of cruelty she saw in the sensual curve of his sculpted lips that tugged so strongly at her senses and made the aura he projected so overtly sensual and masculine?

Close your mouth, Maggie, you're drooling.

In an effort to respond to the ironic voice in her head, she gave herself a mental shake.

It didn't help. Her head remained a swirl of impressions and her nerve endings continued to thrum, sending shivers across the surface of her overheated skin.

She'd had too much sun, Maggie decided, shading her eyes as she struggled to find an explanation for being struck dumb and foolish at the same moment—an explanation that did not involve being in the presence of a six-feet-four black-haired Mediterranean male who looked like a fallen angel who worked out!

The fine lines around his marvellous eyes deepened as he looked down with concern into her face.

'Are you all right? There is someone you'd like me to call, perhaps?'

Oh, my God, even his voice was sexy! Deep and slightly gravelly, his cultured voice contained a faint and attractive foreign inflection.

'I…I…' She gulped, then he smiled and she thought, Wow!

Get a grip, girl. So you were smiled at by a good-looking man—there is no need to act as though you've just been released from a convent.

'You've had a shock. You're shaking…' Rafael pushed aside an intrusive flicker of genuine concern. Save it, he told himself, for Angelina and her marriage.

Besides, in his expert opinion this was about sex, not the sun or a blow to the head. He was not the only one to feel the sexual charge in the air. This was not a thing he could have anticipated, but Rafael knew that such things were easier to work with than fight against—not, obviously, to the extent that he followed the advice of the loud voice telling him that what he really wanted was *to know what she would taste like when he kissed her!*

Though had the circumstances been different, who knew…?

The comment drew Maggie's gaze to the fingers still curved around her upper arm. She made no attempt to break the contact; in fact she was conscious of a strange reluctance to do so.

She could feel the warmth in his long brown fingers through the thin fabric of her cotton top and sense the strength in them…in the man himself.

Her eyes lifted and the impression of strength she picked up from the light contact intensified. He was a big man, broad-shouldered and athletically built—he was both lean and hard.

He projected an undiluted force-field of raw masculinity. It was utterly overwhelming and…*seductive?*

The latter question made Maggie's eyes widen with shock. Curbing the imaginative dialogue in her head, she began to pull her arm away, then stopped as she encountered the flash of concern in his silver grey eyes.

She swallowed past the sudden emotional thickness in her throat and blinked as her eyelids prickled. She looked away, embarrassed by her emotional response to this cursory show of concern.

'I'm fine…oh!' Maggie grunted as a passerby bumped into her. 'Sorry…'

'*You* are sorry?' Her rescuer mumbled something under his breath and directed a glare of such autocratic outrage at the retreating back of the clumsy culprit that Maggie would not have been surprised to see the burly figure disintegrate into a pile of dust.

'You're very kind.'

Her low-pitched voice with the husky timbre came as a surprise—not an unpleasant one. 'You're English?'

Had he needed confirmation, this would have been it. He knew that Angelina had been shipped to England to have her baby.

She had not gone into details, but he could only imagine that the experience of being sent away from family and friends at such a time must have been a terrifying ordeal for a sixteen-year-old.

Maggie saw the flicker of expression move at the back of his incredible eyes and interpreted it as surprise. She had seen a lot of that when people realised she was not Spanish. There had been several occasions on this trip when unable to respond when, someone spoke to her in Spanish, she had had to explain that she was English.

It was difficult not to think about her genetic heritage when for the first time in her life her colouring made her blend in, not stand out.

She lifted a hand to smooth her tousled hair, a frown settling on her brow as she blinked to clear the unbidden image of Simon's excited expression when he had revealed that the firm he had employed to investigate her background *without telling her* had discovered her real mother did not have, as his own mother had suspected, Romany blood, but was in fact a member of one of Spain's oldest families.

'Like Mother said, it explains your temperament and your colouring, doesn't it, sweetheart? The way I see it,' he had mused, 'if this family are willing to acknowledge you it would do us no harm at all. Obviously we have to approach them sensitively…'

Sensitive—he actually said *sensitive* and with no trace of irony. 'You told your mother about this?'

Simon had remained oblivious to the danger in her voice and stilted manner. 'It was her idea.'

He had not appeared to notice her flinch as he'd smiled indulgently before announcing confidently, 'I know what you're thinking.'

Maggie had been pretty sure Simon hadn't or he wouldn't have been standing that close to her clenched fists.

She could remember clearly staring up at his handsome face, and thinking, I've never actually seen you before.

She was engaged to a man who didn't know her at all, a man who under the caring exterior he liked to cultivate, was utterly and totally self-centred.

'You're thinking how did the daughter of a Spanish aristocrat come to be adopted by an ordinary English couple.'

Maggie had recovered her voice in time to silence any further revelations and assure Simon that she had no interest in her birth mother or a family who were strangers to her, and neither did she have an interest in marrying him.

It had taken some time to convince Simon that she wasn't joking, but when he had realised he had been furious, revealing a side to his nature that she had never glimpsed previously.

Maggie flicked her ponytail firmly over her shoulder and equally firmly pushed away the memories.

She had moved on and in a rather unpredictable way, she thought, directing a bold direct stare at the face of the dark, devastatingly handsome Spaniard. Communication was not a problem; he spoke perfect English.

The problem was her inability to stop staring at him or speculate on how good his non-verbal communication skills were.

'You are here with your family?' He arched an ebony brow, his eyes travelling up from her toes to her glossy head.

She shook her head, feeling ridiculously tongue-tied and unable to shake the crazy conviction he could read her thoughts.

Rafael arched a dark slanted brow. 'Boyfriend…?'

Maggie rubbed the finger that had recently sported her engagement ring. 'No…'

Rafael's sharp gaze noted the action and he filed it away for future reference. She was young to be divorced, but he did not discount the possibility.

'I'm here alone. On holiday.' Nice move, Maggie—you've just told a total stranger that you're a vulnerable target. 'With friends,' she added quickly as her natural caution kicked in.

'You are alone with friends?'

She flushed and gave a self-conscious laugh and struggled not to look guilty. Her inability to lie without blushing remained a constant source of irritation. 'I'm with a group of friends,' she lied.

The corners of his sensual mouth lifted as he arched an ebony brow. 'Public place and I'm totally harmless,' he drawled, displaying an uncomfortable ability to read her mind as he stood there looking about as far removed from harmless as a wolf. She tilted her head back to look into his face and qualified further—of the big and bad variety.

'I'm sure you are,' she lied politely, adding, 'Excuse me,' as she fished her phone from her pocket and scanned last night's text from her mum with an expression of interest.

For some women, of course, the bad part would have been a plus, but she had never been drawn to danger. Danger was for women who could live in the moment, and men like him were for women who did not worry about how it would feel the next day.

Maggie had never been swept away by the moment, she had never said to hell with tomorrow and she didn't see the attraction of dangerous men any more than she felt the urge to walk along a crumbling cliff edge because the view was nice.

She studied her companion's dark lean face and couldn't deny that the view was very nice… The skin on her scalp tingled as her glance drifted to his mouth and she corrected her assessment. This man was many things but *nice* wasn't one of them!

Uncomfortably conscious of the flash of heat that washed over her skin, she pressed her hands to her stomach where a flock of butterflies were rioting and lowered her eyes back to her phone.

'Bad news?' he asked, not fooled by the little pantomime but playing dumb and for time.

His thoughts raced.

He needed to warn Angelina and give her the opportunity to tell Alfonso. He owed her that much, as he was the one who had encouraged her in her lie of omission to her husband in the first place.

That one had really come back to bite him, he reflected grimly. The next time he got asked for advice he would politely refuse.

This girl might, for all he knew, be an expert liar, but there were some things that you couldn't control and she was genuinely shaken. Whatever the cause it seemed logical to take advantage of it before she fully recovered her wits.

All he had to do was figure out in the next thirty seconds how to get her some place that wasn't here without breaking any laws… If it involved kissing that would be a plus, he reflected as his heated glance shifted to the full sexy curve.

'Not really…I just missed them.'

'Your many friends.'

Fascinated, he watched the colour rush over her cheeks.

She nodded, not meeting his eyes, but lifted her chin defiantly. 'We're meeting up back at the hotel,' she told him creatively before glancing at her watch and exclaiming, 'It's that time already!'

To her dismay the tall Spaniard did not take the hint; he just carried on looking at her. Looking hard. She lowered her own gaze. The unblinking regard was unsettling on more levels than she wanted to admit, let alone examine.

Maybe the novelty of a man noticing she existed had spooked her. Wincing at the self-pitying direction of her thoughts, she shook her head and laughed.

Rafael raised an enquiring brow. 'Something is funny?'

'Not funny—sad,' she admitted, hoping the enigmatic response would shut him up.

As he watched her soft lips curve into a determinedly cheerful smile that did nothing to banish the despondent shadow from her luminous eyes he felt feelings stir. Refusing to recognise them as concern—definitely not empathy—he reminded himself that his concern belonged with the mother and her threatened marriage, not the daughter.

He was attracted to the daughter—inconvenient, but not a problem. He had never had a problem keeping his libido on a leash. He couldn't allow himself to look at her and think of her as a beautiful woman because she was business and sex and business did not mix.

He had to look at her and think, Disaster waiting to happen.

While he could not *stop* the disaster unfolding, he could control the timing to minimise the impact and give Angelina time to tell her husband that she had a past and that that past had come calling.

There was a problem. Just one? mocked the voice in his skull. Every time he tried to focus on his strategy his train of thought got hijacked and he found himself thinking about her mouth.

He puzzled over this growing obsession.

It wasn't even as if she were as beautiful as Angelina. The resemblance was startling, but she was not, as he had first thought, a duplicate copy. Her face was heart-shaped and her nose, though delicate, was tip-tilted, her mouth was…

His thoughts slowed as his eyes drifted to that full, generous curve.

Her mouth, he admitted, was a problem.

He wanted to kiss her. The weakness angered him.

'Sad?'

Maggie shook her head. 'Just a private joke.' It was joke when she realised that she had allowed Simon to systematically undermine her confidence and make her feel that her wants and needs were always secondary to his.

It took a total stranger noticing her and being kind to bring home the extent to which she was hungry for attention and how invisible she had felt.

For Simon she had come just above…*maybe* above…his appointment with his hair stylist, because whether he liked it or not, as he was fond of telling her, the sad fact was that appearances counted in politics… The first time he had said this he had felt compelled to advise her that the amount of cleavage she was showing in her favourite red dress might give the wrong idea.

Her *blue* dress, he had added, made her look *wholesome.*

And she had been so eager to be the woman he wanted her to be that she had gone and changed, the same way she had stopped wearing her hair loose and had abandoned her killer heels.

Part of the problem was that she had been so young and impressionable when she met Simon, a first-year student on her first ward allocation, and the handsome son of a rather demanding patient had seemed very sophisticated.

And, yes, she had been flattered that he noticed her. For years boys had *not* noticed her, not really until the last year at school when she had finally said goodbye to the ubiquitous braces. The event had coincided with her skin clearing up, and, once revealed as smooth and flawless, her golden-toned complexion made her stand out among her fair-skinned classmates.

Her excess inches had also melted away almost overnight. She had needed a belt to keep her school skirt from falling down—she had a waist.

The boys at school had noticed her then, but their admiration had taken the form of crude comments and clumsy passes and Maggie, to hide her shyness, had responded to them with an icy disdain that had earned the not very inventive nickname of Ice Queen.

To Maggie at eighteen—and in her head still the dumpy teenager—Simon, a nearly-thirty-year-old lawyer with political ambitions, had seemed very sophisticated, and he had been interested in her!

He hadn't been clumsy, he'd been charming, and he had never made her feel awkward or uncomfortable. He had even been sympathetic when she confided how self-conscious her overgenerous breasts and curvy hips made her feel, patting her hand and assuring her comfortingly that nobody was *perfect.* With very limited experience of men and dating, Maggie had been relieved when he had put no pressure on her to go farther than kissing. Though the circumstances of her childhood had made her mature in many ways in other ways, she had led quite a sheltered life.

When he had asked her to marry him a dazzled Maggie had really believed herself in love and fully expected the relationship to move on to another level; her feelings about this had been mixed.

When Simon had said he respected her and he wanted to wait until they were married she was pretty sure that relief should not have figured even fleetingly in her reaction, but it had.

Her fists curled as she reflected angrily on how submissive she had been, how she had let Simon mould her into the person he wanted her to be.

'You wish to share this joke?'

Maggie shook her head. The last thing she wanted was to tell this man above all others that she was not used to male attention. She tried to frame a suitable excuse to make good her escape.

She could always just open her mouth and say, 'Go away,' but, having had good manners instilled in her from the cradle, it was hard for Maggie to tell anyone to get lost, especially when that someone had just sort of saved her life.

'Allow me to walk you back.'

Maggie shook her head and smiled to rob her refusal of offence. 'I couldn't possibly put you to the trouble.'

She thought of cliff edges and pretty views and sighed. No, she would definitely opt for the safe route even if the view was not so thrilling, although for a split second she had been tempted.

The same way you opted for the, oh, so safe Simon and that worked out so well.

Ignoring the contribution of the critic in her head, she folded her phone and held out her hand.

'Thank you very much for saving me, but I won't impose on you any longer.'

The stilted dismissal made Rafael veer between amusement and astonishment, then as his attention was captured by the rapid rise and fall of her rather magnificent breasts both were swallowed up by a blast of raw lust so strong he actually took a stiff half step backwards as his body hardened.

It took him unawares. It was a long time since he had wanted a woman this much, let alone a woman that was out of bounds… Maybe, he mused, that was the attraction…the forbidden fruit?

The fingers that tightened on her arm made her wince. He murmured an apology.

She couldn't see his expression; his heavy eyelids were lowered, leaving only a glittering slit of silver.

For a second she thought he wasn't going to take her hand, then he did, holding it a moment too long, giving time for the electrical tingle under her skin to morph into a shameful throb of awareness that clutched low like a fist in her belly.

Then his brown fingers tightened slightly before falling away.

She stayed motionless her eyes meshed with his compelling silver eyes. His gaze was strangely emotionless considering the electrical charge that shimmered in the air between them—or did it?

She brought her lashes down in an ebony protective screen and sucked in a shaky breath. She clearly needed to get her overactive imagination in line. It made no sense that the brush of a stranger's fingers could… She rubbed her hand against her thigh and dismissed the moment from her mind.

The sexual charge in the air did not diminish even though they were no longer touching.

'You are not well enough to walk.' It was not a lie; she looked pale and shaken.

'I'm fine. I just missed lunch and if I don't hurry I shall miss the paella evening.' Authentic, she reminded herself as she tried to work up enthusiasm for the prospect—the authentic flamenco evening had involved dancers who hailed from Manchester, though in their defence they had been very good.

'I know where they do the best paella.'

'How nice.'

He watched the appearance of the polite smile that was

starting to aggravate him and thought about doing something that would wipe it off her face.

'It would be nicer if I had company…would you come share some paella with me?'

CHAPTER FIVE

MAGGIE stared at Rafael, startled by the invitation.

'With you?' she asked, trying to judge if he was serious; not that it mattered—she was not going to say yes, was she?

His shoulders lifted in a magnificent shrug as he inclined his dark head.

Maggie gave a strained laugh and lifted her flushed face to his… So, all right, it was gratifying that a gorgeous man like this wanted her company, but not reality. 'I couldn't possibly…'

'Why not?'

'Because I don't know you…and I'm not…' she stumbled.

'Not?'

She gave him a direct look.

'You have very beautiful eyes.'

The eyes in question fell from his. 'You don't have to compliment me, and actually I don't like it.' Her heart was thudding so hard against her ribs that he had to hear it above the hum of the traffic.

'If that were true it would make you a very unusual woman, but as a matter of fact it was not a compliment.'

A laugh left Maggie's lips as her eyes swept upwards. 'No?' She arched a feathery brow. 'It definitely wasn't an insult.'

'You have a lot of experience of insults?'

Maggie smiled. 'I have brothers.'

He began to smile back, then as his eyes drifted to her mouth he stopped abruptly. The buzz of sexual awareness that had been pumping through his veins became a loud thrum.

'It was actually a statement of fact—you have very beautiful eyes.'

His eyes were resting on her mouth when he said it and something in the smoky scrutiny made Maggie's heart rate quicken.

And why not? She was allowed to be attracted to a man; it was plain silly to deny it. She was not expert at reading the signs, but it seemed possible he might be attracted to her, although he might be one of those men who were able to make every woman think she was special.

Attraction or not, it wasn't going anywhere. If she had been the sort of girl who could separate sex from emotion he would have been exactly the sort of man she would have chosen—she wondered uncomfortably if she had been sending out the wrong signals.

She gave an apologetic shrug and explained. 'I'm not looking for a holiday romance.'

Though some people had suggested—even her own mother had dropped hints—that this was exactly what she ought to be looking for.

Her friend Millie's typically outspoken parting shot came back to her.

'What you need to recover from Simon is some fun for once in your life—head-banging sex with no strings with, of course, the right stranger.'

Was there such a thing as the right stranger…and was he it? Maggie brought the train of thought, shocked, to an abrupt halt.

Her eyes widened. I am tempted. I'm really tempted!

He gave a sardonic smile. 'I was offering dinner.'

The mortified colour flew to her cheeks. 'Of course you were…sorry…that is, I was…' Wondering if no strings sex was such a terrible thing. And why shouldn't she? It wouldn't hurt anyone; it might even be liberating…it might even be fun.

She doubted this was the sort of fun her mum had had in mind.

He grinned, immediately achieving the impossible and looking even more rampantly gorgeous—he really was the most incredibly *male* man she had ever met—and looked amused.

'That is a yes.'

Flustered, Maggie swept the hair from her eyes. 'Yes, that is, no, I…'

'You wish for references perhaps?'

She flushed and shook her head feeling gauche, foolish and excited; her eyes widened in recognition of this last emotion. 'Of course not.'

'I am Rafael. Rafael-Luis Castenadas.' Holding her eyes, he bowed formally from the waist. He straightened, pushing a dark hank of hair back from his wide brow as he did so, then angled an enquiring brow and waited.

Not recognising the cue to give her own name, Maggie heard herself say, 'That's a lovely name.'

She squeezed her eyes closed and thought, Please, please, let the ground open up and swallow me.

He watched as she bit her lip hard enough to bruise the soft pink flesh and break the skin. He saw a bead of bright blood form and thought about blotting it with his tongue before… He stopped the thought but was unable to stop his body reacting lustfully to the image.

He had never met anyone with a more expressive face. Did

she allow every emotion she felt to register on those lovely features?

It made his task easier that she was so easy to read though he wondered how many men had taken advantage of her transparency—*as he was.*

He pushed aside the sliver of guilt. He had an excuse and he wasn't trying to get her into bed…though in other circumstances that might, he conceded, have been a tempting idea.

Maggie opened her eyes and found he was watching her; the unblinking intensity of his regard was unsettling.

'And you?' he prompted.

'Me?' she echoed, wondering about the expression she had glimpsed on his face.

'You have a name?'

She flushed and struggled to get her brain into gear. She could not believe the effect this total stranger was having on her. 'I'm Maggie. Maggie Ward, well, Magdalena really, but nobody calls me that.'

'Everyone starts out as strangers, Magdalena.'

His deep voice had a intimate quality. Maggie, uncomfortably conscious of the forbidden shiver trickling down her spine, told herself it was his accent. Just because he made her name sound exotic didn't mean she was—she was still the same Maggie who was far too sensible to get silly because a man with a pretty face and a more than all right body noticed she existed.

Her glance skimmed the long, lean, male length of him and the breath left her parted lips in a tiny sigh of appreciation that she hurriedly covered in a cough. Ruefully she admitted to herself he was better than all right—actually he was better than stupendous though a person would have to see him without the clothes to be sure.

Maggie stopped dead mid-speculation, her eyes widening to saucers. I'm mentally undressing a man!

'Even lovers…'

Her wide eyes leapt to his face. *'Lovers?'* she echoed, thinking if ever there was a cue to walk this was it. This was not a subject that total strangers discussed. His next comment made it clear he did not share her inhibitions. She was starting to think he might not have any.

'Lovers start out as strangers.'

He smiled at her with his eyes and her stomach flipped and quivered.

She recalled Millie's friendly advice on how to add some spice to her holiday.

'Act available, Maggie,' she had counselled. 'When your eyes meet his and your heart starts to thud and you get that delicious fluttery kick in your belly, don't look away. A guy needs some encouragement.'

Maggie took a deep breath and didn't look away.

It was just dinner, there would be other people, and she'd be experiencing some of the local culture, which was what she liked about foreign travel.

'Will they have room at this paella place?'

Just for once it would be good to break away from her sensible image—not too far, obviously. And they were not talking the head banging, no-strings sex thing—this was dinner.

Where would be the harm?

As his strangely hypnotic eyes swept slowly across her upturned features. It probably made her pathetic, but she really wished she'd put on more make-up than a swipe of lip gloss and a smudge of eyeshadow.

As he examined the fine-boned features Rafael was struck once more by the startling resemblance between mother and daughter, but now he was equally conscious of the dissimilarities. The younger woman would be considered by most to have less claim to classical beauty, but when it came to sex appeal she was streets ahead.

'They will always make room for me. Come…'

No shocker that he should issue commands—he had that written all over him. The shock was that she allowed him to steer her through the throng.

Looking back on the moment and the ones that followed later, Maggie was left to wonder if her body had not been taken over by an alien.

Maggie paused, ducking her head to look through the door he held open for her. The sumptuous interior looked just as impressive as the exterior of the long, low, powerful-looking car.

'This is yours?'

'You are going to lecture me on my carbon footprint or car theft?'

She slung him a cross glance and slid inside, lifting the newspaper that lay on the passenger seat. The headline was in Spanish but the image was one that had graced several front pages across the world that week—a well-known Hollywood star with his long-term partner making their relationship official at a civil ceremony.

The image of the two hand-in-hand, smiling men shifted her thoughts back to her dad's parting words when Maggie had been startled to realise that her dad, at least, had his own ideas about what had caused her to break off the engagement.

'I respect the fact you don't want to talk about it, love, but the fact is, Maggie, some men…just because Simon has issues with his…*leanings*…'

Maggie had stared, astonished, as her father, red-faced, had cleared his throat before finishing huskily. 'Never think you were the problem or it was your fault.'

'No,' she had responded faintly, thinking, Was I the only one who didn't have a clue?

And she hadn't—not until that final argument when things had got pretty ugly.

Maggie had never seen the normally restrained Simon so angry before, and the trigger to him losing it totally had of all things been a throwaway comment in the heat of the moment, because he didn't have the faintest idea *why* she was angry. 'I don't think you even *like* women!'

'Who have you been listening to? I am *not* gay!'

Before Maggie had been able to assure him she hadn't meant that at all he had grabbed her arm and wrenched her towards him, lowered his face to her and snarled, 'If you spread lies like that I'll…'

Startled by his aggressive reaction, Maggie had frozen with shock, but had not lowered her gaze from his menacing glare. She knew from past experience it was a mistake to show fear to bullies. And Simon was a bully.

Why had she not known that before?

Anger had come to her rescue; her chin had come up and she had asked with cold disdain, 'You'll what, Simon?'

The ruddy colour rising up his neck had reached his cheeks, darkening the skin to magenta as he'd glared at her in furious frustration. 'I…I'll…'

Pretending not to notice the fingers tightening painfully around her wrist, she had cut across him. 'Look, I'm sorry if I touched a raw nerve, but your sexuality is not a subject that interests me.'

Simon had looked at the ring she held out to him and released her arm.

She had dropped it into his palm, walked away and not looked back.

Maggie threw the newspaper into the back seat and fastened her belt with a click. Her chin lifted. Being sensible had got her nothing but humiliation; it was time for a bit of recklessness.

But maybe not this much, she thought half an hour later as they seemed to finally arrive at their destination. The village cut into the hillside was small, in a matter of moments they had driven through.

Keeping her voice carefully casual, Maggie turned her head in time to see the village lights disappear as the road began to climb steeply and asked, 'Aren't we stopping?'

Maggie recognised the extreme vulnerability of her position; she was in a car miles from anywhere with a man who could, for all she knew, be a homicidal maniac and nobody knew where she was.

She should be seriously scared, so why wasn't she?

'Relax, Maggie, I'm quite harmless.'

She looked at his profile and thought, If you were I wouldn't be here. It was a bit late to recognise that it was the danger he represented that had drawn her here.

He was her rebellion against the self-imposed rules she had lived her life by.

'Relax—you will enjoy yourself, you know.' She looked at him with big wary eyes and he expelled a sigh. 'That was not a threat, you know, and you can take your hand off the door—it's locked.'

'Why didn't we stop in the village?'

'Because,' he said, pulling the car onto a patch of rocky ground beside a number of other vehicles, 'the villagers are all here.' He released the central lock. 'You are sorry now that you came?'

Maggie, her lips curved in a happy smile, shook her head. 'No.' When he'd said the village was here he had not been exaggerating; the area of flat ground fringed by trees was full of people.

She felt his eyes on her and turned her head.

Her own smile faded as their glances connected and locked.

The raw hunger in his deep-set eyes made her breath quicken and her stomach muscles quiver receptively.

For a moment their glances clung until Maggie, her heart beating hard, allowed her lashes to fall in a concealing veil.

The heavy thrum of her pounding blood in her ears was deafening. Confused, excited and scared by the strength of her reaction she ran ahead, anxious to distance herself from him and her feelings.

She used the moment to gather her calm around her like a comfort blanket—she wasn't *comforted* but after a little deep breathing she was able to speak without babbling anything stupid like, 'You're beautiful,' when he reached her side.

The tremors that hit her body intermittently she could do little about, so she jammed her hands in the pockets of her jeans, blissfully unaware that while the first-aid measure hid her shaking hands it also pulled the denim tight across her bottom, riveting Rafael's eyes on the feminine flare of her hips.

'This is incredible,' she said, not feigning her enthusiasm as she looked around the mountainside clearing. 'However did you find this place?'

Eyes shining, Maggie stared at the scene, drinking it in: the flickering flames of the open fires, smoke in the night, the strings of fairy lights in the tall pines twinkling above the heads of the people of all ages sitting at the rustic tables, eating, drinking, laughing and some dancing to the music supplied by an accordion player.

The smell of the food cooking in the giant pots filled the air and mingled with the wood smoke, the scent of damp grass, and the wild thyme crushed underfoot.

'Rafael.' The man who greeted her companion stared at Maggie with open curiosity before smiling and making a comment in his native tongue.

The men spoke for a moment before Rafael turned back to

Maggie. 'I did not find it,' he said, responding to her previous question. 'I was brought up not far from here.'

'A country boy!'

He arched a dark brow as he placed his fingers under her elbow to guide her to a seat at one of the long trestle tables. 'That surprises you?'

Considering his aura of sophistication it did, but she had to admit he did seem very relaxed and at home in the surroundings and, judging by the number of people who greeted him with warmth and familiarity, he had not forgotten his roots.

She smiled as people moved to make way for them; Rafael told her to save him a seat while he left to bring her back food.

Maggie sat quietly drinking in the sights and smells, trying to commit this very special moment to memory, she was pretty sure that by the morning it would all seem like a dream.

Rafael returned carrying two plates of steaming paella and, setting one before her, pulled a stray chair to the table and straddled it.

Maggie speared a prawn with her fork and put it in her mouth. She gasped. 'That is incredible!' and refilled her fork.

Her plate was half empty when she realised that Rafael was spending more time watching her than eating himself.

She lifted her eyes to his face and once again he responded to a question before she had framed it. 'I like watching you eat. It is rare to see a woman who enjoys her food.'

'Well, I'd enjoy it more if you weren't watching every mouthful,' she admitted frankly.

Maggie tapped her foot as the fiddler struck up a fresh tune. The man on the accordion finished off his glass of wine before he joined in too. There was a ripple of clapping as people flocked onto the makeshift dance floor. This was clearly a popular choice.

'They all look as if they're having a good time.'

The wistful note in her voice was not lost on Rafael, who was starting to find her undisguised enthusiasm for everything wearing. Every time she looked at him with wide trusting eyes he experienced a need to justify his actions to himself that he did not enjoy.

He knew he was doing the right thing.

So why, asked the voice in his head, do you feel like such a lowlife?

'The paella is very lovely.'

Of course it was.

She was the easiest woman to please he had ever met and by far the most beautiful.

Would she be equally appreciative in bed?

The sybaritic image of her naked body beneath him, her dark hair spread out on a pillow, flashed into his head. Struggling to banish the erotic sequence of images that followed it, he shut his eyes, disconcerted by the strength of the desire that gripped him.

It seemed the moment to remind himself that she was not his type at all.

Luscious, obviously, but there was an aura of wide-eyed innocence about her that under normal circumstances he would have steered well clear of.

He had a low boredom threshold and virtue was, in his experience, boring. It was admittedly not boredom that had him in a constant state of painful arousal, but sexual hunger once quenched did not have a long shelf life. He gave a jaundiced smile; if anyone knew that it was him.

Maybe, he mused, it was genetic. His father's numerous mistresses had never lasted long—pride in his family name had not extended to Felipe Castenadas depriving himself of female companionship after Rafael's mother's departure.

There had been many women and his father had spoken about them with a lack of respect behind their backs and sometimes to their faces that had never sat easily with Rafael as a boy.

Rafael had been in his early teens when he had gone to leave the room in disgust during the middle of one of his father's coarse diatribes about his mistress of the moment.

His father had stood up and blocked the door. Rafael could still recall the smell of alcohol on his breath. 'You know what your problem is, boy, you romanticise women,' he had sneered. 'Don't shake your head, boy, I'm doing you a favour. Do you want a woman to make a fool of you? At heart they are all like your mother, basically whor—'

The crude sentence had never been completed. Felipe had met his son's eyes—realising for the first time perhaps that he had to tilt his head to do so—and what he had seen there had made him pale.

He had moved away from the door maintaining an illusion of macho bluster, but clearly shaken. It had been a turning point. He had never pushed Rafael in the same way, or mentioned his mother again.

In other respects nothing had changed. It wasn't just female companionship his father had not deprived himself of—Felipe Castenadas had lived a lavish lifestyle even when he couldn't afford it. Rafael had been forced to watch silently as his father sold off the estate he'd claimed to love piece by piece to pay for his indulgences, all the time silently vowing to one day restore it.

He had done so now and gained in the process the respect and gratitude of the people on the estate. Though his father would never have accepted an invite to a party like this, Rafael did so regularly, and he frequently enjoyed these simple occasions more than the lavish social events he was expected to attend.

He had never brought anyone along before so he could almost see the speculation in his tenants' faces as they looked at his companion. It was annoying but the speculation would die away.

He studied her through his lashes as she smiled. The man who did end up with her would have to share her—the woman loved the whole world, and paella.

He watched as her smile had a predictable effect on a group of young men who stood a few feet away, staring. He could almost smell the testosterone from here; she remained cheerfully oblivious to the effect it had on them.

Rafael's clenched teeth were starting to ache.

If that smile had turned out to conceal a mean and spiteful agenda he might not be feeling this uncharacteristic guilt.

He had nothing to feel guilty about.

So why do you feel the need to remind yourself of that so frequently?

'You are not counting carbs, then?'

The sardonic observation made Maggie lift her chin. 'Sorry if that offends you,' she said, sounding anything but.

'It was not a criticism.'

Almost certain that, despite this reassurance, it was exactly that, Maggie paused, her fork in the air. The furrow between her brows deepened as she studied his dark face. His entire attitude since they had arrived had been offhand and she was getting the impression he had regretted bringing her.

She ought to be regretting it too, but the hormonal rush she got every time she looked at him had an addictive quality. Then there was the smell of his skin and the way he… She inhaled deep, closing down this chain of thought, which could, if left unchecked, go on for a long time—there was a lot about him she found fascinating!

He might be her hormonal Achilles' heel, but she was not about to apologise for liking food. She had been there, done that before.

'I tried dieting.' Simon had bought her a number of very

useful books on the subject of healthy eating. 'It made me cranky and I almost fainted running for the bus.'

A look of astonishment crossed his face. 'Why would you diet?' His eyes dropped, sliding appreciatively over her lush curves; by the time he made the return journey to her face Maggie's cheeks were burning and her heart was slamming hard against her ribs like a trapped bird.

She was trapped, trapped by the sheer strength of the sexual awareness that had invaded every cell of her body.

'I know I could do with losing my hips and my bottom is a bit…'

A hoarse rattling sound emerged from Rafael's throat. 'You have a magnificent body.'

Heat flashed through her body as their eyes meshed, the sweet sharp ache between her legs made Maggie shift uncomfortably and feel acutely embarrassed—but mingled with the embarrassment was a strong element of dizzy excitement.

'Clothes hide a multitude of sins,' she joked, trying to lower the sexual temperature, she was mortified by the thought of anyone listening in to this conversation.

'It depends on your definition of sin.' His slurred drawl made her shiver. 'Would you like to compare notes?'

Maggie swallowed, the fork slipping from her nerveless fingers. His smoky eyes were eating her up.

'I would really like to know what sinful thoughts are going through that beautiful head right now.' His finger trailed down her cheek.

Maggie gasped and pulled back breaking the spell that held her in sexual thrall. 'I'd really like to dance.'

Rafael laughed at the change of subject and thought I would like to see what those clothes are hiding. 'This is not my sort of music.'

'Your foot was tapping.' Perhaps it was just her he didn't want to dance with?

He heaved a sigh, there was time to ring Angelina and warn her later.

And why should he pass up the opportunity to legitimately hold that soft warm body next to his own?

It looked as if he was not the only person to have this idea.

Recognising the young man who, egged on by shouts from his friends lining the makeshift bar, was approaching, Rafael acknowledged him. 'Enrique.'

The friends, who clearly had not really thought their friend this bold, fell silent.

Maggie watched as the two men spoke; the young man with the bold eyes and macho swagger kept flashing her smouldering looks that made her want to laugh. Despite the physical dissimilarities—he was dark and not very tall; Sam and Ben were tall and fair—he reminded her of her brothers.

When Rafael showed any inclination to smoulder in her direction she felt no desire to smile—in fact her reaction was worryingly close to throwing herself on the floor and screaming, *Take me!*

There had to be a logical reason for her bizarre behaviour… That fish last night had tasted funny…?

'Enrique wants to know if you'd like to dance.'

'And you don't mind?'

His brows lifted at the question. 'Why should I mind?' Rafael shrugged, displaying zero reluctance to relinquish her to the care of the flashing-eyed young man, and said, 'Have fun.'

Maggie looked at him with narrowed eyes. Weren't Spanish men meant to be possessive? Clearly if they were Rafael was the exception to the rule because, far from objecting to the handsome boy—actually he was more than a boy; now she looked more closely she could see he was probably nearer her own age than her brothers', but next to Rafael there was something immature about him—

'Don't worry, I will,' she promised, taking the young man's hand and allowing him to lead her out onto the dance floor.

CHAPTER SIX

RAFAEL drummed HIS fingers impatiently on the table-top as he waited for Angelina to pick up. He felt a jolt as Maggie, who appeared to be rapidly losing her inhibitions, turned her head and smiled at him.

He smiled back, then scowled as she was whirled away by her laughing partner, her dark hair streaming behind her like a silken cloud, her laughter floating on the air as Enrique, his shirt unfastened to reveal a bronzed chest, pulled her closer to demonstrate a complicated step that she copied with ease.

She was very graceful and her laughter and her lack of inhibition made him feel unaccountably annoyed.

Above the sound of her warm laughter he heard Angelina's voice.

'Rafael, are you at a party? Is that why you deserted us so early? Alfonso said you were avoiding the photos.'

Rafael forced his gaze from the dancing couples.

'I'm planning on staying at the *castillo* tonight. Is Alfonso there?'

'Yes, do you want to speak to him?'

'No. Don't talk, just listen.' I'm about to turn your perfect day into a nightmare. He expelled a deep breath and said, 'Your daughter is here.'

The silence lasted a full thirty seconds before she breathed hoarsely, 'That isn't possible! What is she like, Rafael?'

'Like you,' he said, wishing he could not hear the raw longing in her voice. Conscious of a male voice in the background, sharp with concern he added quickly, 'She was going to crash the party.' The ease with which he had diverted her had made Rafael think that the timing of her arrival might after all have been fortuitous—from her point of view—rather than malicious.

Malicious or not, the effect would have been equally destructive. He did not regret his actions and the necessary subterfuge. This was definitely a moment when the ends justified the means.

'I'm playing it by ear,' he admitted. 'I don't think she knows who I am.'

A man who believed in meticulous research, Rafael did not enjoy the novel sensation of working in the dark.

If he'd had a detailed report on his laptop telling him everything that was relevant about Miss Maggie Ward, he would have been much happier. At the moment all he knew about her was that she had a lopsided smile, a husky voice, a mouth that invited sinful speculation and a lush distracting body—and she liked paella.

'If the opportunity arises and she feels able to confide in me I will do my best to convince her this is a bad move, but that's a long shot,' he admitted, thinking of the stubborn firmness of her rounded chin. 'You should tell Alfonso sooner rather than later. I'm sorry, Angelica, it was bad advice.'

He slid the phone into his pocket as a breathless and happy Maggie was delivered by a smug-looking Enrique back to the table.

Maggie, her face flushed from the exertion and her eyes sparkling, smiled as the young man spoke, then looked to Rafael.

'What did he say?' Without waiting for the translation she caught Enrique's hand and flashed a smile of radiant warmth, then, appearing oblivious to the effect it had on the susceptible boy, said, 'That was fantastic. You're a great dancer, but I'm worn out,' she added, fanning herself with her hand and miming a faint.

The young man raised her hand to his lips and spoke again.

'He said that you not only look beautiful but you dance beautifully too.'

'Oh, how sweet!' Maggie said raising herself on her tiptoes to reach up to plant a kiss on the young man's smooth cheek. She turned her head to Rafael, her smile fading as she encountered his stony expression. 'Tell him thank you.'

'He already got that part.' A nerve clenched in his lean cheek as Rafael sought to contain the irrational surge of anger that he had experienced when he had watched her kiss the boy. 'I think he's smitten.'

Maggie's eyes narrowed and her chin lifted at the cold criticism in his manner. She refused point-blank to allow him to make her feel guilty for a spontaneous peck on the cheek, it had just been innocent fun and even if it hadn't been it was none of his business!

It wasn't as if he had wanted to dance with her. Now that, she admitted, would have been a very different experience and not nearly so innocent.

'That's because I'm utterly irresistible, a real man-eater.'

Rafael said something that drew a laugh from the young man who caught Maggie's hand, bowed low over it and brushed it with his lips. Then with a grin and a display of youthful exuberance he ran off to be clapped on the shoulder by his friends before claiming his next partner.

Antipathy shone in Maggie's eyes as she took her seat next to Rafael. Choosing water rather than wine, she filled her glass from one of the jugs on the table.

He raised a brow at her choice and taunted lightly, 'The vintage not to your palate?' The locally made wine, thanks to some clever marketing, had actually started to appear on a number of high-end restaurant wine lists, and his investment in the new winery that many had considered wasteful had not only already paid for itself but brought jobs to an area where young people were often forced to leave in order to find work.

'You're not drinking,' Maggie observed, unwilling to admit she had no head for alcohol—a sniff of a wine gum made her tipsy.

'I'm driving.'

The reminder made her frown. 'What time is it?'

He extended his arm towards her; his sleeve was rolled up to the elbow. Maggie stared for a moment, her throat dry and her heart pounding as she struggled to resist the impulse to run her fingers over the hair that lightly dusted his sinewed golden forearm.

Her voice was husky as she read the time on the metal-banded watch that circled his wrist out loud.

'It's a long way back,' she fretted.

Rafael watched as she nibbled gently at the pouting curve of her full lower lip. This had never been about seduction…but he found himself wanting her more than he had wanted a woman in a very long time.

'Don't look so worried—I am a man who believes that a woman is allowed to change her mind.' This was an attitude that had rarely been tested.

The colour flew to Maggie's cheeks. 'About what?'

He just laughed. 'It's fine if you have second thoughts,' he observed not in reality feeling at all fine as he looked at her lovely mouth. His glance slid lower to the outline of her lush breasts beneath the fine fabric of her top, and he felt even less fine.

He felt hungry.

She didn't know whether to be relieved by his take-it-or-leave-it attitude or insulted.

Had she changed her mind?

Did she have a mind? Now the initial defiant mood had ebbed, allowing herself to be picked up by a total stranger had started to seem less spontaneous and more criminally reckless.

And if she felt this way when the music was playing and the moon was shining how was she going to feel in the morning? she asked herself.

There had to be a less dramatic way to shake her sensible girl image. Next time she would settle for something tamer, like a motorbike or tattoos.

'I will make sure you get safely back.' Maggie's eyes connected with his and her stomach went into a lurching dive. There was nothing safe about the glow in his smoky eyes. 'But what,' he asked, tilting his chair back to avoid a collision with some passing dancers, 'is the hurry?'

Enrique called out and winked at her as he whirled his new partner past.

'What did you say to him before?' she asked suspiciously. 'Were you talking about me?'

'I simply translated.'

Maggie replayed the conversation and her eyes widened in dismay. 'You didn't!'

One corner of his mouth lifted in a mocking smile. 'Actually I gave him a modified version—I told him that you eat little boys like him for breakfast.'

'What if he thought you were serious?' she charged.

His eyes dropped and Maggie was shocked and embarrassed to feel her body respond to the slow, insolent sweep of his densely lashed eyes.

'What makes you think I was not serious?' he countered. His voice lowered a husky octave as he leaned into her and observed softly, 'You are a very desirable woman.'

Tongue-tied and blushing, she looked away, unable to come up with a smart remark to diffuse the fizz of sexual tension.

Did she want to diffuse it?

A thoughtful expression drifted across his lean predatory features as Rafael watched her plunge into a state of delicious blushing confusion. Rather than exploiting her sexuality, she seemed shocked by any reference to it.

'I think maybe I will have some more to eat.' Not looking at him, Maggie picked up her plate.

As she hurried across the grass towards the long trestle table loaded with food she bit her lip to repress a groan. So much for the new improved sexy me—I must have looked like a scared rabbit! What must he think of me?

Unable to stop herself, she glanced back over her shoulder and it became clear he wasn't thinking of her at all. Her place had been taken by a pretty woman in a low-cut blouse who as Maggie watched threw back her head and laughed, her uninhibited spontaneity a striking contrast to Maggie's own stilted self-consciousness.

She felt a stab of something that was obviously not jealousy but was nonetheless unpleasant. It was strange. She was not normally so self-conscious; it was just something about Rafael... Something? Who was she kidding? It was everything about Rafael!

The fact was she had never been attracted to a man this way in her life before. It wasn't just the fact he was incredibly handsome, which he was, it was more...his earthy sensuality... She shook her head, frustrated by her inability to analyse what it was about him.

Maybe it was not possible to analyse; maybe she just had to accept that looking at his mouth made her ache.

One minute she was thinking about his carnal perfect mouth and the things she was shocked to realise she would have liked him to do to her with it and the next she was running.

Later, when she tried to work out the exact sequence of events they remained a confused jumble. In each reconstruction her shocking, shameful thoughts somehow mixed up with the sense of panic and urgency that she reacted to instinctively.

She was never even sure why she had glanced towards a pile of recently sawn timber—perhaps movement caught her eye? She actually looked away, barely registering it as her attention drifted to the children playing a hundred yards or so away.

Then a low rumble just audible above the sounds of merriment made her turn her head again. She froze, paralysed with horror as she saw the stack of felled trees begin to move… Like a house of cards they slipped, fell and began to roll down the steep incline.

Straight towards the group of playing children.

The plate slipped from her fingers. She was told later she yelled—that was what caught the attention of the others who set off in her wake—but she had no memory of that. She just remembered running, praying and the sound of her laboured breathing loud in her ears as she raced towards the children.

By the time she reached them the older ones, alerted by cries, had already started moving, running out of the path of the approaching danger. Some were crying, but the sound was lost in the general pandemonium.

Maggie bent and scooped up two of the smaller children sprinting to the safety of higher ground before depositing them in the arms of women standing, shocked, watching, and she went back, passing men running in the opposite direction with children in their arms.

One child remained, a solemn-eyed little boy who raised his arms to Maggie when she reached him, hefting him into her arms. She turned, pressed his face into her shoulder and tried to run; her legs felt leaden. They worked painfully slowly as she fought against the inertia, struggling to suck air into her oxygen-starved lungs.

She could hear the danger approaching but didn't dare look… Convinced she wasn't going to make it with her last ounce of strength she flung the little boy at a young man who was running out to meet them.

She saw him safe and closed her eyes as the adrenaline rush in her bloodstream dipped dramatically. She tried to run felt her legs give and cried out. Safety was tantalisingly near but she couldn't… Her face scrunched into a teeth-clenched mask of determination as she tried to push herself forward.

Then something hit her. For a brief moment she thought it was the loose timber, then she realised the solidity was warm and male—it was Rafael. She stopped fighting as he carried her from danger.

CHAPTER SEVEN

THE impetus of Rafael's sprint carried them both past the crowd of cheering villagers and to the brink of the grassy slope beyond. He dug his heels in but the momentum he had built up was too great to resist and they went over the top, Maggie still in his arms.

As they landed at the bottom the breath left her body in a painful whoosh as she sank into the mercifully soft ground. For a moment she couldn't breathe or speak…but euphoria made her want to explode. She was alive—that was a big, a massive, plus considering the way things had been looking seconds earlier. A little detail like speech loss was fine, bruises were fine, Rafael on top of her was…

Her chaotic thoughts slowed from a breathless gallop to a slow canter. Rafael was on top of her!

He was breathing like a marathon runner. She was underneath him, a position that if she was honest she had been imagining pretty much from the second she saw him.

She felt fingers frame her chin and heard a deep voice harsh with concern ask, 'Are you all right, Maggie? Can you hear me?'

'Of course I can hear you. I'm not deaf.' She opened her eyes, his face suspended above her was very close.

His heavy-lidded eyes blazed, the heat in them pinning her

as surely as his body; the bones of his face stood out in stark prominence beneath his gleaming golden skin.

She got breathless and it had nothing to do with his weight pinning her down—well, only partly. The veneer of cultured civilisation and urbane charm was totally stripped away, revealing the essence of the raw masculinity beneath.

Without a word or taking his eyes from her, he bent his head and fitted his mouth to hers, kissing her hard, then without a word he rolled off her.

'You went back?'

She turned her head in response to the stark incredulity in his voice. Rafael lay on his back, one arm curved above his head, staring at the sky. She could see his chest rising and falling in sync with his laboured inhalations.

She decided that if he could pretend the kiss hadn't happened, so could she. She could definitely ignore the fact her lips tingled and his taste was in her mouth, a piece of cake!

'I think you saved my life, thank you.' Twice, if anyone was counting.

She expected him to mention the fact.

He didn't.

'I don't want your thanks.'

She lay there on the floor as he got to his feet in one lithe athletic bound. He dragged the hair back from his brow before extending a hand.

After a pause Maggie took it and found herself hauled to her feet.

'You insane idiot, do you have a death wish?'

Maggie was spared from responding to this savage question because at that moment the village en masse swept over them like a blanket of goodwill and concern.

Maggie was carried away on a wave of hugs, kisses and tears, taken quite literally to the heart of the village.

She was declared a heroine bilingually. It was all very

emotional and Maggie, both embarrassed and overwhelmed by the attention, went very quiet.

She lost count of the number of times she said she was fine. It was Rafael who finally rescued her from the love and adulation, saying firmly that she needed rest, could they not all see that she was about to collapse?

She repressed her natural inclination to deny she was that pathetic and allowed herself to be escorted back to his car. It seemed to Maggie from his manner that Rafael's intervention was motivated more by irritation than concern for her well-being.

He had received his share of gratitude too and with every thank-you his mood seemed to have got darker.

Was she paranoid or was she the focus of his annoyance?

Maybe he was actually hurt but was too macho to admit it. She had got the definite impression when they were falling that he was trying to shield her using his body and his arms, which had circled her like a steel barrier to cushion the impact.

And despite his assurances to the contrary the cuts on his dark face did suggest he hadn't escaped as lightly as she had. His dark hair was tousled and his shirt was ripped almost off his back, revealing a very distracting expanse of brown chest, well-developed shoulders and flat, muscle-ridged belly, not to mention a hand-sewn label that explained in part his irritation: his shirt was no more off the peg than his body was.

Maybe he blamed her for everything, including the ripped shirt. She thought about the angry kiss—hard not to—her eyes half closing as she remembered the texture of his firm lips, the warmth of his breath…the brief explosion of mind-numbing passion.

It was lucky, really, that everyone had assumed her numbed state was caused by the trauma of the accident. She wanted them to carry on believing this version. For Rafael to even suspect that a kiss that had barely registered on his radar had turned her the next best thing to catatonic would have been too mortifying.

She lifted a hand to her mouth and tilted her head back to catch a glimpse of his beautiful sculpted mouth, and immediately stumbled on the rocky ground where the cars, including Rafael's, had been parked.

Several pairs of arms reached to catch her but Rafael's were there first. Ignoring her weak protest, he swung her up into his arms, barely breaking stride.

Reaching his car, he deposited her in the front seat.

'That was quite unnecessary,' she said frostily.

'You are welcome.' He inclined his dark head, his grey eyes mocking her.

Maggie managed a stiff smile as one of the women placed a blanket over her knees. The man standing beside the woman waited until she had tugged it snugly around Maggie before he leaned into the car and clasped one of Maggie's hands between both of his and said something in Spanish.

Maggie gave a helpless smile and the old man looked to Rafael.

'The little boy you went back for was Alfredo's grandson. He says to tell you that you are an angel sent from God.'

Maggie gave an embarrassed little shrug, then turning her hand to grasp the teak-coloured gnarled fingers that lay on top of hers, she squeezed and smiled saying huskily, 'I'm glad nobody was hurt.' She glanced at Rafael, bit her lip and, struggling to control the husky throb of emotion in her voice, said, 'Tell him what I said, please.'

Rafael's eyes lingered on her face, moving up in a sweep from the graceful line of her slender neck, the curve of her cheek, the fullness of her lips and her wide-spaced liquid dark eyes. Alfredo's description seemed apt—she did look like an angel, a sad, sexy angel.

This was a situation where seeing both sides of the

argument was not useful. Maggie Ward might have many excellent qualities beyond a kissable mouth and a sinfully sexy body, but he didn't want to know about them. It confused the issue.

She was a danger to the happiness of two people he cared about. Focus on that, he told himself, and forget about her mouth and her courage. Think of her as a problem to be solved and maybe a pleasurable interlude.

And why not? Why was he beating himself up because he found her attractive? He knew the attraction was reciprocated. He was in danger of letting her innocent aura make him lose sight of the facts. He had not kidnapped her, drugged her or sworn eternal love; she had come of her own free will.

Maggie Ward knew that his intentions were strictly dishonourable and she had come along anyway. She was a young woman who wanted to add the spice of a one-night stand to her trip, so why should he feel as though he was taking advantage?

He had been staring at her so long that it crossed Maggie's mind that for some inexplicable reason he might be about to refuse her request.

'Please?'

Responding to the prompt and ignoring the questioning look in her eyes, Rafael translated.

Maggie watched the elderly man's lined face crease into a wide smile as he listened to Rafael. He turned his attention back to Maggie, said fervently, '*Angel.*' And pressed something into her hand before bowing out of the car to join the other villagers who had gathered to say goodbye.

'Watch the door.'

Maggie responded to the abrupt instruction and pulled the blanket closer as Rafael slammed the passenger door with what seemed to her like unnecessary force. There was nothing in his manner to suggest he agreed with the other man's version of her actions. Now she was sure it wasn't her imagination—his attitude towards her since the accident had been terse and unfriendly to a degree that could not be due to a spoiled designer shirt.

Any inclination to flirt with her had presumably vanished along with her make-up and hairgrips. He was obviously a man who could not see past dirty faces.

Or maybe his taste didn't run to angels?

She had no idea why she felt so let down. It wasn't as if she had been thinking of him as deep and meaningful when she looked at him, though a bit of dust on his face had not lessened his magnetism, she admitted, sliding a covert peek at his dark face.

But then it was hard to think of anything that would.

Slightly embarrassed, she waved back to the crowd that had gathered as the car drew away. As they vanished from view she opened her hand.

'Oh,' she gasped. 'I can't take this.' The gold medallion resting in her palm was obviously old; the carving was delicate. 'It must be valuable.' She held it out towards Rafael.

'It's a Saint Christopher.'

'I know. Take me back. I must return it.'

Rafael did not respond to her urgent request. 'You can't do that—it would offend him.'

'But…'

'He wanted you to have it.'

'I'm a stranger,' she protested.

'A stranger who saved his grandson's life, his *angel.*' And was she anybody else's angel? he wondered. Was there a man back home who would not be pleased that she had driven off into the mountains with a stranger?

She wore no ring, but that didn't mean she was unattached. For some women a man back home did not prevent them indulging in a holiday romance, though for some reason he was struggling to put her in that bracket.

The mockery in his voice brought Maggie's chin up. Her fingers tightened around the medallion. His cynical sarcasm made her see red. 'You shouldn't make fun of him,' she said fiercely.

'I wasn't making fun of *him.* I couldn't help but notice you were enjoying the attention.'

This totally unfair scathing evaluation took Maggie's breath away. 'And their heirlooms, don't forget that. I managed to fleece them too.' She allowed her dark eyes to move contemptuously over his patrician profile before putting the medallion over her head. She freed her tangled hair from the chain. 'You do know that you are a very unpleasant man, don't you?'

'Is that why you let me pick you up?'

Colour scored her pale cheeks. 'I made a mistake and assumed you couldn't be as shallow and superficial as you appeared—I was wrong. And you sulk.'

The bitter afterthought drew a startled look from Rafael.

'I'd be happier having cheated death once today if you kept your eyes on the road.'

'Sulk?' Accustomed to hearing the women in his life express rapturous praise, Rafael struggled to swallow this more critical analysis of his character.

On any other occasion his utter astonishment at the accusation might have drawn a smile from Maggie.

'Well, you're obviously in a strop over something, but I'd be grateful if you didn't take it out on me.'

They had passed through the village before reaction hit her. She started to shake. She tugged the blanket closer and made a clinical diagnosis of delayed shock.

'Are you cold?' Rafael asked, adjusting the heating.

Biting back a childish, 'Like you'd care' she compressed her lips and said coldly, 'I'm fine.'

'Then why are you shaking?'

She was bewildered by his continued hostility and accusing manner. Did he think she was acting?

Determined to give him no opportunity to accuse her of being an attention seeker or canvassing the sympathy vote she plastered on a cheery smile.

'I'm not,' she denied. 'I feel fine.' It was only a very small lie, actually. Other than her shaking hands and the scratches on her arm that were stinging she really didn't feel too bad, and she would feel a lot better once this man was a distant memory.

She was a very bad liar, though even a good liar, Rafael thought, his eyes flickering briefly in her direction, would have struggled to deny the chattering teeth and milky pallor.

Accustomed to the company of women who did not know the meaning of 'putting on a brave face,' he realised that stoicism was an overrated quality. And, far from making a woman low maintenance, all it meant in reality was a man could never relax. He would always be wondering if the bright smile actually hid an inner anguish.

Not that her anguish, inner or otherwise, was anything to do with him.

Sweat broke out like a rash over his upper lip as he relived those moments when he'd thought he wasn't going to outrun the avalanche of destruction, that he was going to see her lost under half a runaway forest.

'I suppose you think it was a brave thing to do?'

'I didn't think at all,' she admitted, punching in the hotel number and missing the anger that pulled the skin taut across the sculpted bones of his face.

Rafael could not believe this woman. She was acting as if

nothing had happened—surely she realised what danger she had been in.

He realised it.

His entire body went cold every time he realised it. Even now he could feel the fear that had clawed across his skin as he had been forced to stand by, helpless, and watch, unable to stop her until it had almost been too late.

A fine sheen of sweat broke out across the golden skin of his brow when he recalled the moment that he had thought he would not reach her in time.

He was a man who did not indulge in pointless what-if scenarios, and Rafael's knuckles stood out white on the steering wheel as he found himself unable to stop projecting images, each one more horrific than the last. They all ended the same, with her broken, crushed body, and he would have been at least indirectly responsible.

She wouldn't have been in a position to be harmed if he had not lured her away from the city. He might not have intended her actual harm, but he definitely hadn't had her best interests at heart.

If anything *had* happened to her…? The unaccustomed guilt lay heavy on Rafael's shoulders.

'They will probably inscribe that on your headstone.'

The bitterness in his voice drew Maggie's indignant gaze to his face. 'There's no need to take it out on me and I'm not planning on needing one just yet!'

Rafael, his eyes trained on the road ahead as he swerved to avoid a pothole, asked, 'Don't take what out on you?'

Maggie compressed her lips, aware that if she said she thought he had switched off the charm offensive and started to be so nasty because his expected one-night stand had turned into something more tedious it would be tantamount to an admission she had been expecting the same outcome this evening.

And you weren't?

Frowning at the ironic voice in her head, she punched in the hotel number again.

'You might as well put that phone down.'

Maggie ignored him. 'I need to leave a message.' The tour guide would not worry if she missed the optional evening entertainment, but if she didn't arrive back until the early hours it was possible that they might start to worry. 'I had plans for this evening.'

'So did I.'

She flashed him a look and he added, without looking at her, 'We have no signal here.'

'I saw you using your phone.'

An expression she struggled to interpret broke the impassive stoniness of his expression. 'There is no signal this side of the mountain.'

Despite the information, she tried once more before admitting defeat. 'What time will we reach the city?' she asked, dropping the phone back in her bag.

In the mirror he caught sight of her pressing her nose to the window like a child… Nothing else about her was childish. Recalling the softness of the warm body he had carried sent an indiscriminate pulse of lust through his body.

'You will have to delay your plans,' he informed her shortly. 'We are not going to the city.'

The abrupt afterthought sank in and Maggie swivelled in her seat. 'Is that a threat?'

He looked bored and said, 'A fact.'

'But I want—'

'What you want is not factored into my plans. You know the time—it is not practicable to drive into the city. I have a house nearby.' Beautiful women always thought the world revolved around them and just because she had a reckless streak that made her perform stupidly brave acts did not exclude Maggie Ward from this rule.

'You said you would see me safely back.'

'I did not say when.'

'So when? Next week, next month?' she enquired with silky sarcasm.

The silence stretched.

'Are you trying to scare me?'

A raw laugh left Rafael's throat. 'Scare?' How, he wondered, did you scare a woman who had so little regard for her own safety? Under that soft exterior Maggie Ward had a core of steel. 'Is it working?'

'In your dreams,' she snorted. 'Are you always this rude?'

He turned his head briefly and flashed her a grin that did not reach his steely eyes. 'Yes.'

Her jaw tightened as she angled a narrow-eyed glare of seething dislike at his profile. 'You really must be Mr Popularity.'

'People generally overlook my manners.'

'You're not *that* good-looking,' she lied, then flushed at the implied compliment.

'I'm crushed,' he said, sounding anything but.

'It shows,' she retorted, wondering how she could ever have thought this man sensitive and charming—he was a shallow, arrogant chauvinist.

'But I am that rich.'

This boast drew a scornful snort. 'I suppose you own this half of the mountain,' she said, nodding to the towering bleak presence to their left.

'And the other half and the village and two others actually.'

'And I'm a duchess. I'm not that gullible, and you're not that good a liar and as for your…*wow!*' Maggie let out a silent whistle, her gaze riveted on the illuminated façade of a stone castle complete with turrets that loomed before them.

'That is the most incredible hotel I have ever seen!' she admitted, envying the glamorous people who must stay at a place like that.

Was he planning on staying there?

If so, it was distinctly possible he hadn't been exaggerating the rich part. Well, that was one problem solved—they would have to part company. A place like that would not let her through the door looking like this.

'It is not a hotel.'

'You mean a family still lives there?' What an anachronism, she thought, in this day and age for one family to occupy so much space, but maybe seeing it sold off to a developer might be a worse crime.

Directing his car through large ornate wrought-iron gates that swished open silently at their approach, Rafael shook his head as he drove down the avenue lined with lime trees.

'No, just one person.'

'All that for one person…' She stopped, the colour receding from her already pale face as the penny finally dropped. 'It's yours, isn't it?'

CHAPTER EIGHT

HE confirmed her suspicion with a tiny nod of his head. 'You can use the landline to leave that message about your change of plans.'

'My plans haven't changed.' Maggie found herself protesting to his back.

She was presuming they were expected because as his feet hit the gravel people started to appear. Presumably, she thought sourly, to respond to the commands he was issuing—at command issuing he was definitely not an amateur.

Maggie began to struggle with the car door, her spirits slightly buoyed because she realised that all she had to do was ask the hotel to send a taxi out to pick her up.

She wasn't stranded or reliant on Rafael.

'Allow me.'

Of course the door opened smoothly for him. Maggie nodded her head in an attitude of cold courtesy. 'Thank you.' It was good to feel in control again—*you wish.*

'Can you manage or shall I carry you again?'

Was that a joke? Maggie decided she didn't want to know. She pushed away the memory of being held in his arms and waving a hand in a shooing gesture, snapped crankily, 'I've told you I'm fine.'

Catching sight of her reflection in the wing mirror, she realised that she did not look fine.

The inner masochist in her made Maggie take a second look, she barely repressed a groan.

It wasn't hard to see why the smouldering Spaniard had stopped smouldering, and who could blame him for going off her big time?

Her hair had returned to its natural curly state; surrounding her face in a dark tangled froth and hanging loose down her back, it made her look scary. As for her face minus all make-up and plus a lot of dirt… She closed her eyes and thought it was just as well the seduction idea was off the menu.

'We have mirrors inside.'

His tall figure, backlit by the light streaming through the open door, stood there, his arms folded across his exposed chest radiating impatience.

Maggie gave a grimace, embarrassed at being caught out staring at her reflection. 'I'm coming,' she huffed, jogging to catch him up.

Rafael watched her approach with a frown. 'Slow down. There's no fire.'

Maggie rolled her eyes. 'Make up your mind!' It seemed to her that it didn't really matter what she did—as far as this man was concerned it would be the wrong thing.

The massive metal-banded oak door she followed him through opened directly into what appeared to be an old banqueting hall complete with roaring fire, suits of armour and tapestries on the stone walls.

How many centuries had his family lived here? she thought, wondering what it must be like to trace your roots this far back. Her eyes widened…my God!

She spun around. 'I've forgotten your full name.'

He blinked at the confession. 'Rafael-Luis Castenadas,' he revealed, watching her face carefully for a reaction.

There was none. If she had come to search for her mother, he would have thought she would be more than familiar with the name.

'Ramon will show you where you can use the phone.'

'You…?' She was talking to his back. She wrapped her arms around her body, fighting the vulnerable sensation—vulnerable because Rafael Castenadas's presence did not offer her security.

Quite the contrary was true.

A tall thin man wearing a dark suit and a sombre expression, presumably the Ramon in question, escorted Maggie to a room off an inner hallway. Despite the massive dimensions it was actually quite cosy-looking, with book-lined walls, vibrant-coloured rugs on the polished wood floor and a fire burning in the open fireplace.

To complete the domestic picture a dog of indeterminate parentage lay asleep on one of the large sofas. It opened one eye when Maggie walked in, wagged its tail and went back to sleep.

The thin man nodded towards the phone, and went to leave.

'No…don't…' She dropped her outstretched hand when he turned.

'Can I help you?'

She gave a sigh of relief. 'Great, you speak English. I was wondering, where am I exactly…the address, I mean, of here? Does here have a name?'

If he found the request odd he did not show it, and when Maggie struggled to follow his pronunciation of the *castillo* he produced a notepad and pen from his breast pocket and wrote it down for her.

After her concern that someone might be worried, it appeared no one had noticed her absence! Maggie explained to the person at the other end that she would need a taxi to pick her up. When she gave the address, spelling it out to avoid any mistakes, there was a loud intake of breath the other end, but the hotel agreed it would be no problem.

'Oh, and how much would it be likely to cost?'

The reply to her afterthought took her breath away. 'You're joking.'

The voice the other end assured her that he was not.

Knowing that there was no way her tight holiday budget would run to that sort of money, Maggie thanked him for his trouble but explained that she'd changed her mind.

With a sigh she hung up and sat down beside the dog.

'So what,' she asked, burying her face in his fur, 'do we do now?'

She was still no nearer an answer when fifteen minutes later Rafael walked in.

He made no sound. It was the prickle on the back of her neck that made Maggie turn her head.

She stopped stroking the dog's ears.

'How long have you been standing there?' Nervous tension made her voice sharp.

He had changed and presumably showered, his wet hair was slicked back and he was wearing dark jeans and a white open-necked shirt with no tears. He could have stepped right out of a glossy page advertising…well, actually, advertising anything, because when they said that sex sold they were not wrong.

And every inch of his tall, lean, muscle-packed frame oozed sex, every hollow and plane of his dark face. Maggie's eyes drifted from the full curve of his sensual upper lip to his hooded glittering gaze and her anxiety levels went off the scale.

She licked her lips nervously and drew her knees up to her chin.

'Not long.' He clicked his fingers and the dog lifted his head, his tail thumping loudly against Maggie's legs.

Rafael said something in Spanish and the dog immediately jumped off the sofa and, tail still wagging, went and sat by his side.

'He knows he is not allowed on there, but he likes to push the boundaries…and see how far he can go.'

'Then you click your fingers and bring him to heel.' He probably used the same method with his women, she thought sourly.

And I bet it works. Imagining the sort of women a man who looked like him and lived in a place like this normally shared his bed with did not improve her mood.

Not that she had any intention of sharing his bed, even if she was invited, which now seemed doubtful. No, her loss of sanity had only been temporary she was now fully in control.

You keep telling yourself that, Maggie.

She was no longer amazed that his initial interest had waned, but she was amazed that he had ever been interested in her in the first place. She had seen the sort of woman she was willing to bet he dated, polished and elegant, not a hair out of place, not a nail chipped and not an extra inch anywhere on her svelte silhouette to ruin the line of her designer clothes.

'A reward helps,' he said as the dog took a treat from his fingers before trotting over to the fire and flopping down. 'It is sometimes hard to work out who has trained who,' he remarked ruefully.

Maggie, who couldn't imagine anyone calling him domesticated, shrugged and swept her hair across one shoulder, thinking if he resembled any animal it was a wolf.

'Sorry about your plans.' He walked across to a cabinet,

pulling out a bottle and two glasses. 'Tonight did not go as either of us anticipated.'

She laughed. 'I think you could call that the understatement of the century.' And she was betting things not going to plan was not something that happened to him often.

He didn't just have the looks and the animal magnetism, Rafael was also clearly a rich, powerful man, used to getting what he wanted.

Had he *really* wanted her…?

She breathed through the illicit thrill that raced along her nerve endings at the startling thought. The point was he was used to seeing something and getting it, and equally quickly losing interest. A car, a painting or a woman, and things went smoothly for him because people were there to make sure they went smoothly.

She was sure he had people whose sole purpose in life was to shield him from the unsightly.

Under normal circumstances their paths would never have crossed, but they had and he had thought, Why not…? Had he calculated she was worth the effort of a drive into the country, but when the effort had involved dust, tears and messy hair he had begun to regret his eccentric choice?

She tugged at the medallion that hung between her breasts and watched as he poured some amber liquid into the bottom of both glasses. 'I don't want a drink.'

He shrugged and lifted a glass to his lips. 'Well, I do.' He took the place she had vacated and looked at her over the rim of his glass; his ludicrously long, dark, spiky lashes cast a shadow along his razor-sharp cheekbones.

'Well we've both gone off the idea of a one-night stand.' She laughed and tried to act as though this were something that happened to her every day of the week. 'So where do I sleep? I'm assuming I can cadge a lift back tomorrow morning?'

She was about as convincing as silicone implants. 'You've never had a one-night stand, have you?'

Maggie considered lying, but decided it was doubtful she could pull it off. 'Not as such…' she conceded reluctantly.

A muscle beside his mouth clenched. 'But you came with me. What were you thinking of?'

Outrage with no trace of irony…talk about double standards! 'You invited me, but let me guess—it's not the same thing. God, I haven't actually been missing anything, have I? Simon probably did me a favour.' Now there was a novel thought. 'Men are a total disappointment!' she concluded heavily.

Rafael, struggling to follow the angry diatribe, picked up on one word. 'Who is Simon?'

He took a swallow of the brandy that appeared to have no effect on him, but Maggie, conscious that she was being uncharacteristically indiscreet, wondered if the effect could be passed on to her like a sympathetic pregnancy.

She was a sympathetic drunk; the frivolous imagery made her smile.

'Simon is my…was my fiancé.'

A look of utter astonishment crossed his face. 'You were engaged?'

Maggie lifted her chin. 'Why shouldn't I be engaged?' she demanded in a dangerous voice. 'What's wrong with me?' she asked, banging her chest. 'Just what's wrong with me?' Her voice stalled on a quivering note of self pity.

'Nothing is wrong with you.'

Maggie glared at his rigid blank face and snarled, 'Once more with feeling! I actually prefer you when you're incredibly rude. Mouthing polite platitudes you clearly don't believe. It's just so not you!'

'I am not rude.'

The denial made Maggie roll her eyes. 'No, you probably

call it not caring what people think. Well, newsflash, buster, it's the same thing!' she informed him, tacking on seamlessly, 'I think I will have that drink.' *Buster...?* She really had to cut down on her intake of gangster movies.

'Is that such a good idea?' he asked, wondering about the man who had let her go. Clearly not very bright, that went without saying, but what had attracted Maggie to this loser and did he still have all his limbs intact?

She might look like Angelina, but Angelina's daughter had definitely missed out on the statuesque calm gene; she was a real firebrand and bolshy with it, he thought, unable to repress the flicker of admiration.

Ignoring him, Maggie walked across to the bureau and picked up the glass. Surprised by the weight of the antique lead crystal, she weighed it in her hand before she lifted it in a silent toast. Rafael watched one brow raised, as fifty-year-old vintage brandy vanished down her throat on one gulp.

'That must have hurt.'

Maggie lifted a hand to her throat, feeling the burn all the way down to her stomach. 'It still is,' she admitted, covering her mouth politely as she coughed.

Rafael found himself laughing. He went from being furious with her to enchanted. She really was delicious and not like any woman he had ever encountered. It was as if the less she tried to please him, the more he was fascinated.

'Do they actually let you out without a keeper?'

'Time off for good, possibly *angelic* behaviour. You know what my mistake was?' The burn, she realised, had become a glow settling warmly in the pit of her stomach.

'I know I will probably regret asking this, but what was your mistake, Maggie Ward?'

'I thought I could become another person just like that.' She snapped her fingers to illustrate her point. 'But you can't... I should have started with a motorbike or a tattoo...with you I was…' She watched him shake his head in utter confusion but didn't try to explain—he'd never understand. 'You've got to keep it real and know your limits.'

Rafael, to whom *real* was fast becoming a dim and distant memory, took the half-full glass from her hand. The scary part was she was still well under the legal limit. 'And I am not real?'

'You're a mistake,' she admitted. 'Jumping in the deep end. I wanted to prove to Simon…Millie, my mum…no, *myself…*' She looked shocked by the admission and sat down abruptly. 'I really don't know what I was or am doing…a lot of things have been going on in my life just lately.' And he really wants to know this, Maggie, she admonished herself.

'Sometimes the past is better left undisturbed.' He could see how delving into a background, searching for roots, might make a person question their life.

Maggie lifted her eyes, a little bemused by the intensity of his fixed regard.

Did he think she had a past? She almost wished she did have. Either way, she wasn't about to admit she was actually a blank boring page, especially when it came to men and sex.

God, I don't want to die a virgin.

She tried to think of a suitably enigmatic response and blurted, 'But doesn't the past make us what we are?' His past had to be littered with glamorous, beautiful women.

'I like to look forward, not back.' And when he looked back on tonight, would it be with regret?

Regret that he had resisted the temptation that was driving him slowly out of his mind? Or regret because he had ignored the nagging voice of his conscience?

Did he want her so much because she was out of bounds? he speculated. And why was she out of bounds? What had changed between first seeing her and now? They were two consenting adults—why should they not enjoy each other?

'What were you thinking when I came in? You looked very deep in thought.'

'Isn't that looking backwards?'

'Touché!'

Her eyes slid of their own volition to the sensual curve of his sculpted lips.

Simon had never made her feel attractive.

The way Rafael had looked at her when they'd met, she had felt more aware of her femininity than Simon had made her feel in four years.

'You have a very impressive home.' He was a very impressive man.

'Are you changing the subject?'

'Yes.'

He released a laugh. Maggie tilted her head back as he got to his feet, and shuffled to the far end of the sofa as he sat down beside her.

'Are you feeling better?'

'Better, but a bit…' Her voice died to a whisper when he reached across and trailed a finger down her cheek. 'Near-death experiences will do that.'

She felt intense relief mingled with troubling regret when his hand fell away. 'I just keep thinking what if I hadn't met you tonight?'

Was she wondering about the confrontation with her birth mother? For the first time he considered today from Maggie's point of view.

She might have dreaded the meeting. It might have taken her weeks to work herself up to the moment and, perhaps not fully committed, still wondering if she was doing the right thing, she had stepped back.

Was she regretting it now? Was she wishing she had not allowed herself to be diverted?

'If you hadn't brought me there, would those children have…?' She shook her head.

He watched a visible shudder pass through her body and realised it was another 'what if' that was plaguing her.

'They are fine, you are fine…' A nerve in his lean jaw jerked as the slow-motion replay of the event in his head reached the moment when he had thought she would not be fine. 'You can't live your life thinking what if…' he continued hoarsely.

Maggie turned her head, their eyes meshed and Maggie felt some of the tension leave her body. She sighed slowly and nodded and said, 'But what if…?'

He loosed a husky laugh and lifted a finger to her lips. 'Enough.'

It wasn't the firm admonition that silenced Maggie, but the confusing combination of sensations that was coursing through her body.

His thumb stayed at the corner of her mouth, his eyes sealed to hers; the air was thick with an almost electrical charge that made it hard for her to breathe.

He leaned into her close, very close, but not touching. Her heavy lids half closed as she swayed closer as though drawn by some invisible thread that connected her to him. 'Your skin smells…' He exhaled and she felt his brandy-scented breath on her cheek.

He stopped and she thought, Bad…good? Say something…do something…touch me.

'It's late. We should go to bed.' He had never in his life felt a need so raw, so primal to possess a woman.

She gave a fractured sigh. Her heart rate quickened but her body relaxed. It seemed right. 'Yes.'

He met her eyes shining with promise and trust and he heard himself say, 'Perhaps this is not a good idea.'

She felt her smile slide off her face, and flinched as if he'd just thrown cold water in her face. Not water, Maggie, just a reality check. This is what happens when you start thinking you're irresistible.

She lifted her chin. 'I am a bit tired.' She gave an artistic yawn to demonstrate the point, then spoilt the pretence by adding, 'I'm not drunk, you know.'

'I know you're not.' Scruples, he decided, were very overrated and painful, and what would be achieved by depriving them both of an experience that would, he knew, be pleasurable?

She felt the mortified heat reach her cheeks. To have one man politely excuse himself from her bed was one thing; two… There had to be something seriously wrong with her.

'This day started quite well, and this may sound dramatic but it really is turning into the worst day of my life. You'll laugh, but actually I thought…' She stopped, shook her head. He wasn't laughing; he was staring at her with a fixed intensity that she was not going to mistake for blind lust. 'I really do feel like an idiot.'

'You're not an idiot.' He took hold of her elbows and looked down into her heart-shaped face, gazing deep into her liquid dark eyes. 'But you do have a smudge on your nose…right there,' he said, kissing the spot.

Do not read anything into it, Maggie… 'It's fine—you don't fancy me…perfectly understandable…look, you're not the first man to be able to resist me. I'm not going to take it personally. I'm not really—'

'Shut up!' He hooked a finger under her chin and he captured her eyes and like a primal blast the blaze of hunger in his drove the air from Maggie's lungs in one shocked gasp.

She melted, paralysed by a combination of raw lust and desperate longing, unable to catch her breath; her fingers closed around the hard muscles of his upper arms.

'Do you want to spend the night alone, Maggie?'

Maggie's eyes closed as he kissed the corner of her mouth, her body twisting and arching as she tried to insinuate herself closer. 'No,' she whispered against his mouth. Then she opened her eyes, looked at his lean dark face so close to her own, and said, 'No!'

He smiled at the defiant declaration, a slow, predatory smile that sent her stomach into a spasm of raw excitement. The tension in the air between them thickened; it shimmered.

'Neither do I.'

CHAPTER NINE

THE raw hunger in his kiss blazed along Maggie's nerve endings, vaporising any lingering doubts or fears. This was what she wanted, Rafael was what she *needed.*

She held his face between her hands as his lips moved expertly over her own, the slow, languid exploration a torment and a revelation. At the first erotic incursion of his tongue into her moist mouth she moaned deep in her throat and opened her mouth to invite him deeper, meeting his tongue with her own.

They kissed with a frantic hunger and all the time he touched her, his hands sliding over her soft womanly curves, dragging moans from her lips.

When he did lift his mouth fractionally from hers it was to rasp, 'I love your mouth. It is a miracle. You are a miracle…so soft.' He ran a finger down her throat, his eyes darkening as he felt the deep shiver that rippled through her body. 'So sensitive to my touch.'

'You won't stop, will you?'

She felt the rumble of laughter vibrate in his chest as he pulled her under him and laid her full length on the sofa. There was no laughter in his face as he stared down at her, just a fierce, relentless hunger that tightened the knot of excitement low in her belly.

'Not any time soon,' he promised huskily as he lowered his body onto hers. 'I don't believe any man could resist you. It is not possible… *Madre mia,* I have wanted you from the moment I saw you.'

Maggie gasped, her eyes flying wide as she felt the pressure of his arousal against her belly. Her arms slid around his middle, pulling him closer. She was revelling in the amazing feel of his lean hard body against her and pleasurably conscious of the fresh rush of liquid heat between her thighs.

The heat burned between them as they kissed, he touched her everywhere. Maggie slid her hands under the hem of his shirt. She heard him gasp at the touch of her fingers on his bare flesh and would have pulled her hand away but he caught her wrist and, holding her eyes, placed it back on his body, spreading her fingers and saying huskily, 'I want to feel your hands on me, *querida.*'

Maggie's throat was too congested with emotion to speak. She nodded mutely and trailed her fingers slowly across the ridges of muscle on his flat belly.

Rafael closed his eyes, sucked in a breath, then lowered his head and kissed her with a driving ferocity that made her head swim. His mouth still connected to hers, he raised himself off her, unfastened his shirt with one hand and stroked her face with the other, his fingers tangled in her hair.

Maggie opened her eyes just as the fabric parted. Weak with lust and longing she stared, her passion-glazed stare moving hungrily over the gleaming hard lines of his greyhound-lean, muscle-ridged bronze torso.

A deep, sobbing moan was wrenched from her throat. The sound made the hairs on the nape of Rafael's neck stand on end and propelled him into frenzied action.

Slowed only by the tremor in his fingers, he unbuckled his belt and slid his jeans over his hips before kicking them away.

Kneeling astride her, clad only in boxers—the erotic image,

she knew, would be permanently etched in her brain—he began to undress her.

Every brush of his fingers on her hot skin sent shimmies of tingling sensation along her sensitised nerve endings.

As he peeled her bra from her shoulders a deep gasp was wrenched from deep in the vault of Rafael's chest. His golden skin glistened with the need that drove him as he stripped off her pants, sliding them with tantalising slowness over her smooth thighs.

Suddenly overwhelmed by self-consciousness she gasped, 'This isn't me!' And tried to cover herself.

Rafael caught her hands and pinned them above her head, holding them lightly there with his hand.

'Look at me.'

Maggie reluctantly turned her head. Without a shred of self-consciousness he divested himself of the boxers she had imagined concealed nothing; it turned out they did. She swallowed and felt her cheeks burn as guiltily she wrenched her eyes higher.

'This is me, and you are allowed to look, and want and touch. There is no shame, just sex. This is natural and good.' He had a very poor opinion of the person who had made her feel differently. 'This *is* you…and I will look. I will look because you are—' he swallowed as his glance dropped '—*Dios mio,* your are perfect…so unbelievably perfect.'

He cupped one pink-tipped breast in his hand, drawing the straining point between his fingers, rubbing the sensitised flesh before he lowered his head and applied his tongue to the engorged nub.

Maggie writhed under his touch, her fingers sinking deep into his hair. Her hips lifted as he ran his tongue down the soft curve of her belly, then lower.

As he parted the delicate folds, stroking her, Maggie

squeezed her eyes tight closed and cried his name over and over until she could bear no more.

'This is…please…'

Satisfied that he had brought her to the brink and barely able to control his own driving hunger, Rafael settled between her parted thighs.

His hot, hungry eyes broke through the last shreds of Maggie's shredded control. Face flushed, dark velvet eyes glazed with passion, she spread her thighs wider and, reaching for him, whispered, 'Please, I need you inside…'

And then amazingly he was and she had not come close to imagining how impossibly marvellous, how *incredible* it could feel to have him throbbing hard and hot, filling her.

He registered her incredible tightness and her cry as he entered her and it took a few seconds for his brain to link the two and produce the explanation.

Her body tightened around him and Rafael could no longer resist the temptation to sink deeper into her silky smoothness.

Maggie's legs wrapped around his hips. It was incredible. She kissed his chest and hung on as each thrust of his body sent her deeper into a blissful delirium.

Above her his face was a rigid mask as he struggled to control himself to give her a taste of the pleasure she had never experienced.

When it hit her, the first wave of orgasm shocked a fractured cry from Maggie. Her head went back and she clung to him as another and another hit her, then exploded into a deep pulse of pleasure that went all the way to her toes… As the wave receded she felt Rafael stiffen above her and shiver as the heat of his release filled her.

Holding her head against his chest, Rafael stroked her dark hair. Their bodies slowly cooled. Maggie lay listening to the beat of his heart slow before she lifted her head and smiled at him.

Rafael did not smile back. He didn't say a word. He just lifted her up and, draping a throw around them both, carried her from the room and through the silent maze of hallways into a room that was dominated by a large four-poster bed.

He didn't take her to the bed. Instead he walked into the adjoining bathroom, a massive room of startling decadence with a vast sunken marble bath, armchairs and a carved fireplace with candles set in the grate and along the mantle.

With her in his arms he walked straight into the walk-in shower and switched on the water. As she watched the spray run over his dark face, making his skin glisten, he set Maggie on her feet.

Then still without a word he took the citrus-scented gel from an applicator and began to lather her skin. Gently but thoroughly he washed her, moving his hand in firm circular motions until she tingled everywhere.

Maggie didn't break the silence she just stood passively, her throat constricted by a myriad conflicting emotions she didn't want to analyse. The warm water was soothing, easing the aches and bruises on her body.

There was nothing remotely sexual about his ministrations, even though she could hardly *not* notice the fact that he was aroused.

It was all a little surreal. She felt as though she were watching the scene from outside her body, and strangely the experience was on one level even more intimate than what had preceded it.

Finally he switched off the water. He carefully wrung the excess moisture from her hair and swathed her in a towel, using another to dry her from head to toe before picking her up once more and striding back into the bedroom. The fire in this room was lit. Flames crackled as he pulled back the covers on the bed and laid her naked body on the crisp sheets.

She watched as Rafael used the damp towel to cursorily

blot the moisture on his own body before climbing in beside her.

He pulled her to him, fitting her curves into his angles before tilting her face up to his.

Finally he broke his silence.

'Now, *querida,* we will do this thing the way it should be done.'

'I thought it was fine the first time,' she admitted, feeling so relaxed that she was boneless, though sexual awareness remained like a prickle under her skin.

He kissed the pulse spot at the base of her slender neck and the prickle became an itch.

'You are not a woman who should settle for "fine" and I am not a man who delivers it.'

He delivered this not as an arrogant boast but more in the form of a simple statement of fact, and Maggie accepted it as such. When it came to matters carnal she was quite prepared to accept that Rafael was the expert.

'But?'

He touched a finger to her lips. 'And afterwards we will discuss how it is that you were a virgin.' His eyes darkened; the discovery was one that would stay with him for ever. 'I could have hurt you and that would have...'

The expression of self-loathing on his face as he broke off and swallowed hard drew a cry of protest from Maggie. 'You didn't—you were perfect.'

His mouth curved into a complacent smile. 'Yes, you mentioned that. Don't blush—a man likes to be appreciated.' The smile faded from his face. 'Now let me show you how much I appreciate you.'

Maggie's eyes darkened. 'Please,' she whispered.

Much later as he lay still sheathed in the heat between her thighs Rafael struggled to make sense of his reluctance to break the physical connection even though his sexual hunger and hers were satisfied—finally.

He looked at her face pressed against the curve of his shoulder her lashes dark on her cheek as she surrendered to sleep and he realised it was foolish to analyse such things. It was not as if it were a meeting of souls; they were sexually compatible. Maggie was an amazingly passionate woman and an incredibly intuitive lover.

Rafael suspected there was still more passion there just waiting to be awakened. It was a pity that she would not be here long enough for him to unlock that promise.

CHAPTER TEN

MAGGIE put down her coffee cup and stared at Rafael. She waited for the maid who had fetched fresh coffee to leave before she replied to his invitation.

'You're suggesting I spend the rest of my holiday here, with you.'

Rafael refilled his own cup. 'It seems logical.'

His idea of logic and hers were very different. 'Not logical—mad.'

'How so?'

She looked at him in astonishment. 'It's totally crazy.'

'That is not an argument and, anyway,' he said, considering her freshly scrubbed image with a smile, 'I think you need some crazy in your life.'

She shook her head. 'Last night was enough crazy to last me a lifetime.'

'I seriously doubt that.' He planted his elbows on the table and leaned towards her, a knowing look on his face. 'You're thinking about it, aren't you?'

She responded to the goad with a frown and firm denial that she almost immediately cancelled by saying, 'I couldn't?'

'But you want to.'

'I have plans.'

Rafael, who knew about her plans, said, 'Dump your plans.'

She tried to look amused when she asked, 'Do women always dump their plans for you?' Because of course she knew they did and she knew why.

Last night had been the most mind-blowing experience of Maggie's life, and she would cherish it forever. Walking away this morning was hard—in a week's time just how much harder would it be?

The thought frightened her and made her hesitate.

'You will not regret it, I promise.' While she was here with him Angelina was safe.

You're such a saint.

Rafael ignored the sardonic voice in his head and added, 'Did I not fulfil my promises last night?'

Maggie closed her eyes, hearing his smoky voice in her head promising her a glimpse of paradise and more. And he had made good on the promises more than once.

'I've got nothing here, no clothes…no…'

He glanced at the watch on his wrist. 'I am having your luggage brought from the hotel. It should be here shortly.'

Maggie laughed. 'You were that sure I'd stay?'

'I was that sure that I want you to stay. I will make this a holiday to remember.'

'It's already that.' It would be strange going back to her normal life after this.

'So why do you look sad?' He had never experienced a desire to make a woman smile before, but he did now.

She shook her head. 'I'm not sad…mad possibly,' she conceded, 'but not sad, just…' She screwed up her nose and gazed around the room. 'This is not my life.'

'What is your life?' Rafael heard himself ask and frowned. This situation had been a lot simpler when he had thought of her as a problem to be solved. When, he wondered, had she become a person?

A beautiful and desirable person, and her smile made him happy.

The question seemed serious. She stared at him and then to lessen the intensity of the moment she summoned a smile. 'If you have a spare five minutes I might actually take you up on that invitation. But seriously…'

He cut across her. 'I was being serious.'

Her eyes fell from his. His intensity was unsettling; actually, he was unsettling.

She gave a strained little laugh. 'I'm sure you're not really interested…'

'I asked, didn't I?'

'I work in a city casualty unit. I'm a nurse.'

'A nurse?'

She tilted her head to one side and studied his face. 'You sound surprised.'

'I am,' he admitted, though now he thought about it he could see her in the role. 'The last time I was in a casualty department in England my nurse was a rugby player called Tomas. I'm feeling cheated.'

The glow in his eyes made her dizzy and excited.

'So its not just last night—you spend your time saving lives.'

Maggie gave an embarrassed shrug. 'It's not normally so dramatic and there is no danger involved, except of course when a drunk decides to take a swing.'

Rafael tensed. 'At you?'

Maggie who couldn't stop staring at the muscles clenching and unclenching beside his mouth, nodded. 'It has been known,' she admitted, blinking as he loosed a stream of fluid, angry-sounding Spanish. 'Don't worry,' she added, patting the clenched hand that lay nearest her and saying cheerily, 'I can take care of myself and I have very quick reflexes.'

'What sort of world are we living in when a nurse takes being assaulted for granted? *Madre di Dio,* your family allow this?' he grated incredulously.

'It's not really a question of allowing, is it? I'm over eighteen…I'm over twenty-one, and I've never been assaulted. It happens, but not to me.'

'But it could. Well, I,' he announced autocratically, 'would not permit it.'

'Well, I'm glad I'm not your sister.'

'So am I, but I have no sister.'

'Your father and mother?' she asked, wondering about this man whom she was alone with and realising he had told her nothing about himself. She had slept with a stranger and she had agreed to stay with him.

His shoulders lifted in a shrug. 'Both dead.'

The pragmatic statement did not invite sympathy but Maggie's tender heart ached. 'I can't imagine what that would be like.' A shadow crossed her face as she imagined a life that did not contain her family.

'So you have a family…?' Having pushed the Angelina question to the back of his mind, he did not enjoy the topic being front and centre where he could not ignore it.

She reached into her bag and pulled a family snapshot she always carried from her wallet. She held out her hand and offered it to him.

Maggie frowned as she watched an expression of astonishment wash over his dark face. He was looking at the snapshot as if it were an alien.

'Is something wrong? You don't have to—' She began to withdraw her hand but he caught her wrist.

'No, nothing's wrong,' he promised, taking the photo, not

because he actually felt any interest but because he knew it would have injured her feelings if he had refused.

Feelings were entirely new territory for him and he saw no urgent need to explore this development.

'I'm more used to being offered bills for designer shoes.'

Her brow furrowed in confusion at the comment. 'Why? Do you have a business interest?'

He regarded her in much the same way she imagined he might had she just announced that she believed in Santa Claus.

'No, I have girlfriends with expensive tastes who like me to pick up the tab.' He did not begrudge the expense, he considered himself a generous lover.

The plural was not wasted on Maggie.

Good God, where is your pride, Maggie?

I'm sleeping with a man who, not only does not promise something as basic as exclusivity, he probably doesn't understand the meaning of the word.

'If you ever pay for my shoes I will feed them to you.'

He stared. 'You don't like shoes?'

'You may not mind women who sleep with you for your money, but I mind being mistaken for one.' She pinned him with a wrathful glare and yelled, 'I'm sleeping with you for the sex! On a temporary basis, obviously.'

'Obviously, and I promise not to offend you with shoes, though I would like to point out that I like to think it is not just my money they sleep with me for.'

Maggie's eyes narrowed. She knew they didn't and she hated them all with a vengeance. 'You really do love yourself!'

His lashes lifted from his cheek and he levelled a direct look into her eyes. 'Love is not something I encourage.'

Maggie blinked. The warning was unmistakeable. Then before she could respond to it he began to study the snapshot, saying, 'Those are your brothers?' The young men in the slightly out of focus snapshot were both blond and broad-shouldered and duplicates of their father. All three men towered over their sister, and the woman in the wheelchair.

She nodded, wishing she had remembered sooner that this was not the most flattering photo she had ever appeared in. 'I still had my braces then.'

'Which accounts for the lack of a smile? The woman in the wheelchair…your mother?'

'Yes.' Maggie did not want to go into details, but added, 'But she's not in the wheelchair any more—at least, not all the time.'

'Your brothers are not much like you.'

Maggie grinned. Talking about her family made this abnormal situation seem less surreal. 'You mean because they're six feet four or because they're blond?' she suggested, raising a hand to her dark hair and grimacing as she realised it had come free of the ponytail and now hung loose in a tangled skein down her back.

'Your colouring is very…Mediterranean?' His glance moved across the glowing contours of her face. Her skin was flawless and had a peachy sheen that was almost opalescent. The idea of carrying her back to bed became more urgent than eating breakfast.

Maggie's eyes fell evasively, her long lashes brushing the soft curve of her smooth high cheekbones, but not before Rafael had seen the emotion flicker across her face.

'Actually, I wouldn't look like Ben and Sam. I'm adopted.'

'That must have been a shock…discovering you're adopted.' Rafael suggested, watching her push the gleaming strands of hair back from her heart-shaped face with both hands, looping it into a heavy bunch before letting it fall down her back.

She shook her head. 'Not really. I didn't *discover*—I

always knew I was adopted. Mum and Dad always made me feel special because they picked me.'

'But your brothers, they are…?'

'Big surprises, with an emphasis on the big,' she added with an affectionate grin. She felt some of the tension slip from her shoulders as a mental picture of her younger siblings formed in her head. 'Mum and Dad thought they couldn't have children so they were pretty shocked when Ben came along and then, a year later, Sam.'

'So your real mother?' he probed, wary of pushing too hard.

Her smile vanished. 'Let's talk about something else,' she suggested.

Rafael gave a casual shrug and didn't push.

'I really envy you being bilingual… Spanish is such a marvellous language and you have an incredible home. I have never met anyone who lived in a castle before.' She stopped, drew breath, and prayed for the floor to open and swallow her.

She had just taken inane babble to an entirely new level. On the plus side, at least she had run out of breath before she asked him about his heating bills!

No, actually there was no plus side.

'We don't have to talk at all.'

The invitation in his smoky, sinfully sexy voice would have been obvious no matter what language he chose to use. Maggie's breath snagged in her throat. Her eyes fused with his and Maggie's insides melted.

She reached for the coffee pot and refilled her cup. 'This is great coffee,' she enthused.

'Or we could…?' Rafael conceded drily.

Maggie, who couldn't stop staring at his long tapering fingers—she had never looked at a man's hands and thought about them on her skin, but now she had she couldn't stop—blurted with incurable honesty, 'I feel very out of my depth.'

She levelled her candid gaze at his face and wondered how she had ever been mad enough to think a one-night stand with him was a good idea.

'Once you learn to tread water, depth is not a problem.'

'I can't swim.'

'But you are a very fast learner.'

She blushed and looked at him through her lashes. 'You're a passable teacher, but you're also the sort of man I'd normally cross the road to avoid. You're not my type at all. It's crazy, but from the moment I saw you I…'

'You what?'

Maggie shivered. He had a voice that was the auditory equivalent of having your skin stroked against the deep pile of rich velvet.

'The moment I saw you I wondered…I wondered what sort of kisser you were.' And you had to tell him that why, exactly?

Rafael didn't move, didn't blink, but she heard the breath leave his lungs in one audible hiss.

She carried on looking at him.

It was said and there was no way she could unsay it. Near-death experiences did not make you braver, they clearly made you more stupid!

'God, pretend I didn't say that. I'm embarrassing myself…' she admitted, not looking at him. 'I'm embarrassing you.'

'I am not easy to embarrass.'

Her eyes lifted. 'I know,' she conceded unable to take her eyes off his dark face. 'Not that I'm suggesting that's a bad thing. It wasn't a criticism,' she added hastily, thinking not many people looking at his face would find much to criticise.

Her embarrassed little laugh transmuted into a sharp intake of breath as he left the table and came round to join her.

Holding her eyes, he took her hand and drew her up to him. Placing a hand behind her head, he tilted her face up to him.

'I too wondered when I saw you how you would taste. I wanted to find out right there in the street.' And what man would not? How could any man with red blood in his veins resist the combination of warm sexuality, wide-eyed innocence and a body made for pleasure? 'What would you have done if I had?'

'Screamed, called for help…?' she suggested, struggling to inject amusement into her voice and failing totally—her breath was coming in short choppy spurts that made it difficult to breath and impossible to raise her voice above a whisper.

'And now?' he asked, running his thumb across the cushiony pink surface of her lips.

She closed her eyes because looking at the flame burning deep in his—a trick of the light, probably—made her dizzy, and said, 'Are you going to kiss me or torture me?' She held her arms wide in a come and get me gesture and, eyes still tight shut, tilted her head back in invitation.

'When you put it like that I see it would be an act of charity to put you out of your misery.' The fever in his blood as he looked down at her made him shake—literally shake with need.

She tensed in anticipation of the plundering pressure of his lips; the light touch on the corner of her mouth took her by surprise.

Maggie's eyes flickered open. They were still open, welded to the silver gleam in his, as he increased the pressure slightly as his tongue followed the curve of her mouth, leaving a damp trail.

The heat and frustration inside Maggie mounted as she noticed just how ragged her breathing was.

'How was that for you?'

'You know your way around a mouth. Thank you.'

'Don't thank me yet,' he breathed against her mouth.

So I would get a good score, hmm?

His wicked grin flashed as he took her face between his big hands.

'That was not a kiss, that was merely the beginning… foreplay. I love the way you blush…I love your skin…'

'There is only so much foreplay, Rafael, a girl can take.'

The touch of his warm lips as they claimed her sent a tide of heat through her body. Rafael's arms slid around her body, pulling her close into him. Maggie's arms curled around his neck as she raised herself up on tiptoe and leaned into the male hardness of his lean body, excited by the leashed hunger that made him shake.

The excitement spiralled at the first sensual stab of his tongue into the warm, moist recesses of her mouth. She moaned with need and kissed him back, her hands bunching into fists as she grabbed the fabric of his shirt.

'I'm so sorry, darling, I had no idea.'

Maggie jumped away from him as if shot. Blinking as she struggled to clear the sexual fog in her brain, she stared. For some reason the star of a top American detective series was standing in the doorway.

CHAPTER ELEVEN

In the flesh and without the benefit of lighting and make-up and minus the skin-hugging trademark leather trousers Camilla Davenport was even more beautiful than the wise-cracking detective she played on the small screen.

Five ten in her bare feet, which she wasn't—her heels had to be at least four inches—she was dressed in what was probably the latest fashion. It was hard to find fault.

And Maggie tried!

In real life the actress's eyes were actually bluer, her lips even more incredibly pouty, and her breasts—was it even possible—more perky. And the people who said the camera put on ten pounds were obviously lying.

Was he sleeping with her?

Of course he was sleeping with her.

Maggie felt sick and stupid and plain. A plain, stupid woman throwing up—that would leave a great lasting impression, because obviously she was leaving. It would save him the bother of asking her to go.

'Camilla, what are you doing here?'

Rafael dragged a not quite steady hand through his dark hair and turned a less than welcoming glare on his ex-lover.

'And how did you get past Security?'

'Oh, don't blame them—nobody told the darlings I am yesterday's news. Rafe, *darling,* you look absolutely scrummy…' She advanced with a purposeful sexy sway and kissed him on the cheek, not from intention, but because he turned his head before she landed the kiss.

She gave a sigh and stroked a red-painted nail down his cheek. 'As always,' she said, adding with a pout, 'you are a spoilsport.'

Rafael issued her a glare of seething impatience and her hand fell away.

'Oh, all right, look, I can see my timing is absolutely lousy as usual—' she flashed Maggie a friendly look apparently totally all right to find her lover with another woman '—but I was up here to check on the house. I'm thinking of putting in a new pool. I have a little villa just across the valley,' she explained to Maggie. 'Rafael makes a *very* friendly neighbour.'

'I can imagine,' Maggie said, trying hard not to, but Camilla's attention and her fluttering eyelashes had already returned to Rafael.

'So I thought I'd come and say sorry in person and I am truly…'

Rafael struggled to contain his impatience. 'For what?'

She widened her eyes in amazement. 'God, you don't know! Wow, that's…awkward.' She lifted her brows and grimaced in Maggie's direction. 'He always reads the papers from cover to cover, doesn't he? But not today. I guess he was busy.'

Maggie blushed and Camilla gave a husky laugh and said, 'You're different.' Her attention swung back to Rafael. 'All right, I'll come clean. You remember that gorgeous weekend we spent on your yacht?'

'I remember.'

Would anyone notice if she slipped out? Maggie wondered bitterly. Or on second thought she might make a scene, a big, noisy scene, and smash a few things because dignity was not, in her opinion, any substitute for broken crockery.

Different—presumably that translated as not glamorous.

Camilla took a folded newspaper from her bag and spread it on the table. Rafael, oblivious to Maggie's violent plans, did not even glance at it.

He can't even take his eyes off the woman, Maggie thought miserably…and who can blame him?

'That afternoon on the deck when we got… It turns out we weren't alone. Tragic, I know, and so shocking—there's absolutely no privacy these days. I think it must have been that speedboat that passed…'

'Just as you took off your top.'

Maggie closed her eyes and thought, Just kill me now, let me die or, failing that, let me come up with a really good exit line!

'Timing is everything.'

Rafael walked over to Maggie's side. She tensed as she felt his fingers massage the tense muscles of her neck. 'You all right?'

Maggie moved away and, unable to come up with an exit line of any variety, mumbled, 'No, if you'll excuse me…'

He moved to block her exit and declared autocratically, 'No, I won't. I want you to hear this.'

Tears of anger and humiliation formed in her eyes. Did he want to rub her nose in it for some reason, or was he genuinely unaware of how humiliating this was for her?

Maggie wasn't sure which explanation was the worst.

'So why are these photos appearing now, Cami, three months after the event?'

Cami and *Rafe?* She really wanted to throw up now. A choked sound escaped Maggie's throat.

'What's wrong?'

That he could ask the question spoke volumes about his sheer titanic insensitivity.

'I always knew there was something missing, now I know what it is…a pet name for you, *darling*.'

The corners of Rafael's mouth twitched. 'I'm sure you'll think of something, *honeybunch*.' He turned back to the other woman and folded his arms across his chest. The levity left his eyes as he snapped coldly, 'Come clean, Cami.'

'All right, I can see you've guessed—you always do. The studio are meeting this weekend and there have been rumours flying around that they are going to cancel the show. The viewing figures were low, but that was because they killed off my love interest…I always said—'

'Cami!'

'All right, all right. I arranged for the photo to be taken as an insurance policy, and it turned out I needed it, and,' she added, clapping her hands and releasing a squeal of delight, 'it has worked. The photos are all over the Internet, your name guarantees that, and the studio have been on the phone all morning. They are *definitely* going to commission a third series and give me a pay hike. Aren't I brilliant?'

Rafael was at his most dry as he responded, 'Not the word I would have used.'

Cami gave a wide complacent smile. 'I knew you wouldn't be mad if I explained things.'

'You are a very devious woman, Cami.'

Maggie had struggled to follow the explanation—the American spoke very quickly and her brain was on a go-slow—but if she had got the facts even half right Rafael's attitude made no sense. The woman had used him and the apparent public appetite for stories about him, and he didn't even seem mad.

That made no sense at all unless…unless he was in love with the beautiful actress.

'Darling, a girl has to watch her back in this business if she doesn't have a man to do it for her.'

'Your agent would sell his soul for you, always supposing he ever had one.'

'Gus is a treasure but he doesn't do it for free.' She picked up a croissant from the table. 'You know, I'm totally starving.'

Rafael put his hands on her shoulders and turned her around. 'Say goodbye, Cami.'

She gave a philosophical smile. 'Goodbye...' She waved over her shoulder to Maggie, who stood like a small statue and watched Rafael steer her through the door.

When he returned a few moments later she was still standing in exactly the same place.

'Your luggage has arrived,' he said, setting her cases on the floor.

Maggie expelled a deep shuddering sigh and felt the life return to her body, and the anger and the burning humiliation.

She marched over to him and picked them up. 'I won't be unpacking.'

'Fine. I will buy you new clothes.'

She scrunched up her face in a grimace of loathing. 'I would prefer to walk around naked!' she yelled.

'I can work with that.'

She compressed her full lips into a thin line. 'I have no interest in being part of your harem!'

He studied her angry face for a moment in silence. 'Do you not think that perhaps you are overreacting?' he suggested calmly.

'Mildly!'

She stood her ground as he walked across to her, though by the time he reached her side her knees were shaking.

'You're crying.'

'Not because I give a damn about your sleazy sex life, I'm mad, that's all.'

'You're jealous.' The first display of jealousy was his signal to walk, but Rafael could see that this situation was different.

In what way exactly? asked the pedantic voice in his head.

Different required a different approach—not compromise, because he did not do compromise, but an explanation perhaps?

'You have no cause. Cami and I were lovers…'

She rolled her eyes. 'Shock, horror, call the press—oh, I forgot,' she trilled. 'They already know.' The world knows and he appears to care less. 'And save your explanations. I'm just someone you picked up—you don't owe me any.'

'Do not speak of yourself in that manner!' There was a reason he had spent his life facing problems head-on and not manipulating and nice talking his way around them—nice talk didn't work!

She blinked at the lash of anger in his voice.

'It's the truth.'

'It is a crude version of the truth and you are deliberately trying to provoke me.' A spasm of impatience tightened his lean face as he snapped, 'Shut up and listen. Past tense—we were lovers. I do not have a harem, I have one lover in my bed at a time and at the moment it is you.' And for some reason even though she drove him insane he wanted it to stay that way.

'You're not sleeping with anyone else.'

'I do not make a habit of explaining myself to people.' So what was he doing now?

'All right, you may not be sleeping with her, but you wish you were. It's obvious. You weren't even angry with her and she used you.'

'That was always a possibility.'

The calm admission made her stare.

'Cami is without scruples—charming,' he conceded, 'but utterly self-centred.'

'And good in bed,' Maggie, slightly mollified by his scathing assessment, inserted with a sniff.

He did not deny it, but no matter how expert a lover he had taken he had always been conscious of an empty, knowing sense of dissatisfaction even after the most satisfactory sex.

The feeling had been absent last night and this morning. Possibly her inexperience added a challenge that he needed?

'There are a hundred Camis—a thousand. I meet them wherever I go.' He studied the tear-stained face turned up to his and wondered if he would ever meet a Maggie again.

As she watched him dismiss the actress with a click of his long fingers she wondered if he would dismiss her in the near future in a similar fashion. He almost certainly would and the knowledge gave her a horrid sinking feeling in the pit of her stomach.

'Look, I could lock myself away behind high walls and massive security and never have an unflattering photo of me snapped. But I consider the price too high.'

'But you have a lot of money.'

The observation drew a grim smile from Rafael. 'It is not a question of cost.'

'Something only a very rich person would say.'

Rafael ignored her wry interjection and said quietly, 'I would become a virtual prisoner. Instead I walk the middle ground. I do not actively seek publicity and on occasions I go out of my way to avoid it, but I do not lose sleep over every insane story that appears about me.'

Maggie frowned, considering his words. 'All right.'

He regarded her warily. 'I believe you and I might have overreacted slightly.' *Slightly!* She had broken out with a bad case of the green monster; the amazing thing was he hadn't run for the hills.

'So we can go back to where we were before the interruption?'

The sultry look she flashed him through her lashes sent a pulse of lust through his already aroused body. 'I think we'd got past the foreplay.'

'Do not be so impatient,' he charged, slipping his hands around her waist. It was so tiny that he could almost span it. 'I am still waiting for you to score me on my kisses.' He pressed an open-mouth kiss to her neck and her head fell bonelessly back. 'Be generous,' he pleaded huskily.

CHAPTER TWELVE

MAGGIE forced her heavy eyelids open. Rafael's face was so close she could see the gold tips on his lashes and feel the warmth of his breath on her cheek. 'I'm thinking possibly above average.'

He inclined his dark head fractionally without taking his eyes from hers. 'Thank you.'

'You're welcome,' she said, breathing in his warm male musky scent and feeling dizzy—in a good way.

'You're a very beautiful woman.' He slid a hand into her hair and let the silky strands run through his fingers. 'A sensual woman.'

'You really think so?'

The indentation between his brows deepened. 'If you have any doubts, then I've been doing something wrong.'

'No, Rafael, you do everything right…so right it hurts…' She pressed a hand low on her stomach to show him where her agony was centred.

His smouldering eyes slipped to her mouth. Very slowly he lowered his head and kissed her; he kissed as if he would drain her, then he lifted her up into his arms and strode from the room.

'You do know all this macho stuff does nothing for me,'

she said, teasing the sensitive skin behind his ear with her flickering tongue.

'You are very bad for my ego.'

'Well, you're incredibly good for mine,' she confessed struggling even now to get her head around the fact the marvellous man fancied the socks off her.

Rafael removed more than her socks and she enjoyed every single second of it. She was determined to savour every moment of their short time together.

Over the next few days Maggie did not lose sight of her vow.

She did indeed extract the last ounce of pleasure from everything, from the sound of his laughter, to waking and feeling the warm weight of his arm across her waist, and the intimacy of a candlelit meal and a shared bottle of wine.

She savoured everything and firmly pushed away the lurking knowledge that it would all shortly end. It was getting harder to ignore the ticking clock.

She woke on the Wednesday and thought, Two days left.

She opened her eyes and the cheerless thought slipped away. Rafael's head was on the pillow beside her, his long lashes lying in dark fans across the chiselled contours of his cheekbones, his jaw darkened with a layer of piratical dark stubble.

Sleep had ironed some of the severity from his patrician features and the hank of dark hair flopping across his high forehead made him look younger.

She could have carried on looking at his face for ever.

Over the days some of his defences had come down and he had opened up and spoken to her about his family and the uncomfortable relationship he had had with his father, who sounded to Maggie like a sadistic monster.

When Maggie had voiced her opinion he had laughed, and told her that his father had never been that interesting.

She had learnt about his mother more slowly. Sometimes she had caught a look of surprise on his face when he'd spoken of her. She got the impression that it was not something he did often.

Then the previous night as they had lain, their bodies still cooling in the aftermath of lovemaking so intense that it had made her weep, he had explained abruptly why he had reacted so strongly to her tears.

'I was ten when my mother left. I never saw her again. She was crying.'

The association, it seemed, had stayed with him always.

He had not revealed the story in one go, it had slipped out in fragments that Maggie had joined like a puzzle to see the big picture, and it was a very sad picture that had made her tender heart ache for him. Though, knowing how allergic he was to any form of sympathy, she had made her response practical, contenting herself with hugging him hard until he'd laughingly asked if she was trying to break his ribs.

Amazingly he was not bitter that when faced with the stark choice his mother had chosen her lover over her son. He was not even sorry she had left, because, he'd explained, her marriage was killing her.

Maggie had realised that he wasn't speaking metaphorically.

She had fought back tears as he'd described watching her being reduced to a shadow of herself by her destructive marriage.

Aching with empathy, Maggie had felt his frustration—a child who had had to stand by and watch helplessly the systematic destruction of someone he loved.

No, it seemed that the thing that haunted Rafael was the angry words he had yelled at her while she left. Things he had never been able to retract because she and her lover had died not long afterwards in a train smash.

Maggie, her tender heart bleeding for the vulnerable child he had been, had wrapped her arms tight around him, laying her head on his warm chest.

'She would have known you didn't mean it. She must have known you loved her. And the last thing she'd want is for you to carry on beating yourself up over it. I mean, *she* must have been eaten up with guilt.'

She wasn't sure if her comments had helped but she hoped so. It had been late before they had slept and, not wanting to wake him now, she slipped from their bed careful not to disturb him. Shrugging on a towelling gown, she went downstairs to the big kitchen where she helped herself to coffee from the fresh pot on the stove before pulling a warm roll from the basket. Tossing it from one hand to the other as it burnt her fingers, she reached for a plate and the butter.

She was topping the butter with jam when Ramon entered the kitchen looking uncharacteristically flustered.

'If you're looking for him, the boss is still asleep.'

She hesitated to add, 'Can I help?' because, although the staff rather surprisingly acted as though her position in the household were permanent and had developed a habit of consulting her on domestic issues, Maggie was very conscious of her temporary status and always referred them to Rafael, who was not always appreciative of her tact. Only the previous day he had become extremely exasperated and referred the problem back to her after she had refused to mediate a minor domestic dispute.

'That is the problem. Sabina took it on herself to wake him when the guests—'

'He has guests?' Maggie tightened her robe.

This was the first time the outside world had intruded on her little idyll and it was an unwelcome reminder of how flimsy the foundations her happiness was based on actually were.

The world was out there and, like it or not, she had to go

back into it. She had wondered what she would say if Rafael suggested continuing their relationship after her holiday ended.

She had agonised over her response, finding the thought of never seeing him again hard to contemplate without horror. But would drifting slowly apart, as they inevitably would, be less painful? A cancelled visit, a missed call, watching the gradual disintegration of their relationship? Wouldn't a clean break be easier in the long run to bear?

In the end the question might be academic; he might not suggest it. While he never mentioned it ending, he never mentioned it carrying on either. And Rafael had never given any indication that he considered their time together anything other than a pleasant interlude.

For her part Maggie had resisted it, but she had finally been forced to ask herself why when she was around him her heart reacted independently of her brain.

He was the love of her life, and though she had always scoffed at the better-to-have-loved-and-lost theory she would not have had it any other way.

Him not returning her love was a tragedy, but not ever meeting him would in her mind have been an even greater one. She had embarked on the affair thinking that sex might liberate; in reality love had.

'I think I'll take my coffee upstairs.'

'Well, if you think that…' Ramon stopped. 'Perhaps that might be best, but I thought…' He shook his head and vanished, leaving Maggie to stare after him in perplexed bemusement.

The reason for his stress became more obvious when she entered the grand hall, her intention to take the short cut up the main staircase to their room.

She came to a halt and tried to blend into the background. Rafael was standing at the far end in the company of a man and woman, who was pushing a pram up and down with her foot.

The raised angry voices of the two men made it clear she had wandered into the middle of a private argument. Unsure whether to retrace her steps and use one of the rear staircases or try and slip unnoticed up this one, she hesitated uncertainly.

While she stood there the seated woman turned her head and the blood left Maggie's face. The plate and mug slipped from her nerveless fingers and she shook her head slowly from side to side.

This could not be happening.

The face she was looking at demonstrated how slim the line between beauty and average was; it was *her* face if her features had been perfectly symmetrical, if her lips had been less generous and her nose had been straight.

The woman stood and Maggie thought she could be looking in the mirror if she were four inches taller and half a stone lighter.

Nobody was shouting any more; they were all staring at her. She never had liked being the centre of attention, she thought, struggling to control the bubble of hysteria lodged in her throat.

The silence that had followed the shouting was unbearably loud.

'I dropped the plate.'

Her voice was the catalyst for a fresh bout of yelling. This time the woman joined in and the baby—no, *babies*—in the pram started to cry.

Feeling strangely disconnected from the drama unfolding and, for that matter, her own body, Maggie listened to the exchange of insults and accusation—a lot of accusation, and most of it aimed at Rafael, who made, it seemed to Maggie, only a token effort to defend himself.

His attention was constantly straying from those who were energetically jabbing the finger of blame at him to Maggie.

'How could you, Rafael! My daughter…you have betrayed every trust I ever had in you!'

'What gave you the right to assume…? I am not like your father…I thought we were friends…'

Maggie sucked in a breath, caught up in this strange nightmare moment but distant from it—distant from these people who were not her people.

The need for the comfort, the familiarity, of those she knew were there for her no matter what rose up inside her until she had to act on it.

'Nice to meet you, but I have to go now.'

Even though her voice had been barely more than a whisper the acoustics in the room were such that every word echoed around the room.

Silence broke out all over again.

Maggie dropped to her knees. 'I'll just…'

Rafael was at her side, taking her hand and cursing as he saw blood oozing steadily from the superficial cut.

'I could do with a dustpan, really.'

'Madre di Dios!' he breathed, lifting her into his arms.

He turned his head, murder in his eyes in response to an angry comment from the male half of the couple, before he strode up the stairs with Maggie in his arms. She didn't resist, she did not do anything—the blank look in her eyes scared him more than anything in his life!

He sat her on the bed and cleaned and dressed the wound. He pushed a glass of brandy into her hand. For a moment she looked at it blankly, then he saw something move at the back of her eyes a moment before, with calm deliberation, she tipped the contents on the floor.

'Was that who I think it is?'

'Yes, it was. Your mother is married to my cousin.'

The muscles along her jaw quivered as she looked at him with dark unfriendly eyes.

'No, she isn't, because my mother,' she said in a voice that quivered and shook with emotion, 'my mother looked after me when I had chicken pox and wanted to scratch the spots—she stopped me. She read my teacher the Riot Act when I was being bullied at school. She listened to my spellings when I had a test. I only need one mother and *that* woman is nothing to me…a stranger.'

'I know it must be hard for you to understand now, but Angelina was very young and her family—'

Maggie shook her head and covered her ears. 'I don't want to know her name. I don't want to know how sad and sorry she is. I want *nothing* from her. Do you understand? *Nothing!*'

'You're pretty judgemental. Haven't you ever made a mistake?'

The question drew a bitter smile from Maggie. 'Several, but the one I'm looking at right now makes the others fade into insignificance.'

She saw him flinch as her words hit home and she didn't care. She was glad. She wanted him to hurt as much as she was, even though that was impossible.

The burst of anger had actually cleared the fog of confusion in Maggie's brain, leaving cool, clear clarity in its place. As the argument's main points sifted through her mind she looked at her bandaged hand and noticed it had stopped shaking.

'Let me get this straight—is it true what that man said?'

'Alfonso my cousin.' Who now, it seemed, hated and despised him—there was a lot of it around! The next time anyone asked his advice he was going to develop selective deafness—not that this was likely to happen any time soon;

most, if not all, of the people he cared about were not talking to him.

'Was he right? You slept with me to stop me confronting *her* and spoiling a family party. You could,' she suggested bitterly, 'have just explained it wasn't a good moment. And I wasn't…'

'You weren't?'

'I have never wanted to trace my birth mother. I even split up with Simon because he did just that and now you…' She dropped her head into her hands. Rafael had seemed so different, but actually he wasn't.

He was worse!

She pressed her fingers to her pounding temples. Rafael covered them with his own and tilted her face to his. 'I admit it started out that way…'

'And then you fell desperately in love me…yes… Save your breath, Rafael, for the next starry-eyed fool who thinks every word you utter is gospel.'

'I have never lied to you, Maggie.'

'No, but you were pretty economic with the truth and anyway you didn't need to lie, did you? Because, let's face facts, I was easy!'

Rafael swore.

Maggie flinched away from his outstretched hand. 'It was all an act, wasn't it? And in the end such a waste of your *valuable* time, because I never presented any danger. I was not a scandal waiting to happen. I was just a silly girl who believed you were as special as you seemed. And you're not, you're not special, you're…' Her voice quivered as the tears began to seep unchecked from her eyes. 'I hate you and I wish we'd never met!' She raced to the wardrobe and began to pull her possessions off the rail. 'I'm going home.'

The dark lines of colour scoring Rafael's razor-edged cheekbones deepened as he watched her. 'I did not ask you to stay with me only because of Angelina and you did not stay because you hate me.'

Maggie spun back, her dark eyes glowing with scorn. 'Like you said yourself, I'm a fast learner, and actually hating is not so hard!' Maggie drew a hand across the nape of her neck to free the hair trapped under her shirt before sweeping it back from her face and securing it behind her ears.

'Do not be dramatic.'

The terse recommendation drew a low growl of incredulity from Maggie's throat.

'You could not regret the sex any more than I do…'

Maggie's head went back as though he had struck her. She bit her trembling lip.

'You were not so open,' he charged angrily. 'You did not tell me you were a virgin.'

Maggie's jaw dropped as she shook her head in disbelief—as if what he had done could compare. 'What was I meant to do—carry a sign around my neck? Call me an idiot, but I had this crazy idea I was missing out on something marvelous, that the experience would be liberating! How was I to know that it was all hype and no substance?'

He received the information with an aggravating air of disbelief. She wondered what it would take to dent this man's ego. More than a bad review from her, clearly—though it had been noted on more than one occasion that she was a bad liar.

'That is not what you said last night.' The memory sent a surge of lust through his body that Rafael was powerless to control…

Maggie gave a sniff and fixed him with a glittering glare, channelling cynical woman of the world as she admitted, 'I'm a great actress…sigh…gasp.' She let her head fall back and moaned, *'Please…please…you're so good at this,'* before straightening up and smoothing back her hair.

'You're so marvellous blah…blah…blah… Women have

been saying what men want to hear for ever. It was a good holiday, end of story, and now I'm going home.'

He took one last look at her angry, accusing face and shrugged expressively before turning and stalking stiff-backed towards the door. He paused in the opening and turned back.

'It may suit you to play the unwilling victim now, Maggie, but we both know that you were not!'

He had vanished before she thought of a suitable response. Tears streaming down her face, she ran to the door. He was nowhere in sight but she shouted down the corridor anyway.

'My fiancé turned out to be a complete and total loser and I decided that anything had to be an improvement. I was wrong!' she threw after him, before sliding to the floor and crying her heart out.

CHAPTER THIRTEEN

IT was a month later when Rafael made a discovery: it was actually quite easy to enjoy anonymity—all a person had to do was stand in a busy casualty department on a Saturday night.

He been standing in a corner of this noisy, crowded Casualty waiting room for an hour and nobody had approached him. He got the impression that if he stayed quiet he could stand there all night and nobody would; this, however, was not his intention.

He had a plan, well, not a *plan* exactly—for the first time in his life Rafael was winging it.

Another thirty minutes passed and the novelty value of being invisible began to lose its charm for Rafael. It occurred to him as he shifted his weight from foot to foot that he might have taken the under-the-radar approach a little too far.

His jaw clenched as he continued to scan the room. He had still not caught even a glimpse of her dark head and he was losing the struggle to control his frustration.

Inaction was not his thing for a reason—it was a very unproductive method of achieving a desired end.

And his desired end remained elusive. He shifted his weight from one foot to the other and wondered how she worked in this place surrounded constantly by all this ugliness and suffering.

Rafael watched a man dressed in a security uniform approach, stop a few feet away and wait expectantly.

'Can I help you, sir?'

Rafael flashed him a look. 'I should not think so.'

The security guard, who had all the responses to belligerent or threatening behaviour—not that he wasn't extremely relieved that this tough-looking customer was displaying neither—struggled for a response to this polite but unhelpful reply.

'Have you given your details at the desk?'

'I am waiting for someone.'

'I'm afraid…Mr…?'

'Castenadas,' Rafael supplied.

He watched the inevitable flicker of recognition in the other man's eyes, and gave a philosophical shrug. Security guards tended to have a lot of time to flick through tabloids.

'Do I know you? Your face…'

Rafael was saved the necessity of responding because a smashing sound, loud enough to be heard over the general babble in the waiting area, followed by raised voices caused the man to break off.

Like everyone else Rafael turned in the direction of the sound, then he heard the cry—a cry of pain followed by the distinct sound of breaking glass.

Rafael, responding to the rush of adrenaline that flooded through his body, hit the ground running. He was through the swing doors and parting the curtain before the security guard had finished summoning help.

The scene was chaos: an overturned trolley, broken glass, instruments all over the floor and a large thug slurring a string of loud abuse at the figure crouched on the floor.

Some gut instinct had told him the cry had come from

Maggie's lips. Even so, seeing her there made him reel as though a blow had landed through his defences.

She lifted her head, saw him, gave a sob of relief and said, 'I'm fine!' despite the evidence to the contrary.

He advanced and felt his foot slip; he glanced down, saw the blood on the floor and the colour seeped out of his face. It only took him a second, a second that was long enough to realise that the gore came, not from Maggie, but from her attacker, who was standing barefoot in the broken glass, oblivious to the pain.

The realisation that the thug was going to feel it once his anaesthetic of choice wore off afforded Rafael a brief moment of savage satisfaction before he placed his hand on the man's collar and hauled him across the room.

Rafael, grimacing in distaste, moved his head back as he was hit by alcohol fumes.

He glanced over his shoulder and was relieved to see that Maggie was getting to her feet, helped by another nurse.

The drunk did not understand a word of the staccato Spanish directed at him but he did recognise the cold light in those eyes.

Rafael's lip curled in distaste as he watched the rapid transformation from aggressive to pathetic when the drunk recognised he had lost the upper hand.

The two security men relieved him of his burden and Rafael swung back to Maggie.

'What are you doing here, Rafael?' Something twisted hard in his chest when he saw her face.

He struggled to control the rage lodged in his throat. 'I am not a medic, but if you want my unqualified opinion I'd say ice might be a good idea.'

'What are you doing here, Rafael?'

Of course she knew, she had known the moment she saw

him standing in the waiting area and pointed him out to Security as a dangerous-looking character.

He was here to speak on behalf of her birth mother, Angelina Castenadas.

She could think the name now, even say it out loud, and she'd had a series of long discussions with her mum. The discussions had involved a lot of tears but she felt less threatened by the situation. It definitely helped that she now believed Mum and Dad would not feel she was being disloyal if she did have contact with her birth mother.

'Other than saving you?'

She studied his dark face hungrily, loving every strong plane and hollow. Seeing him again had made her realise that she would never be over him, she would smile, she would laugh, she would seem normal, but there would always be an empty space inside her that she *knew* he was meant to fill.

'Thank you, Rafael.'

Her brow furrowed with concern she struggled to conceal. There were lines around his mouth she had not seen before, and shadows under his eyes that made them appear haunted.

Had he lost weight?

Had he been ill?

'Who saves you when I am not around?'

'These things only happen to me when you are.' She sucked in a deep breath. 'Look, I can save you time and energy.' She lowered her eyes as her composure slipped and added huskily, 'I know why you're here.'

He stiffened, wariness sliding into his grey eyes as he met her candid gaze.

'You're here to plead my birth mother…Angelina's case.' Maggie bit her lip. 'I know I sent her letter back unopened, but since then…I've thought about it a lot and spoke with Mum and I can see that I have been unfair. I know she had reasons for giving me up and things couldn't have turned out better for me. I have a marvellous family. I would like to meet her…later…' She still struggled with the idea that it could be the positive experience her mum suggested, but she was willing to try.

The silence stretched.

'I'm sure that Angelina will be pleased that you feel this way, but that is between you and her.'

'But I thought…?'

'I came because we had something that…it was not over.' And until it was he would remain unable to function. 'I want you back.'

The breath left her body in one startled gasp. 'You want me back.'

His lifted a shoulder in an irritated shrug. 'No, I was just passing.' His eyes narrowed as he hissed, 'Why else would I be here?'

'And what I want? I suppose that is irrelevant.'

'You want me,' he charged. It was a struggle to think past the fog of sexual hunger in his brain, but this much he did know.

The predatory gleam in his eyes when he made this arrogant pronouncement sent a stab of excitement through Maggie's hopelessly receptive body.

'We can work out some sort of arrangement,' he continued casually.

'Arrangement?'

'Families need not be involved.' For the first time in his life he understood the attraction of being stranded on a desert island with no distractions.

Maggie shook her head as if waking from a daze. 'Believe me, Rafael, you're not the sort of man I'd take home to meet my parents.' What did you expect, Maggie? she asked herself bitterly. That he came here because he's interested in you anywhere outside the bedroom?

He studied her flushed, angry face with a baffled expression. 'Why are you behaving as though I have insulted you?'

She pressed a finger to her chin and pretended to consider the question. 'Could it have something to do with the fact that you think all you have to do is snap your fingers and I'll provide sex on tap?'

His face darkened with anger at her sarcasm. 'You would have sex on tap also.'

The mortified colour flew to her cheeks at the taunt. 'You're not the only man in the world or, for that matter, my life,' she lied.

For a moment Rafael could not breathe past the swell of molten hot anger in his chest.

'I'm curious,' she continued, oblivious to his titanic struggle for control. 'Are we talking about just while you are in town, days or weeks…hours? Or are you asking me to move in and be your full-time mistress?'

'You wish to formalise the arrangement?' His shoulders lifted. 'Fine…yes!'

The mocking smile slid from her lips. 'You're not serious!'

'I would not be here unless I was serious.' Or insane, he thought, dragging a hand through his dark hair. 'You walked away from me. No woman has ever done that.'

'So this is about pride.' Maggie was furious with herself for imagining even for one brief second that it might be more. 'We're not finished until *you* say so…'

He regarded her with an expression of intense irritation. 'Why do you always twist what I say? I have come here—'

Her lips twisted. 'I'm flattered.'

'You should be. I've never chased after a woman in my life.'

Maggie's eyes swept upwards and connected with his brooding molten stare; her breath caught. 'You're chasing me?'

His fascinating mouth curved upwards. 'I've caught you.'

A shiver slid down her spine and she swayed towards him as though drawn by an invisible thread.

'Mags…?'

A nurse popped her head around the curtain that someone had pulled across and Rafael stepped back, the muscle in his lean cheek clenching as he swore under his breath.

'Mark will give your eye the once-over shortly.' The girl slid a curious and appreciative glance toward Rafael. 'He's just seeing to our friend. The guy's feet are in a mess—he was walking on glass.'

'No problem, I'm fine. I'll be out in a minute.'

'Can I get your friend anything…coffee, tea…?'

Maggie, who heard the unspoken addition of *me,* glared and heard Rafael respond with an abrupt, 'No.'

Rafael, who had listened to the brief interchange with growing disbelief, waited until the other woman had left before he spoke. 'That man—he is being attended to before you.'

'Well, it is a matter of priorities.'

Indeed it was, and the ones he was witnessing were to his mind, sadly skewed.

'You are planning on continuing to work?'

She nodded. 'It's a really busy evening and we're short staffed…'

Rafael unable to contain his outrage a moment longer held up his hand. 'Listen to me—you are *not* going back to work.'

'Really, Rafael, you don't understand—'

'No, you don't understand—this is not a debate.'

'You can't walk in here and order me about. I'm not your live-in girlfriend yet…not yet, I mean…' She closed her eyes and thought, What do I mean? Her head felt as though someone were inside her skull trying to hammer his way out. 'All right, I'll go home once I've been checked.'

Rafael's feelings were not soothed long. When the doctor did put in an appearance he looked as though he had not begun shaving and his manner towards Maggie was far too familiar.

The doctor pronounced her fine, though he suggested she might like to wear dark glasses for a few days because she was going to have quite a shiner.

He also said there was no way she should go back to work. This time Maggie did not argue; the man with the hammer in her skull had been joined by friends. Maggie looked up as Rafael stepped back into the room.

'You're still here?'

Rafael's dark brows shot up. 'You expected me not to be? We have things to discuss.'

Maggie's lashes fell. 'Not tonight…'

'Certainly tonight,' he retorted, his attitude displaying no room for manoeuvre.

'Fine. I can save you some time, Rafael. I can't be…with you.'

A muscle clenched in his cheek. 'Why?'

'Because I can't be with a man who can't promise me an exclusive relationship that lasts more than a few weeks.' With a highly sexed man like Rafael, she thought dourly, there would always be someone waiting to take her place.

A nerve clenched in his lean cheek and he remained silent as he pushed open the swing doors for her to pass through before him.

'And if I was prepared to do that?'

Eyes round in amazement, she swung back just as a blinding light flashed in her face. Beside her Rafael swore, raised his arm to shield her, moving to stand between her and the paparazzo.

'Just keep walking.'

A good plan in theory, but she stumbled and Rafael swept

her up into his arms and across to the waiting car, all the time being snapped.

Maggie gave a sigh of relief as the car pulled away.

Rafael flashed her a quick sideways look. 'We should be at my place in about half an hour, traffic willing.'

'I want to go to *my* place and it will take five minutes.'

It actually took less than the five minutes she predicted and Rafael hadn't said another word after his abrupt, 'Fine!' when he turned the ignition.

It didn't occur to Maggie to ask how he knew where she lived as she responded to his urging to hurry because the paparazzo would not be far behind.

The flat door closed and the tension slid from Maggie's shoulders and she flopped down onto the sofa. 'God that awful man.'

'There will be more awful men when you move in with me,' Rafael felt obliged to warn her as he pulled down his sleeve to cover the nick on his wrist that was still seeping blood.

'If I move in…' Maggie stopped, her eyes drawn by his actions to the stain on the cuff of his shirt. 'You're bleeding!' she accused, leaping to her feet.

Rafael gave an impatient shrug. 'It's nothing—a piece of glass, I think…'

'Let me see? You should have let someone look at it.'

Rafael backed away. 'It's nothing.'

'It should be cleaned.'

He stifled his impatience and gave a sigh. 'Fine, where's your bathroom? I'll wash it if that will make you happy.' Nothing but feeling her body beneath him would make him happy.

Maggie directed him and sat listening to the sound of running water.

It was a few moments later he emerged, his face and hair both dripping wet; he barely seemed to register the fact.

Dazed was the only word she could think of to describe his expression.

Oh, God, maybe he had a thing about blood?

She shot to her feet. 'Sit down, you look…'

Acting as if he hadn't heard her, he walked straight past her and headed for the door. 'Rafael!' she called after him, seriously spooked by his strange behaviour. 'Where are you going?'

He swung back and she saw the dazed look in his eyes had been replaced by a grim but purposeful gleam. 'I will make things right. Stay indoors until I get back.'

And with that he was gone.

CHAPTER FOURTEEN

MAGGIE covered her ears as the phone began to ring again. She clenched her teeth, willing it to stop. When it did she let out a long sibilant sigh of relief and felt like an utter coward as she carried on searching for her other shoe.

Where had she put the damned thing?

'Calm down and think, Maggie,' she muttered, recalling that she had been sitting in her armchair when she began to cry.

She had sat puzzling over Rafael's enigmatic words while she had waited and waited some more, but he hadn't come back. At some point in the early hours it occurred to her that she could spend the next few months doing just that—waiting.

What sort of man, she asked herself suggested living together and walked out before they had discussed it? A man who had cold feet? It was then she realised that it was never going to work—they had no sort of future together.

She resumed her search, angrily dashing tears from her cheeks, but it was unsuccessful and the respite before the phone started ringing again was brief.

She knew who it was without checking the caller ID again. He had called the first time an hour earlier and without thinking she had picked it up; the sound of his deep voice the other end had caused her to drop the receiver.

It had been ringing every few seconds since and she had been ignoring it. Maybe not ignoring—ignoring suggested she was tuning out the sound and carrying on with what she was doing, which was of course thinking about Rafael. When wasn't she thinking about Rafael?

She was just not answering because she was a pathetic coward. While she didn't answer she could pretend he had a perfectly good explanation for running out of there last night.

The only solution—why hadn't she thought of it earlier?—she decided, was to get out of the flat with or without her shoes. Of course, she *could* answer, but that would mean hearing his voice and how badly she wanted to—simple *want* didn't really describe the intense, deep, gut-wrenching longing—was so utterly terrifying that she just couldn't do it.

It could be the first step on the slippery slope: this time answering the phone, the next time ringing his number just so she could hear his voice!

Last night he had literally run from her flat as though he couldn't bear to be in her company—if ever there was a case of actions speaking louder than words, that was it!

Ditching her shoe search, she ran to the door where she'd left her trainers—why had she fixated on the black heels anyhow?—and began to lace them up with shaky fingers.

It was far too easy, she reflected to get into the mindset of thinking she had no control.

'I do have control. I won't love him.'

She angrily wiped a tear from her cheek and almost immediately realised she couldn't *not* love him.

Halfway down the stairs, her thoughts in utter turmoil, she realised she had not got her car keys. She retraced her steps and discovered she had left her door wide open.

I'm losing it, she thought.

Rafael's dark features flashed into her head and she sighed, thinking, You lost it the moment Rafael-Luis Castenadas smiled at you and since then you've been in denial big time.

Denial didn't seem so bad when she considered the alternatives.

She was reaching into her bag for a tissue when she walked straight into the blinding volley of flashes.

Confused she blinked and lifted a hand to shield her eyes as the waiting press pack advanced.

And this time they were here in force.

They were all talking at once, several were waving newspapers in her face, and all she could think as she stood there was how odd that they knew her name.

'Miss Ward, are you going to press charges?'

'Maggie, has this ever happened before? Has he hit you before?'

'Miss Ward, is it true that Rafael Castenadas attacked you while you were trying to save the life of a—'

The questions hit her like missiles as the cameras kept flashing. Maggie shrank back in horror, her feet nailed to the spot.

'Maggie, if you give us an exclusive we can get you out of here.'

Maggie focused on the man that had come close, his face right in hers. She could smell his aftershave and she stopped being scared and started being angry—very angry.

He took another step towards her, his face arranged in a sympathetic smile, and suddenly the feeling returned to her paralysed limbs.

He extended his hand towards her and she lifted her chin and said, 'I don't think so. Now move out of my way.'

He looked taken aback by the low note of cold authority in her clear voice, but he didn't budge. None of them did; it was a scrum.

Like pack animals scenting blood—hers, which was not a nice thought—they continued to yell and jostle, physically blocking her exit and trapping her.

Head down, struggling to emulate the air of cold indifference with which Rafael treated the press intrusion, and failing miserably, Maggie tried to push her way through the screaming mass.

Of course, they would not have bumped and shoved him, not even the keenest paparazzo would have made that mistake.

'Is it true the police want to question Rafael?'

Maggie's head came up; the red dots dancing before her eyes formed a red mist and, eyes blazing, she rounded on the man who had spoken.

'What did you say?'

'Are the police questioning Rafe, Maggie?'

Wrapping herself in a cloak of icy dignity, Maggie lifted her chin and fixed the man with a direct unblinking regard. 'The police are *not* interested in questioning *Mr Castenadas,* but they will be interested in questioning you if you don't take your hand off my arm.'

She held his eyes until his hand fell away, then she nodded and said quietly, 'Thank you.'

She managed to move another couple of feet forward before the pack closed in around her once more.

'Do you think you're setting a bad example to other abused women by not bringing charges?'

Maggie could almost hear the sound of control snapping. She threw up her hands as anger coursed through her veins.

'That's it!' she cried, swinging back to face the general direction the question had come from. 'How dare you take the moral high ground and preach to me?' As if they were interested in anything but a headline.

In this situation Rafael would have acted as if they didn't exist and he would never have tried to defend himself.

But she wasn't Rafael and she couldn't stand by and let them say these things about him while he wasn't even there to defend himself—she just couldn't!

'I don't know how you lot get away with saying things like this about a man who…' She stopped, her throat closing over with emotion as she added furiously, 'God, you're not fit to breathe the same air as him. For the record, my black eye is courtesy of a patient who got nasty in Casualty, but a drunk hitting a nurse isn't much of a story, is it? It's the stuff that happens every day.' She paused and let her contemptuous gaze move over the now silent crowd.

'You don't send out the cameras for that, do you? Oh, no, that's not *sexy* news,' she spat scornfully. 'You'd prefer to make up lies about a man whose only crime is not crossing to the other side of the street when someone needs help, I wonder how many of you can say the same?'

The silence grew and, shaking with emotion, Maggie looked directly into the camera lens pointed at her face. 'I don't know how you're going to sell this as being in the public interest. Rafael's only crime is being successful and good to look at.'

She paused to catch her breath and thought, Maybe, just maybe I have got through to them—when one small voice broke the silence.

'So what's it feel like to be the girlfriend of a billionaire, Maggie?'

The question signalled the return of hostilities after the brief lull. The questions came thick, fast and frequently offensive. Maggie stood, her fists clenched, unable to defend herself from the onslaught. Her emotional outburst had utterly exhausted her emotional defences.

She wanted to run, but she couldn't; they were pressing in on her from all sides.

She stiffened as she felt arms slide around her waist and instinctively began to hit out wildly.

Her flailing elbow made contact and Maggie felt a spurt of savage satisfaction when she heard a grunt of pain.

'I come in peace.'

At the familiar voice Maggie stilled. She had elbowed Rafael. She stifled a totally inappropriate desire to giggle—probably hysteria—and said his name.

She said it again because it sounded good, then added, 'Some people say better late than never, but I don't.'

'That is something we will speak of soon. For now just relax—we'll be out of here in one minute. Trust me.'

Maggie did utterly, which was totally crazy because he didn't represent safety and he had gone all weird and left her high and dry last night. Rafael represented rampant sexuality, dangerous excitement and misery because he couldn't love her.

Even while she acknowledged this she leaned back with a sigh of relief into the hard solidity of his lean male body feeling his strength seep into her—a physiological impossibility, but true nonetheless.

On one level she recognised that her reliance on him was foolish. Hadn't she always solved her own problems? She was no wilting flower. Yet here she was, leaning, and not just physically, on Rafael… It was actually just good to be able to let go and know that someone else would pick up the pieces…was that wrong?

The thoughts passed through her head in a matter of seconds, though time had little meaning to Maggie as around them the flashes became one continuous blast of light and the barrage of questions and requests to look at the camera became a hysterical babble.

Rafael, partially shielded from the press pack by the physical presence of the two broad-shouldered figures, with a combination of expertise and their sheer bulk, were shielding the couple, turned Maggie around to face him and winced.

The sight of her poor face sent a blast of outrage through him, followed swiftly by an equally powerful stab of protective tenderness.

He had spent his entire adult life keeping, not just women, but his emotions at arm's length and succeeding—until Maggie came along.

His emotional detachment had been crumbling from the moment he had laid eyes on her, he'd just been too blind to see it, but last night when those baby clothes had spilled out of the boxes in her bathroom and he had realised she was carrying his baby it had disintegrated and his vision had cleared!

Marriage, love, children—they were all things he had never wanted or needed. Ironically the very things he had actively avoided were now the things Rafael wanted more than anything.

He wanted Maggie, but after the way he had behaved he knew he had a lot of ground to make up. But he had made a start, and he would do whatever it took to convince her that he would be a good husband and father.

'You do know you've turned my life upside down, don't you, Maggie Ward?' He touched her uninjured cheek and tilted her head a little to one side to examine the bruises.

If he had that loser from yesterday here now… His hands tightened into fists and he told himself that violence never solved anything. On the other hand it would make him feel a lot better.

Pushing away the thoughts of retribution, he curled his fingers gently around her chin and turned her face to examine the damage that appeared to be limited to the right side.

Maggie withstood his silent scrutiny with difficulty. Where was a paper bag when a girl needed it?

'The bruising has come out today.' Rafael, without her experience of similar injuries, probably found the sight more shocking than she had; he might not realise it was actually very superficial.

Maggie knew that tomorrow when the swelling began to subside she would be able to disguise most of the damage with make-up, but it had been a lost cause today.

Rafael swore through clenched teeth and, without taking his eyes from her face, lifted a hand to signal to the two men who had exited the car that had pulled up on the kerb behind the chauffeur-driven limo he and the first security contingent had arrived in.

Maggie, totally unaware of them moving into place beside the limo, unconscious of anything but Rafael, shook her head when he observed in a strained, thickened voice, 'It must be very painful.'

'Actually it—'

He laid a finger against her lips. 'If you are about to say, "It looks worse than it is," do not.'

How did he know?

'And if you go into brave little trouper mode I will not be responsible for my actions.'

Maggie did not get the opportunity to ask him if he preferred she have hysterics as at that moment one of the big minders said something in Spanish. Rafael listened and nodded. Maggie, who up until that point had not even realised Rafael was not alone, watched as the man, complete with dark suit and mirrored shades, spoke into a mouthpiece, then said something in rapid Spanish to Rafael, who nodded in agreement.

'You brought reinforcements?'

Rafael, recalling the moment he had drawn up and seen her in the middle of the media feeding frenzy, swallowed a retort.

If it had not been for the intervention of Luis, he might have waded in metaphorical guns blazing and made a bad situation worse. The way he was feeling now made him think it might have been worth it.

Dios, at that moment he hated diplomacy; he loathed tactics. Frustration at being forced to stifle his natural impulses left the adrenaline with no place to go but notching up the tension in his body to a painful level.

'This is my Head of Security, Luis,' he said, introducing the man at his shoulder to Maggie.

The man with the mirrored shades inclined his shaved head and might have smiled, it was hard to tell, but Maggie smiled back just in case. He struck her as the sort of man you didn't want to offend.

'If I'd known you would be *stupid* enough to walk into this I would have fetched a small army.'

Maggie's attention swung back to Rafael, eyes widened indignantly as she launched into a robust defence of her actions. 'How was I to know that they'd—?'

'Save it!' he snapped, cutting her off with an impatient motion of his dark head.

Her chin went up in response to the autocratic decree. 'But I—'

'Just do what I say and do not argue, also do not speak.'

Maggie nodded meekly, her eyes dropping as she recalled her diatribe.

The entire face-the-press-and-yell-at-them thing was all a bit of a blur. But she had yelled, yes, there had definitely been volume—this she knew even though the content of her rant remained frustratingly elusive.

Around them there was noise and frenetic activity, but everything about Rafael, from his carved features to his steady regard, was still. But nobody would mistake that stillness for tranquillity.

Fascinated by the resolution she saw etched into every

stunning angle of his lean face, Maggie stared. Resolution, not to be confused with coolness, and the light gleaming in his eyes had a combustible quality that was echoed in his body language.

His black leather jacket open to reveal a blue shirt that deepened the intense startling colour of his eyes, he reminded Maggie of a dark avenging angel.

A shiver trickled down her spine and things shifted and clenched low and deep inside her as she stared, her eyes drawn to the muscle clenching and unclenching along his shadowed jaw.

She was frightened by the dangerous idea that surfaced in her brain: to touch him, run her fingers over his hair-roughened cheek. Once planted, the impulse was almost impossible to resist. She pressed her clenched hands to her chest, and silently mouthed, No!

Either he could read lips or she had not been so silent because Rafael bent forward and said, 'There is no need to be frightened of them.'

Just of you she thought. 'Easy for you to say—you're the sort of person who gets a kick from chasing hurricanes.'

'A hurricane,' he observed bitterly, 'is child's play compared to you!'

It was always good to have the man you loved inform you that you were a nightmare. Maggie opened her mouth to deliver a suitably ironic response and was horrified to feel her eyes fill.

Rafael watched her luminous eyes fill and felt a pain that was roughly the equivalent of having a dagger plunged into his chest.

He snarled something very un-angelic and wrapped an arm supportively around her waist. She saw the muscles in his brown throat work as he framed her face with his free hand, angling it up to him.

His eyes swept her pale features again, a spasm twisting his lips into a pained grimace as he made himself look again at the extent of the damage to her cheek and eye.

Maggie went instinctively to lift a protective hand to her face, but found she couldn't. Her hand was trapped between their bodies and the fingers of her free hand had somehow become interlaced with Rafael's.

Maggie stared at the brown fingers wrapped around her own wondering when that happened as Rafael swore soft and savage under his breath as one of his minders spoke.

The muscles along his jaw tightened as he turned his attention back to Maggie. This madness was his life, not hers—what had he got her into?

'This,' he said, self-condemnation putting a harsh uneven note into his deep voice as he flicked a harsh glare at the media pack. 'It should not have happened.' He touched the bruised, discoloured skin tenderly with the pad of his thumb and swore again, turning his head as he closed his eyes and clamped his jaw.

Maggie's eyelashes came down in a protective sweep, a turbulent cocktail of emotions lodged tight like a weight in her chest as she struggled to hold back the hot tears that stung her eyelids.

She was vaguely conscious of a flurry of movement as one of the minders confiscated the camera someone had pushed under Rafael's nose. He acted as though nothing had happened.

Maggie wondered enviously how he managed that.

And how did he put up with this sort of invasion on a daily basis? How did he tune out the press who dogged his footsteps?

Presumably this was why he had adopted a strict policy of 'say nothing, not even yes or no' and, though the details still remained a bit of a blur she was pretty sure she had said more than that and it would probably be edited to suit whatever angle they were pursuing.

She took a deep breath. Better to come clean now before she lost her nerve.

'I didn't keep my mouth shut. I said…stuff.'

The guilty admission brought his eyes to the mouth in question. Lust slammed through his body. That was predictable, if painful, but the protective instincts that accompanied it were so alien to him still, so strong, that his normal restraint snapped.

Didn't consider the audience or their cameras, but the need that drove him as he framed her face in his hands.

Didn't consider them as he bent his head.

Didn't consider them as he fitted his mouth to hers and with a groan of male need slid his tongue deep into the soft heat of her mouth.

The paparazzi, unable to believe their luck at the cool, controlled Rafael Castenadas' public display, went crazy as they snapped the kissing couple.

Rafael lifted his head.

Dazed and clinging to Rafael's jacket Maggie was vaguely aware of Rafael's extended arm protecting her and bodies, encouraged by their escorts, parting to let them through to the waiting car.

The door, held open and flanked by another two tough-looking suited figures who were both talking into headpieces, was closed with a decisive sound after Rafael slid into the back seat beside her.

Rafael spoke to the driver and leaned back in his seat as the car moved off and the smoked-glass partition between them slid into place.

Maggie willed herself not to lower her gaze, while for the first time she started asking herself why he was here.

His glance skimmed her profile. 'I am sorry that you had

to go through that,' he said, sounding angry, which, considering he was the one that had done the kissing, struck Maggie as pretty unreasonable.

'I told you to stay in and I did try and warn you,' he added.

'Did you?'

Maggie could not recall any warning.

Just the memory of his mouth, she mused her glance drawn irresistibly to that strongly sculpted sensual curve. And his probing tongue sliding—that was very clear. She huffed a shaky breath and, sliding her fingers into her heavy hair, pushed it from her face. The memory was not so easy to remove; it lingered like the heat lying low in her pelvis.

'I've been ringing all morning.'

'Ringing?' she echoed blankly.

'You were not picking up.'

'I was busy,' she lied.

His public display had been totally out of character, so possibly she was irresistible?

If that were true he would hardly have walked away last night.

Or—a less flattering though possibly more likely explanation—it had been a dramatic way of telling the circus that dogged his footsteps that they did not make any impact on his life—Rafael's way of thumbing his nose at them.

He clenched his teeth in frustration and pushed his head back deep into the soft upholstery as he closed his eyes. 'You were not busy, you were simply punishing me because I walked out last night.' His eyes opened. 'There was a reason.'

Maggie shook her head and betrayed no interest in hearing it.

What was the point? Nothing, with the exception of hearing him say he loved her, would make anything better—and that was not going to happen.

He studied the obstinate angle of her averted chin and said softly, 'Look at me, Maggie.'

Maggie ignored the instruction and carried on staring at the smoked-glass window.

She listened to him curse fluently, then turned her head. 'I want to go home.'

'We are.'

She looked at him, a question in her narrowed eyes.

'Going home, to my London house. We can be private there.'

'I don't want to be private,' she retorted, thinking that it was a pity he hadn't been so keen on privacy before he gave the photo opportunity of a decade to the paparazzi.

'Why did you agree?'

She was thrown by the question and her startled gaze flew to his face, her first mistake—his compelling metallic stare shredded her thin veneer of composure.

She cleared her throat and tugged fretfully at the neck of her top. 'Agree to what?'

'To meeting Angelica—why did you agree?'

'Why the third degree? I thought that's what you wanted.'

'And you always do what I want?' He loosed a dry laugh and reminded her, 'Before you gave the very strong impression that your mind was made up, you were totally inflexible on the subject, unwavering…'

Maggie's eyes fell from the disturbing speculation in his silver gaze.

'I wasn't.'

'You were dead set against it.'

Maggie focused at some point over his shoulder God if only it were that easy to ignore him! She was painfully conscious of him.

'Things change,' she countered.

'And what changed with you?'

Maggie lifted her head in response to the pressure of his fingers under her chin. She shook her head mutely.

'Susan thinks you might be pregnant.'

CHAPTER FIFTEEN

MAGGIE'S eyes went wide with shock. For the space of several heartbeats her breathing was suspended. The colour seeped from her already pale cheeks before she took a deep gulping breath.

If she had not been sitting her legs would have failed her.

That statement did not work on more levels than she could count.

'Susan…Mum…?'

He confirmed her incredulous query with a calm nod of his head. 'An incredible woman,' he said. "Like her daughter."

Talking long into the night with her parents had helped him understand what had made Maggie the woman she was today—too mature for her years in many ways, yet untouched…*until he came along.*

He clenched his teeth against the self-condemnatory stab of self-loathing that sliced into him like a dull blade when he considered the impact his selfish actions had had on the one person in the world he wanted to protect.

Madre di Dios, he seemed to have inherited an uncanny ability to mess up when it came to the people he loved…

He could only imagine how Maggie must be feeling.

She'd spent all her life weighed down by responsibilities. This was her time, her time to finally put her needs and desires above those of others, her time to be carefree, and if her mother's suspicions were correct he was responsible for clipping her wings before she had spread them.

Maggie had no control over the rush of pleasure she experienced at the compliment. Her throat clogged with emotion she struggled not to show, it was one of the nicest things that anyone had ever said to her.

'You do know that I'm not her real daughter?' She stopped—of course he did.

With an expressive sweep of his hand Rafael brushed aside the comment as irrelevant. 'She has passed on her qualities to you, strength, compassion, and, I suspect,' he added, flashing a grin that sent her sensitive stomach into a lurching dive, 'bloody-minded stubbornness.'

Maggie stared at him in a daze. 'You *really* spoke to her? *When* did you speak to her? She thinks I'm…' A slow flush worked its way up her neck until her face was burning.

Rafael's eyes didn't leave her face. 'And is she right, Maggie?' he asked quietly.

Maggie struggled to tear her eyes from the nerve pulsing like a metronome beside his mouth, and she was not fooled by his conversational tone. Even though his hand had fallen away, she could feel the waves of tension rolling off his lean body.

'How can you have spoken to my mum?' It seemed better to deal with one extraordinary comment at a time. 'You don't even know her phone number.'

The moment the words left her lips she knew how stupid they were. It was hardly beyond his capabilities to pick up a telephone book or have a flunky do it for him.

Delegated or not, why would he want to?

'I did not phone your mother—'

'I didn't think so—'

'I called on her. The term "jaw dropped" has just taken on

an entirely new meaning,' he observed, placing a helpful finger under her chin. Maggie's mouth closed with an audible click as she continued to stare at him.

He stared back, allowing himself the luxury of examining the delicate features turned to him, committing each soft curve and delicate hollow to memory. As emotions that he had finally stopped fighting welled up he tried to put them in words, but for once in his life the words wouldn't come.

Instead he mumbled huskily, 'A better look for you I feel.'

Maggie shivered as he trailed a finger over the curve of her cheek.

He thinks you're pregnant.

Her brows twitched together in a dark line of distrust as she wrinkled her nose. 'How do you mean "called on her"?' she quizzed suspiciously.

'What part of "called on her" do you not follow? You wish for me to describe my actions step by step?'

He gave every appearance of being amused, relaxed even but, noting the more defined foreign inflection in his voice—something she had previously noticed occurred at moments of heightened emotion—Maggie wondered if he might not actually be so stress free as he appeared.

Of course he's not stress free, dunce, she told herself scornfully. He's trying to figure out if you're about to lumber him with a baby he definitely doesn't want. Wow, was he going to be happy when she set him straight—he might also feel less inclined to tell her she was beautiful.

Ignoring the stab of pain administered by this timely reality check, she snapped, 'Do what you like.' Spoiling the delivery by allowing a quiver of emotion to ruin her snarl.

She saw him register the quiver, felt him tense for a moment, and thought he was about to reach for her. When he didn't the relief—or was it the anticlimax?—was intense.

'I knocked on the door, and she let me in, or to be precise

your brother let me in…Sam, I think? They are both very alike.'

This comment dragged her wandering thoughts back from the confused dark place they had fled. Wide eyes flew to his face.

'Sam has the broken nose.' This conversation had gone past surreal.

'Then it was Sam,' Rafael confirmed. 'Susan was late back from her physiotherapy appointment.'

Maggie blinked at the casual familiarity of the comment. 'Will you stop talking as if you know my family?' she pleaded, pushing both hands into her dark hair.

'*Know* might be overstating it,' he admitted. 'But I felt we got on well.'

'You really went to my house?' She eyed him with suspicion, and wondered if this was his idea of a joke.

'I did, last night.'

'You went to my house.' She shook her head as she tried to imagine Rafael in his immaculate designer suit and handmade leather shoes in her parents' chintzy living room, complete with its out-of-tune piano and large shaggy dog, and failed.

Talk about worlds colliding!

He crossed one ankle over the other and raised his brows. 'Why do you find this fact so extraordinary?'

'Why?' She laughed. 'Because you're—' her gesture took in his elegant person from sleek dark head to gleaming handmade shoes '—*you* and my family are…' She stopped. 'What were you doing there anyway?'

'I wanted to explain the situation to your parents before they woke up this morning and saw this.'

Maggie's eyes shifted to the paper he rustled. She was turning back to him when she registered the photo splashed across the front page and felt the pain behind her eyes kick up several uncomfortable notches.

She closed her eyes and breathed deeply, her freckles standing out against the marble pallor of her skin. Rafael, a breath trapped in his throat, frustration lodged like a fist in his chest, felt every protective instinct he possessed screaming for him to make her feel better, but how?

He was reaching out when she opened her eyes.

'Fame at last,' she said faintly. 'Some people try all their lives to make the front cover.' It was a struggle to treat the situation like a joke when she thought of all the people she knew who would be looking at it. 'Not very flattering,' she finished hoarsely.

Rafael, his eyes welded to her face, watched her lips quiver and cursed. The violence of the mumbled epithet brought her eyes to his face.

'It could have been worse.'

Maggie stared at the brown fingers covering hers and gulped, resisting a mad impulse to throw herself into his arms. As if that were going to solve anything…though it would feel nice while it lasted.

Maggie didn't believe him but appreciated the white lie.

'I didn't think…' she admitted with a shamefaced grimace as she thought of her parents picking the newspaper up off the mat and seeing that.

He took the newspaper away and slung it over his shoulder. 'You have other things on your mind.' Like carrying my baby. 'I have been there before, though not with anyone like you.'

The concession made her stiffen. He did not need to labour the point that he was not normally photographed with a woman who looked as seductive as a scarecrow.

'I'm so sorry if it's injured your reputation to be seen with a woman who is fully dressed and not drop-dead gorgeous!'

Dark head tilted to one side, he regarded her with an air of frustrated incredulity. 'You have a positive genius for misinterpreting everything I say. The women I have been photographed with previously have been with me because they want to be photographed, not because of my charming personality. They want their five minutes of fame.'

'Well, don't flatter yourself. I wasn't with you because of your charming personality. You're not charming, you're a…a…' She stopped and thought, The man I love, before adding with a husky note of enquiry, 'Mum and Dad…'

'They know that you are all right. I wanted them to stay with friends but they preferred to sit it out.'

'You mean the press are there too?' Maggie asked, startled. That had not even occurred to her.

'A few when I left this morning.'

Maggie groaned.

'Look on the bright side—your brothers are anticipating an upsurge in female interest in the near future.'

The comment drew a reluctant laugh from Maggie. She could almost hear the boys. 'You really were there,' she said wonderingly.

'I like your family, Magdalena.'

'Me too. I suppose I should thank you for making the effort…?' Her eyelashes came down in a protective sweep. 'So what did you say to them?'

'We had quite a long talk…'

She clenched her teeth in frustration at the evasion. 'About?'

'You, mostly.'

Maggie found this cryptic utterance deeply disturbing. 'Sure because I'm such a fascinating subject.'

'I wouldn't call you a subject.'

'No, just a total pain in the neck, probably.'

She tensed when Rafael leaned across without warning and fastened the clasp on her seat belt. 'A legal requirement.'

Rigid, Maggie sat as still as a statue while he performed his task, staring through the mesh of her lashes at the top of his dark head, her nostrils flaring in response to the evocative scent of his clean washed hair. In her head she could see herself pushing her fingers deep into the luxuriant mass.

She released a small sigh of relief when he straightened up. It was becoming increasingly difficult to maintain a semblance of sanity when she became a mass of craving hormones every time he so much as glanced her way.

As he leaned back in his seat Rafael's eyes brushed her flushed face. Maggie, her palms damp with the effort of maintaining eye contact, was too caught up in her own struggle to notice the dark bands of colour etched across the angles of his razor-edged cheekbones.

'You inspire strong feelings in everyone who meets you.'

This cryptic response drew a frown from Maggie. Thanks for nothing, she thought. 'How tactful.'

'Tact is not something I'm known for.

'You didn't tell me that you were your mother's carer when you were younger.'

Maggie's air of studied nonchalant defiance fell away at this, she felt a surge of anger.

'I was not her carer. We all mucked in. Mum was always very independent.'

'That's not what she said.'

'I wouldn't know—I wasn't there. You were talking about me behind my back.'

'Did you never resent that you didn't have a normal childhood?'

His curiosity made Maggie see red. She drew herself up poker-straight, ignoring the pain from the belt digging into her bruised shoulder as anger burned away the last shreds of her restraint.

'Of course I never resented Mum or anything else—I had

a great childhood. Don't you *dare* feel sorry for me!' she growled. '*I'm* not the one with the hang-ups and emotional scars, I can express my feelings. I don't have to reduce everything to the lowest common denominator—' She stopped, appalled by what she had said. 'I'm sorry, I shouldn't have said that…' Maggie cast a stricken look at his face before her eyes fell. 'My parents would never discuss me with a total stranger.'

'You had sex with a total stranger.' He watched her flinch and shook his head, regret etched in the drawn lines of his strong features. 'Now we have both said things we should not have. I'm not a total stranger, Maggie.'

The emotion she heard in the husky addition brought her head up, but it was not anger she saw stamped on his dark features; it was a raw need that made her stomach muscles contract and flip.

Her eyelids, suddenly heavy, half closed as she registered the sensual glow in his eyes. She struggled to retain control; she felt an erotic shiver trickle down her spine.

Control…? She swallowed and ran her tongue over her dry lips. Who was she kidding?

She definitely had more control over the direction her glance drifted than she did the dramatic dilation of her pupils. As her eyes moved slowly across the sensual curve of his incredible mouth she thought about his lips on hers, his tongue sliding into her mouth.

'Maggie.'

The sound of her name brought her eyes back to his, the tension climbed as she read the silent message in his hot hooded stare. A tiny gasp left her lips as desire tightened like a fist low in her belly.

The fog of sexual tension in the confined space grew denser, almost tangible and totally unbearable, she felt torn apart as conflicting desires and fears battled inside her skull.

She lifted a hand to her heaving chest as she struggled to draw enough air into her lungs.

She could almost see the breaking point she was about to collide with when a sudden thump on the car broke the spell. She jumped instinctively towards Rafael.

'Relax.'

Maggie was too tense to register the rough-edged strain in his thickened voice as he soothed her.

'What?' she asked as the car slowed and she heard several more thuds.

Then Rafael was drawing her towards him. 'It's just the reporters camped outside my place. This will only take a minute and we'll be inside.'

Maggie silently accepted the support of the arm he placed across the back of the seat; she tried to tune out the sound of muffled yells outside and the further thuds on the paintwork of the limo as she responded to the pressure of the fingers on her shoulder and shuffled her bottom across the space separating them.

She allowed her head to rest on his shoulder closing her eyes as his arm tightened around her. It was such a relief to stop fighting for a minute and give her natural instincts free rein. She felt his fingers light on skin as he brushed the hair from her brow, and she sighed, allowing herself to enjoy the intimacy that she craved.

'We're here.'

Maggie lifted her head. She hadn't even been aware of the car stopping, but the driver was standing holding the door open. She saw that they were in what appeared to be an underground parking area.

Maggie in the grip of emotions too strong and unfamiliar for her to put a name to, felt a strong reluctance to move and break the intimacy of the moment. Misinterpreting her hesitation, Rafael placed an encouraging hand between her shoulder blades.

Once they left the limo he immediately went to speak to the man he had introduced as Luis, who had climbed out of the second limo that had been travelling close on their tail the whole way. Of the car that had preceded them there was no sign.

Trying to orientate herself, Maggie stood and watched the two men speak. The shaven head of the shorter man turned in Maggie's direction several times and she felt increasingly uncomfortable. What, she wondered, were they saying about her?

Behind the respectful attitude, what were Rafael's staff saying about her?

Was she just getting paranoid?

She watched as the other man got into the car, which reversed at speed towards large electrically controlled doors that opened, letting in a blast of noise before silently closing behind it.

'Where are we?' she asked as Rafael joined her.

'This is my London home.'

'Is this where you wanted me to come yesterday?' she asked. 'Go on,' she added. 'Say it—you're right…'

Rafael's dark brows lifted at her accusing tone but the corners of his wide mouth lifted as he dragged a hand across the dark shadow on his normally clean-shaven jaw and he nodded agreement. 'Generally, but could you narrow it a little? What particular *rightness* are we discussing at the moment?'

'If I'd let you bring me here last night none of that craziness would have happened.' Maggie shrugged in the direction of the big electric doors that shielded them from prying eyes.

She turned her head and found his eyes were welded to her face, a raw, hungry expression that made her hopelessly susceptible heart thud loud against her ribs glowing in the grey depths.

'Don't look at me like that.'

The husky plea made him blink and shake his head as if dispelling a mental image.

'The women I know dress to impress,' he said, still seeing the jewelled collar around her neck.

The collar he had found himself buying two days ago because he had *known* the rubies he had glimpsed in the display cabinet would look incredible against her luminous skin.

He had stood outside the exclusive establishment with the boxes in his pocket—once inside he had seen other items that had tempted him—when he had realised that he had just bought jewels worth a small fortune for a woman he never intended to see again.

Well, not intentionally see again—for a man not given to fantasizing, he had been spending a considerable amount of time imagining scenarios where they accidentally bumped into one another.

She would of course have realised in the interim that she had made a massive mistake and discovered that actually she could not live without him.

In the imagined scene he took her back, of course on his terms.

And as he stood there he recognised that there was a flaw in this scenario: the accidental part.

He was not a man who had ever left things to chance.

Why, he had asked himself, start now?

He had walked back to his office with a new sense of purpose—purpose that had been sadly lacking over the last few weeks.

He needed to work her out of his system. *Dios,* had he really been that stupid? Then he would regain the focus that had deserted him. He needed to tire of her because it was obvious that the woman and her damned eyes and the soft skin he woke up craving to touch were only still in his head because she had left him, she had walked.

Something no other woman had ever done, and she had done so before he had exhausted his interest in her.

Then he could move on.

It was rational to seek her out.

His self-delusion now seemed ridiculous in the extreme, but ridiculous or not it had lasted until last night when the truth had hit him with the force of a proverbial lightning bolt.

Why had he been afraid of admitting he loved her?

Maggie flushed at her own stupidity. She was seeing what she wanted to. He wasn't overcome with lust—he was just wondering what he had ever seen in a bag lady.

'Colour co-ordination wasn't high on my list of priorities this morning, and anyway,' she dismissed, 'you don't look so hot yourself.'

With a rueful expression Rafael ran a hand across his jaw. 'I would have asked your father to lend me a razor but he—'

'Has a beard,' she completed for him.

'And I don't think your brothers have started shaving yet.'

Maggie was distracted by the image of him in her home. 'You actually spent the night there?' She experienced a spasm of alarm as she noticed the greyish tinge to his normally vibrant skin. 'You obviously didn't get much sleep,' she observed concealing her anxiety behind a spiky attitude. 'You look worse than I do.'

CHAPTER SIXTEEN

MAGGIE stepped out of the lift from the garage and stopped, a small laugh drawn from her parted lips.

'Just how many houses do you have?' she asked, tilting her head back to look at the massive chandeliers suspended from the high ceiling. The wide sweeping staircase was perfect for making an impressive entrance. As she looked at it she could almost hear the swish of a silken skirt and feel the sensuous smoothness of the fabric on her bare skin.

'It's like a film set.' And I'm a character from another film, she thought, glancing down at her scuffed trainers that made no sound on the marble. Her jeans were a long way from the ball gown in her head and she was a long way from the sort of woman Rafael invited to host his London parties.

'What film did you have in mind?'

Maggie resisted the temptation to respond in a hushed tone—appropriate to this awe-inducing setting—and levelled a glare at his lean face, waiting until he had stopped speaking to a uniformed figure who had materialised before she narrowed her eyes and said, 'A film about someone with tasteless wealth, who kidnaps women!'

A flicker of impatience appeared in his eyes. 'This is not a kidnap—and we both know it—any more than it was the first time.'

Unable to bring herself to concede the truth of his edgy observation and feeling churlish because she supposed most people would acknowledge that he had actually rescued her, she pursed her lips and lowered her eyes.

'Myself, I always had a soft spot for misunderstood heroes.'

This comment brought her head up; her scornful scowl faded as she was hit by a badly timed debilitating surge of lust.

God, he was utterly gorgeous and his gorgeousness was not diminished by the dark shadow of stubble on his jaw or the exhaustion etched into his bronzed face.

The camera would love those strong angles and planes, and if it had been able to pick up even a fraction of the dark, smouldering, sexy aura he projected he would have been box office gold.

'Your problem is I do understand you,' she lied, thinking he had to be the most complex man on the planet; just when she thought she had figured him out he did something that totally threw her.

'But you think I am a hero—I'm flattered.'

'I might believe you if I didn't know you don't give a damn for anyone's opinion.' She stopped, wondering why they were wasting time on semantics.

She folded her arms over her chest and adopted a businesslike manner, always easier to do when your shaking hands were tucked safely out of view, and glanced at the doors leading off the hallway.

To her dazzled and slightly disorientated eyes there seemed to be dozens.

'So what next?' It was a question she hardly dared ask, let alone think about.

How did your life go back to any sort of normality after you had your face plastered all over the tabloids? How long in this situation did it take for the furore and speculation to die down…or maybe it never would?

Would she always be labelled the woman that a billionaire playboy gave a black eye?

On the brink of total panic she took a deep breath; all this speculation right now was pointless—what she needed to do was sort out one thing at a time.

Prioritising was not hard, and it was one of the few things in her life she still retained control of. She could at least concentrate on the positive: that she was not pregnant.

Struggling to capture that elusive positive frame of mind, she squeezed her eyelids closed, but the freeze-frame image that had formed in her head did not vanish.

For several moments she was forced to stare at Rafael gazing down proudly at the baby in his arms before she successfully banished it.

Dabbing the beads of sweat along her upper lip, she put a name to the tight, achy feeling in her chest: loss.

'Are you all right?'

Maggie's eyelashes lowered in a protective sweep. The sooner she cleared up the baby issue, the better, and how hard could it be to say there wasn't one?

He would probably break out the champagne.

He might even see the funny side of it, then again maybe not, she thought as she read the suspicion in his narrowed-eyed scrutiny.

Pasting on a smile brittle enough to break at the lightest touch or wrong word, she said brightly, 'I'm fine, it's just I think…'

Rafael, who had been watching the fluctuations of colour in her face, felt a stab of anxiety at the bluish discoloration of her lips. 'Are you going to faint?' He extended a hand that she patted irritably away.

Maggie breathed through a wave of nausea, tried to remember when she had last eaten and couldn't. Damn!

'I don't faint, just a blip. I'll be fine in a minute.'

'You are clearly not fine.' And it was his fault—everything was his fault.

Maggie lifted her head. 'Just a blood-sugar dip. I could just do with a cup of tea, that's all, and maybe a biscuit.'

Rafael was relieved to see that, though she was still pale, the blue discolouration around her lips had faded, but brave-face attitude did not fool him.

He studied her pale face, loving the curve of her cheek the tilt of her nose, her delicious mouth, loving even her stubbornness and fierce independence, but seeing past it to her fear.

She was holding it together, but only just. The need that rose up inside him, the need to remove the weight from her shoulders, to care for her, was totally outside his experience.

It was as strong in its own way as the wild, elemental attraction that existed between them. He was shaken to recognise it as part of the whole—it came with loving.

'Look, I know you must be scared. I know you must feel as if your life is over before it had begun.'

Maggie, confused by the intensity of his manner, looked startled and warily shook her head.

'But it doesn't have to be this way, Maggie. You may not believe it but if you could—'

He stopped abruptly and Maggie's level of bewilderment deepened as, in an utterly uncharacteristic action, his eyes slid from hers. He paused, the ripple of the muscles in his brown throat visible as he swallowed hard.

It was almost as if he were struggling to find the right words, which couldn't be right. Sure, Rafael was nobody's idea of chatty, and he never saw the need to fill a silence, but he was also extremely articulate.

As his head lifted the bands of colour along his cheekbones

drew Maggie's attention to the slashing contours. If this had been anyone else she would have said they were self-conscious—but this wasn't anyone else, it was Rafael, supremely confident Rafael, who she had never seen display anything approaching insecurity, even when he was stark naked. Palms damp with the effort, she pushed aside the erotic image of his lean, streamlined, golden-skinned body gleaming as shafts of moonlight hit… Focus, Maggie…

Moonlight and his body out of the equation one thing remained obvious: she was misreading the signs.

'One day you might look back and think this is the day your life, it began.'

She was startled not just by his words, but by the driven intensity of his manner and the emotion packed into his words. Her eyes lifted to his face and she saw the same intensity reflected in his smoky eyes as their glances locked.

'This is not something that you have to do alone.'

The husky resonance in his voice made her shiver. 'What do you mean?'

'I'm saying that I will not be an absent father. When we are married you will not have to worry about being a solo parent. I have much to learn,' he admitted.

The uncharacteristic display of humility passed right over Maggie's head. All she heard was *married…* He had said it so matter-of-factly that Maggie thought she had misheard.

'It's just as well I know your opinion of marriage, Rafael. For a moment there,' she admitted with a hollow little laugh, 'I thought you said *married.*'

Rafael did not share her mirth. 'A man can change his opinion.'

Maggie stared, drawn as always by the brooding strength in his face, but totally sure this was a case of crossed wires. Anything else was, well…*impossible!*

'You're suggesting we get married?' This time the laugh got locked in her aching throat.

His head reared back and he looked at her, hauteur and offence etched into every line of his dark patrician features. 'You thought I would not?'

Maggie blinked, realisation sending a soft pink wash over her skin.

He was serious.

This was a proposal. The fact he would hastily withdraw it did not alter the fact that he had made it.

Maggie admired the misplaced sense of honour that had made him propose, and even though she knew marriage under these circumstances was totally and utterly wrong she was unable to dispel the unsettling suspicion that, had she been carrying his baby, she could not have lived up to her own principles without a struggle.

She looked at him, a punch-drunk glaze in her wide eyes. 'I…I didn't think,' she admitted.

It looked to Rafael as if she wasn't thinking now; she looked as if adrenaline alone was keeping her upright. He grimaced and silently cursed the impatience that had made him prematurely blurt things out that way.

The priority was getting a medical all-clear because he still felt little confidence in the hospital's assurance she was fine. In his view they were simply covering their backs against litigation. He would not relax until they had a diagnosis from a non-biased source.

'Wow, Rafael, I really appreciate the gesture, a really lovely gesture,' she began thickly. 'But you see—'

'You "appreciate"…!' he echoed.

'Yes, really, it's—'

'Yes.' He swallowed. 'You said—a *lovely* gesture.'

Maggie winced at the sardonic note in his voice.

'It is not a gesture, Maggie. We will speak of this afterwards.'

'No, I have to tell you now.'

Ignoring her anguished wail, Rafael walked over to a door and pushed it open. He turned and gestured for her to enter before him.

She sighed and, left with little choice, she acceded to the silent request and walked past him.

The room she found herself in appeared to be a large drawing room. It was not, however, the décor or antique furnishing that caught Maggie's attention, but the man standing next to the Adam fireplace.

'Maggie, this is Dr Metcalf…James,' he said, turning to the older man. 'I am grateful you came so promptly.'

Maggie watched the two men shake hands and felt her resentment stir. Did Rafael really think she would sit back and let him take control of her life this way? Maggie scowled and said loudly, 'I do not need a doctor.'

'Possibly,' Rafael conceded. 'But as he is here now it would be foolish, not to mention rude, to make this a wasted journey.'

Her jaw clenched. 'Don't patronise me, Rafael. If you want to waste your money on a totally unnecessary consultation that's your business, but I don't have to waste my time when I already know I'm fine.'

'So you are a doctor now.'

Maggie threw up her hands in utter exasperation. 'No, but I'm not a hypochondriac by proxy either.'

'Is that an accepted medical term?'

'Shut up, and in case,' she added coldly, 'you forgot, I was examined by a doctor after the incident.'

All humour evaporated from Rafael's manner as he scowled darkly. 'Not an incident,' he corrected. 'An assault, and not a doctor, a medical student.'

Maggie, who was not about to explain the intricacies of the

medical hierarchy, sighed. 'It doesn't take a Harley Street specialist to diagnose a black eye.'

Neither man denied the job description, but then this was no surprise. Rafael would only consult the best.

'For the record James—' his gaze was trained, not on the medic, but on Maggie '—and I explain because I understand that things such as uncharacteristic mood swings are sometimes diagnostic of an underlying problem with head injuries—but, no, she is always this unreasonable and difficult.'

Maggie's dark eyes flashed in response to this display of deliberate provocation. 'Thank you. I am in the room, and you are embarrassing the doctor.'

'Not at all,' the older man intervened smoothly. 'Now if you just give us a few minutes, Rafael, I'm sure I'll be able to put your fears to rest.'

Maggie rather enjoyed seeing the startled expression when Rafael realised he was being asked, albeit politely, to leave the room.

His steel-reinforced jaw tightened imperceptibly, but after a pause and what she suspected was a tough internal struggle—clearly his natural response to an order, even one couched as a polite suggestion, was not to smile—he nodded and produced one anyway.

Not that Maggie found the sardonic grin in her direction at all apologetic, but he did leave.

Maggie's shoulders sagged with relief when the door closed. It was a temporary reprieve, but at least it gave her breathing space and the opportunity to explain to the doctor that she really did not need a consultation.

The doctor agreed totally with her, which begged the question how did she end up being examined, anyway?

The examination was thorough but not lengthy. The doctor

pronounced that her facial injuries were superficial and advised she take painkillers to ease the discomfort.

Maggie said, 'I fine with pain, actually. It's just a bit uncomfortable.'

The doctor, who didn't look impressed by her stoicism, produced a bottle from his bag and handed it to her, saying, 'Just in case you change your mind and they won't harm the baby, but then you're a nurse—you already know that.'

Maggie's fingers tightened around the bottle as she managed to produce a half-hearted smile. She was not going to take her anger out on this man. She intended to reserve that for Rafael, who was a control freak of the first order.

Or maybe he wanted confirmation of the pregnancy? Ironic when if he'd only let her get a word in he'd already know there was no baby.

'I know Rafael is concerned that the attack could have harmed the baby…how far along are you?'

'There is no baby, doctor.'

CHAPTER SEVENTEEN

THE doctor had been gone a few minutes when, after a tap, the door opened. Maggie, who had been nursing her anger while she waited, spun around with a wrathful glower.

The maid holding the tea tray looked as startled as Maggie felt. She forced herself to smile and said thank you as the girl nervously put the tray down on a console table and beat a hasty retreat.

It was five minutes later when Rafael walked through the door, by which time Maggie had eaten several of the delicious smoked salmon and cream cheese sandwiches from the tray to revive her flagging energy levels and silence her growling stomach.

'How dare you go around telling people that I'm pregnant?'

'Shall I be mother or you?'

'Very funny.'

'I am not laughing,' he pointed out as he lowered his rangy frame onto a leather armchair.

A quick survey of his face through her lashes revealed that this was an accurate assessment; it was easy to read what he wasn't. What he was was more of a challenge and one beyond her capabilities.

'And I would not call one medic "people"—but as I was

asking him to examine you and make a diagnosis it seemed logical to give him all relevant medical information. And before you start accusing James of revealing confidential medical details, I can assure you the only information he imparted was that you are well.'

'But you tried?'

He flashed her an incredulous look as he crossed one ankle over the other and gritted, *'Dios,* you make me dizzy with your pacing. Sit before you fall down.' Rafael had to dig deep into his reserves of self restraint to stop himself leaping to his feet and physically enforcing his suggestion.

To see the pallor of sheer exhaustion etched into her delicate bruised face was a torment; not to respond to it intensified the agony.

'Of course I tried. It embarrassed me that I had to.'

Maggie winced as her sense of fair play kicked in hard. Shaking her hair back from her face, she lifted the stray strands that had crept down the neck of her top with her hand and flopped in an attitude of weary defeat into the chair opposite Rafael.

'All right, let's get this over with.'

'You make it sound like pulling a tooth.'

A procedure, she reflected grimly, that generally involved a local anaesthetic. This offered no such luxury. She expelled a shaky breath and watched as he left his seat to pour tea from the pot.

'Drink,' he said, handing her a cup before retaking his seat.

Maggie winced as she took a sip. 'I don't take sugar.'

'You look like you need it.'

'You're the one who will be in shock, not me.'

Rafael expelled a deep sigh and leaned forward, his hands planted on his knees.

'Susan's right—you are pregnant.' It emerged as a statement and not a question.

Maggie exhaled. 'No, I'm not,' she said, wondering whether he would be able to hide his relief.

There was no relief because it soon became clear he didn't believe a word she was saying. 'She is hurt you didn't feel able to tell her.'

'Of course I'd feel able to tell her—if I was. I'm just not.'

'She thought perhaps that you wanted to tell the baby's father first?'

'And you told her that was you…great, have you not been listening to me, Rafael? There is no baby!'

'Your mother is sure—'

'My mother has been sure that I'm pregnant ever since I got engaged to Simon.'

At the mention of the other man's name Rafael tensed.

'It was her worst fear. She never thought he was good for me—my entire family were relieved when we split up.' The same family that, it appeared, had welcomed Rafael with open arms.

One of life's little ironies.

Rafael's anger and frustration at her denial escalated.

'That won't wash. She didn't seem afraid to me—hurt because you hadn't told her and concerned because you bottle things up—'

He stopped as a hissing sound escaped through Maggie's clenched teeth.

'What's wrong?'

The question drew an incredulous laugh from Maggie. 'Why would anything be wrong?' she asked with bitter irony. 'My family has been discussing my character flaws with a stranger who walked in off the street!' she exploded.

'Not walked, exactly—I drove there.'

'Well, don't think you got preferential treatment because they were impressed with your big car. My family are not like that.'

'Yes, I did get that.' Having been born with a name that had been opening doors for him all his life, he had found it a strange experience to have a door stay firmly closed—until he had said the magic word: Maggie. 'I think they just liked me.'

'That's because she thought you were the father,' Maggie returned gloomily.

The smile that briefly lightened the brooding intensity of Rafael's expression had a definite hint of smugness. 'So you finally admit it.'

'No!' Maggie flicked a glance at his dark lean patrician profile and thought, She took one look at you and decided you were the catch of the century.

'I think Mum's mindset is almost anyone is better than Simon.'

It was name that he was fast growing to hate. 'If ever I need my ego deflated I will know where to come. This has nothing to do with...*Simon*. I am your first sexual relationship.' His glance drifted to her lips.

'But Mum doesn't know that, unless you told her?' Which was becoming a less ludicrous possibility by the second.

'It was not a subject that came up.'

'Well, thank God for that,' she breathed, thankful for small mercies.

'You are obviously very close. I assumed—'

'Can we leave my sex life out of this!' she cut in, not even making a pretence of being able to match his casual, almost careless attitude to that particular subject.

Meeting his eyes, she caught her breath and thought, Cancel careless. There was nothing that could be categorised careless in the glow reflected in those platinum depths.

'I have never discussed my sex life with Mum.'

'We will leave your sex life out of this, though I think it is very much part of it.'

He was struggling to be patient. He understood she was in denial, but her continued refusal to face up to facts was hard to take.

He had to make Maggie understand that he appreciated how she must be feeling and that he was going to be there for her—that she wasn't alone.

'I think Susan is a pragmatist. You are pregnant and, like any mother, she wants to know that you will be looked after.'

Maggie lifted her hands in a gesture of utter frustration.

'And,' he said, ignoring the interruption, 'I reassured her on the subject.'

'Oh, God!' Maggie groaned, lifting her knees to her chest and wrapping her arms around them. 'I'm not pregnant!'

A hissing sound of anger escaped through his clenched teeth. 'Will you stop pretending, Maggie? I saw the baby clothes.'

She watched in bemused silence as he got to his feet and stalked to the opposite end of the room with the grace of a restless caged panther. He was so damned gorgeous that even the sight of his broad back made her ache.

The swell of longing that tightened in her chest made it hard for Maggie to speak as she echoed.

'"Baby clothes"?'

He spun back, dragging a hand over his dark hair as he pinned her with a lethal steely glare of disapproval. 'Isn't it about time you stopped this act?'

'I'm not acting.'

Her response did not soften the grim severity of his expression. 'In the bathroom, the boxes.' He saw the realisation wash across her face and said, 'Finally! Now can we start discussing this like two adults?'

Maggie covered her mouth with her hand. 'You saw the clothes and thought…' She stopped, exhaled a shaky sigh. 'So that was why you left so suddenly?' It was totally illogical of her to feel hurt by the fact he had been so spooked that his first instinct had been to run.

The fact was he had come back, even though a baby was the last thing he wanted in his life, because despite his reputation Rafael was a thoroughly decent man, and with a strong sense of responsibility.

And because he was a decent man he would try to hide his relief when he realised the truth, she thought bleakly.

'I'm not pregnant, Rafael. No!' She held up her hand and said quickly, 'Please, just hear me out.' She paused, choosing her words with care, ashamed that for a split second she had wished there had been a baby and she would have an excuse to keep him in her life.

'There were baby clothes in the boxes. A friend at work passed them on to me because she knew—'

'That you are pregnant.'

'No, she knew about the work I do at the shelter.'

His dark brows twitched into a frowning line above his hawkish nose. '"Shelter"?' Was this yet another diversion?

'When Simon was campaigning during the by-election he visited a shelter. It's a place,' she explained, 'where women who are escaping abusive relationships go. They stay there while they get back on their feet. Some have children with them.'

Simon, happy with the results of the photo opportunity, had seen no reason to go back, privately confiding that he had found the entire experience depressing.

When asked if she felt the same way Maggie had admitted she had been shocked but not depressed; actually she had found her visit to the shelter, if anything, uplifting.

The people who worked there, she had explained to him, had been so tremendously dedicated, and the courage and resilience of many of the women who, despite all they had been through, were looking forward to starting a new life inspirational.

Simon had been unable to understand her attitude and he had been less than happy when she had continued the association with the shelter, not on any formal basis, but she had become quite involved with fundraising.

'Some of the women have children and babies.'

He leaned his broad shoulders against the wall and studied her face in silence for what felt like an eternity to Maggie.

'This is true?'

She nodded.

'And the clothes, they are for them?'

She nodded again.

'How do you have time for this shelter? You work impossible hours and—'

'So do you.'

'That is not the same…' He exhaled slowly and met her eyes. 'So you are not pregnant,' he said, not portraying any particular relief, but then maybe it was still sinking in.

'No, so you can relax—you're not going to be a father.' It was difficult not to notice that he didn't look relaxed.

Rafael passed a hand across his eyes and peeled himself away from the wall. His demeanour as he walked across the room toward her was not one she would have associated with a man who had just had a narrow escape.

As he got closer Maggie's levels of nervous tension soared. There was something ominous about his body language and she began to talk, the words tripping over each other in her nervous haste to get them out.

'I'm sorry you had all the worry and my mum made it worse. Some men would have walked away.'

He stopped a few feet from her. 'I did.' In shock or not it was a response that he would never forgive himself for. 'I was a coward.' He had not known how to tell her he loved her.

'A bit harsh.'

He gave her a long level look. 'Not harsh enough.'

The depth of self-condemnation in his voice made her blink.

'You did come back and it's all a happy ending. No baby, no wedding bells.'

Rafael continued to stare back at her, not looking like a man who was celebrating his lucky escape.

Maggie's control snapped. She didn't need this. It was tough enough putting a cheerful face on the fact that there was nothing beyond a physical attraction which by his own estimation only had a short time to run before it fizzled out—at least on his part—to keep them together.

Rafael was going to walk away some time soon and this time he wouldn't come back, and he was standing there acting as if it were his life that had just fallen apart.

'It doesn't change anything.'

Maggie was startled by this incomprehensible interpretation of the situation.

'It changes everything, Rafael. You came here to ask me to be your mistress, not your wife.'

His upper lip curled in an expression of contempt and he reviewed his behaviour. He took her chin in his fingers and with his free hand brushed the strands of dark hair from her face. The tenderness in the action brought a rush of tears to her eyes. 'I spent a long time trying to work out why I came here, but last night I realised it is not complicated.'

'It isn't?' Maggie whispered. The tender glow in his magnificent eyes was sending all sorts of messages that she didn't dare believe.

'The answer is just as simple as when you asked me earlier did I have to kiss you.' A distracted expression appeared in his smoky eyes as his thumb moved along the curve of her soft lush lips. 'I *had* to come to you.'

The throaty admission was good, but suddenly Maggie wanted more—she dared to think that there was more. 'Why?'

'I do not function without you in my life. It was a shock to learn you were pregnant, or I thought you were,' he corrected, flashing her a bitter grin.

'Look, you were allowed to be unhappy. No man wants to be saddled with a baby from a casual fling.'

'Is that what we were?'

Her eyes fell, she swallowed…was it possible…? She could not let herself believe. She felt his hands on her shoulders and lifted her face to his. The incandescent glow in his eyes made her gasp.

'It was never a simple fling for me, Maggie,' he said quietly. 'I told myself it was but that was just a front because I didn't have the guts to admit the truth.' He shook his head in disgust.

'And what is that?'

'The truth is I stopped refusing to admit the truth about us. And, for the record, once the initial shock wore off I was delighted about the baby, and not just because it bound you to me.'

Maggie shook her spinning head, unable to take in what he was saying. 'What are you saying? You want me to be your mistress?'

'Mistress?' He took her face between his hands and gazed down into her eyes with an expression that brought tears of emotion to them. 'No! I want you to be my wife.'

'Marry…me…you…'

'That,' he said lovingly, 'is the general idea.' He fitted his warm lips to the quivering outline of her mouth and kissed her until she was breathless. 'I love you,' he breathed against her mouth. 'And I have been lost without you.'

'This is real.' She pressed a hand to her mouth, but was obliged to remove it when he kissed her again. 'You love me?'

Finally allowing herself to believe that this really was happening, Maggie let out a euphoric whoop of joy and flung her arms around his neck.

'And I love you, I adore you…' she declared, punctuating each word with a kiss. Breathless she lifted a loving hand to his face. 'You do know, don't you, that I would do anything for you?' she husked emotionally.

'This is good to know, but I discovered that my needs are actually quite simple, *mi querida.*'

'They are?'

He took the hand laid against his face, holding her eyes with his as he pressed her palm to his lips. The heat in his eyes made her insides tighten. 'Yes. It turns out after a life of driven achievement, all I actually need is you.'

She blinked away the tears of happiness that filled her eyes. 'Are you saying I'm simple?'

'I'm saying that you are infuriating, stubborn, argumentative!' Stilling her protest with a brush of his lips that made her tremble, he added huskily, 'And I wouldn't want you any other way. Without you I'm not even sure I exist, Maggie. If that makes sense.'

Maggie nodded. 'It does to me, and if that is the case then I think I'd better stay for more than a week this time.'

'A lifetime would not be long enough for me to show you all the ways I love you.'

She laughed up into his dark beautiful face and said solemnly, 'Then as time is an issue maybe you should start now—showing me, that is…'

It was an invitation that Rafael found he had no problem accepting.

'Out of curiosity,' he added as he lifted her into his arms and looked with love into her eyes. *'Dio!'* he groaned, distracted by the love glowing back at him. 'You are beautiful.' After a pause for a kiss that left her aching for more he added,

'I know your feelings on shoes, but what is your attitude on jewellery? I like the idea of rubies on your skin.'

Maggie who liked the idea of *Rafael* on her skin nodded happily. 'Anything you say.'

'No arguments?'

'Me?' she said innocently then laughed huskily when he rolled his eyes. 'I concede that it is just possible I might occasionally disagree with you. But if all our arguments end this way I have no complaints!'

'I think I find that I believe in happy endings.'

'Surely not,' she teased as he strode from the room.

'I must—I have found mine. Now we will begin the tour of the house. Starting, I think, in the master bedroom, which you might like to redecorate.'

Maggie linked her arms around his neck. 'I wouldn't change a thing.'

Why change perfection?

EPILOGUE

THE doting grandmothers had been reluctant to relinquish their burden, but Rafael remained firm as he took possession of the irritable baby.

And no wonder he was irritable, Rafael thought, able to identify with his son's demeanour.

Left to him this would have been a small intimate celebration with guests whom you could tell to go home at the appropriate moment without causing outrage. This was *definitely* the last time he would open his home to his family.

Until the next time Maggie smiled and said, *'Please, Rafael,'* he thought with a wry grin.

His focus shifted to the other side of the room where his wife, looking totally drop-dead gorgeous in a striking red dress and oblivious as always to the fact half the men in the room were lusting after her, was doing her perfect hostess thing.

When people asked, as they always did, if he knew how lucky he was, Rafael was able to honestly say—yes.

The conversation with Rafael's elderly aunt was stretching Maggie's novice Spanish to the limit. It was Angelina who rescued her.

'Thanks for that.'

Angelina smiled. 'You looked as if you were struggling. Oh, not again,' she sighed, turning at the sound of a cry.

Maggie watched amused as Angelina ran gracefully across the room to pick up her sobbing toddler from the floor. Her twin half brothers had reached the terrible two stage.

Only a second behind her Susan Ward was on the spot, bending to lift the remaining twin into her arms, a handful of his brother's hair still clutched triumphantly in his chubby fist.

They had had a noisy and very happy family party when Mum's operation had been officially declared a total success.

Maggie watched as the two women—her *mothers*—their heads close together, laughed. The previous night Maggie had found herself taking snaps of her mum teaching Angelina the dance she had learnt at her salsa class!

Now how weird was that? she thought. Only it wasn't. The first few times she'd met up with Angelina had been strained, but over time they had become quite close. Not in a mother-daughter way—they were too close in age for that—but they had become friends and Angelina had really helped her settle into her new life, not to mention persuading Rafael not to wrap her up in cotton wool during her pregnancy.

Maggie hadn't asked about her natural father, and she knew the other woman was grateful she had left this painful subject alone.

Maggie feared that being outed as illegitimate might have made her some sort of social outcast, but she had been wrong. There had of course been gossip, but far from being an outcast she had been embraced by both Spanish clans, who seemed anxious to claim her as their own.

Angelina's reaction to having her secret made public had surprised Maggie. It was a relief, she insisted, to finally have everything out in the open, and though Maggie had no idea what had gone on behind closed doors Alfonso certainly appeared to have totally accepted the situation.

Maggie reached Rafael's side just as he was tucking their son expertly against his shoulder. An emotional lump swelled in her throat as she watched him supporting their son's small head tenderly with one big hand.

Though she teased Rafael about his protective attitude to their son, she totally understood it. Alessandro had been so tiny and fragile when he was born that she had been almost too scared to touch him, but he was catching up fast.

She lifted a hand and stroked his silky head. They called him their 'wedding-night baby' because he had been due nine months to the day following their wedding. Alessandro had, however, decided to do his own thing and arrive six weeks early.

Maggie had spent that first couple of weeks when he was being monitored in the special care baby unit in a state of constant anxiety. If it hadn't been for Rafael, who had been incredible supporting her through that scary time, Maggie wasn't sure she could have coped.

His dark lashes curled from his flushed cheek and Maggie smiled as their perfect beautiful baby boy looked directly at her.

'He looks more like you every day.'

'Is that a good thing?' Rafael asked with a teasing smile.

'Ask me the same question in eighteen years' time when he is breaking hearts and if he's like his papa, rules, too.' She smiled, cheerful when considering this moment that was still safely distant.

'Sixteen,' Rafael corrected. 'We Castenadas are early developers.' The baby in his arms chose that moment to give a loud cry. 'He needs a nap. I'll take him to the nursery.'

'I'll do it if you like?' she offered.

Rafael shook his head, meeting her eyes above the soft froth of baby curls. 'I need a break from our guests.' The scowling glance he threw around the room drew a laugh from Maggie. 'Shouldn't they be going?'

'Play nice, Rafael. Remember we did them out of a wedding,' she reminded him.

Rafael, it turned out was not a fan of long engagements. Theirs had lasted only as long as it took to push through the legalities before she had walked the hundred yards to the church from her parents' house.

The only guests present had been her parents and brothers and she and Rafael had spent the next month in a villa owned by Rafael's Greek billionaire friend Theo Leonidis.

'I think we owe them today.'

'Owe them!' he ejaculated, shaking his head before adding, 'How you ever persuaded me to say yes to this!'

Maggie feigned innocence and angled a wide-eyed look at his face. 'You don't remember?'

Rafael's eyes darkened as they slid to her wide lush lips. 'You can remind me later.'

Their eyes connected and a familiar bolt of lust slammed through her body. 'A date,' she agreed huskily, laying a hand on his arm and raising herself up on tiptoe to kiss her son's forehead. 'Yell if you need me.'

'I always need you.' His eyes travelled from the baby in his arms to the face of the woman he loved, loved with such an intensity that it still took his breath away just to see her smile. He suspected it always would.

Maggie tilted her head to one side, a wicked smile playing over her lips as she said huskily, 'Our guests don't seem to want to leave, but there's nothing stopping us, is there? They probably won't even notice,' she predicted.

Rafael a gleam in his eyes, nodded. 'I like your thinking, Magdalena,' he said admiringly.

Maggie grinned and slanted a sultry look up at him through her dark lashes. 'Is there anything else you like?'

'It depends on what's on offer.'

She lifted herself on tiptoe, this time to whisper a suggestion in his ear. Rafael raised his brows and grinned.

'I could be persuaded,' he admitted, sliding his free arm around her waist as he headed for the open door.

'I think he's asleep,' Maggie whispered.

'Of course he's asleep—his timing is as good as his father's.'

'Says you!' Maggie teased.

'No,' he contradicted smoothly. 'Says you…often. Have I ever mentioned that you turned my world upside down?'

'Only once or twice a day.'

'You know,' he mused, his glance sliding from the flushed face of his sleeping son to the glowing beauty of his wife's upturned features, 'I don't know if I'm standing on my head or my heels, but I love the view from here.'

'It's not bad from where I'm standing either,' Maggie returned, her loving gaze glued to the face of the tall Spaniard who had captured her heart. 'Sometimes,' she confessed, 'I think this is a dream and I'll wake up and all this will be gone.'

Rafael bent his head and kissed her tenderly. 'When you wake up I will be there, *mi querida.* Now come, before our guests spot us and decide to follow us to our bedroom.'

Maggie gave a sigh of contentment. 'God, but I love being irresistible!'

'And I love you.'

THE SECRET SPANISH LOVE-CHILD

BY

CATHY WILLIAMS

Cathy Williams is originally from Trinidad, but has lived in England for a number of years. She currently has a house in Warwickshire, which she shares with her husband Richard, her three daughters, Charlotte, Olivia and Emma, and their pet cat, Salem. She adores writing romantic fiction and would love one of her girls to become a writer—although at the moment she is happy enough if they do their homework and agree not to bicker with one another!

CHAPTER ONE

GABRIEL heard his secretary's sharp rap on his office door with a sense of relief.

Perched on his desk, with her high, *high* heels dangling from her feet and her short, *short* skirt provocatively and purposefully riding high enough to expose a generous eyeful of thigh, Cristobel had been in full flow for the past twenty minutes.

She needed to *really start doing the shops*, the wedding was getting closer by the day and *everything had to be perfect* and there was just no way that she was going to leave *all the details* to that *ridiculous wedding planner* his mother had insisted on hiring.

She had punctuated each statement with a flick of her long, curling blonde hair and a jabbing motion with her finger, taking care to lean forward so that he couldn't fail to notice her deep cleavage and the full swell of her breasts under the tightly pulled silk top.

Cristobel was nothing if not sweepingly confident about her ability to use her body to its maximum advantage and while Gabriel would concede that he had been distracted by it for all of two minutes, right now he just wanted her out of his office and safely tucked away in whatever mind-blowingly expensive shop she favoured. He really didn't care. He had calls to make and several reports to look at and the high pitched, insistent staccato of her voice was beginning to give him a headache.

Naturally he had contained his impatience because she was, after all, his fiancée but he had almost given his secretary a standing ovation when she had tactfully suggested that she had checked the personnel files and found a Spanish speaking employee who would be delighted to take Cristobel to Knightsbridge, where she would be able to shop to her heart's content before she headed back to Madrid.

'But I want *you* to come with me,' Cristobel pouted now, leaning further forward and sweeping aside several documents as she planted her hands flat on his desk. 'It's important for you to get involved with the planning.'

'You don't want me involved with the planning, Cristobel,' Gabriel told her dryly. 'At any rate, you know how I feel about these things. Lavish weddings are not my cup of tea.' Nor, he mused now, were weddings of any sort, at least in so far as they pertained to him, until a year ago when he had finally and philosophically ceded to loving but insistent parental pressure.

His parents were both keen to see him married and settled. They were getting older. They wanted grandchildren. Whilst they were still at an age to enjoy them. Before they died.

And Gabriel had finally acknowledged that perhaps the time was right to take a wife. There was a very thin line between the desirable bachelor and the oldest swinger in town. He was now in his thirties and life had a habit of racing on.

Cristobel would make a perfectly suitable wife. Her family tree was as old as his was and as wealthy. She understood the unspoken rules of the way his life operated and would abide by them. Whatever she wanted, she would have and in return she would understand that his work was a priority for him. She was also a beautiful woman, small, voluptuous and well groomed.

On paper, it was a union brokered in heaven and any doubts were expertly fielded by using common sense and reason, two things which had never let him down in his life before.

'You'll enjoy Harrods with another woman.' His phone rang and he answered it, his mind already on work, watching distractedly as Cristobel slid off his desk and stood up, smoothing down her tight cream skirt with her hands and pouting at him.

She was moving towards her bag when the door opened and in walked his Spanish-speaking saviour. A number on a file somewhere in the bowels of his cutting-edge glass building, a name he hadn't even been told because it was such an insignificant detail. But that face. The memory of it leapt out at him as though it had been lying just below the surface, nudging the edges of his consciousness.

Gabriel had a moment of utter speechlessness, while Cristobel continued to sort herself out, dabbing some lipstick on her mouth and angling a little compact mirror so that she could inspect her handiwork.

Alex Mcguire. He didn't need Janet to announce her because he realised that he could put the name to the person in an instant, even though it had been years since he had last had anything to do with her. She was as tall as he remembered, as tall as Cristobel was tiny, and she still had that coltish, boyish grace he had once found so unusual and so appealing. Short dark hair, which she had always defiantly refused to grow because she just *wasn't that type of girl*, the type of girl who wore stilettos and push up bras and red lipstick and tight clothes. In fact, he had never, not once, seen her in anything smart, but she was dressed smartly now, in a sober grey suit, although the shoes were still flat and the nails were still short and she still didn't wear much by way of make-up.

Alex, a newcomer to the Cruz business empire, had followed Gabriel Cruz's secretary along the opulent top floor of the offices in a state of nervous tension. At first, when she had been summoned from her lowly office on the first floor, she had steeled herself for a worst case scenario. Had she sent the wrong invoice to the wrong, very important client? Mistyped something critical? Used the wrong tone of voice to the wrong person on the telephone? She might just be a small cog in the finance department, but rumour had it that nothing escaped the mighty Gabriel Cruz's eagle eye and mistakes were never allowed to slip through the net. She needed this job. The salary was so much higher than what she had been getting before and when she thought that she might have blown it by doing something stupid, something that might require a personal summons by the great man himself, then her stomach had twisted into desperate knots and brought her out in a cold sweat.

But then she had been told that she was wanted for her translating abilities and she had relaxed a bit. She could speak Spanish fluently, had been assiduous in maintaining it even though she hadn't been back to Spain for a little over five years. Mr Cruz, she had been told, needed someone to visit the shops with his fiancée because he couldn't possibly spare the time and his fiancée's grasp of English was limited.

Now, as she stared at the legendary Gabriel Cruz, sitting behind his desk, a massive handmade creation which blended various shades of wood and looked as though it cost the earth, she felt the room begin to swim around her. Her throat felt dry, her brain seemed to decelerate to a standstill and a hot, burning tide of horrified colour swept into her face. She had to blink because the sight of the man in front of her was so extraordinarily, terrifyingly unexpected.

Reason tried to push its way through the tangled chaos of her thoughts, telling her that this couldn't possibly be the guy she had known all those years ago, because the guy she had known had not been called Gabriel Cruz and he certainly hadn't been some kind of mega-billionaire, but the testimony of her eyes was telling her otherwise.

She had to take a deep breath to steady herself. But she couldn't look at him. The resemblance was just too uncanny. Maybe it was just seeing this *type*. The sinfully good-looking Mediterranean *type*. Her brain had formed some weird ridiculous link, hence her feeling of being catapulted back in time.

'Well?' Cristobel demanded in Spanish. She looked at Gabriel sourly. 'Is *this* the girl who is supposed to come shopping with me?'

Gabriel was back in control. There was no point in playing catch up games now. 'She speaks Spanish. And, as I have said, I can't spare the time at the moment.'

'Look at her! How is she going to know where to take me?'

'Excuse me?' Alex interrupted, clearing her throat and forcing a polite smile on her face. Did they think that she was a pot plant to be spoken about as though she wasn't in the room? 'If you tell me what sort of stuff you're looking for…' She couldn't bring herself to look at the man lounging indolently behind the desk. Her imagination had been working overtime but she still wanted to get out of that office as quickly as possible.

Any longer and she might just start wondering what would happen if Gabriel Cruz really *was* her Lucio and there was no way that she was going to play mind games with herself and get lulled into visualising how catastrophic that would be.

'I need clothes,' Cristobel snapped. 'I need trinkets for my boxes to go on the tables. I need something exquisite for Vanya.' She moved behind the desk and wrapped her arms around Gabriel. 'And I cannot imagine this girl being able to help me. She has barely said a word since she entered! Darling—' she brushed her lips against his neck and he gently but firmly disentangled her from him '—is there *no one* else in this place who speaks Spanish? I need someone on my wavelength. She doesn't even know how to dress!'

Alex gritted her teeth together. 'I apologise for being a bit lost for words…' she reluctantly allowed her gaze to flit over Gabriel '…but for a minute you reminded me of someone I used to know, Mr Cruz. Sir.' She hurriedly averted her eyes to Cristobel, who didn't look dressed for a shopping trip in the middle of winter. 'I tend to dress in a practical fashion but I know where all the trendy places are.'

'I am not looking for trendy. I am looking for classic.'

'Yes. Well. Those too.'

'I suppose you will have to do. My coat is in the cupboard.'

Feeling as bulky as a bodyguard, Alex fetched the coat and followed in Cristobel's imperious wake, half listening to the further list of things that needed sorting out, half thinking her own thoughts because just seeing Lucio's doppelgänger had opened a door to a bank of memories and now they wafted through her mind, overpowering her attempts at control like a poisonous gas.

Making love to Lucio, laughing, talking until the early hours of the morning and then making love again so that she was exhausted when she rose in the morning to help out in the kitchens where she had been working for part of her gap year. Learning the hotel business while polishing up her Spanish and also developing a healthy tan. And, disastrously, falling in love. Eighteen and in love with the most gorgeous man alive. Boys had always been a known quantity for her. She had four brothers, for heaven's sake! She had known how to relate to them, how to talk about football and rugby and cars. She had even had a couple of boyfriends, drank beer with them and got freezing cold watching football matches in the depths of winter but nothing had prepared her for meeting Lucio. He had been everything a girl could ever dream of, a raven-haired, black-eyed, broodingly and impossibly sexy Spanish alpha male, not a boy but a man and one who had taken her girlish inexperience and turned it on its head.

Five years' worth of uninvited memories were her companions for the remainder of the day and Alex returned to her desk six and a half hours after she had left the office, wrung out and with barely any time to spare. For the first time that day, she succeeded in relegating the disturbing procession of memories out of her head because she was in such a rush to get back to her little terraced house in West London.

She was rummaging in her bag, trying to locate her Oyster card for the underground and save herself the daily embarrassment of holding up a queue of belligerent rush hour office workers while she frantically tried to find the elusive little plastic folder, when her telephone rang and she automatically picked it up, sticking the receiver under her chin so that she could continue her hunt.

Gabriel Cruz's voice, that deep, lazy drawl with its slight foreign intonation, brought her to a screeching halt and she felt her heart speed up. She had done a pretty good job convincing herself that her boss was not a spectre from her past. Gabriel Cruz had never been a broke, nomadic hotel worker. He had always had bucket-loads of money. His family, apparently, could trace their heraldic roots back to the dawn of time. She had managed to elicit that much from Cristobel and the information had finally silenced any lingering fears, but hearing his disembodied voice now made her think that time had somehow managed to rewind, throwing her back to that small hotel in Spain.

'Come up to my office. Now.'

'I'm...I'm sorry. Sir. Mr Cruz. I can't. I'm on my way out. Perhaps it could wait until tomorrow?'

'How long have you been working for my company?'

'Three weeks,' Alex said weakly, glancing frantically between the door and her watch.

'Long enough, in that case, to know that I do not appreciate my employees clock-watching. So that you are crystal clear on the matter—I wasn't issuing an invitation to my office; I was giving you an order.'

'Everything went fine today! I think your fiancée managed to get through most of what she wanted to...'

'In my office. I will give you five minutes.' He disconnected and pushed himself away from his desk. It bugged him that he had not been able to get Alex's image out of his head. He told himself that it was a futile exercise to dwell on what had happened between them. He had enjoyed many women in his life and had never had any problem in relegating them to history once they had ceased to be a part of his life. So why had he found it so difficult to stop thinking about this one? Was it because she had appeared out of the blue and had caught him unawares? Or was it because she held the unique position of having been the only woman he had bedded who had never had an inkling of his material worth? He didn't know. What he *did* know was that she had played havoc with his concentration. He was also keenly aware that thinking about another woman when he was engaged to be married in four months' time was entirely inappropriate.

He drummed his fingers impatiently on the gleaming surface of his desk. It was Friday. It was nearly five forty-five. He had dispatched his secretary, who was accustomed to routinely working overtime. The majority of his employees who occupied the outer offices would have packed up and gone and the remaining directors on the top floor would be ensconced in their offices, cutting deals and making calls until they were summoned home by irritable wives and partners. He should be doing the same. Working. But his brain seemed to have malfunctioned and he had found himself hunting down the company internal directory and then tapping in to Alex's extension because hell, he couldn't allow her to continue to wallow in the illusion that he was a stranger, could he? A stranger who bore a remarkable resemblance to someone in her past! She couldn't really believe that, could she? But, just in case she did, it was his job to disabuse her because she worked for him now and such a delusion would be downright unethical.

When she finally knocked on his door, he found that he was looking forward to their little chat.

'You wanted to see me.' Alex could feel her stomach churning as she hovered indecisively by the door, ready for flight.

'I did.' Gabriel didn't stand. Instead, he sat back and devoted one hundred per cent of his attention to acknowledging how little she had changed. Remarkable. She must be what now…? Twenty-three? Twenty-four? And she still hadn't succumbed to the polish and finesse to which most young people in the capital seemed to aspire. 'Come in.' He gestured expansively to one of the chairs positioned in front of his desk. 'Have a seat. I would offer you coffee but Janet, my personal assistant, has already left.' He shrugged and offered an apologetic smile.

Alex wondered whether a man of his importance was incapable of working a coffee machine. 'I…I really can't stay…'

Gabriel frowned. 'Maybe you didn't quite understand me when I told you that I don't tolerate clock-watching in my employees.'

'I know. And I'm more than happy to work overtime, but I need a day's notice. As it is, I'm already really late for…'

Gabriel raised one imperious hand. 'Not interested. Whatever date you've got lined up will have to wait. There are a few things we need to discuss.' He thought that he had swept all traces of her from his mind but he must have been mistaken because there was a familiarity about her that was strangely disconcerting and he was aware that the faintest colour scored his slashing cheekbones. Déjà vu slammed into him with pulsating intensity and suddenly he could remember everything about her, right down to the smallest details, the tiny freckles across her shoulder blades, the way she always smelt of the pine soap she liked to use, the sounds she used to make when he ran his hands all over her body.

The memories stole into his head like destructive gremlins and he banished them without conscience.

'What things?'

'You said that I reminded you of someone you used to know. Tell me.'

'Wh…what?'

'And stop clinging to that door knob as though you're on the verge of collapse! I told you to sit down!'

Alex could barely hear herself think. The blood was rushing through her and, even though she could see a precipice yawning open at her feet, she was still desperately happy to kid herself that everything was fine. She was having an inconvenient conversation but that was the extent of it.

'I…I really have to go, Mr Cruz. I have…obligations. I know you hate clock-watchers but…'

'I told you. Cancel your date. It'll be a lot easier than you think.'

Alex tried not to look resentful in the face of his implacable smile. In fact, she was trying hard not to look at him at all.

'Okay.' She angled her body away from him and spoke in a low, hurried voice, explaining the situation and lacing her request with a thousand apologies. Then, feeling a bit calmer, she turned to face him.

'So.' Gabriel watched as she gingerly sat down. Her body language was shrieking discomfort. 'This guy you tell me that I remind you of.'

'It's not important. I thought you called me here to find out how my day with your fiancée went.'

'Okay. Shall we use that as our starting point? How did the day go? Feel free to speak your mind. It's something I encourage in all my employees.'

Alex refrained from pointing out that he hadn't much liked it when she had spoken her mind and told him that she had to leave the office. 'The day went very well. She's demanding but I think she got a few things accomplished.'

'Yes,' Gabriel mused thoughtfully, 'I can imagine that you might have found Cristobel a little challenging. What else did you think of her?'

'I don't think it's my place to say, sir.'

'There's no need to keep repeating *sir* at the end of every sentence. So I take it that you two didn't get along…'

'I think she found my translating skills very useful.'

'I'm beginning to get the drift.'

'She's a very…a very…*polished* woman…' She had broken out in a film of perspiration because she suspected that traps were being laid, except she had no idea where the traps were. If she inadvertently stepped on one, would it signal the end of her career? Women, apparently, had a great deal of influence over their men, or so she had read somewhere, and if the mind-numbingly empty-headed socialite Cristobel decided to blacken her name, then she might very well find herself out of a job before she had had a chance to even get her feet under the table. But there was no way that she could pretend a rapport where none had existed. Nor was she finding it comfortable to look at him, which meant that she was addressing her answers to her feet. Hardly the sign of an efficient rising executive in his dynamic company.

An uncomfortable silence lengthened between them until Alex was eventually driven to look up at him and, as their eyes tangled, she felt her skin begin to prickle. The thread of reason that had held sway throughout the course of the day, the notion that there was no way that this man was the same one who had invaded her life and turned it upside down, began to fray at the edges.

When he said softly, 'Would that guy you remember have gone by the name of Lucio…?' Alex barely heard him. His words floated around her head and then, like laser-guided torpedoes, shattered through her protective barriers and her eyes widened in shock and dawning horror.

'How…how did you know?' The truth had already sunk in but, in her determination to block it out, she had subconsciously created all sorts of pointless justifications in her head as to why the guy sitting in front of her, oozing sex appeal and power, couldn't possibly be the Lucio she remembered from years ago. Lucio had been broke. He hadn't descended from the Spanish hierarchy. And surely he hadn't been as tall or aggressive or dangerously masculine as this man?

'I'm surprised you don't recognise me, Alex. I recognised you the second you walked through my door. You know, in a way, I'm a little offended but I'll rise above that.'

'But...but your name's not Lucio...it's...it's...' A great chasm was opening up at her feet and she tried not to stare down into its dark abyss.

'Lucio is my middle name.'

Having laboured to avoid looking at him at all, Alex now felt driven to stare as her memory of Lucio overlapped and merged with the reality of Gabriel Cruz, one and the same person, and of course she had been a complete fool to have thought otherwise. His was not a face to be forgotten, even with the benefit of some serious wishful thinking, and if she had found him good-looking back then, he was scarily sexy now. Time had taken the guy of twenty-six and honed him into staggering perfection.

And he was engaged.

'I don't understand,' Alex stammered in complete confusion.

'What don't you understand?'

'You lied to me? All those years ago? When I saw you in this office, I just thought you resembled the guy I used to know. Why would I think that you had lied to me? I knew someone who didn't have much money and liked the simple things in life. Who *were* you?'

Gabriel's lips thinned and he flushed darkly at the wounded accusation in her voice. She had always been upfront and honest. It had been one of the things he had enjoyed about her. No games, no subterfuge, no hidden agendas. No way was she going to understand his harmless pretence and now he felt like a bastard, which didn't sit well with him because he was someone accustomed to always feeling pretty good about himself.

'I indulged in a piece of innocent fiction,' he drawled with a shrug of his broad shoulders. And it *had* been innocent. Saddled with the weight of responsibility from a young age and already prematurely jaded by the nature of women and the lengths they would go to in order to fall into the bed of a man with money and power, the lure of allowing Alex to believe that he was no more than an ordinary guy who happened to be working at a nearby fancy hotel, had been irresistible. For the first time in his life, he had left his gilded cage and tasted a certain freedom. The vague, nebulous feeling that somewhere, buried deep inside, he had protected that memory, was something that Gabriel barely registered on a conscious level. He was not one of those weak men who wasted time indulging in a load of pointless introspection. He certainly wasn't going to start now.

'*A piece of innocent fiction?* What's so innocent about lying to someone?' She was momentarily distracted by the shocking concept of having been wilfully duped. She had fallen head over heels with a guy who had thought so little of her that he had found it okay to spin her a bunch of lies about himself. How big an idiot had *she* been? 'I believed every word you told me about yourself!'

'Your memory's playing tricks on you. I never told you anything about myself.'

'You allowed me to believe that you were an ordinary guy! You took walks on the beach with me and we ate out at cheap and cheerful restaurants and you sympathised with the fact that I was broke and all the time you were actually Gabriel Cruz, mega-rich and mega-powerful! You played with the truth and, as far as I'm concerned, that's the same as lying! You weren't really working at the Tivoli, were you?' On the fringes of her mind, she knew that this was all irrelevant but she shied away from confronting her truly ugly dilemma. It was easier to postpone that by taking refuge in the details of his deception.

'I was, in a manner of speaking.'

'What manner of speaking would that be?'

'I own the Tivoli Hotel. At least, I do now. At the time, I was in the process of acquiring it.'

Alex's mind reeled. How was it that she had never questioned his self-assurance? His confident charm? The effortless way he seemed to command the space around him? She had just found it unbelievably thrilling. So different from the boys she had known who had seemed like toddlers in comparison.

She wondered whether they had gone to cheap places because he would have been safe from recognition. Rich people wouldn't have been seen dead in cheap tapas bars frequented by local fishermen so the chance of him inconveniently bumping into a fellow millionaire acquaintance would have been nil.

And, hard on the heels of that thought, came another, even more sickening one. She had committed the grave error of telling him that she loved him and he had scarpered. Sure, he hadn't done a midnight flit, but as good as. He had let her down gently, explained that she was young, that they had had fun, that she had her whole life in front of her. He had been immune to her distraught expression and had kindly set her aside when she had clung to him. It had been a sobering experience but over time she had managed to persuade herself that she had had the misfortune to have invested all her youthful love in someone who hadn't felt the same towards her. These things happened. The music charts were littered with singers crooning on about broken hearts and unrequited love.

She was working out now that, even if he *had* been madly in love with her, which he hadn't been, he *still* would have walked out of her life because he was Gabriel Cruz and there was no way he would ever have hitched his wagon to a nobody.

Hadn't she met his fiancée first-hand? Hadn't she seen for herself what he was all about? Rich men needed all the right trappings and that applied to everything, from houses to cars to fiancées. On every level she was waking up to the fact that she had been an even bigger fool than she could ever have imagined possible.

'So,' she said slowly, very, very angry now, 'let me get this straight. Five years ago, you pretended to be someone you weren't *for a bit of fun*. I'm right about that, aren't I? Were you bored with fawning rich girls? Was that it? So you decided that you'd take a bit of time out and pretend to be just like everybody else and I just happened to be the poor schmuck who landed up in your path.'

'You're overreacting!'

'I am *not* overreacting! You may be rich and powerful but that's no excuse to manipulate other people! I *trusted* you!'

'I didn't *manipulate you*,' Gabriel muttered, 'and I didn't do anything with you that you didn't enjoy!' He raked restless fingers through his black hair and Alex followed that graceful movement with a compulsion that terrified her. She didn't want to think about exactly how much she had enjoyed all those things he had done with her.

'That's not the point! The point is, I might have liked having an idea of the person I was dealing with!'

'Why? Would you have behaved differently? Expected a bit more? Five-star hotels, perhaps? Four-poster feather beds and my limo to ferry you everywhere?'

'That's a horrible thing to say!'

'Why is it horrible? Call me cynical, but I've noticed that a healthy bank balance brings out all sorts of predictable behaviour patterns in women.' From the unusual position of self-defence, Gabriel fell back on the dispassionate air of someone delivering self-evident truths.

'Yes, well, believe it or not, there are some women who would run a mile from a man with a *healthy bank balance*.'

Gabriel gave a roar of incredulous laughter, which made her even more furious. 'Really? Let me think about that... No-o-o...don't think I've ever met that particular species...'

'Would you mind telling me why you summoned me here?'

'Why do you think, Alex?' He linked his fingers behind his head and leaned back. 'You don't seriously imagine that you can carry on working for me and kidding yourself that you don't know who I am, do you?'

Alex steeled herself to meet his gaze levelly, without flinching. She was thinking fast now, thinking about all the different ways his reappearance might jeopardize the life she now led, thinking that the last thing she wanted was for him to start picking her out from the herd. It wasn't likely. He was almost a married man. But what if he decided to play catch up games, just for the heck of it? There was too much at stake.

'You're right,' she conceded quietly. 'I shouldn't have... have let my feelings run away with me. It's been a bit of a shock but I'm over it now. You caused me a lot of sleepless nights when you walked out of my life...' she forced herself to smile wryly at him '...but that was a long time ago. It was just an eye-opener hearing the truth about who you were. If I reacted a little over the top, then I apologise...'

Gabriel was watching her carefully, his eyes narrowed. Her volte face was almost as dramatic as her outburst had been. His initial thought was that she was waking up to the fact that there was such a thing as kicking up too much of a fuss. She could reasonably get away with a little, given their past connection, but he was her boss and she was expendable. Hence her strategic back down.

Less welcome was the suspicion that she was trying to get rid of him, but he decided to discard that option.

'Apology accepted,' he drawled, his sharp eyes picking up the way her mouth tightened at that. Sorry, he realised, was something she certainly wasn't feeling.

God, he'd forgotten how feisty the woman was. He'd forgotten how refreshing it had been to be with a woman who didn't tiptoe around him. He'd put into mental cold storage that memory of being able to drop his cynicism and function with an openness he had never had and didn't have now. Crazy, inappropriate memories.

'If that's all, then…?' Alex sprang to her feet and snatched up her bag from where she had earlier dumped it on the ground next to the chair.

It didn't take a genius to figure out that she couldn't wait to get out of his office. Gabriel stood up with his usual lithe, easy grace and strolled over to where she was making a hasty beeline for the door.

'So…' His voice exuded the lazy confidence of a man who expected to be obeyed the second he opened his mouth and, sure enough, Alex paused in her tracks and turned to look at him. 'Where can I find you…?'

'What?' Her face drained of colour. *Find her? Why would he want to find her?*

'I mean, which department do you work for?'

'Why?' Alex asked cautiously.

Gabriel could feel irritation getting the better of him. 'Because I might need your services again,' he told her bluntly. 'Cristobel comes to London on a regular basis. It would be helpful if you could act as her tour guide if I am not available.' Had he meant to say that? Maybe not, but her desperation to get away from him was annoying.

Alex lowered her eyes, cut to the quick. Was he *that* thoughtless that he could suggest some kind of bonding experiment between his ex-lover and his wife-to-be? How thick could one guy get? But then hadn't he proved that his only concern was himself? He had wanted time out five years ago and so he had lied to her and used her. Now, he might need a Spanish translator and so he would demand her services and to heck if she found the arrangement inappropriate.

Put in an impossible situation and already coming to terms with the fact that there was too much at stake for her to remain in her job, Alex raised her eyes to his and ignored the way her pulse quickened as his dark gaze swept over her. She remembered the way he could make her feel. She reasoned that that was why her body felt so tingly, as though she had suddenly become uncomfortable in her own skin.

'That's not going to happen,' she told him quietly. 'I'm not paid to babysit your fiancée whenever she happens to be in London. I also didn't enjoy my duties today. You may be crazy about your fiancée and I'm really happy for you, but there's no way that I'm going to be ordered to go shopping with her again. We aren't similar and we didn't get along. We tolerated each other because neither of us had a choice.' She took a deep breath and found that her hands were shaking so she stuck them behind her back and bunched them into fists. 'Today's been a bit of a shock. It's a weird coincidence that I've ended up being employed in your company but there's no reason why we should have anything further to do with one another. We've both moved on with our lives. I wish you all the best but when I walk out that door, I really don't want to see you again.'

She fled with the last word, even resorting to taking the stairs rather than wait in mounting anxiety for the lift to arrive.

She'd always wondered how things might have turned out had she been able to get in touch with him all those years ago…tell him about Luke. Now he was getting married and his life was in a different place. He had moved on, found the perfect partner. Alex realised that she would just have to accept that there were some waters that could never be disturbed.

CHAPTER TWO

ALEX handed in her resignation the following Monday. There were a lot of questions and raised eyebrows but Alex played it down, using the old time worn favourite about *family problems*. No one liked to ask too many questions when confronted with someone else's *family problems*, especially when the someone else in question had only been employed by the company for less than a month.

She felt a pang of sharp, bitter regret as she quickly and efficiently cleared her desk, but she had had a night to think over the situation and there was no way that she could continue working in the same company as Lucio/Gabriel. He would have had no qualms about ordering her to flit around London with his fiancée, looking at stupid bits of fabric and translating ridiculous questions about shoe colours and flower arrangements. He might even have seen it as fitting punishment, considering she had laid into his wife-to-be with brutal honesty.

She barely gave consideration as to how this development would impact on her meagre finances. She had been too busy making sure that she vacated the smoked glass building with the minimum of fuss and under the radar of Gabriel's eagle eye, should he happen to be around. It was just a stroke of luck that his offices were on the top floor, safely out of harm's way.

One week later and she had managed to land herself back into her old job, which had seemed a miserable step backwards but she could hardly afford to turn the money away. And her old boss had been nice enough about her slinking back with her tail between her legs. No awkward questions. No snide remarks. He had accepted her vague waffle about *things not living up to expectation* and installed her right back into her swivel chair in front of the computer in the small reception area.

Which was where she was precisely eight days later when Gabriel showed up.

She didn't see him. She was busy putting the finishing touches to a document she had been given to edit, racing against time, which was what she always seemed to do the minute the clock struck four-thirty.

From the small corridor, Gabriel's eyes quickly and efficiently scanned the room, for the office was really just one big room, amateurishly divided into cubicles by flimsy partitions. The weather had turned chilly and it was cold. So cold, in fact, that, as his eyes rested on her downbent head, he became aware that she was typing quickly, wearing fingerless gloves and with a woolly hat pulled down low so that only the ends of her short dark hair were visible. The smart get-up in which he had last seen her dressed as she had sat across from him in his office had been abandoned in favour of a pair of jeans and a grey jumper. He guessed that she would be wearing trainers. She had once told him that she had not possessed a pair of high heeled shoes until she turned seventeen and had to attend her grandfather's funeral.

Gabriel wasn't entirely sure why he had attempted this trip halfway across London but she had lodged in his brain like an irritant and he hadn't been able to clear his head of her image.

He had finally persuaded himself that he should see her to make sure that she was all right. She had quit without notice and he had, after all, once been her lover. He felt duty-bound to satisfy himself that she hadn't done anything crazy. She could be impetuous. And she had seemed pretty overwrought the last time he had seen her.

Having successfully attained the moral high ground, he had done the unthinkable and cancelled his meetings for that afternoon, choosing to drive instead to her office, having had someone verify that she was back working there.

It was some minutes before anyone noticed him and then his presence was announced via a network of urgent whispers and giggles until someone who must have been the section supervisor headed towards him.

Alex, he noted with dry amusement, was lost in a world of her own, immune to the flurry of attention his appearance had aroused.

It took no more than a curt nod in her direction to halt the supervisor in her tracks and he felt a moment of gleaming satisfaction as Alex looked up, met his gaze and instantly blanched.

She pulled off the woolly hat and her hair responded by sticking up in little dark spikes before she made an attempt to smooth it back into obedience, standing up and pulling off her gloves at the same time, the focus now of all attention as he continued to lounge indolently in the doorway.

She was red-faced when, after a whispered conversation with her supervisor, she eventually made her way nervously towards him.

'What are you doing here?' was the first thing she said, barely containing her anger.

'Do you know, I had forgotten how tall you were.'

'You haven't answered me!'

'I don't like having prolonged conversations in doorways.'

'And *I* don't like being hunted down!'

'Why don't we go and discuss this somewhere a little less in the glare of your colleagues? Anyone would think they had never seen a man before.'

They hadn't, Alex thought resentfully. At least not a man like him. She was maintaining a healthy distance and trying to work herself up into an appropriate lather of anger and condemnation but, even so, she was still acutely aware of the power of his presence and the latent strength that vibrated under the veneer of his expensive tailored suit. That she had once known that body as well as she knew her own was just something else that threatened to undermine her defences.

'What do you want?' She glanced at her watch as they walked out into the fading light.

'I want to know why you quit your job.'

'Why do you think?' Alex raised mutinous eyes to his, remembering her old self and how much she had moved on from that place. How much she had been *forced by circumstances* to move on.

'I have no idea. Do I still get to you that much?'

'Don't flatter yourself, Lucio! Or whatever you choose to call yourself!' She turned on her heel and his hand shot out, catching her by her wrist.

'The name is Gabriel. Use it!'

'You're hurting me!'

Gabriel dropped her hand and she rubbed her wrist with her fingers, making a production out of nothing. He hadn't hurt her. Far from it. That feel of his flesh against hers was like having a branding iron planted on her skin. Her whole body was on fire and trembling and *tingling*. Under her jumper and her fleece, she could feel her nipples tighten and begin to throb as they rasped against her lacy bra. It was an appalling reaction.

'So tell me why you quit. Did you have a nostalgic yearning to return to an office where the central heating's obviously broken and the dodgy fluorescent lighting is enough to induce seizures?'

'What does it matter?' But there was resigned weariness in her voice now and she had stopped walking.

As if sensing the shift in atmosphere, Gabriel remained silent and stared down at her upturned face. It was nearly five and the pavements were busy with the usual trawl of workers leaving their offices and kids heading back from after-school activities. He pulled her out of the weaving crowd.

'You were pretty upset the last time we met.'

'Can you blame me?'

'It's been a long time.'

And I can still get under your skin. Alex read that wryly accurate postscript to his baldly spoken statement and blushed, although she didn't say anything, just started walking again, heading towards the bus stop.

'Where are you going? I'll drive you.'

More silence and Gabriel clicked his tongue impatiently. Always alert to the nuances of other people's reactions, he was picking something up now, something unspoken and unsettling. He quickly dismissed that airy-fairy notion as his imagination and instead chose to focus on the surprising fact that this woman from his past, whose image must have been floating really close to the surface of his memory banks because three seconds in her company and he could recall every detail about her, was still affected by him. Why else would she have quit her job? He had done a bit of checking, found out how much more money she had been offered for the post in his company. Walking out on it would not have been the response of someone who had relegated him to the past.

He was only human to have felt a kick of satisfaction at that idea.

'Could you give me a minute, please?' She made a hurried phone call and then turned back to face him.

'Who the hell do you keep calling?' Gabriel demanded irritably.

'Why do you ask? Is it forbidden for someone to make a phone call when they're with you?'

'I don't remember you being so *stroppy*.'

'There's a café just around the corner. If you can't talk in an office, then I can't talk in the middle of the street.' And talking was something they had to do except there was no way that she was going to do, that in his car. It didn't take the intelligence of a genius to figure out which one was his. The office was located in a fairly busy side street but it was by no means a classy area. The parked cars were uniformly serviceable, except for the gleaming black top-of-the-range BMW tucked away between a scooter and a hatchback. She imagined slipping into the passenger seat of his car, with the door shutting firmly behind her and knowing that there was no escape route unless she chose to hurl herself out of the car at forty miles per hour.

Gabriel shrugged but his levels of irritation were rising steadily. He wasn't sure what he had hoped to achieve by descending on her at her workplace but it was beginning to rankle that his reception was somewhat less than warm. He had, after all, only traipsed over out of the goodness of his heart because he wasn't comfortable with the notion that she had quit her job because of him.

'I can understand that you might be a little upset,' he began as soon as a cup of black coffee had been placed in front of him. 'You think that you were lied to…'

'I *was* lied to…'

'You've got to get your head around the fact that the world is a different place for the seriously wealthy.'

'You mean it's a playground,' Alex responded bitterly, staring down into her coffee, which had been stirred into a swirling brown whirlpool. If she shifted just a tiny bit, her knees would touch his and, to avoid that happening, she made sure to tuck her legs to one side. 'You can do whatever you want to do and then sit back and blame the fallout on the fact that you play by a different set of rules.'

'There's no point going over all of this,' Gabriel offered with a slight shrug. 'You deserve an apology and I'm big enough to provide you with one. Does that make you feel better?'

'Why did you bother to come here?'

'To offer you your job back,' he was surprised to hear himself say, although, once the words had left his mouth, he was pretty happy with the decision. Was it possible, he wondered, for a man to be more generous?

Alex looked up at him in surprise and inwardly flinched because just being so physically close to him was like being hit with a sledgehammer.

'Why would you do that?'

'You were being paid twice as much as you're getting at that hole you've thrown yourself back into. Thanks to me—' he let her think about that for a few seconds, happy to take the credit for his magnanimity '—you felt obliged to leave a perfectly good job with excellent prospects and a shed-load of benefits. That situation does not sit well with me.' He took a sip of his coffee and sat back, eyeing her thoroughly over the rim of his cup.

He had always wondered what he had seen in her because she was so unlike the women he had dated. Not just physically, but mentally and intellectually. He was still wondering. The woolly hat and the fingerless gloves had been secreted in the bowels of her oversized bag, but her face was bare of make-up, aside from a bit of mascara and the remnants of some lip gloss. Her nails were unpolished and, sure enough, she was wearing a pair of trainers, which were eminently practical but hideously unfeminine. She worked in an office but she would have looked right at home in the middle of the countryside mucking out. He caught himself wondering what kind of house in the country would suit her, favouring something small and thatched and totally impractical when it came to mod cons, and he nipped his wandering thoughts in the bud.

'In fact, I am willing to up your salary as compensation for the headache.'

'When are you getting married?'

'Come again?'

'Your fiancée didn't mention a date. I think she was too busy being indecisive about the flowers.'

Gabriel frowned. He didn't particularly want to talk about Cristobel. In fact, she hadn't once crossed his mind since she had returned to Spain three days ago.

'March,' he said abruptly.

'A spring wedding. How nice.'

'I didn't come here to talk about Cristobel.'

'How did you meet her?'

'Is it of any importance?'

'I'm curious.'

'I met her at…a party. Something arranged by her parents.' Broadly speaking, it was the truth. He had met Cristobel exactly one year ago and, were he to be brutally frank, he would have described their meeting as contrived, just as he would have described their wedding as arranged. It suited him. His parents were keen for a grandchild and, as his middle thirties loomed, he too felt the time right to get married and settle down. He had played with some of the greatest beauties in the world and tying the knot with someone of equal social standing as himself seemed an acceptable arrangement. He didn't want to think beyond that.

'When did you meet her?'

'This is ridiculous!' He stirred restlessly in his chair and beckoned the waitress across for a refill of coffee. He was irritated to see Alex glance at her watch again. 'I met her a year ago.'

'And was it love at first sight?' One glance at Cristobel had told her that she was just the sort of woman Gabriel would have found satisfactory. Good wife material. And spending a day in the other woman's company had solidified that impression. Cristobel would make the perfect society wife. She had an inbuilt contempt for people who were not of equal social standing and the self-confident, demanding manner of someone whose life has been cushioned by wealth. Alex could see the diminutive, curvaceous blonde rattling off orders in a sprawling mansion in Spain somewhere and bossing around the hired help while her husband worked all the hours God made and multiplied his already shockingly vast fortune on a daily basis.

How strange to think that this was the same guy who had worn jeans and old T-shirts and eaten paella from a plastic plate at a great little café on a beach. She cut short the thought. Right now, he thought all her questions were pointless. Maybe he thought that she was still so consumed with him that she was desperate to know *everything*, even though knowing *everything* was just twisting the knife in an open wound.

Would he die a thousand deaths if he knew how important it was for her to find out about him?

'Where are you going with this?'

'I'm playing the catch up game.' She tore her eyes away from his disturbing, fabulous face and settled her gaze on the less stressful sight of her slowly congealing coffee.

'In that case…' Gabriel leant forward, resting his elbows on the small table and shoving his cup to one side; the sudden closing of distance between them was as dramatic as a blow-torch directed at a lump of wax and Alex instinctively pulled back in alarm '…why don't you tell me a little bit about yourself? For example, why you've looked at your watch six times since we sat down? In a hurry to meet someone?' As far as Gabriel was concerned, this could only signify the presence of a man in her life. Maybe she had to scuttle back to the domestic front to do some vital house cleaning chores. Not for her husband. No wedding ring there and if there was something he knew about this woman, it was that she was nothing if not in love with the idea of romance.

He watched intently as pink colour seeped into her cheeks and felt a sudden, inexplicable rush of anger. So there *was* a man in her life. Why should he be surprised? She might not conform to the stereotype of a beauty, but there was certainly something about her that appealed. Hadn't that something drawn him in all those years ago? Made him forget himself? Made him wonder if sanity didn't lie in overthrowing convention and allowing the unexpected to dictate his responses? In the end, years of ingrained reason had won out.

He wondered what the mysterious guy was like. Obviously no kind of big earner or else she wouldn't have gone shooting back to her averagely paid non-job the second she had walked out of his building. But then, to be fair, money had never been a big deal for her. Still, what kind of guy forced his woman to work at a job she clearly didn't want to do? The picture forming in his head was of someone weak and poorly paid. Who knew? Maybe *she* was the breadwinner!

'Well?' he pressed, keen to find out whether his conclusions were on the right track.

'There *is* someone in my life,' Alex confirmed softly.

Having anticipated a positive response, Gabriel was stunned to find himself at a complete loss for words. He almost wished he hadn't brought up the topic of conversation because what she got up to in her private life was hardly his concern. He had enough on his plate with his own private life and a fiancée who was driving him round the bend with her elaborate wedding plans.

'I'm glad about that,' he said briskly. 'So, about my job offer…'

'I think I'll stay where I am, but thanks anyway.'

'There's no profit in being a martyr, Alex. You obviously need the money…'

'What makes you say that?' she asked with surprise and he pushed himself away from the table, all the better to really look at her. She had, he admitted to himself, the most amazing eyes. Large, dark pools that were once as transparent as glass and full lips that promised laughter. He knew the shape and the feel of her small, high breasts, now totally concealed under her functional jumper. A flash of uncomfortable warmth surged through him and he quickly gathered himself.

'If you didn't need the money, you would have taken your time to find another job. Also, I recognise the trainers. Five years is a pretty long time to hang on to a pair of shoes because you like the sparkly bits on the side…'

Just like that, Alex was catapulted right back to the past, to those glorious, heady days when every single day trembled with promise. It was precisely the last place she wanted to be. She rustled in her bag and fished out her wallet with trembling hands, not looking at him and not caring what he read into her abrupt reaction.

'I really don't think memory lane is appropriate, do you?' she said curtly, pulling out some change and dropping it on the table. 'Considering you're engaged to be married!' She had thrown that at him as a timely reminder, in the hope that he would be stung into retreat, but it had the opposite response.

Instead of embarrassment, Gabriel threw his head back and laughed and, when his bout of amusement had subsided, he said softly, 'You always *did* look very fetching when annoyed. And, speaking of inappropriate, isn't it inappropriate to be jealous when you have someone in your life as well?'

'Don't flatter yourself!' Alex said through gritted teeth, red with anger.

'And there's no need to pay your way.'

'There's *every* need to pay my way!' She knew that she was teetering on the edge of sounding childish but her head felt as though it was going to explode. She just wanted to scream to an unkind fate *Okay, you win! I give up!*

'Your car!' She spun round to look at him and was further enraged to see the traces of amusement lingering on his beautiful mouth. What did he have to snigger about? 'That great big gas-guzzling BMW I spotted outside the office, I take it?'

'Tsk, tsk. Don't tell me you're going to deliver a sermon about global warming.'

'I wouldn't waste my breath!'

Gabriel was enjoying this rampant display of fire. The Alex he had known had been outspoken, yes, but her sharp tongue had never been directed *at him*. Oh, no, in his company she had been all soft and pliant and wonderfully warm and willing. He should have been outraged at most of what she had said to him since their unexpected crossing of paths, but he wasn't. He was intrigued.

'Okay. Hands up, in that case. The gas-guzzling monster is mine.' He beeped it open from a distance and was surprised as she stormed towards it and then stopped dead, with her hand on the passenger door. 'You're asking me for a lift?'

'You offered me one earlier.'

'And you informed me that the bus was good enough.'

'I've changed my mind.'

'In that case, hop in. Give me your address. I'll put it into my sat-nav…' Now he was seriously curious but more than willing to go along for the ride. He wondered if these were delaying tactics before she accepted his wildly generous offer to give her back her job on a silver platter and decided that it probably was. Pride was all well and good, he thought dryly, but it didn't pay the bills. He was slightly disappointed at this pedestrian conclusion to their little meeting, but she would have been a complete fool to have resisted his offer. Especially if she needed to support a half-baked layabout.

'Did you own this when I met you? When you were riding around on a motorbike? Was this in storage somewhere? Having a little holiday while you passed the time of day with the hired hand?'

Gabriel's good mood vanished like dew on a summer's day and his lips thinned. 'Don't put yourself down. I don't like it.'

Alex hadn't realised the depth of her bitterness and was shocked by it. Yes, she still thought about him, which was only natural, but she'd really believed that she had come out the other side of the tunnel. Now a little voice whispered that surely she hadn't. If she had, wouldn't she have found someone else by now? Moved on? It was what people did after they had learnt their lessons. *He* had moved on. He was on the threshold of getting married! He had moved on *big time*!

She gave him her address and watched as he expertly typed it into the gizmo on his dashboard. She noticed that he hadn't answered her question about whether or not the car had been his when he had been busy pulling the wool over her eyes and decided that it probably hadn't. Didn't really rich people change their cars as frequently as most normal people changed their toothbrushes?

'You were going to go into hotel management,' Gabriel remarked, pulling away from the kerb and glancing across to where she was as still and as stiff as a marble statue. Why had she asked for a lift if he was going to be treated to the silent treatment? he wondered.

'Plans changed.'

'How so?'

Alex twisted so that she was looking at his profile. When he turned and their eyes met, she forced herself not to look away. She was also, she decided, going to make a heroic effort to drop the bitterness, which wasn't going to get either of them anywhere. She had had her say and now was the time to take a deep breath and move on.

'You'll see.'

For the first time, Gabriel felt a twinge of unease. He looked at her but she was staring out of the window. Her neck was long and slender, all the more apparent because her hair was so short, and at this angle the lashes framing her large almond-shaped eyes were long and thick. She had confessed early on in their relationship that she had always been a tomboy, the consequence of having so many brothers. She looked anything but a tomboy, even in her sloppy clothes and the woolly hat which she had stuck back on.

Shockingly, his body kicked in and that shook him so much that he tightened his grip on the steering wheel and applied his mind to the business at hand. The areas through which they drove alternated between cramped and rundown to just cramped until she pointed to a tiny terraced house at the end of the street and instructed him to get parked wherever he could because it was always hell finding an empty slot.

'So you have a car?'

'No. I only go on what I see.'

Her heart was beating fast and hard and nerves had kicked in with a vengeance. She literally felt sick and she had to take a few deep breaths before she opened her car door.

'I'm…I'm really sorry…' she said in a low voice, glancing at him over her shoulder.

'Sorry for what?' Gabriel threw her a sharp look but she was already turning away and slamming the door behind her.

'Sorry for *what*?'

She didn't reply, leaving ample time for him to brood over her enigmatic statement as she yanked off the woolly hat and inserted her key in the lock, pushing open the front door to a flood of light in the small hallway.

Gabriel had a few seconds, during which he took in that it was a bright, welcoming space but small. Much smaller than his place in Chelsea, which was only a two-bedroomed apartment but probably three times the size of her house. There also seemed to be a great deal of clutter. Coats, jackets and various other items of clothing were hung on a coat rack that was groaning under the weight and there was a little collection of shoes which seemed to have started out life in a neat line against the wall but had ended up in a chaotic heap.

Did the guy share the house with her? For some reason, he didn't like that idea.

'Wait here.'

'With the door open? Or am I allowed to shut it?'

'Just wait here and I'll be back in a couple of minutes.'

Gabriel discovered that he was too bemused to argue the toss. He closed the door and leaned against it, his hands in his pockets while he idly scanned the space around him. Yellow walls, a small staircase leading up to what could only be one room, surely, and a bathroom. To his right, the door was ajar and he could glimpse pale walls and the edge of a flowered sofa. Ahead was probably the kitchen and some sort of study, he expected. Not much more.

She returned so silently from a door to the side that he didn't initially register her presence and, when he did, it took him a second or two more before he registered another presence. A kid.

'You never answered my question. Are you going to reconsider my job offer? It's pretty generous, if I say so myself. In fact, I can't think of any other person who would put themselves out to re-hire someone who had walked out of their job for the reasons you gave.'

'Gabriel…this is Luke…'

Gabriel, forced to acknowledge the child, nodded and resettled his gaze on Alex.

'Mum…can I have some ice cream now? Can I? Susie said I could…'

'Susie said no such thing, you cheeky little monkey!'

From behind him a tiny round girl emerged, grinning as she slung her bag over her shoulder and she ruffled Luke's hair, which produced a little frown before he straightened it.

All of this Gabriel noticed in a daze because his brain had seized upon that one word—*Mum*—and stuck there. He had straightened and was scarcely aware of the enquiring look that Susie directed to Alex before she bustled out of the house.

'Luke, say hi to Gabriel…'

'Only if I get some ice cream.'

'Out of the question, big boy!' But Alex was laughing as she lifted him up and walked towards Gabriel. He looked like a man who had opened an envelope only to discover a letter bomb inside. Alex, on the other hand, was aware of a spreading sense of relief. This had been an inevitable meeting from the very first moment she had stepped into his office and realised that her past had finally caught up with her. She had made a half-hearted attempt to tell herself that things would be better left alone. That Gabriel was engaged, due to be married to a woman he loved and on the brink of starting his own family. That she would be doing him a favour in keeping this secret to herself. She had quit her job, prepared, in the heat of the moment, to just do a runner and deal with the fallout when it happened later down the road. But, time and again, her thoughts had returned to the glaring, naked, unavoidable truth: Luke deserved to know his father, even if it would forever be in the context of a less than ideal situation.

'How was playschool? You're a messy little grub!' He was twisting in her arms now, curious to find out who the stranger in the house was.

Without the benefit of direct comparison, she was only now waking up to the startling physical similarity between father and son. The same dark hair, although Luke's was a curly mop…the same dark eyes…and that olive tint that spoke of his Spanish ancestry. Also that smile and the tiny dimples that came with it. Her heart restricted and she felt a fierce, overwhelming, protective love for her son.

'I'm going to give him a bath and settle him down,' she said quietly. 'You can leave if you want to or you can wait for me in the kitchen. I won't be much longer than half an hour.'

Gabriel could no sooner leave than he could have grown wings and flown through the window. His brain, while taking in everything and already working out a series of consequences, was not functioning at all on another level. He was a father. In what could only be classified as a complete screw-up, he was a father, because there was no doubting paternity. Yes, he could make a song and dance about dates and times and then request a DNA test because he was nothing if not suspicious by nature, but the proof of his genetic link to the child was glaringly obvious. He could have been looking at a picture of himself aged four and a half.

He remained frozen to the spot for a few minutes after she had disappeared up the tiny staircase. He was aware of noises drifting down. Very slowly, he made his way to the kitchen and this time, when he inspected his surroundings, it was with renewed interest.

He had a child. And his child was being brought up in conditions that were, if not completely basic, then certainly bordering on it.

He felt the slow build of anger and brought all his formidable willpower into play to stamp on it. From where he was sitting, life as he knew it was over but he would still have to deal with the consequences.

All the paraphernalia of a young child imprinted itself in his head like a tattoo. There was some kind of booster seat gadget attached to one of the kitchen chairs and various plastic utensils on the draining board. He walked across to the fridge and examined the infantile drawings randomly spaced under fruit magnets.

Happy family drawings that ostensibly did not include any father figure.

So there was no guy in her life. When she had talked about her involvement with someone else, she had been referring to her son. *Their* son. He barely deciphered the strangely proportioned pictures he was staring at or the spidery writing underneath. In his head, his eyes were still locked in unwilling fascination on his son's.

There were a thousand questions pounding through his head. In short, he couldn't wait for her to return.

CHAPTER THREE

OF COURSE he wasn't going to leave. Alex had given him the option but she had no doubt that Gabriel would be waiting for her when, after forty minutes, she eventually made her way down the stairs. Luke, sensing tension in the air, had played up, demanding story after story and finally holding her to ransom by extracting a promise of ice cream for the following day before he grudgingly consented to close his eyes.

Without her son as a physical barrier between her and Gabriel, preventing any displays of anger, she felt naked and vulnerable and fairly terrified as she made her way quietly down the stairs to the kitchen.

She reminded herself that she was no longer the impressionable teen she had been years ago when she had fallen under his spell. Then, she would have done anything he asked. She was the puppet and he the puppet master. When he had walked away from her she had fallen to pieces but pregnancy and having a baby, making her way in life as a single mother, moving to London so that she could build a career for herself, which had been nigh on impossible at home, with her family in Ireland, had toughened her up. She might be scared of his reaction but she wasn't going to cower.

Those bracing sentiments were nearly blown to smithereens as she walked into the kitchen to find him sitting on one of the chairs. There was a half drunk glass of orange juice in front of him and he had swivelled the kitchen chair away from the table so that he was facing the door. Waiting for her like an executioner.

'Would you like something hot to drink?' she said, opting for some semblance of politeness before open warfare began. 'Tea? Coffee? Or more orange juice?'

'Is that all you have on offer? What about some whisky? Or gin? I think I'm in need of something a little stronger than tea or coffee.' Faced with the unthinkable, Gabriel could feel himself descending into that unknown territory known as The Emotional Response. It was a route to be avoided at all costs. He had been presented with a problem and the problem would not go away because of his reaction to it.

'I have some wine. It's not very good but it's the best I can do.' Alex poured them both a glass and suggested they sit in the lounge. His silence as they walked there was even more unnerving than if he had been bellowing in her wake. In fact, it sent shivers racing up and down her spine.

'So,' he said once he was seated, 'when were you going to tell me? Or were you going to bother to tell me at all?'

Alex gulped down some wine and then nursed her glass as she stared with a wildly beating heart at the rug on the floor, given to her courtesy of her parents, who had campaigned against her moving to London but, having finally bitten the bullet, had proceeded to kit her small house out with stuff they vaguely labelled *unwanted bits and pieces* but which she knew had been bought new. She visibly jumped when he repeated his question in a voice with icy bite.

'When did you find out?' Gabriel changed tack, enraged by her silence. Was he supposed to feel sorry for her? Her drawn face and miserable, sagging demeanour suggested it but, having had his foundations rocked to their core, his sympathy levels were non-existent. He had never considered the whole issue of children but, when he had, it had been in an abstract way. They would come along at some point in time, as yet undecided. He was engaged to be married but not once had he considered Cristobel as a mother, although he would have been hard pressed to analyse why. If pushed, he would have said that he just wasn't into kids. He would be a father because that would have been the expectation.

Now, faced with the reality of his own child, he was outraged that he was five years late in having any input. During that time, had there been any men on the scene? Of course there would have been! She might not be all curves, but she was as sexy as hell. Any guy with two eyes in his head would see that.

'Well?' he asked in a clipped voice, keeping his unwanted thoughts about other men well to the back of his mind. 'Are you going to answer me or are you going to sit there in silence and expect me to mind read?'

'You're making me nervous!'

'You deserve to *feel* nervous.'

'Why would that be?' She raised angry eyes to him and clenched her hands into tense fists. 'You're the one who did the vanishing act because you didn't want to be tied down to a foreigner you met in passing! You're the one who lied about his identity so that when I found out I was pregnant and tried tracing you I kept running into a brick wall!' Suddenly the room seemed way too small and she stood up and walked across to the window ledge, perching on it and gripping the wood so tightly that her knuckles were white. She felt as though she had to put a little distance between them because the closer she was to him, the less capable she was of thinking rationally. It was like being eighteen all over again and she didn't like the feeling. Being held hostage by her emotions once could be called an excusable error of judgement. Being held hostage by her emotions a second time would definitely come under the heading of suicidal.

'I was nearly four months pregnant when I found out and already back in England. In fact, at university. Thinking that my life could carry on as normal after…after Spain.' She could remember the shock of finding out as though it had happened only yesterday. The dawning awareness that she hadn't seen her period, always erratic, in a while. The home testing pregnancy kit. The horrible feeling of the whole world falling away from under her feet when that telltale little line had appeared. And then everything that came afterwards.

Gabriel flushed darkly. Mistakes, he acknowledged, had been made. Not wilfully, but even so. They would have to be rectified. That was life.

'I tried to contact you.' With a sigh, she resumed her place on the flowered upholstered chair facing him. She couldn't quite meet his eyes so instead she stared at the pattern on the sofa, also flowered. Both generous gifts from her parents, who had dug deep into their savings to help her out. *They* were the ones who had been there for her. Not the guy sitting opposite, who had cleared off with no forwarding address.

'Of course that was impossible.' Her huge brown eyes were bitter. 'I asked at that hotel you were supposed to be working at and they had never heard of a *Lucio*, never mind a *Lucio* with no surname. Hardly surprising since *Lucio* had never existed. I tried describing you, but naturally they would never have put two and two together and come up with the big shot owner of the hotel.'

Guilt found its way through his iron-clad defence system. 'No one could have anticipated this situation,' he said grimly.

'We should have been more diligent with the contraception. More careful.' The Pill had not agreed with her. Instead, they had relied on barrier protection and there had been times when spontaneity had got in the way of common sense. Like a complete idiot, she had airily imagined that there would be no consequences. Her periods had always been irregular. She had vaguely concluded that pregnancy would therefore be less likely than in someone with a tip-top menstrual cycle.

'There is no point going down the *what if* road…' But another stab of guilt penetrated his austerity. At the time, he had told himself that walking away from her had been in her best interests. She had been young, only just out of school, as he had discovered along the way. Definitely not experienced enough to take on or even need any sort of committed relationship, especially with a guy like him. A guy she didn't even really know. She was a free spirit, about to begin her journey through life. He was already marching upwards, an only child programmed to adhere to unspoken expectations.

But, with malign treachery, the image in his head of her, young and frightened, had wormed its way in and was refusing to budge.

'If it is any consolation, I put my hands up and admit that my little white lies may not have been one hundred per cent justifiable.'

'Oh, well, thanks very much for that belated apology.' Alex's voice was laced with sarcasm. She had never been the sarcastic sort. Funny how experience had a way of changing a person.

'My family were very good. I hid out there for a while but in the end I knew that I had to follow the jobs and London was the most likely place for me to get one so I moved in with a friend and then got this place.' She was pleased at how this dispassionate rattling off of the past few traumatic years of her life managed to sound so *ordered* when in fact she had lived in a semi-permanent state of stress and exhaustion.

'And then you happened to run into me.' He was making a determined effort to stay away from the emotive topic of his son being in a house that was barely big enough for one person. This was not going to do. But he would bide his time for the present.

'It was a shock.' She glanced across at him warily. 'You seem to be taking all this very well,' she ventured hesitantly. 'I thought you'd be furious.'

'What would be the point of that?' Gabriel questioned with chilling self-control. 'Would it change anything? My son would still be upstairs sleeping and life as I know it would still have ceased to exist.'

If at any point in time she had daydreamed about a happy-ever-after ending, some surprise meeting which might have concluded with joyous exclamations of love, then those words conclusively put any such fantasy to rest.

For Gabriel, the knowledge that he was a father meant that *life as he knew it would cease to exist*, and since his life had been very happy indeed without either her or their son in it, then he was looking at a bleak future and that hurt. Even after all these years.

'Tell me something,' he said in the same ultra-controlled voice. 'Having quit your job, presumably because running away was the only solution you could come up with, having the dilemma of seeing me again, would you have made any effort to let me know that I was a father if I hadn't sought you out? Or would you have disappeared off the face of the earth and watched my son grow up without my input in his life?'

Alex felt the colour rise to her cheeks. Would she have said anything? She would have years ago, when she had first discovered that she was carrying his child. And she really wanted to think that she was an honest enough person to have done the same now, but he was engaged. In love with another woman. On the brink of settling down and starting a family with Cristobel. She might have grown up over the past few years, but *that much*?

'I see,' Gabriel said softly, reading into her silence.

'You don't understand!'

'Enlighten me.'

'We...we're in different places,' she began weakly. No nod of agreement greeted this remark. She wished his eyes weren't boring into her head. It was disconcerting because, underneath the ice, she could glimpse the seething, passionate core and just thinking about that did strange things to her body. 'I...I've moved on since we knew each other...'

'Moved on how?' Instantly Gabriel was on red alert. *Moving on* was a phrase with which he was well acquainted and it usually indicated from one person to someone else. All of a sudden he was questioning his easy assumption that *the person in her life*, the person to whom she had vaguely referred before this whole bomb had detonated, was Luke. All of a sudden the notion that she might really have met someone else slammed into him with the force of a freight train. 'Is there some guy in your life?' he demanded, leaning forward and resting his elbows on his knees.

'No!'

'Good.' He relaxed fractionally.

'What does that mean?'

'It means that, now I am aware of the situation, a boyfriend on the scene would be entirely inappropriate.'

Alex felt a red mist of anger envelop her like a cloud, smothering all her good intentions to keep things cool, composed and adult. If she had had something heavy and breakable to hand, she would have flung it at his deceitful, arrogant head and hang the good intentions.

'Would you mind repeating that?' she asked in a tight, unnaturally high voice.

'No man on the scene.'

'No. Man. On. The. Scene. And yet it's all right for *you* to have a *fiancée* on the scene, is it?

What were his expectations here? she wondered. Carry on with his life, get married and lock her up in a state of permanent celibacy because he didn't want another man around his son? She was trembling with anger.

'You're overreacting.'

'I am *not* overreacting!'

'I am being honest. Isn't that what you would want? The truth? And the truth is that I would not welcome anyone else having an influence over my son. What's so difficult to understand about that?'

'I don't want to talk about this,' Alex said tightly. 'I don't want to get into an argument with you. Now that you know about Luke, we can try and sort out…the practical stuff…'

'Does he know who I am?'

'No. I haven't told him yet.'

The enormity of their situation struck Gabriel forcibly at that bald statement. He had an instant picture in his head of his son, all black curly hair and big drowsy eyes, and from nowhere sprang a crazy, confused feeling of time wasted.

'I'm sorry,' Alex said quietly, at which his expression became shuttered once again.

'When do you intend to tell him?'

'As soon as possible.'

'Try again.'

'Okay! Tomorrow! I'll tell him tomorrow! He's very inquisitive, anyway. He'll probably wake up with a hundred questions about you.' Her eyes skittered from Gabriel to the window behind him to the mantelpiece, on which sat a row of pictures of Luke at various stages of his young life. Gabriel followed her eyes and he slowly stood up and moved across to the mantelpiece, where he proceeded to hold and examine all of the pictures. All seven of them. From infancy to the one she had taken last month.

While he had been blithely pursuing his goals with the relentless drive that came so naturally to him, while he had been adding to his fortune, building his empire and congratulating himself on his well run, well oiled, no-unpleasant-surprises-life, his own flesh and blood had been growing up without him around. Frustration rocked him because it wasn't as though he could blame her. Of course, she might have been lying. She might have never bothered trying to find his whereabouts, but he seriously doubted that. He would have been an instant and permanent meal ticket. Why would she have turned that down? He replaced the last of the photos and turned slowly round to look at her.

'When are you going to...tell the people that you know? Your family? Your fiancée?' she said awkwardly, to cover the silence.

'Immediately.'

She breathed a little sigh of relief. Once that hurdle was over, once the shock was absorbed and the situation accepted by the people who mattered to him, they would be able to discuss arrangements for him to see his son. She wondered how Cristobel would receive the news. Not well, she anticipated, but it was hardly as though he had been unfaithful.

'Then, maybe, when you've done that...well, and I will have told Luke about you, of course...we can try and sort stuff out...'

'Sort stuff out...?'

'Yes. You know. Visiting rights. I'm really happy for you to see Luke whenever you want to...' She had stood up in preparation to seeing him to the door but now her voice trailed off because he wasn't saying anything. And he was looking at her as though she had a screw missing. And neither of those things added up to a man on the verge of departure, having settled matters.

'Visiting rights?'

Alex detected the odour of a trick question and she looked at him warily. 'Yes? Visiting rights? You come to see Luke and take him somewhere for an afternoon?'

'You don't really think that that's going to work, do you Alex?'

'Not going to work?' Alex repeated in dumb founded confusion. 'Why wouldn't it work? It's what everyone else does when their relationship falls apart and there's a child involved. Not that we ever *had* a relationship.'

'Since when am I *everyone else*?'

She was struggling to get the gist of what he was saying but her mind wasn't obliging. Had she misread all the signs and signals? Was he implying that his intention was to stroll out through her front door and disappear over the horizon without a backward glance at his son? Since that seemed highly implausible, she settled on the other, more likely option. He was engaged, he had his life in order. He didn't need a murky, unwanted past misadventure rising up to wreak havoc with his perfect life and so he would keep it a secret.

'I don't intend Luke to be hidden away!' She sprang to her feet, shaking, her hands on her hips. 'He deserves better than that! So, if that's the road you're going down, then you'd better clear off! I can't believe this. I really, can't, Lucio! Gabriel!'

'Sit down!'

'Stop giving me orders when you're in my house!'

'Then stop behaving like a child!' Gabriel had no idea what she was talking about and he recognised that she was in a pretty hysterical frame of mind. She thought he was a louse and, while he was prepared to concede some mistakes made on his part, they were mistakes only in retrospect and only in view of the current extraordinary circumstances. While he was, once again, dealing with the unique temptation to lose his temper, he noticed that she was no longer shouting. Like a burst balloon, she seemed to have suddenly deflated. Her shoulders were slumped and, as he stood up and approached her, he could see tears leaking from the corners of her eyes.

She wasn't a crier. She'd once told him that crying was for small, dainty girls, that tears just didn't suit her. Even when he had walked away from her *for the best possible reasons*, she had been distraught and her eyes had filled up and her lips had wobbled but she had managed to hang on to her self-control. So to see her so utterly crushed did something to him.

'Why are you so good at making me feel so bad?' he murmured half to himself, reaching into his pocket and extracting a pristine white handkerchief. He didn't think she had heard him but once the words were out of his mouth, he realised that no truer ones had ever been spoken because, lurking just below the surface, just beyond the reach of consciousness, there had always been the unpleasant suspicion that he had not behaved properly towards her. Seeing her again had brought all those hidden feelings rushing to the top.

He pushed the handkerchief into her hands and then, still working on automatic, he put his arms around her. It was electrifying. His mind cleared of everything but the sensation of her against him. It was hauntingly familiar, from the length of her to the slenderness of her boyish frame. Her breasts, small and rounded and soft, pressed against his chest and he was overwhelmed by a suffocating desire to shove up her top and slide his hands underneath her bra so that he could caress her. The swiftness of his response, almost as though his body had been waiting for just this moment for a very long time, galvanized him into action and he released her abruptly and turned away.

Alex sniffed into the handkerchief, missing the sudden lack of warmth while cursing herself for having disintegrated like a fool in front of him.

'What sort of man do you think I am?' Gabriel demanded, sinking into the chair, half conscious of his inappropriate arousal. 'What would give you the idea that I intend to keep my own son out of sight?'

'You're not interested in visiting rights.' Alex blew her nose and subsided back into her chair. For once, she wished that she was blessed with long hair so that she could let it fall against her face like a silky curtain, blocking out her weepy, puffy eyes and blotchy skin. 'Which means that you're not committed to seeing Luke. I realise that all this must be a terrible shock for you, but…'

'Stop trying to second guess me. I intend to take my responsibilities head on. I won't be abandoning my own son because he doesn't happen to fit in with my lifestyle. But you're right. It's a great shock and it will be an enormous upheaval.' He sighed heavily and ran his fingers through his hair.

'It's not as bad for you as it could be,' Alex said with a stab at optimism.

'Run that by me?'

Her eyes tangled with his dark, piercing gaze and she felt her bones turn to water. This was precisely the sort of out-of-control feeling that she had to stop.

'I'm sure Cristobel would understand. I mean, it was something that happened before you met her! In fact, chances are that she'll feel sorry for you.'

'Really? I'm not seeing it.'

Frankly, nor could Alex but, before she could plough on with her upbeat approach, he raised his hand to silence her.

'I will naturally have to announce this situation to the world,' he said heavily. 'Starting with my parents.' He imagined their disappointed faces. They had both seen it as their mission to marry him off and the upcoming wedding had been planned meticulously for months. He had distanced himself from as much of the tedious detail as he could get away with, but he still knew that his parents were like a couple of kids on Christmas Eve with their excited preparations and never ending lists of people to invite.

'Then there is Cristobel. There is no question that the wedding will have to be called off.'

For a few seconds, Alex wondered whether she had heard correctly and she stared at him with a blank, uncomprehending face.

'What are you talking about?' she asked in genuine bewilderment.

Gabriel wondered whether she could really be that naive. Hadn't she already clocked that, by detonating her little hand grenade, she was, in passing, doing herself a massive financial favour? A quick glance around him was enough to confirm that hers was a life devoid of any luxury.

'You don't think that I would really agree to have my son brought up in these conditions, do you?'

'These *conditions*? There's nothing wrong with where we live! Have you any idea how hard I've worked to be able to afford this place? Even with Mum and Dad having to help out now and again?'

'Yes, and here's where I come in. You can start relaxing.'

Having digressed, Alex brought the conversation back to its origin and again asked him what he meant by having to call off his wedding.

'I have a child and no child of mine will be raised illegitimate. Connect the dots, Alex.'

'Are you asking me to *marry you*?'

'I don't see all that many choices staring me in the face, do you?'

Alex felt the weight of pain settle in her chest like a rock. Five years ago, she could have thought of nothing better than to receive a marriage proposal from this man. She would have abandoned all thoughts of a university career without a backward glance. Now here he was, years down the road, proposing marriage because he could think of no other choice, given the situation in which he had found himself dragged. Did he expect her to feel *grateful*? She sincerely hoped not because gratitude was way down the list of things she was currently feeling.

'Okay. So let me get this straight. You would break off your engagement to Cristobel, dump all your wedding plans to marry me because I happen to be the mother of a son you never knew you had.'

'Like I said. Not too many options staring me in the face.' Gabriel was surprised to find that he felt a lot less disturbed at this eventuality than he would have expected. Why was that?

Never given to the pointless luxury of introspection, it crossed his mind that his choice to marry Cristobel had perhaps been the result of silent pressure from his parents and a general logical awareness that marriage was the next step. Cristobel ticked all the boxes and she had been more than eager to oblige. On paper, it had had everything going for it. Until now. On paper, this arrangement he was proposing not only made more sense but was, in fact, a necessity.

'We'll have to get it done sooner rather than later,' he mused, thinking of his parents and bracing himself for the inevitable ugly fallout. 'My parents will doubtless be disappointed at the turn of events but knowing that we have married and given my son the Cruz surname should go a little way to easing the situation.' He thought that Cristobel would be a rather different matter. And then there were all those wedding arrangements to un-arrange. And the further hassle of press intrusion. Like it or not, his was a public face. He would have to act swiftly to avoid even the merest whiff of a scandal.

'I could arrange something quiet for the weekend.' He glanced quickly at his watch and frowned. 'Once that's out of the way, we can go somewhere abroad until the fuss dies down. Naturally, I will only be able to be with you for a very short while. It would be impossible to leave my business concerns for too long...'

'I don't believe I'm hearing this.'

'I know.' Gabriel's mouth twisted into a dry smile. 'You must find it almost beyond belief that you've managed to hit jackpot. Who would have thought it?'

'I have no intention of marrying you.'

'You really don't mean that,' Gabriel said patiently.

'No, but I really *do*,' Alex said, her pulse leaping with anger and loathing. 'First of all, we're not living in the Dark Ages. *You* might think that sacrificing your life because of some warped sense of family honour is the thing to do, but *I* don't. *Secondly*, Luke deserves more than the two of us trapped in a loveless marriage!' She could see his face becoming more coldly disapproving by the second but there was no way that she was going to be browbeaten into doing something that was all wrong. 'Do you really imagine that I'm so pathetic and desperate that I would accept marriage to you in these circumstances?'

'Wasn't it the thing you wanted most when we were together?' Gabriel said with cutting smoothness.

'That was *years* ago! Believe it or not, I'm a different person now!'

'How different?' Gabriel murmured and, just like that, Alex could feel the atmosphere between them subtly alter. His eyes did a lazy sweep of her body and came back to rest on her flushed face. That kick of awareness that had sprung from nowhere earlier on resurged back into life. He had a rich, graphic fantasy of taking her to bed again, feasting on the body the way he used to. He wondered how pregnancy had changed it and the craving to satisfy that curiosity hit him swift and hard.

So wouldn't that be a great bonus to the whole sorry situation? he wondered. If he was to be married to her, then why shouldn't sex play a part in its success? As if his imagination had suddenly been given the green light, the urge to take her was more powerful than anything he had known before and, why kid himself, it had been there the second he had seen her in his office. He shifted uncomfortably in his seat and tried to focus.

Alex looked at him and fought against the tingly feeling she was experiencing, as though she were being intimately caressed, even though he wasn't even near her. 'I think it's time you went home, Gabriel and gave some thought to how we're going to deal with this *in a realistic way.*'

'This is a supremely realistic way of dealing with the situation.'

'Not for me, it isn't.'

For the first time, it was beginning to dawn on him that his marriage proposal might truly have met with a negative response. Her lips were tightly pursed and her tilted face smouldered with stubbornness. What the hell, he thought, was the problem here? Hadn't he just done the most decent thing possible?

'I don't intend to be shackled to someone who would rather be somewhere else,' Alex continued, just in case he wasn't getting the message.

'This isn't about you; it's about our child.'

'A child you don't even know!'

'Naturally, getting to know him will take time.'

'Good. I'm glad you said that,' Alex inserted quickly, thinking on her feet, 'because that should be your first step.'

Gabriel frowned. 'First step?'

'Get to know Luke. Take him out. Incorporate him as part of your life. It's not going to be easy. You've suddenly found yourself landed with a four-year-old child and you have zero experience of children…'

Gabriel's sharp brain moved rapidly on to another track. 'Of course. And what are the other steps in this realistic scenario of yours?' he asked with a slow smile that sent shivers racing through her. 'Should I do the modern day thing and proceed with my marriage plans?' There was no chance of that but he allowed a few seconds of silence, during which she might contemplate that alternative route. 'Needless to say, Cristobel, as my wife, would have enormous input into all decisions taken regarding Luke. How do you feel about that?'

Not good, was the first thought that came to Alex's mind. She didn't like the thought of Cristobel being any kind of role model for her child. Complicating the scenario came a sneaking thought: sharing Luke with Gabriel was one thing, but what if he wanted more of his son somewhere along the line? She blanched and cleared her throat.

'And naturally my parents would want involvement as well. They live in Spain. It's possible that there might be occasions when Cristobel would take him across for holidays…'

'Holidays?'

'So tell me how you see things working out…. Sell it to me.'

Alex threw him a venomous, trapped look from under her lashes. 'How do you think I feel, knowing that you would ditch the woman you love just because mistakes were made years ago and I got pregnant as a result?'

'I know how you *should* feel.' He had no intention of getting wrapped up in some caring, sharing, ridiculous conversation about his feelings for Cristobel. If Alex was finding it hard to appreciate the enormous generosity of his gesture with her, then she would be at a complete loss to understand a marriage that might have been more of a suitable arrangement than a match made in heaven. 'You *should* feel a certain amount of respect for a guy who's willing to do the right thing. Not many would.'

Alex wondered in confusion how she had managed to turn into the *bad guy*.

'And you should feel a certain respect for a woman who's willing to turn down a wedding ring and an easy lifestyle because she has principles! Not many would.'

Gabriel's steely control slipped and he was subjected to a rush of aggressive anger. Where was she coming from? What airy-fairy planet did she inhabit? But, then again, out of all the women he had ever known, she occupied a unique spot and not just because she was the mother of his child. She was feisty and her failure to be impressed by money was staggering. The harder he pushed for what he wanted, for what he considered *inevitable*, the faster she would retreat. But he *would* get his own way. He always did and he wasn't going to break the habit now.

CHAPTER FOUR

THE first Alex knew of what was happening behind the scenes was when she opened her newspaper three days later, as usual scanning the headlines and then sitting down to relax with the gossip pages in the centre. This was her favourite time of the day. Seven-thirty. Luke safely tucked up in bed, having, as usual, cunningly contrived to keep her reading bedtime stories to him for as long as possible. Small glass of wine on the table next to her and the television turned on but with almost no volume because, whilst she liked the comforting background noise, she wasn't too interested in what the noise was actually about.

It irked her that since everything had come out in the open with Gabriel, she had been able to think of nothing else but him. He hadn't contacted her. On day one she had assumed that the shock of the situation had driven him into a temporary retreat, time out to consider his options and think about what he was going to do next. But now, after three days of silence, she was beginning to think that he had simply chosen to disappear.

Which, she told herself repeatedly, meant no change for her. He hadn't been on the scene for the past five years and so the fabric of her life would remain exactly the same. She also told herself repeatedly that it was just as well that Luke was none the wiser that the stranger who had appeared and then just as quickly disappeared had been his father.

In fact, to count even more blessings, wasn't she glad that she had reconnected with him? Put to bed all those haunting *what if* and *if only* scenarios which had continued to jostle around in some weird Pandora's Box in her head, clamouring for a hearing? Wasn't it *healthy* that she had finally seen him for the person he really was? A man who had knowingly deceived her. He'd disappeared from her life because she hadn't been good enough for him, hadn't been like the Cristobel airhead to whom he was now engaged. He was a guy who made all the right noises when confronted with a difficult situation but then scarpered as fast as he could the minute he was through the door. In other words, a fully signed up, one hundred per cent member of the Creep Club.

The fact that he was still managing to get under her skin and give her, *yet again*, sleepless nights infuriated her.

And her low level, never-quite-gone-despite-all-efforts fury was seething just below the surface as her eyes fell on the hot gossip headlines in the tabloid which announced the end of the perfect engagement between *billionaire whizz-kid Gabriel Cruz and Cristobel Rivera, daughter of import/export magnate Geraldo Rivera*. It took Alex a few stunned seconds before she could read and then reread what was clearly being touted as the scandal of the year. She even had to switch off the television so that she could concentrate on the article, which carried on over the page, and also stare at the photograph of the tiny blonde scurrying away from the limelight wearing a pair of oversized designer sunglasses and shielding her eyes from the intrusion of, presumably, a barrage of cameras. Another photo depicted Gabriel dressed in a suit and looking unruffled at the chaos his announcement had provoked. Typical.

There was an awful lot of background information on the ditched fiancée, which only proved her eligibility for a guy like Gabriel. Moneyed background, at home in the playground of the Rich and Famous, as opposed to the playing fields of the Hard Working and Almost Always Broke. And there was wild speculation as to what could have generated the break up but, even on a fourth reading, Alex could find no mention of either herself or Luke.

The shriek of her mobile interrupted a compulsive fifth reading of the article and Alex nearly spilt the glass of wine in her shaking hand.

Even before she heard his voice, she knew that it would be Gabriel. It was as if her antennae had been put on to red alert and primed for his presence in her life.

'Sitting down, I hope?' he enquired in a silky voice that made her glance furtively around just in case he happened to be hidden somewhere in the vicinity and could see the reaction his voice had on her mangled nervous system.

'I...I've just read...'

'I thought you might have.'

'You...should have warned me that...'

'You had all the warning you needed. I told you that I would be breaking off the engagement. You must have known that it would hit the news. I'm a public figure, whether I like it or not.'

'Yes, but...'

'You can hold that thought. I'll be over in forty minutes. It would probably be better if I used a back door. Is there one?'

'Use a back door?' Alex was fast remembering the past few days of silence, during which her entire life had been turned on its head as she tried to find ways of reconciling herself to his disappearance. She felt as though she was now destined to start the endless cycle of highs and lows all over again.

Just like that. He had walked back into her life and instead of finding her defences in place, she had discovered a gaping lack of body armour. *'Use a back door?'* she repeated in a higher voice. 'You're not playing the lead in a spy thriller, Gabriel! And yes, I have a back door and you're more than welcome to use it but you'll still have to get to the front of the house first because it's at the side!'

'Are you in a mood because I haven't been in touch for the past couple of days?'

'I'm not in a mood.'

'Good. Then I'll see you shortly.'

Alex was treated to the sound of the dial tone as he rang off and she glared at the phone for a few seconds before springing into action. The constant frustrating whirlpool of nagging, unwanted thoughts about Gabriel was replaced by a frantic rush of blood to her head as she scrambled upstairs, changed out of her sloppy jogging bottoms and baggy T-shirt into a pair of halfway decent jeans and a short-sleeved checked shirt that nipped in at the waist and ran her fingers through her hair.

Her cheeks were flushed and her eyes were over-bright. It shouldn't have mattered what she wore but his disparaging remark about her house not being good enough for his son still rankled. As did the fact that she knew, without a shadow of a doubt, that the remark also applied to *her*. House too average for his son, and ex-girlfriend way too average for him.

She was in a fighting mood by the time the doorbell rang forty-five minutes later and she swung to open the door, making a great show of checking the road behind him.

'Phew. Doesn't look like you've been followed. Maybe you'd better sneak in, just in case.'

'Hilarious, Alex. Just open up and let me in.' Gabriel couldn't help himself. His eyes darkened as they took in the tight faded jeans and the small plaid shirt with the top two buttons undone so that just the shadowy promise of breast was visible.

The past few days had been fairly hellish but, even so, he was feeling pretty good about life in general. As he would, he had smugly acknowledged, doing the right thing as he was.

Cristobel had been a nightmare and he couldn't blame her. She had watched her future crash and burn and he had offered nothing by way of a reasonable excuse. Time enough for the situation to be explained in its entirety. Instead, he had attempted some consolation by pointing out their fundamental differences and informing her that she would be well rid of him. He didn't love her. She didn't love him. When she had shrieked that *there was more to marriage than love*, his mouth had tightened, even though she was preaching to the converted. After all, wasn't he the prime proponent of that theory?

He had left her apartment with the peculiar feeling that he had been given a reprieve. What would this woman, perfect on paper, have been like as a wife? She had grown from a rich, indulged girl to a rich, indulged woman and it wouldn't have been long before she became a spoiled, dissatisfied spouse, intolerant of anyone outside her gilded social circle. How was it that he had never seen that promise before?

Surprisingly, his parents had taken the news well, although it had been hard to tell from the other side of the Atlantic and on a phone link. He would fly over very shortly, he had told his mother. Speak with them face to face. But certainly, at the moment, he realised that he had allowed a situation to develop that would not have been right in the long-term.

'Your mother would probably agree with you, son,' his father had said in a low voice. 'Although this is between us men. She always had her reservations about Cristobel. Nice girl, I am sure, and of course it certainly would have made for a powerful merger, but, let me put it this way, do not feel as though you are disappointing us…'

Gabriel had not known whether to believe that statement or if it had just been his father putting a brave face on things. But now, he at least felt as though he was starting with a clean slate.

'You *could* have told me what to expect.' Alex stood back from him and folded her arms, thereby providing some much needed protection against the brutal power of his presence.

'Is Luke asleep?'

'Of course he is. I have very strict guidelines about his bed times.' This just in case he got it into his head that she was a bad mother.

'Stop playing the injured party.' Gabriel swept past her, divesting himself of his jacket in the process and slinging it over the banister. He went straight to the kitchen, opened the fridge and proceeded to help himself to a glass of wine while Alex trailed behind him and gaped at the high-handed way he had just *made himself at home*.

'Why didn't you get in touch?'

He looked at her over the rim of his glass and a slow smile curved his mouth. 'You sound like a nagging wife. Why? Did you miss me?'

'Like a severe case of flu!'

Gabriel threw back his head and laughed. 'I had forgotten your quirky sense of humour.'

Alex watched him with seething resentment. 'I'm glad you find this situation such a bundle of laughs, Gabriel.'

'Let's get one thing straight right here and now…' He deposited his glass on the small pine table and leaned against the kitchen counter and looked at her grimly. 'This is the least amusing situation I have ever found myself in and if you think you can stand there, fuming and behaving as though you're due the sympathy card, then think again. *I* am the one whose life has come to a grinding halt! *I* am the one now faced with a series of decisions which will affect the lives of more than just myself! *You* behaving like a brat isn't going to help matters! Am I making myself understood loud and clear?'

Alex stared down stubbornly at her feet, acknowledging that there was more than an element of truth in what he was saying but still resenting his tone of voice.

'I never asked you to change your life for me,' she mumbled indistinctly.

When she raised her eyes, it was to find that he had pushed himself away from the counter and was towering above her. She wished she had worn heels instead of a pair of socks. At least, with the benefit of heels, she would have been more or less on eye level with him.

'I'm not changing my life for *you*,' Gabriel ground out. 'I'm changing my life for my son.'

You mean nothing to me. That was the implied, unspoken rider to his statement, Alex thought. He intended to do the right thing for his son and in the process she would be dragged along, whether she liked it or not. He couldn't have reminded her more forcibly of his take on events than if he had printed a sign saying *you're someone I happen to be stuck with* and shoved it in her face.

She took a deep breath. 'Maybe we should talk in the sitting room. I…I haven't eaten dinner yet. There's a casserole in the oven. It could just about stretch to two.'

It was an olive branch of sorts and Gabriel knew better than to snap it in two. But her stubbornness did things to his normally cool head that he wouldn't have thought possible.

'I thought you hated cooking.' She had worked in a hotel to practise her Spanish but she had once confessed that kitchens made her dizzy. All those items of food and ingredients in bottles baffled her. He wanted to smile at the memory.

'I've learnt…to…I prefer to give Luke home-cooked food,' she said reluctantly. 'I can manage a casserole but anything fancier than that is out of the question.'

'So he's yet to sample a soufflé…'

Alex dipped past him towards the sitting room at the front of the house. She knew that this polite banter was his way of making the best of a bad situation and she would have to go along for the ride or else make life a constant battleground for them both, and inevitably for Luke. She couldn't do that. But dredging up memories of their brief shared past was more than she felt she could handle. Yet where was the common ground between them now? They were operating in an unreal space, where the normal rules of social engagement were suspended.

'What happens now?' she asked abruptly, as soon as they were sitting. Gabriel on the sofa, she on the comfy chair by the fireplace. Her half finished glass of wine was still there and she took a sip but it had gone warm.

'I didn't see any mention of Luke in that article…' she carried on, drawing up her long legs and then resting her chin on her knee.

'Because I didn't mention him. There was no point getting into the nitty-gritty and, besides, I have little respect for reporters. The world will find out about you both when I'm good and ready.'

'You mean you haven't told your fiancée *the truth*?'

'*Ex*-fiancée. And no. Time enough for that.'

'What on earth did you tell her?'

Gabriel shrugged. 'I told her that ours was not a relationship that was destined to last the course and, as such, we should break it off before we both made a mistake.'

'That little speech should have come easy to you, Gabriel. You must have had years to practise it.'

Gabriel looked at her broodingly. There would be no profit in taking up this futile conversational thread. His mission was to get her on board and the only way he could do that was via dialogue. 'Cristobel will have no trouble in finding my replacement.'

'That's not as easy as you think!' The words were out before she could do something useful, like swallow them back and give herself a stern reprimand for even going there. There was a thick, pulsating silence, during which Alex could feel the slow crawl of embarrassed colour into her face.

'What are you trying to say?' he murmured in the sort of lethally sexy undertone that had always been able to send her pulses skyrocketing into the stratosphere. 'That I'm still on your mind?'

'Of course not!' Alex shot back wildly. Their eyes met and, for a brief moment, she could feel her senses go into agonised, melting free fall. With a sense of deep mortification, she was aware of a dull ache between her legs and the tickle of dampness that proved the effect he was having on her.

'Because it's nothing to be ashamed of…I still happen to find you a very attractive woman…'

'How can you sit there and say something like that when you've only just broken off your engagement? How fickle *are* you?'

In the space of a heartbeat, Gabriel could feel the tables turn on him. She seemed to have developed a talent for doing that. From nowhere, she could generate an argument of ridiculous proportions. 'I was never in love with Cristobel,' he heard himself say and then immediately wondered why the hell he had felt the need to justify himself. Since when did he ever do that?

'You weren't in love with her?' Her heart skipped a beat and she put that down to her surprise at his flat, unvarnished statement. She also had a moment of pure elation and she put *that* down to the fact that, without love in the equation, there would be a lot less to feel guilty about. And wasn't that cause for elation? Her life had suddenly become so complicated that any help in reducing her stress levels was a reason to celebrate!

'No, I wasn't in love with her, Alex,' Gabriel said heavily, frowning at her disapproving expression. 'You should feel better because of that,' he pointed out through gritted teeth because he seemed to have lost the reins of the conversation, which had been going very nicely. 'You weren't responsible for destroying the love match of the century.'

'Why were you going to marry her?'

'Why is any of this relevant?'

'You should never answer a question with a question.' Alex smirked. 'I distinctly remember you telling me that once.'

Gabriel threw his arms up in a gesture that was exotically foreign and muttered an oath under his breath. 'It was a union that made sense,' he offered.

Obviously the wrong choice of words because she looked at him squarely and then mused, '*A union that made sense.* A bit like what you had in mind for us...'

Gabriel opened his mouth to correct her on using the past tense when it was very much still his current intention to settle upon his son the mantle of legitimacy, whether she liked it or not, but he decided to steer clear of reminding her of that.

'I hope you appreciate the fact that, as yet, neither you nor Luke have been mentioned...'

'Remind me why I should appreciate that?'

'Because I don't suppose you'd want the paparazzi camping on your doorstep.'

Alex could feel her brain lagging behind. She was still caught up in the fact that he would have approached marriage as a sensible business arrangement. Proof that there was a block of ice where his heart should be, was fairly piling up.

'You never used to be so *cold*,' she said, thinking aloud. 'I mean, unless you hid it really well.'

'You've lost me.' Gabriel flushed darkly and scowled. Thinking back to those heady times with her was like remembering a different person. He hadn't strolled on a promenade eating an ice cream cone since he had been with her. Incognito. Being Lucio had been a far cry from being Gabriel Cruz. Unfortunately, this was his life. Promenade strolls eating ice cream and pretending the world as he knew it didn't exist had been enjoyable but it was a thing of the past. And being reminded of that served no purpose. Nor did he care for the implication that he was some kind of soulless monster because he happened to take his responsibilities seriously.

Nor, for that matter, did he care for the expression she was wearing on her face, which seemed to be a combination of incomprehension and pity.

'Have I?' Alex asked, staring off into the distance before settling her thoughtful gaze on his face.

'But all this is by the by. I haven't come here for a character assessment, Alex.'

'No. Well, I'm hoping you haven't come here to repeat your offer of marriage because I haven't changed my mind. Cristobel,' she added for good measure, 'might be prepared to enter into a loveless business arrangement with you because the perks are good, but I'm not.'

'Whoever mentioned anything about marriage?' Gabriel shrugged. 'I offered to do the decent thing; you turned me down because you'd prefer to occupy the moral high ground.'

Alex was disconcerted to discover that she was vaguely disappointed at his rapid retraction of his marriage offer. 'I'm not occupying any moral high ground.' Her voice had risen fractionally and she took a deep breath.

'*No importa.* It doesn't matter.'

'No. No, it doesn't. So…thank you for sparing me the paparazzi camping on the front lawn, although if the world is dying to know the details of your broken engagement, then I guess it's just a matter of time before it all comes out in the wash and the paparazzi get here. I can handle it. I'm very good at saying *no comment* and, believe me, I don't want my life disrupted any more than you do.'

'You misunderstand. Disruption is inevitable for both of us,' Gabriel drawled. 'However, it will be lessened by your being out of the country until after the story breaks and the fuss dies down.'

'Out of the country?'

'Out of the country.'

'You're going to shuffle us off to some remote place in the middle of nowhere, hide us away for an indefinite period of time…'

'Don't be ridiculous.' Gabriel stood up and Alex watched him in confusion. 'The casserole. I can smell it.'

Alex leapt to her feet with a little shriek of alarm, temporarily distracted by the prospect of eating the charred remains of chicken and peas.

'I'm not being ridiculous!' She reverted to his sweeping solution to the problem of unwelcome publicity as she dished out two plates of extremely well cooked chicken and rice.

'I'm not going to *shuffle* you off to any remote place. Frankly, I can't think of one woman who would be less amenable to being *shuffled off* anywhere than you.'

'Meaning what?'

'Meaning that you're like a Rottweiler off the leash.'

'That's a horrible thing to say.' She wondered how they had reached the point where insults were being traded back and forth like two combatants fighting in a ring. A belated sense of fair play made her realise that perhaps, and only a very small perhaps, she wasn't being quite as helpful as she could.

His life had been a lot more disrupted than hers and he *was* trying to deal with it without drama. A pack of reporters in front of her house, she reluctantly acknowledged, *would* be hellish. If he resented her sudden, disastrous reappearance in his life and all the chaos it had brought in its wake, then how much more was he resenting her now, when she stubbornly refused to listen to a word he had to say because she was just too busy shouting at him?

'But point taken,' she muttered, sliding her eyes to him and then just as quickly sliding them away again. She reacted against every single thing he said because he just seemed to rouse frightening, primitive feelings in her that made a nonsense of her normally phlegmatic, upbeat personality. Hadn't she coped with the fear when she'd discovered that she was pregnant and the loneliness of having her child without the support of the father around? Yes. So that surely pointed to an inner strength, even though one look at that darkly handsome face made her feel weak and panicky. But if he could be an adult about the situation, then she could as well.

'Finally. We're getting somewhere.' He pushed aside his empty plate and angled his long body back from the table so that he could cross his legs. 'My parents have yet to find out what's really happening. I have only told them about breaking off the engagement.'

'I bet they were overjoyed at that,' Alex mumbled with a sinking feeling. Just when their son was about to tie the knot with the perfect woman, along came a serpent in the garden of Eden to wreck the whole plan.

'They have accepted it. But I wanted to tell them about Luke face to face. Which is where you come in. I will arrange for us to have a little…holiday in Spain. We can break the news to them together and introduce them to their grandson. It will also allow me time to…get to know Luke. Undiluted time. As a bonus, we will be out of the country and away from media speculation.'

From a detached point of view, it certainly sounded like a brilliant idea. However, Alex felt far from detached when she considered the suffocating prospect of her and Luke spending *undiluted time* with Gabriel.

'What about your work?' she asked, drifting off with sickening ease into all sorts of scenarios that would prove a constant, unremitting threat to her mental health. Gabriel eating meals with them, lounging around a beach with a towel slung over his broad shoulders, laughing and relaxed and horribly, horribly disturbing. 'You have an empire to run!' she blurted out, fighting against the image of the old Lucio slotting neatly into this new Gabriel, thereby blurring the lines of hostility that were so useful.

'Needs must.' He shrugged, coolly polite as he detected the horror in her voice. 'Sacrifices must be made. I am prepared to make them.'

'Your parents will hate me!' She speared a piece of chicken with her fork and looked at it miserably. 'They must be so disappointed at how things turned out between you and Cristobel and, when they find out the reason why, they're going to have me hung, drawn and quartered.' Having never met his parents, she was already imagining them as older versions of Gabriel. Cold hearted, ambitious, fabulously wealthy and one hundred per cent approving of a marriage based on suitability. She didn't think that they would be falling over themselves to welcome a jeans-wearing foreigner from a humble background who had been silly enough to have a fling with their highly eligible son and get pregnant. She cast her mind around for a punishment that would befit such a crime and could come up with nothing.

Gabriel felt his lips twitch with sudden, unannounced amusement. She had always had a flair for the dramatic.

'Maybe you could face them on your own,' she carried on, her voice adopting a wheedling tone. 'Luke and I could stay somewhere...else and then they could come and visit. For a couple of hours to start with...'

He was already shaking his head before she could get to the end of her sentence and she threw him a baleful, sulky look from under her lashes.

'You're being unrealistic. And they won't have you hung, drawn and quartered. They're not barbarians. Naturally, they are deeply conventional people and they will find it odd that we have no intention of legalising our union for the sake of our child, but I'm sure I can bring them round to your point of view.'

'Right.' Alex was not in the least bit mollified by his reassurances.

'So, now that you have agreed to this small step, we have to discuss the practicalities. I will get my people to see about selling this place and you can refund any money you borrowed to your parents. You will have to hand in your notice at your job, but that will be a formality because you'll be leaving for Spain next week. Is your passport in order? Is Luke on it?'

Alex looked at him open-mouthed. She felt as though she had suddenly been tossed inside a washing machine which had been turned to the spin cycle.

'I can't sort all this stuff out in a matter of a few days!' she gasped at the first immediate difficulty staring her in the face.

'You don't need to.' Gabriel paused and looked away for a few seconds before returning his dark, brooding eyes to her face. 'You were on your own once. You won't be on your own again.'

His words, low, husky and uttered with driven intensity, brought a flush of colour to Alex's face. They also gave her an incredibly warm feeling somewhere deep inside her. She had carefully cultivated a spirit of independence, knowing that one small person depended on her, but to know that she was no longer on her own was a seductive thought.

'I...I will want to meet my son before we head off to Spain,' Gabriel said abruptly. It had only been a matter of a few days and he hadn't known whether keeping away had been a good thing or not. Should he have rushed to bond with Luke? No precedent had ever been set in his life for this sort of situation and he had found himself immobilised by indecision, finally falling back on a businesslike approach to the problem. Sort out the details first and then meet his son, get to know him. It was a thought that made him curiously nervous and Gabriel was not a man accustomed to nerves. He cleared his throat and helped himself to another glass of wine. 'Is there anything I should know?'

'Anything like what?' Alex enquired, mystified.

'Likes? Dislikes?' He had barely registered the boy when he had last seen him and had serious doubts about his ability to bond with the child, partly because he had been absent for such a long time and partly because children had never figured in his life at any level. They could have belonged to another species. He just didn't have a natural empathy with kids and he couldn't see how that was going to change now, whatever the circumstances. He had avoided dwelling on that, choosing instead to focus all of his attention on the nitty-gritty of calling off the wedding and getting his secretary to initiate the process of rearranging all of his forthcoming meetings. Now, however, lay the unknown territory of meeting his son. It was a terrain charged with unseen landmines. What if the kid hated him? What then?

'He likes all the usual things a four-year-old boy likes,' Alex said slowly. 'You know…'

'Well, actually, no. I don't.'

'Are you *nervous*?'

'Of course I'm not nervous!' Gabriel thought it right that he should dispel any such hint of weakness. 'He *must* be into certain things, though. Trains? Cars?' Or was he too young for things like that? Gabriel didn't know. He was an only child. There were no nieces or nephews clamouring for presents and interaction on birthdays and Christmas. He had friends and a couple of them had young children but they had always been safely out of sight whenever he had been around.

'He likes planes,' Alex told him. 'He has a collection of them.'

'Good. We already have something in common. I own two.'

'Which is something we have to talk about,' Alex told him, laying down her ground rules before she discovered that each and every one of them was being broken. 'I have tried to bring Luke up to be grateful and happy for small things. I don't want him growing up to be a spoiled brat. So don't think that you can swan in here and shower him with expensive stuff.'

Gabriel frowned. For a start, he didn't like being told what to do. He also didn't care for her questioning his parenting methods before he'd even met his son properly.

'Don't expect me to sit back and watch my own child live in poverty…'

'Of course I expect that you want to contribute financially to his well-being! I'm just saying…'

'You're just saying that you have a right to lay down whatever laws you want. For the past four years, you've had it your way. Now I'm here and things are going to change. I have offered you marriage. You turned that down. Fine. But the alternative will not be constant warfare. We will present a civil and united front to my parents. And when we return from Spain, you will move out of this house into something I deem suitable for my son.'

'What do you deem *suitable*?' Alex asked in genuine curiosity because a guy who owned a couple of planes probably had a very different idea of *suitable* to most other normal human beings.

'Somewhere close to me, for a start.' He held up one imperious hand, cutting her off before she could establish her protest vote. 'Remember, Alex. This was your choice. The twenty-first century option. An amicable relationship working together to do the best by our son. What we had is history. This is what we have now and you will not fight me on it.'

Except, *was* it history? When the sight of her body sparked something inside him and the curiosity to see what that body looked like now, having given birth to his child, was like a slow-burning fire?

For the moment, though, this was the road he would take. God knew, she thought he was a complete bastard and, that being the case, he would keep all inappropriate impulses under wraps. No problem there. Hadn't he perfected the art of self-control?

CHAPTER FIVE

ALEX settled into the comfortable seat on the plane and closed her eyes. She felt as though she was closing her eyes for the first time in three days because life, in the space of seventy-two hours, had become a crazy roller coaster ride.

Gabriel had taken charge with a ruthless efficiency that had given her very little time to think and even less time to argue. Had he thought that, given half a chance, she would have dug her heels in and refused to go along with his plans? In actual fact, she would have loved to because the thought of meeting his parents and being subjected to their certain disappointment and hostility was terrifying, but there were no grounds on which she could object. She had rejected his offer of marriage and had thereby somehow ended up removing her ability to contradict any further proposals without sounding uncooperative and selfish, two traits which were unacceptable when there was a child to consider.

So her house had now been valued and was in the hands of an estate agent for sale. Even though she had tried to insist on a rental.

'No can do.' He had shaken his head without any apparent remorse at flatly turning down that request. 'Rental carries the unacceptable whiff of lack of commitment. The minute you don't get your own way, you'd be back in your little terraced house and I would be back to square one, with my son living in a place of which I don't approve, and subjected to a traffic-laden drive every time I wanted to visit.'

Of course, that was a blazingly obvious piece of exaggeration but she just had to accept that Gabriel was never going to consider her modest little house as anywhere near what his son deserved. And any trip spent crawling on a busy London road for longer than twenty minutes would always constitute an arduous and unacceptable journey.

Alex had folded her arms and muttered under her breath and given him a look of open incredulity, all of which he had contrived to ignore.

But her hands had been tied. And it didn't seem to help that he was being the perfect gentleman. She had stood on her platform and spoken her piece about not wanting either of them to sacrifice themselves to a marriage made for all the wrong reasons, had asserted her independence, had scoffed at something as Victorian as marrying for the sake of a child and had proclaimed that they could be perfectly good parents, adult, civilised and connected only by their son. She had got what she had wanted. He had been adult, civilised and perfectly friendly. In a detached, polite way that she hated.

And then she hated herself for being silly.

It had all been exhausting.

The only positive had been Gabriel meeting Luke.

She reached out her hand with her eyes still closed and placed it gently over the chubby arm draped on the cushioned arm rest separating them.

Her mouth twitched. Gabriel might have conducted the technicalities with military precision, but it had been a different story with his son. Of course, she had sat Luke down and explained to him that Gabriel, the man he had glimpsed for a few seconds, was his father, wishing heartily that there were books on how to deal with conversations like that. But

Luke had accepted what she had told him with a little frown, then he had nodded slowly and proceeded to ask her about a toy he had seen on television which he had to have because his best friend had one. He was too young to fully understand the implications of what she had told him, although she was pretty sure that he would wise up soon enough.

So when Gabriel had appeared at the door and introduced himself by shaking Luke's hand, the child had hidden behind Alex and only peeped out when Gabriel had extended the set of toy planes which he had bought as an ice-breaker.

'I obeyed instructions,' he had said, looking at Alex. 'Nothing too expensive.'

They had all sat at the kitchen table and Gabriel had asked awkward questions while Luke messily wolfed down his plate of spaghetti bolognese and looked up now and again to answer something in childish detail.

Now, Luke was sleeping between them, his head drooping against her shoulder, while, on the other side of him, Gabriel frowned at something on his laptop.

Alex half opened her eyes and glanced surreptitiously at him from under her lashes. No amount of tough talking to herself could minimise the impact he had on her every time she set eyes on him. Five years on and he was still drop dead beautiful. He had discarded his jacket and now, as though aware of her staring at him, he snapped shut his computer and turned to her before she had the chance to close her eyes and feign sleep.

Gabriel looked down at the sleeping Luke and thought how easy it was when he didn't have to wear his paternal gear. He had foreseen difficulties in bonding and he had been right. Meeting his son formally for the first time had been an uncomfortable experience. The boy had hidden behind Alex, clearly terrified at the sudden intrusion in his life of a complete stranger. Today had not been much better. He had been gratified to see Luke carrying the set of toy planes over which he had agonised for a ridiculous length of time at Harrods, but he had still looked at Gabriel with barely concealed suspicion and gripped his mother's hand as though terrified that he might be left with the guy he had yet to refer to as *Dad*.

'This isn't going well, is it?' Gabriel asked abruptly and Alex frowned and straightened in her seat.

'What isn't?'

Unaccustomed to dealing with failure on any level, Gabriel looked away and said nothing.

'You're not used to young children,' Alex told him reassuringly. In his dealings with Luke, she could glimpse the vulnerability that was so alien to his nature and she knew, with some deep, inborn instinct, that recognising that vulnerability would be a mistake. 'He really likes the set of planes you bought for him.'

'He was less impressed with the real thing.'

'Maybe he takes after me.' Alex looked around her at the high level comfort afforded by a private jet. She could have been sitting in a tasteful lounge with very helpful waiting staff who seemed to appear on cue, without needing prompting of any sort.

Gabriel relaxed a bit. He slid his eyes over her long jeans-clad legs and the fitted striped jumper that would have been a glaring fashion mistake on any other woman but seemed to be just right on her. If he had picked a person out of a hat, he could not have picked someone less like Cristobel. Physically and intellectually, they barely seemed to come from the same planet.

'Don't tell me you're not impressed to death,' Gabriel said lazily, almost forgetting the whole friendship thing she had encouraged. Under the jumper he could make out the jut of her breasts and the usual host of lustful thoughts sprang out of their loosely contained cages.

'I'm not!'

'Liar,' he said softly, with one of those killer smiles that made her break out in nervous goose bumps. 'I remember when I showed you that Ferrari all those years ago and told you that it belonged to a local celebrity. You were awe struck.'

'I was a kid!' Alex said loftily, trying and failing to drag her eyes away from his face. 'Did it belong to *you*, by the way?'

'Will you throw something at me if I tell you that it did?'

'Well, I'm not impressed with that sort of stuff now,' she said. She had a sudden image of them making love in the back of the red Ferrari, which *had* impressed her to death at the time. It would have been a disaster, of course. They were both way too tall to ever do anything serious in the back seat of a sports car, but that sleek BMW he now drove…

She went bright red and thanked all the saints that he couldn't read her mind.

Then she wondered whether his politeness was so horrible because she didn't feel polite around *him*. Did she secretly want him to still fancy her? Even though she knew that his taste in women ran to a completely different sort and probably always had? Even though he was the kind of guy she had repeatedly told herself over the years she would never again get involved with?

'And I hope you don't expect me to bow and scrape to your parents just because they're rich…'

'I expect you to be yourself.' Gabriel could sense her withdrawal. Just when the conversation relaxed between them, she would pull back and it enraged him because, whatever she thought of the man he was, she should open her eyes to the guy he had become, a guy who was willing to stick around for a son he had never known he had. Did it get more praiseworthy than that?

'How much longer before we land?'

'Very soon.'

Alex's stomach clenched. He had told her that his parents now knew everything. His plan to tell them face to face had been scuppered by his inability to get over to Spain in time and he could hardly show up with a ready-made family in tow and expect them not to jointly collapse from the shock. So Alex knew that she would be entering the lion's den with no defensive suit of armour. She only hoped that they would be charmed by their grandson, even if they loathed her on sight, although if they were as stiff as Gabriel then she could look forward to some heavy going.

And they would be out there for nearly four weeks!

Alex had been stunned when Gabriel had casually inserted that into the conversation as they'd boarded the plane to Madrid. Two weeks of possible hell with his parents and then a further two weeks criss-crossing Spain, where he apparently had a series of houses in various places. He needed to get to know his son and he intended to do it on his home turf. What could she say to that?

'They're not monsters,' he told her with a hint of impatience. 'You won't be eaten alive.'

Between them, Luke stirred and curled closer towards Alex. She saw Gabriel note that imperceptible shift away from him and for a few painful seconds her heart constricted. Before she could be sucked in by her emotions, however, she felt the plane begin to dip and circle and then Luke was flying his pretend plane in his hand and bombarding her with questions. Somehow considering himself eliminated from the magic circle, Gabriel stared frowningly through the window and watched as the land beneath them got closer and closer until the plane was bumping along the runway and then, at last, coming to a smooth halt in the airfield.

Between the cluster of other small planes, against which his gleaming black jet stood out like a sore thumb, he could see his parents' driver waiting behind the fence.

'Alonso has come to meet us—' he turned to Alex, who was looking uncertainly around her as if waiting for the captain's voice to come across the tannoy telling her that she could safely unclasp her seat belt and disembark '—so you can put your nerves on hold temporarily.'

'That's easy for you to say,' Alex mumbled, finally galvanising her body into action and turning her attention to Luke, who was busily occupying himself in her arms, making plane-like noises and pretending to give orders to an imaginary crew.

'My turn will come,' Gabriel said dryly. 'When I confront your family and get beaten to death by your brothers.' His fabulous dark eyes met hers and she gave him a reluctant smile.

'I can't imagine you being nervous.'

'Good,' he drawled, tipping her face up to his before she could begin leaving the plane. 'I like that.'

That was so typically Gabriel, even the Gabriel she used to know, that she laughed and he felt his breath catch in his throat. With driving intensity, he focused on her soft, full lips, her pearly white teeth and then the nervous way her fingers raked through her short hair as she tuned in to his wavelength. For a second, the rest of the world disappeared.

Alex's breath caught in her throat and, when he reached out to brush a strand of hair from her face, she inhaled sharply before turning away with a slight stumble. She was horrified to find that she hadn't wanted that sudden electric connection to end and if it had to end, she had wanted it to end with him kissing her. How could she have so completely forgotten the nerve-racking present in favour of a treacherous, erotic fantasy? Luke had stopped the random twirling of his toy plane and was now contorting his little body in her arms so that he could stare directly into her eyes.

Flushed with guilt, Alex dropped him to his feet as soon as they were on the tarmac and her polite chit-chat about the heat dried up as she saw him reach out and unconsciously slip his tiny hand in his father's.

Above his curly dark head, Gabriel's eyes met hers and there was a moment of wordless communication before she looked away.

The long black limo waiting for them rescued her from dwelling on her nerves as it was a source of boundless fascination for Luke in a way the plane had failed to excite him. While she grappled with the ever advancing and dreaded meeting with Gabriel's parents, he squirmed and investigated everything there was to investigate in the car, from the little drinks bar to the dark windows to the various high-tech gadgets, there to make life more comfortable for the average billionaire. In the process, he babbled a running commentary on nothing in particular, peppering random insights into some of the other children in his pre-school class with a hundred questions about what in the car did what and why.

'He seems highly intelligent,' Gabriel remarked, looking at Alex, and, for the first time since they had stepped into the limo, she gave him a genuinely warm smile.

'I think that's called parental bias.'

With a mere forty minutes left before they reached his parents' impressive mansion on the outskirts of the city, Gabriel determined to employ distraction tactics. There was no way that he wanted Alex to be on the defensive when she met his parents. It would be a sure fire way of ensuring that the two weeks spent with them was a crashing failure. He hadn't been able to gauge the level of his parents' disappointment with the abrupt change of wedding plans via a phone call but he was banking on severe. Nor had he been able to decipher the depth of their shock at what he had had to tell them a scant twenty-four hours previously but he was also betting on severe. To add a defensive and belligerent Alex into the mix could be a catastrophe.

So he maintained a light-hearted murmuring banter about Luke throughout the journey, making sure to fill any pauses with conversation and focusing so hard in his efforts that he was barely aware of the casual ease with which he scooped his son on to his lap and ruffled his silky dark hair.

Released from his own self-imposed inhibitions, he was communicating with his son without even being aware of it and Alex was surprised at the tightness in her chest as she witnessed that unconscious breaking of the ice. When she had been pregnant, and when she had first had Luke, she had daydreamed about what might have been had she and Gabriel—or Lucio, as she had thought of him back then—ended up together. She had fantasised about being a normal, happily married couple. In her fantasies, he had related to his son pretty much the way he was relating now, holding him on his lap with those big, strong hands and bending to smile distractedly at something his son said.

She was surprised when she next glanced out of the window to discover that they were no longer on the main road but navigating through a series of small side roads, on either side of which orchards stretched away into the distance. It couldn't have been further from the dreary listless grey weather they had left behind in London and, for the first time, Alex felt a little kick at thinking that perhaps it had been right, after all, to remove herself and Luke from their familiar territory. He had never had the chance to go abroad. It was occurring to her that this would be just one of the things that he would be able to enjoy, being the son of Gabriel Cruz.

Trips abroad, big houses, fancy cars…they had been the stuff of Gabriel's life, not that she had known that when they had met. Was it any wonder that he passionately wanted the same for his son?

'We're here.'

Alex blinked and gazed at the sprawling mansion looming into view at the end of the private avenue. A massive circular courtyard, elaborately landscaped at its centre, fanned out to impeccable lawns on either side. Whilst it bore no resemblance to the stately homes in England, it was much too big to be classified as a villa.

'Your parents live here…*on their own*?' Alex asked weakly.

'There's staff.'

'Right.'

Gabriel looked at her incredulous saucer eyes and was catapulted back to that heady teenage feeling of having successfully impressed a girl. It was a feeling he hadn't experienced for a very, very long time and it felt good.

Against him, Luke stirred out of the catnap he had fallen into with the ease of a child and Gabriel looked down at the flushed little face staring drowsily up at him, weirdly confused and surprised. His instinct was to return the child to his mother, but he resisted the impulse and was gratified when Luke showed no signs of wriggling away.

'I can see why you thought my place was a bit on the small side,' she whispered to cover her nerves as the driver moved around to open the door for her. On top of everything else, she felt horribly underdressed for the occasion. She had dressed casually as a protest vote, wanting to establish from the start that she was her own person and would not be bullied by anyone. She was regretting it.

'Will we be living here?' Luke asked Gabriel with keen interest.

'For a little while.' Gabriel smiled. 'But you'll be able to come and visit any time you want to.' He shot Alex a warning look, just in case she was about to protest. 'Your grandparents would love to have you whenever you want.'

'Nan and Gramp live in Ireland.'

'And your other grandparents live here.'

Luke accepted that simple fact with a slight nod.

Alex barely registered that because the impressive front door had opened on a beaming couple. The man was tall and, as she drew nearer, she recognised those classically austere features, and the woman, coming towards them now, was small and round and amazingly unlined.

'Didn't I tell you that they weren't monsters?' Gabriel murmured, taking her hand, a piece of moral support which Alex knew she should object to but for which she was inordinately grateful.

He was smiling as he bent to kiss his mother and something else clicked into place in her head. Gabriel loved his parents. His marriage proposal had been his way of trying to capture what they had and provide it for his own son. Of course, there was no love in the equation and so it would never have worked out, but Alex was beginning to understand his motivations.

'Antonio Cruz…it is a pleasure to meet you…' He was extending his hand and smiling, as was the woman, who had also moved forward to introduce herself in accented English, but their eyes were on their grandson and Luke was positively basking in the sudden attention, allowing himself to be lifted by his grandfather and shown to his grandmother like some amazing long lost treasure, although twisting round just to make sure that Alex was still in sight.

This was hardly the cold, condemnatory greeting she had expected.

She was ushered inside the house and, when she began to awkwardly explain how sorry she was that they had not met their grandson sooner, her apologies were waved aside amidst affirmations of delight that they were meeting him now. Every compliment was paid to Luke and, waiting in the grand drawing room, an anachronism against the opulent, traditional decor, was a shiny three-wheeled bicycle of the sort Alex had never seen before.

'It is their way of expressing their enthusiasm about meeting him,' Gabriel murmured softly to her. He was as surprised as she was at the warmth of their greetings and wondered whether there had been truth in his father's remarks that the cancellation of the wedding had not been the disaster he had anticipated for them both. 'Please refrain,' he continued in the same low breath, 'from giving a speech about the evils of money.'

'I wouldn't have dreamt of doing any such thing!'

'Good.'

While Gabriel moved to chat to his father, his mother, Maria, drew her to one side. 'We can watch Luke in the garden on his new bike,' she said, not seeming to mind that he had already climbed on it and was experimenting with their gleaming polished floor as a possible racetrack.

'You must be very proud of him,' the older woman confided as they followed him outside, leaving Gabriel with his father. 'Gabriel explained the situation.

'He told us that you were unable to contact him when you fell pregnant. Distressing though it is to know that I could have met my grandson when he was a baby, we are both pleased that we are meeting him now and that Gabriel will finally be happy. As a mother, you know that is all we wish for our children.'

Alex flushed and guiltily wondered how this charming woman would react if she knew that her son *finally being happy* was not really on the agenda.

'Cristobel was not the right one for Gabriel,' Maria confided, chuckling when Luke paused to flash her a crooked sidelong smile that made him resemble a mini Gabriel even more than he already did.

Alex said nothing. Maria had romantic delusions about her son. She would be stricken if she knew that what was right for Gabriel *was* a woman like Cristobel who ticked all the right boxes except for that big box labelled Love, which didn't interest him anyway.

'You, on the other hand. The very minute I saw you, my dear, *I knew*. A mother *knows these things*.'

'Knows *what* things?'

Completely lost, Alex turned to Maria with a perplexed frown but Gabriel and his father were emerging from the house and any explanation for that weird remark was lost as Alex was plied with questions about Luke, who had the look of a child suddenly let loose in a sweet shop.

'Now, you must be tired,' Maria announced once they were all inside.

Alex realised that she was. It had been a long, wearying few days and, with the horrifying hurdle of meeting his parents behind her, exhaustion slammed into her like a brick wall.

'Your bags have been taken up and, if it is all right with you, Antonio and I would enjoy so much settling our grandson.'

Alex looked down at Luke, who looked as bright eyed and bushy-tailed as any four-year-old boy who had slept off and on and was now brimming over with boundless energy and excitement in his new surroundings, even though it was already past his normal bedtime. It would take more than a handful of stories to send him to sleep but, whilst she hesitated, Gabriel stepped into the silence and assured his parents that Luke would love nothing better.

'We bought a few books…' Maria smiled down at the child and held her hand out. 'Made the room as special as we could in the small amount of time...I hope you do not mind...' A quick look at Alex, who shook her head and gave in to the warm feeling inside her of being accepted. More than accepted...*apparently welcomed with open arms*. Her mind drifted sleepily back to what the older woman had earlier said but she was literally too tired to analyse anything.

'Of course, he will be in the blue room next to you...'

'You're practically asleep on your feet,' Gabriel said, amused. He looked hesitantly down at his son, unsure whether the affection displayed earlier had been an anomaly, but, risking it, he stooped down to lift Luke up and was rewarded with a shy smile which was fairly thrilling. He grinned back and ventured a more robust sign of affection, throwing him up in the air and catching him as if he were as light as a feather. Alex watched, feeling vaguely left out when Luke gave a shriek of laughter and begged for a repeat performance. He had no experience of men. Alex had had no boyfriends since she and Gabriel had parted ways. There had been opportunities and she knew that some of them had ticked all the right boxes, but she had never felt inclined to take any of them up. Her life had been too busy, she reasoned to herself, with Luke and with just making ends meet and carving out an independent life for herself, for her to make space for the arduous business of getting to know a guy. Sometimes, underneath that robust reasoning, she'd thought that no man had ever come along who could hold a candle to the Lucio she had known then. But she didn't like thinking like that and it scared her to imagine that he was now back in her life, harnessed to her against his will, a nightmare living reminder of her foolish teenage dreams.

The little game with Luke ended as Gabriel gently set him down. For a few seconds Alex knew that she had been entirely forgotten in the aftermath of his boisterous few minutes of fun with his father. From the sidelines, Maria and Antonio were looking on with every semblance of enjoying the sight of Gabriel playing with his son and, when Maria caught her eye, the older woman's beam became even broader so that Alex couldn't resist smiling back, even though it was a little disconcerting to witness this much delayed bonding finally beginning to take place.

'And now up to bed, both of you!' Maria urged them up the magnificent staircase that forked in opposite directions at the top to accommodate the various wings of the grand house.

'I'm sure Gabriel would like to stay and catch up with you.' Alex shot him a telling glance which she hoped he would correctly interpret as *tell your parents the full story of our situation.*

'Time enough tomorrow,' Maria said comfortably. 'And this little man will be following very soon.'

'Since I've been good—' Luke directed this question to his new found grandparents, taking full advantage of a once in a lifetime opportunity but making sure that he wasn't actually looking at Alex when he did it '—am I allowed some ice cream?' He flashed them a winning smile. 'Or even some chocolate?' And then, finally realising that permission might be required from a higher source, he shot his mother a pleading look and she sighed resignedly.

'You're a horror,' she told him grinning. 'But first, come and have a look at your room and I'll be checking to make sure you're in it in an hour.'

Thoughts of a lovely warm bath gave her a renewed sense of energy as they all trooped up the stairs and turned left at the top. For the first time since she had arrived, she really paid attention to her surroundings. There was nothing restrained about the opulence of the massive house. Lush carpet was soft underfoot and numerous traditional paintings adorned the walls, conferring the impression that this was a house that had seen many generations of the same family. It was odd to think that Gabriel had lived here as a boy. Was that why it had been so tempting to string her along under a phoney name when the chance had presented itself? Had the novelty of being anonymous been as powerful for him because of his fabulous background as the lure of celebrity might have been for someone who had come from nothing?

If only he had had a crystal ball and had seen that for every act there was always a consequence. Maybe then he might have stuck to what he had always known.

She blinked with a start when Maria paused to push open the door to Luke's room and then, a few minutes later, the heavy wooden door that was next in line.

It was a vast room dominated by a four-poster bed, not the modern, undressed, minimalist version, but a four-poster bed of the old-fashioned variety that was only ever glimpsed nowadays in magazines or seen in period movies. It was spectacular enough to produce a gasp from Alex, as were the rest of the furnishings. The large, ornate dressing table, the rich royal-blue of the floor to ceiling curtains, the wardrobe with its panel of exquisitely fashioned glass, which was reflecting their images back at them as they stood in the doorway.

'I have put you here...Gabriel's room is in the other wing and I know you would have wanted to be close to your son in the room next door...'

Maria's words echoed around her head and then crystallised slowly but surely as Alex's wandering gaze finally alighted on the clutch of suitcases tucked neatly away in the corner of the bedroom. Hers, Luke's...and Gabriel's. Louis Vuitton rubbing shoulders with cheap and synthetic department store.

She looked round in confused horror, trying to meet Gabriel's eye, but he was busy talking to his father while Luke hopped from one foot to the other, bored with the house tour and eager to get to the kitchen for whatever untold delights awaited him.

'Um...' Alex cleared her throat. 'I don't think this is quite right...' she ventured hesitantly into a sudden bemused silence. 'I can't help but notice...well...' She gestured to the offending pile of suitcases on the ground.

'We will take care of these,' Gabriel said smoothly, inserting himself between Alex and his parents and Maria's puzzled face uncreased into a smile. Luke had slipped his hand into hers and was tugging.

'Look—' Alex gave it another shot, although she had to angle her body awkwardly just to avoid addressing his back '—there seems to be a misunderstanding here...'

Tall though she was, he was, however, taller and broader and she was forced to watch helplessly as the troops departed and she was left standing in the room with Gabriel, who slowly closed the door behind him and turned to face her.

'I thought that went well. Better than expected, in actual fact.' He strolled towards the window and glanced outside before turning to perch against the broad window ledge, on which were arranged a pair of solid black marble sculptures of galloping horses.

'What's going on?' Alex demanded, folding her arms, refusing to be drawn into polite chit-chat and infuriated by his attitude of casual indolence when she was itching for answers.

'I don't get you.'

'Oh, don't pretend you don't know what I'm talking about, Gabriel!' Alex resorted to an explosive outburst and pointed at the stack of cases on the floor. 'Why has your bag been put in the room I'm supposed to be sleeping in?'

'Because this isn't *your* room; it's *our* room. And I am as surprised as you are. I wouldn't have thought that my parents were quite so liberal minded. Then again, today has been full of surprises.'

Alex looked at him in seething silence. 'I'm not sharing a room with you,' she said through angrily gritted teeth.

'You haven't got a choice.' Gabriel spoke with utmost politeness. When she bent down to reach for her two nylon suitcases, he was at her side before she could straighten and this time there was an implacability on his face that sent shivers down her spine. As did his proximity. As did the intimacy of their situation, with that hulking great bed behind her, significant and shockingly evocative.

'What do you mean? Of course I have a choice! Luke's room is big enough to hold a small party! It'd be no problem if I slept with him tonight until this misunderstanding is sorted out!'

'Didn't I mention to you that my parents are ultra-traditional?' His voice was like dark chocolate swirling around her, suffocating her ability to think on her feet. 'They haven't considered the possibility that there is no relationship between us.'

'But didn't you tell them…?'

'Tell them what? That you are happy for Luke to remain illegitimate? So that you can *do your own thing*? That they will only see their grandson when visiting rights are allowed? That he will be the innocent victim of an unstable background? Surprise, surprise. I thought that delicate matter should be addressed to their faces and by both of us. In the meantime, they have reached their own conclusions.' He spread his hands wide. 'Shall we interrupt their enjoyment with Luke so that we can break the news to them that they're still in the Dark Ages and that single parent families are the done thing?'

'That's not fair!'

'Right now, it's all we've got. We can think of a way ahead in the morning. In the meantime, it's been a long few days and I am not inclined to stand here arguing with you. The bed's big enough for the two of us. And now I'm going to take a shower. I suggest you get down to the business of unpacking…'

CHAPTER SIX

GABRIEL took his time in the shower. Alex wouldn't be going anywhere. Firstly, she didn't know the layout of the house and, secondly, she would never want to risk the deluge of questions that would be raised should she be discovered bunkering down next to Luke in the room next door. She had expected the worst and, having been showered with warmth, she wouldn't want to risk destroying it all by creating a scene. At least not tonight. Tomorrow was another day and he would cross whatever bridges required crossing when they appeared.

Right now, he would give her time to calm down because she had been ready to explode. In the shower, he grinned to himself. Women tiptoed around him, always desperate to get on his good side. Alex did the opposite. He wondered how it was that although she was the least girly girl he had ever met, she was also one of the most maddeningly feminine.

He felt revived after his shower and utterly relaxed, despite the disruption to his highly well organised and well oiled everyday life. He had left his computer downstairs and he decided to forgo the joys of being on constant call in favour of whatever the evening had in store for him.

Which appeared to be nothing when he finally emerged from the steamy bathroom with only a towel round his waist. The bedroom was conspicuously empty, although a quick check told him that the suitcases were all still intact.

Without bothering to go through the hassle of trying to find something suitable to wear to bed, Gabriel headed for Luke's bedroom and, sure enough, there she was, sitting on the side of Luke's bed and in the process of finishing a story in a low, soothing voice to a child who was fast asleep.

'The sleep of the innocent,' he murmured and Alex gave a little squeak of surprise because she hadn't heard him coming in.

And little wonder why! She looked down at his bare feet and her heart skipped a beat. She had come to check on Luke, make sure that he had brushed his teeth because there was no way that she intended to wait in the bedroom for Gabriel to emerge from his shower. She hadn't banked on him following her through to Luke's bedroom, least of all with…

Her eyes travelled upwards and she released a little sigh of relief at the sight of the fluffy towel wrapped round his waist.

'Couldn't you have got dressed?' she snapped, rising to her feet and depositing the book on the little bedside table.

Maria hadn't quite been telling the truth when she had said that they had done what they could to Luke's room, given the short notice of his arrival. The bed was in the shape of a racing car and every picture book imaginable had been provided on a bookcase that was cleverly designed in the format of a cartoon character. A giant faux fur beanbag rested in one corner of the room, right alongside an electric racetrack, complete with miniature sports cars and remote controls. Lord only knew how they had managed to kit out a child's bedroom to such an exquisite standard in the space of a couple of days but that, Alex assumed, was how money talked.

It was spoiling taken to extremes but she didn't have the heart to tell them off because they were so conspicuously thrilled to have a grandson, even one they hadn't planned on.

They had been gracious and charming and at great pains to conceal the bitter disappointment they must surely be feeling and for that she was grateful.

'I wondered where you were.' Gabriel lounged against the door frame, beautiful, indolent and off-putting, and waited for her to join him. 'I thought for a minute that you might have scuttled off to some far-flung corner of the house but then I spotted the cases on the floor and figured you had come here.'

Alex brushed past him and shut the door quietly behind her. The temptation to feast her eyes on that magnificent body was making her feel a little weak but she was heart-stoppingly aware of him as he fell into step alongside her and even more heart-stoppingly aware of their bedroom door closing behind them.

The room was big. In fact, vast by any standard. But not so vast that she could possibly direct her eyes to a safe spot. She reluctantly turned around and looked at him and her skin tingled and her pulses raced and she had to fight down the inappropriate desire to swoon. She wished he would just put something on but there was no way that she was going to repeat that simple request for fear of him jumping to the conclusion that she was affected by the sight of him. Which he would, in a heartbeat. Gabriel was anything but dim when it came to reading female responses.

Then another thought struck her. Did he even *possess* pyjamas? He never had when she had known him. Of course she had loved nothing more than that, back in those heady times, but, in their current situation, she could think of nothing worse for her peace of mind.

'You're staring,' Gabriel drawled. 'Should I feel flattered?'

Alex bristled. His behaviour had been exemplary over the past few days. She had demanded a businesslike approach to their situation and he had obliged. But this was his home turf and she suddenly felt very vulnerable.

'I hope you brought something...*decent*...with you...'

'Something decent?' Gabriel's brows knitted together in a perplexed frown. 'What does that mean?'

'Pyjamas. Long johns. Something of that nature.'

'Why would I have done that? It's not as though I was actually expecting my parents to put us in the same room.'

'Which they wouldn't have done if you had had the common sense to explain the situation to them.'

'Old ground, Alex. We've been put in the same bedroom. Get over it.'

'Fine!' She folded her arms and glared at him belligerently. The naked torso was really getting under her skin. As was the way he was deliberately making no effort to conceal it. 'But, just so that you understand the ground rules, I didn't have to come here and sharing a room with you wasn't my choice! I have no option but...but...'

'But I'm to keep my wandering hands to myself. Is that it?' Gabriel asked in a cool, amused voice. He strolled very slowly towards her and felt her exerting every ounce of will-power in her body not to cringe back. Cringe back *in what*?... he wondered. Fear? Repulsion? Did she think that he was going to do something to her against her will? He had had the foundations of his entire world thrown into chaos and yet he had risen to the occasion and done his utmost to make life easy for her. And his thanks? *This.*

Her silence confirmed her mute agreement with his question.

'Let's get one thing straight, Alex. I am not in the habit of making a nuisance of myself as far as women are concerned.'

'I never said that…'

Gabriel held up one peremptory hand. 'What gives you the idea that you are so fantastically irresistible that I wouldn't be able to pass a few hours in the same bed as you without trying to make a pass?'

'Nothing,' Alex muttered, turning scarlet. 'I just thought I should put down some boundaries.'

'Have I given you any reason to think that I am not a man of honour?'

'No, but…'

'You presented me with a son years after the event. I did not question paternity. Nor did I threaten to take you to court to win custody. In fact, I did the opposite. I offered to legitimise our relationship for Luke's sake. You turned me down because you felt your own needs and desires overrule the well-being of our child. Fine. You want a detached, amicable relationship. I have granted your request. Moreover, I have done my very best to protect you from aggressive and unwanted paparazzi by bringing you both over here, where I can offer seclusion of the highest order until our news becomes tomorrow's fish and chips newspaper. My parents have not censured you. They have not asked questions. They, too, have accepted the fact of Luke's appearance with grace and dignity and have welcomed him to their hearts. And assuming, mistakenly, that this is more than just a simple business arrangement for us, they have overcome their own natural prudishness and stuck us in the same bedroom, thinking no doubt that they were doing us both a favour. And, bearing all that in mind, you have the cheek to stand there and treat me like a sex-starved teenager who can't wait to jump you.'

Alex felt as though she had been assaulted by a mental battering ram. His choice of words was contrived to demolish her defences. He had been nothing but reasonable, fair and frankly second to none, his little speech implied, and yet she persisted in treating him like a common criminal.

He had managed to take the wind out of her sails as effectively as a pin applied to a balloon, even silencing the little voice in her head that reminded her just what Gabriel was like. One hundred per cent red-blooded male with more than his fair share of an enthusiastic libido. But, hard on the heels of that little voice, came another, telling her that perhaps she was no longer the target for that enthusiastic libido.

Now she felt an utter fool. He was probably repelled at the thought of sharing a bed with her but had been big enough not to make a deal of it. He respected and loved his parents and wouldn't throw their good intentions back in their faces.

She opened her mouth to tell him that they should set the matter straight with his parents so that they didn't have to endure a full two weeks in the same room, but knew that he would see no point in doing any such thing. At least not when they were obviously in their honeymoon period of misguided delusions. After all, resisting her would prove no problem for him, so why bother with the fuss?

'What do your parents think…um…our relationship is?' Alex enquired tightly.

'Naturally, they imagine that their son would have done the honourable thing and offered marriage.'

'They *said* that?'

Gabriel gave an eloquent shrug of assent. Not in so many words, he thought to himself, but they had jumped to that conclusion. He was sure of it. They would not have conceived a situation of shared custody and visiting rights. How he disillusioned them of their fanciful notions remained to be seen.

'What on earth are we going to do about that?' Alex asked aloud and Gabriel frowned. It still angered him that she found it so outrageous that he had asked her to marry him. Five years ago she would have leapt at the idea.

'We are going to do nothing about it at the moment,' he told her baldly. 'They're old. They deserve one or two illusions, at least for the time being. So get your head around the shared bedroom scenario and rest assured that your body is safe as houses with me.'

'Okay.' Alex lowered her eyes because he was just too much in her face for comfort. 'I'm going to have a bath.' She hoped that by the time she finished he would be asleep, and preferably would have done the decent thing and removed himself to the sofa. It might be uncomfortable and his feet might have to dangle a bit over the side, but needs must.

Gabriel watched as she flounced off to the adjoining bathroom and he heard the meaningful click of the door being locked behind her.

She would take as long as she possibly could in there. Hours, if she could pull it off. Anything to avoid the darkened room and the intimate silence. But face both she would have to and, outraged as he was that she would think him loser enough to try it on when she was a reluctant recipient, he was still in a pleasantly contented frame of mind as he unpacked his suitcases, whistling as he went and then, eventually, chucking the towel over a chair and slipping under the duvet.

With true gentlemanly consideration, he switched off the overhead light so that when she finally emerged from a bath that could go down in the record books as the longest ever, she was obliged to feel her way to the bed.

Having not foreseen a scenario in which she would be forced to share a room with Gabriel, Alex had given absolutely no thought to her sleepwear or else she would have bought something suitably hideous. As it stood, she was in her normal garb of a pair of small shorts, which left an awful lot of leg exposed, and a vest.

But at least Gabriel appeared to be asleep. She slipped into the bed, huddling as far to the side as she could without falling off and when, after fifteen minutes of barely being able to breathe for fear of waking him, she was still wide awake, she discreetly got out, found her way to the cushions on the sofa and quietly began stacking them on the bed into an impromptu partition format.

Watching her from under his lashes, Gabriel wondered how long he should remain silent and motionless before he got rid of the ridiculous barrier between them.

No time, he thought, like the present.

Without warning, he heaved himself onto one elbow and, with his free hand, he casually tossed every single carefully arranged cushion on to the floor and focused his eyes on her appalled face. His eyes had long adjusted to the silvery darkness in the room and he had fully appreciated the spectacular view of her fumbling her way to the bed clad only in the briefest of nightwear imaginable. It was the sort of nightwear that would have sent a shudder of horror racing down Cristobel's spine. No lace, no ribbons, no silk. The sort of nightwear that he would have considered highly unsexy on any other woman on the face of the planet, but on her rangy, leggy body looked amazing. She might not have had the long swinging hair or the drop dead good looks, but there had always been something curiously appealing about her and his body reacted to that *something* with knee-jerking intensity.

'Forget it,' he drawled. 'I'm not having my space restricted by a pile of cushions.'

Having thought him to be safely ensconced in the land of nod, Alex could only stare at the beautiful angles of his face as he looked at her. The super-king-sized bed was suddenly reduced to the suffocating dimensions of a carrycot. He was propped on one elbow and the duvet left her in some doubt as to whether the towel had been replaced by anything suitable. Or anything at all, for that matter. She could spy the sleek, muscular curve where his waist dipped to his hip, even though her eyes were strenuously averted.

'Why aren't you asleep?' she snapped accusingly.

'Is this another of your crazy rules?'

'My rules are *not* crazy!' Which was more than she could say for her misbehaving body!

'Are you telling me that erecting a foot high barrier of cushions is the behaviour of a sane woman?'

'I just thought,' Alex replied grittily, 'that it would be helpful…'

'Why? I've told you I'm not going to ravish you. Besides, it's not as though we haven't shared a bed in the past.'

'That was different!'

Gabriel was finding that hard to concede, considering that his body was reacting in exactly the same way as it had done years ago.

'I want those cushions back!' Alex was almost weeping from sheer frustration.

'Okay.' Gabriel gave an elaborate sigh and began to slide out of the bed, which elicited just the response he had predicted. A high squeak of alarm as soon as she realised that he was completely naked.

'Forget it!'

'Sure?' He turned to look at her over his shoulder, his face a study in earnestness. She could have thrown her pillow at him. Instead, she made a low, inarticulate sound under her breath and he subsided back into the bed.

'It's stupid,' he said in a seductively unthreatening tone, 'to make such a big deal about this…' In the process of getting back under the covers, he had managed to gain a few inches closer to her. She smelled good. Clean and fresh and soapy. She never had liked perfume of any sort.

Alex looked at him suspiciously. It was hard to read the expression on his face because of the darkness but she didn't trust him an inch and she didn't want to. It was hitting her hard that she couldn't *afford* to trust him. Her anger and her wariness and her distrust were the only weapons she had against the power of his personality. If she abandoned those, where would she be? She shivered whenever he was around and the sound of his voice was enough to induce a maddening meltdown of her nervous system. At least when she was spitting fire, she was keeping him—and *herself*—at bay.

'And, while I'm about it…' He lowered his voice a couple of notches and reached out to idly play with her splayed fingers. Alex was barely aware of the gesture. She was mesmerised by the honeyed gentleness of his voice. The silvery moon was touching light fingers across his face and the shadows and angles heightened the beauty that had always had her in thrall. 'You're right.'

'I am? Right about what?' Her voice sounded pathetically feeble. And he was still doing that playing thing with her fingers although she pretended not to notice because she liked it. It was dangerous but she liked it.

'Maybe I should have told my parents the whole unvarnished truth. Told them what you want and that they would have no choice but to accept it, but I was…' for a minute, he almost used the word *weak* but that would have been going too far; *weak* was a word that could not possibly be associated with him and she would never have fallen for that '…concerned about their mental welfare. Coping with the wedding being called off and then plunged into what they might have considered an unbearably stressful situation…'

'Understood.'

'You have no idea how relieved I am to hear you say that…'

'You are?'

'Of course I am. I can't think of anything worse than fighting with you.'

Alex had no idea how he had managed to get so close to her. She felt the heat from his body and, when he shifted, the brush of his thigh against hers. Her head was telling her to briskly wind the conversation up but, instead, with a frightening recklessness, she angled her own leg and the shock of nudging him and knowing the extent of his arousal was like being hit with a power surge of live electricity.

Gabriel made no effort to move. Instead, he smiled and murmured ruefully, 'Just ignore me.' By which he meant *just ignore my unruly body and the fact that I'm unbelievably hot for you*. How likely was it that she was going to do that? When she had pressed herself closer to him? When she was staring at him with hot, dark eyes and those slightly parted lips that were begging to be thoroughly kissed?

The ice queen with her issues about their past and her high moral principles about their future was melting fast but Gabriel wasn't going to be the one to make the first move.

But he *did* wonder what he would do if she took him at his word, rolled over to her side and fell asleep. He had discovered a streak of stubbornness in her that had not been apparent the first time round, when she had been gloriously his for the taking.

The prospect of a cold shower was not pleasant.

'And, while I'm in the mood for wholesale contrition,' he continued in a voice that whispered over her like a caress, 'I think it's important to know that I would have stood by you had I known about the pregnancy…' Gabriel realised that he *would* have and they would have married and there would have been none of this ongoing nonsense about her asserting her independence and not wanting to sacrifice her life for the sake of their child. Five years ago, there was no way that she would have turned down an offer of marriage. He could remember her youthful, adoring enthusiasm for him as though it was yesterday.

'It would never have worked in a million years,' Alex mumbled, thrillingly tuned in to his proximity even though she was fully aware of the health hazard it presented. 'Look at Cristobel.'

'Cristobel?' Gabriel was beginning to wonder how he could ever have conceived of marrying Cristobel. She seemed like a distant figure belonging to a different and somehow irrelevant life. Still, he didn't care for her name cropping up in conversation.

'You would always have wanted someone who fitted the role.' Alex felt a stab of self-pity and her eyes blurred. 'I was your time out and you would have gone mad if you'd ended up stuck with me for the rest of your life.'

'You're being ridiculous. And don't put yourself down like that. That *time out*, as you call it...' this whole confidence exchanging thing was crazy...but still '...it felt good.'

'I'm just being truthful. But it's sweet of you to say it anyway...'

'*Sweet?* Since when have I ever been described as *sweet*?'

There was such genuine outrage in his voice that Alex's lips twitched and she eventually laughed.

'I would have wanted to have seen you growing inch by inch with my baby inside you,' Gabriel told her huskily. 'I would have wanted to have seen the changes in you...'

With that powerful admission, Alex felt that *danger* alert sign flashing frantically in her head go completely off the scales and she drew in a trembling breath.

'You wouldn't have liked them,' she whispered, assuming that if there was one thing certain to put him off, it would be the thought of her getting fatter and fatter by the day until she resembled a beached whale.

'Did your breasts get bigger?'

Alex stifled a choking gasp. She had edged her leg back but just a couple of centimetres and she knew that he would be hard as steel against her and the thought was an impossible turn on.

'We...you...shouldn't be saying stuff like that...'

'Why not? I wasn't there with you at the time. It's only natural that I would be curious about what I missed.'

He made it sound so reasonable but there was nothing reasonable about the way her body was on fire.

'So...' he prompted, enjoying the exquisite physical ache of his throbbing erection and his erotic fantasies of her ripe, pregnant body. 'Did they?'

'Of course they did,' Alex mumbled.

'I have an image in my head...'

Alex moaned softly and her eyelids fluttered.

'Did you say something?' Gabriel enquired in a concerned voice.

'It's time for us to get some sleep. This arrangement...it's just not going to work...'

Gabriel ignored that half-hearted protest. 'Not that your breasts aren't exquisite the size they are now. Small but beautifully formed.'

'Please don't...'

'Don't what...? Turn you on...? Because you *are* turned on, aren't you? I know I am...but I also know that I gave you my word that I wouldn't touch you and I'm a man of my word... So, if you want to be touched, then you just have to reach out...'

A flare of wicked, reckless craving rushed through her body like a tidal wave, obliterating everything in its destructive path. Common sense, reason, bitterness, resentment…all the things she had been holding on to caved in like a house of cards.

Well, why not? she thought with sudden, furious intensity. She hadn't been touched for such a long time. No one since Gabriel. She hadn't even been *attracted* to anyone since him. So what if she had one night of pleasure? It wasn't going to commit her to an ongoing relationship with him. Things would stand just as they had before! Except she might have got this terrible thing out of her system. In fact, she *would have got* this terrible thing, this awful attraction, out of her system and she would feel a lot more comfortable around him instead of acting like a cat on a hot tin roof every time he came within two metres of her.

'Just this one time…' she murmured slowly. 'Just tonight…'

'One night of wild passion…'

Alex released a long sigh of relief that they were of the same mind. She missed his grim smile as she obeyed him and reached out to splay her fingers across his flat, hard stomach. She could no longer contain the groan that escaped her lips or the way her hips jerked forward instinctively.

'I'm not rushing this…' Gabriel told her thickly, pulling her towards him and grinding provocatively against her so that she couldn't help but feel the abrasive rub of his hardness against the soft cotton of her loose pyjama shorts.

He heaved his big body up and then lowered his head, plundering her soft mouth with his lips, liking the way she moaned and sighed as he continued to kiss her. He had the crazy feeling that he had spent the past five years starved of significant sex which, he told himself, had to be a load of rubbish because he hadn't been short of beautiful women in the interim.

He curled his fingers into her short hair and tilted her head so that he could trace a hot trail along her slender neck with his mouth. He hadn't forgotten what she liked, what turned her on. She was sensitive behind her ear and just there, along her shoulder blades…

He smiled with satisfaction at her little whimpers of pleasure as he retraced that familiar territory.

'You feel exactly the same as they you…'

'You surely can't remember what I *felt like*,' Alex protested, her eyes fluttering open to stare at him with drowsy heat.

'You'd be surprised what I remember about you,' Gabriel told her truthfully. 'For instance, I seem to remember that you like me paying a lot of attention to your breasts…' He shot her a wolfish smile as she blushingly looked away. 'Believe me when I tell you it was never any hardship…' He pushed up her vest to expose her body and had to close his eyes briefly to control the shudder of rapturous pleasure that slammed into him.

Her breathing was rapid and shallow and her skin was dewy moist and flushed. The feel of her long body was silky smooth under his fingers. He wanted to turn the lights on so that he could stare at her and fill his eyes with the sight of her body. He didn't. He figured that that would be one sure-fire way of ruining the atmosphere and that was the very last thing he wanted to do.

'I think your breasts are a little bigger, actually.' He cupped them expertly and then rolled his thumbs over her swollen, tender nipples. 'I wonder if they taste the same…'

The verbal foreplay was driving Alex crazy. She moaned softly and felt wild and wanton as she arched upwards, inviting him to satisfy his question. He had always made her feel wild and wanton. He had taken her virginity and taught her how to be proud of her passion. It was all coming back now and she could indulge herself because it was going to be just for one night. He had promised and somehow that had eradicated all sense of wrongdoing.

'Would you like me to taste them...?' Gabriel circled one pouting disc with his finger and smiled with hungry satisfaction when she ordered him to stop teasing her. 'But I *like* teasing you and you haven't answered my question...'

'Yes! Please...'

She gasped with pleasure as his mouth found her nipple and he sucked hard, tugging it into his mouth and caressing it roughly with his tongue until she was squirming and writhing. She was making up for years of celibacy but she didn't want to hurry the pace. She didn't want it to be over. But the way he was taking his time, moving from one thoroughly ravished nipple to the other, was driving her out of her mind.

Did he know how much he was turning her on? She opened her eyes and looked at him and a slow smile curled his beautiful mouth.

She ran her fingers lightly along his broad shoulders, like a blind person tracing patterns of Braille, enjoying the feel of his defined muscle.

He, in turn, parted her legs with one hand and, still looking down intently at her flushed, averted face, slowly slid his finger to explore her ripe wetness, testimony to her arousal. He watched her moan and toss under his exploratory touch, as he rubbed her clitoris with the flat of his fingers and felt it softly throb under his touch.

When her movements became more uncontrolled, he regretfully cupped her firmly, bringing her down before she could tip over the edge.

There was the whole night to play with, though…She badly wanted to touch him. He knew that. And she would. In due course.

Right now… He lowered his big body and his mouth replaced his fingers as he stroked that sensitive bud with his tongue, rasping it over and over and pinning her hand down when she would have tugged him away.

'No…Gabriel…*stop* or I won't be able to control myself…'

Gabriel looked up just long enough to say, 'I don't want you to, my darling. We're in no rush and I want you to climax beneath me…'

A shudder of uncontrolled pleasure, yearning and desire rammed into her heated body and she let herself go, her body taut and then quivering as she was rocked by an orgasm that seemed to last for ever.

Gabriel waited for her to surface and then he kissed her tenderly on her lips and stroked her cheek with one finger.

'You should have let me wait, Gabriel…'

'Like I said, sweetheart. Don't plan on getting much sleep tonight…'

And she didn't.

CHAPTER SEVEN

ALEX shifted on the low futon-style bed and opened her eyes slowly. In terms of perfection, this moment of waking, with the mosquito net fluttering in the fragrant breeze that wafted through the open louvred doors, had to be right up there.

Gabriel would be walking along the beach with Luke, looking for shells or interesting pieces of driftwood. It had become something of a morning ritual since they had arrived on the island seven days ago.

Or was it six? Or eight? It had been alarmingly easy to lose complete track of time once they had left his parents' home in the city and headed down to his secluded beach house that perched majestically above a cove where the water was as turquoise and as calm as anything she had ever seen in her life before. It was a setting that could have leapt straight out of the pages of a tourist brochure advertising exclusive homes. The house was open and modern, with a sprawling wooden veranda and bedrooms that opened on to the front lawns and overlooked spectacular views of the sea. To one side, the rectangular infinity pool was the perfect setting for their evening meals, light suppers prepared by one of the two housekeepers who kept everything in order when Gabriel wasn't around. Which, she gathered, was actually most of the year. Ana and Edna had also proved to be immensely popular with Luke and, for the first time in four and a half years, Alex had been able to do what many women with young children occasionally took for granted when they weren't having to cope on their own. She had been able to relax.

And Gabriel had aided and abetted that. From that very first night sharing that bed, he had chipped away at her defences with his humour, his obvious enthusiasm to win over his son after their shaky start. So she had vowed to stick to her guns and not repeat their lovemaking… He had allowed her. Until, on night three, she had cracked and gone back into his arms.

And since then she had been on a self-justifying bandwagon. She had been weak, yes, but didn't she deserve to snatch this time before grim reality back in England could take its toll? There would be no question of anything permanent in their relationship. In fact, Gabriel had said that himself, had told her that they were just getting closure. And if that had sent a shiver of bitter disappointment through her, she had quickly talked herself out of it because she was no longer the gullible kid she had once been. She had been a single mother for years. She had grown up and out of that obsessive, consuming love she had once felt for him. She was safe.

Now, she would happily argue with Gabriel if she didn't agree with what he said. No longer did she creep around behind him with lovesick puppy eyes, deliriously happy to say *how high*? whenever he said *jump*.

She wasn't sure what her parents, or her brothers, for that matter, would make of the situation. They knew that she was in Spain but their version of events had been severely edited. She had phoned and spoken to her mother a couple of times and had been vague in the face of direct questioning. Mostly, she had communicated with them by text and had been thankful for its deliberately short, uninformative format.

That awkward situation lying ahead was just something else that joined the other *something elses* waiting to be sorted out when the time came.

Stretching pleasurably, Alex slipped into a pair of shorts and a halter neck top which she had bought on one of the various shopping expeditions she had done whilst in the city.

Outside, the sun was already getting ready to unleash its full force and it was warm.

She took a minute to look round at her surroundings. Beautiful lawns, thickly planted with flowers of every bright hue, the glittering blue of the pool, the cool, airy luxury of the house behind her with its expansive wooden flooring. Every day, she felt the need to commit something new she had observed to memory, ready to be dusted down and examined at some future point in time when the reality of it had been lost.

She had even sneaked a few pictures on her mobile phone, although she knew that Gabriel would probably disapprove. He was passionate about his privacy. Which was why they were there in the first place.

She had only to walk for a few minutes before she spotted Luke and Gabriel on the beach, squatting by a rock pool, Gabriel's hand protectively resting on his son's stomach as Luke peered into the water.

The shadow she cast as she approached them alerted Gabriel to her presence and he looked up at her, shading his eyes with one hand.

His dark eyes gave her a leisurely once-over and he grinned as the colour crept into her cheeks. They had made love in more positions than he could remember and she *still* blushed whenever he looked at her!

'Nice,' he commented, while Luke frowned and poked his finger into the water, curious to see what the tiny fish in the rock pool would do.

Alex stooped down and made random conversation with her son while she waited for her heated blush to subside. But it was to no avail because back it came when Gabriel reached out to stroke the side of her arm with one finger.

'Today,' he said lazily, 'I'm taking you somewhere special.'

'I didn't think we could get anywhere more special than this.' In one quick flash her greedy eyes had taken in the khaki shorts, the loose T-shirt, his lean brown legs as he stooped to accommodate his son and she felt that familiar tingle in her breasts, the way her nipples tightened in expectation of being touched. The intensity and immediacy of her responses to him unsettled her but she had learned to deal with that by telling herself that she was just getting her fill of him while she could.

And it hadn't escaped her notice that all talk of marriage had fallen by the wayside, even though she knew that it was the path his parents expected, although the subject had not once been openly breached. They undoubtedly knew their son well enough to realise that he didn't take kindly to his boundaries being broached or perhaps they were giving him space to deal with the sudden developments in his life before trying to push him in another direction. Alex didn't know.

'Ana is going to have a special day with Luke…'

Luke's ears pricked up at the sound of that and he demanded to know what was in store for him. The sun had darkened him and he slung one thin brown arm around Gabriel's neck and looked at him with the same brown-eyed intensity that was so typically his fathers. More and more, when she looked at the pair of them, she was struck by the uncanny physical resemblances connecting them. Had Luke carried all those similar mannerisms, inherited from Gabriel, while he had still been in the womb?

While Gabriel told him about one of the local guys from the village, a personal friend and specialist kite maker who would be coming to teach him how to make his own kite, his every utterance was peppered with a deluge of excitable questions. Every so often Luke's eyes would flick over to Alex, silently looking to her for support, then back to his father. To the innocent outsider, they would, she thought, seem to be the perfect family unit, which just went to show how deceptive outward appearances could sometimes be.

'And now.' Gabriel drawled lazily as they strolled back towards the house, 'you and I are going to have a day out. I have a boat and you can't see it from here, but it's a twenty-five minute ride to an island. Just you, me and nature… Trust me, you'll never have seen anything like it before…'

Luke was soon happily out in the back garden, intently watching Marco as kite number one was meticulously constructed. It had taken some doing to arrange this day to themselves and Gabriel intended to make full use of it. He had brought all his energies to work on making himself an indispensable part of Alex's life, the challenge being that he did so without her even being aware of it. More than ever now, he knew that the unconventional relationship she advocated was not what he wanted. Having never felt any particular urge to procreate, he had now reached a point where the prospect of a ridiculous twenty-first century caring, sharing situation with the mother of his child and his son was unacceptable.

But he had known better than to voice his thoughts, instead allowing her to believe that the hotly passionate relationship in which they were now indulging was little more than a brief stroll down memory lane. She was clinging to the illusion that she wanted her independence but she would come to him. He knew it. Hadn't she come to him with her body? Crept over to where he had been pretending not to notice her presence and blissfully surrendered to something that was bigger and more powerful than she could control? The answer to that one was yes.

On all fronts, Gabriel was completely satisfied.

'Who is going to drive the boat?' she asked a little nervously. 'You know I'm not good with all that sailing stuff.'

They had headed back to the bedroom and she was busy rummaging through her drawers in search of a bikini. Where they were going, she wouldn't be needing one, but he let her rummage anyway, asking her to change in front of him.

'You know how much I enjoy that,' he said, his eyes caressing her as he lay on the bed and folded his hands behind his head.

'Incidentally, I am going to drive. I refuse to have my day of peace and solitude with you cluttered by the presence of a boatman. Take your top off *very slowly* and then come closer.'

'Don't give me orders on how to change into a swimsuit!' But Alex was laughing as she undid the little bow at the back of her neck and at her waist so that the flimsy halter top slid to the ground.

Gabriel's bitter dark chocolate eyes flared with naked appreciation and she sauntered over to him, hands on her hips, her full mouth curved into a smile of pleasure and satisfaction. Out of all the uncertainties in her life just now, the one thing she was very sure of was the power of their mutual attraction. Gabriel wanted her, he really *wanted* her, even if she wasn't a blonde bimbo with pneumatic breasts and big hair. He wanted her as much as she wanted him and, at least on that front, there was equality.

'Closer,' Gabriel growled, catching her hand and yanking her over so that she collapsed, laughing, on top of him. While she protested about getting dressed, heading off, leaving early because she wouldn't go unless he promised to drive the boat really, really slowly, he positioned her on top of him.

'I agree with everything you say. Keep talking.' He drew her down to the perfect level so that he could fasten his mouth around one breast and begin suckling on it as she supported herself in an arched position with the flat of her hands. The little shorts felt like an impossible barrier between them and she knew that she was getting wetter and wetter as he continued to lave her nipple with his tongue and mouth.

'Now, now…' he said, reluctantly pushing her away from him. 'You really must stop distracting me. If we don't get going…well…I'll probably have to drive the boat really, really fast and I know how much you'd hate that…'

The boat, when they eventually made it there, was moored out of sight beyond the bend in the cove. Ana had prepared an elaborate picnic for them and Luke was so wrapped up in the business of trying to get a metre of tissue paper off the ground that he was barely aware of their departure.

The trip to the island was so beautiful and the weather so balmy that Alex forgot that being on the water induced seasickness. Or at least it had when she had been a child and had travelled to Normandy on a school trip in foul weather.

Also Gabriel was helpfully distracting her from the onset of any symptoms by insisting she see how to sail the boat and then making her recite all the technical terms, like a professor, so that they were at the island before she had time to think about herself and her queasy sea stomach.

And the island was beautiful.

'I used to come here often,' Gabriel confided. 'The house has been completely modernised and renovated but it belonged to the family and we used to take a lot of holidays there. I can remember sailing across to this gem of an island with my father when I was a boy.'

Alex could imagine him doing the same with Luke but she didn't say anything.

Out to impress, Gabriel gave her the full tour of the tiny island. The white sandy beach on which they had landed gave way to a thicket of trees and shrubbery but a path had been cut into the density and, in the heart of the island, a small, roughly fashioned cottage was the only sign of habitation.

Alex was impressed to death, as she had been with pretty much everything he had shown her over the few weeks they had been in Spain. Everything was testimony to a lifestyle which was ridiculously opulent and beggared belief.

'Do you like it?' he asked casually when they were finally back on the beach.

'It's beautiful, Gabriel. Everything I've seen since we came over here has been beautiful. Like out of a magazine. It's amazing to think that you grew up with all of this.' She now fully understood why he had been tempted to keep her in the dark about his fabulous legacy all those years ago. It must have been refreshing not to have dated a woman who knew exactly how much he was worth.

'Of course—' he gave an elegant shrug and pulled off his T-shirt '—my parents come from a different generation and a different place. Now, it would be madness to encourage Luke to think that all of this gives him a right to be lazy.'

'Even though *you* obviously didn't let it go to your head?'

'I'll take that as a compliment—' he grinned at her and patted the space next to him on the towel, which he had spread on the sand under overhanging branches that reached out towards the sea '—considering you've told me a million times that I'm the most arrogant guy you've ever met. Not your kind of man at all.' He waited for her to contradict the last part of his statement and was disproportionately irritated when she failed to take the bait.

'You work hard.' Alex approved of what he had said. She, too, didn't want Luke to end up a spoiled brat. 'Maybe that's what I should have said.'

Gabriel hid his frown. 'Of course, however down-to-earth we strive to be with him, he will always be able to enjoy considerable comfort... Frankly, I would like to bring him over to Spain as much as possible. Not just for the sake of my parents, who would be more than happy to travel to London to see him, but I find it extraordinarily relaxing to be in his company. It strikes me that I may have forgotten some of the simpler pleasures in life.' He wondered whether he should press his point by insinuating that she, too, could enjoy such trips with them. He had tactfully avoided all mention of the future lying inevitably around the corner but perhaps his diplomacy had been misguided. For the very first time, he felt suddenly unsure of success. They made the perfect lovers and she was as obliging as he could ever have hoped for the minute she fell into his arms, but was it only lust that motivated her?

Gabriel uneasily did a quick mental comparison of the woman he had now and the girl he had once possessed. The sex was as good...better even, if that were possible, but there the similarities ended. She was relaxed with him but no longer was she a slave to his every demand. Did he like that? Gabriel wasn't sure. Given their situation, it would have been a lot easier if she had just surrendered to his superior logic.

'I didn't think you liked those simple pleasures.' Alex sat down, clasped her arms around her knees and tilted her head to the sun, closing her eyes and enjoying the feeling of warmth on her face.

'I liked them five years ago...'

Alex stilled. She had to fight against the temptation to be encouraged into thinking that the man lying on the towel, inches away from her, was the same man she had innocently gone out with, believing him to be a carefree wanderer with great looks and an uncomplicated personality. He wasn't. That guy was a myth. The real Gabriel snapped his fingers and watched while the rest of the world saluted and jumped to his orders.

'The simple things in life are always the best,' she said non-committally, which was not what Gabriel wanted to hear.

'Are you going to follow up that statement with the cliché about the best things in life also being free?'

Alex glanced down at him. His proximity was having its usual effect of scrambling her brains. She could hear the cool, jarring note in his voice and she was assailed by an intense desire to avoid arguing with him at all costs. The past three weeks had been a glorious ceasefire and she didn't want to resume hostilities.

'No. I've really enjoyed my time here and none of it was for free.'

'Some of it was.' Gabriel's voice dropped a level and he pushed himself up to drop a kiss on her shoulder. 'You smell of the sun, *cara*.' He licked her shoulder, a quick, delicate flick of his tongue, and had her twisting round to face him.

Making love on the beach was something they hadn't done. With Luke ever present and knowing that the two retainers at the house, along with the other incidental staff, were always liable to be somewhere in the vicinity, they had restricted themselves to the bedroom. Now, the prospect of making love with the sun on their bodies and the gentle rhythmic sound of the sea as background music was like a shot of adrenaline to Alex. When he carefully pulled down the strap of her bikini, she helped him along by unclasping it at the back, then she placed her hand on him, feeling his arousal and loving the way it throbbed at her touch.

A consummate lover, he had always been the one to insist on satisfying. This time, it was her turn to be in charge. If she had had some of her scarves and a couple of handy posts sticking out of the ground, she would have tied him down, but instead she was obliged to order him not to move.

'I'm not usually the one taking orders,' Gabriel said with a sharp sense of anticipation, 'but I'm willing to give it a go this time…'

It turned out to be easier said than done as he was forced to watch her do a leisurely, provocative striptease. There wasn't much to remove but off came her top with agonising slowness and, by the time she was wriggling seductively out of her bikini bottoms, he was on the verge of losing control.

He had to close his eyes a couple of times because she was just such a turn on. Long rangy body, high breasts, no evidence of the baby she had borne years ago, although there were times when he had caught himself fantasising about how she might have looked as her belly grew with his baby inside her. No way was he going to add that further fantasy to the stockpile right now.

She offered every part of her body to his hungry mouth, allowing him to feast for a while before pulling back until he had to stop following orders and take her with a deep, possessive hunger that left them both spent and perspiring.

Between uninhibited lovemaking, and another session during which *she* was obliged to keep still while he tormented her with every sensuous touch imaginable, and their frequent trips to the sea, which was gloriously calm and warm, the exquisite picnic lunch was almost an anticlimax.

'Enjoy yourself today?' Gabriel asked, watching as she daintily nibbled at one of the sandwiches. He didn't think that she was aware of what a splendid sight she made. Having rubbed her entire body with sunblock, taking his time over certain parts, which had reduced her to a quivering wreck, he had forbidden her to put her bikini on again so he could fully appreciate every bit of her body as she sat, cross-legged, watching him with the same hunger as he was watching her.

'No. It's been hateful!' She laughed and fed him some of her sandwich and then shivered as he took her finger into his mouth and sucked it thoroughly, his fabulous eyes never leaving her face.

'One more night and then work beckons,' he said, which was like a bucket of cold water being poured over her and she looked at him with consternation.

'But...I thought we had a few days left...'

'You and Luke have. Unfortunately, I received an email last night; there's something of a crisis in one of my deals. I have no choice, my darling.'

'So this whole *thing* was my equivalent of the last supper!' She stood up and turned her back to him so that she could stick her clothes back on. She knew that she was being ridiculous. This *interlude* was not going to last for ever. She had known that all along. They had fallen back into bed because the lust was still there, hard and strong, but no amount of lust could change the reality of what was waiting for them back in England.

And she couldn't let it. Because...because...

A tide of mortifying emotion swept to her face as she contemplated the pass to which she had come. Sleeping with the guy she had sworn to keep at a distance ever since he had returned to her life. The same guy who had used her and dumped her years ago had managed to infiltrate her system all over again. She had foolishly imagined that time had immunised her against his devastating personality. How wrong she had been! He had showered her with his undivided attention and single-minded sexual assault and she had fallen like a house of cards in a high wind.

And now she was in love with him all over again.

Released from the box in which she had desperately tried to shove it, the unvarnished truth rose up to stare her in the face. She couldn't even use the excuse that he had pursued her because he hadn't. No, he had waited and she had gone to him. Had he planned it that way or had that been just a pleasant train of events which he had seen no point in derailing?

'Sit back down. You're being ridiculous. Overreacting.'

'Why didn't you tell me that you were going to be leaving tomorrow?'

'Does it matter? I would have brought you here anyway.' Gabriel stood up and put on his clothes.

'Why?'

'*Why?* What kind of a question is *that*?' Gabriel was finding it difficult to understand where she was coming from. From his point of view, his behaviour from day one had been impeccable. And now, out of nowhere, she was throwing a hissy fit over nothing in particular. Hissy fits were normally the equivalent of death warrants as far as women were concerned, but of course he was in a place where his options were limited.

'One last day of lust and passion before reality kicks in.'

'Is that what you think?' Gabriel spotted the chink in her reasoning before she had time to withdraw her impulsive remark. 'That I'm going to get back to London and put what we have behind us?' He walked up to her and tilted her adorable, suspicious face to his.

'It's what we agreed.' Confusingly, Alex couldn't quite remember the precise details of this agreement. They had been eroded by his stealthy, subtle attack.

'Since when do we have to stick to an agreement that was made before we found out that what we had forgotten about each other wasn't worth remembering?' He kissed her tenderly on her full, sulky mouth and felt her instant response. No matter that her head was shrieking at her to resist. Her body was obeying its own rules and he liked that.

Having not quite worked out how he would set about getting what he wanted, the opportunity now presented itself to him and since when had he ever been the kind of man to ignore a perfectly good opportunity?

He gave her time to breathlessly surface for air and then ran his hand along her side, down to her thighs, lingering on her inner thigh with delicate teasing fingers.

'Stop it, Gabriel.'

'You know you don't want me to… You *like* me touching you…your mouth…your breasts…you like it when I get between your legs and taste your arousal…'

'You're not playing fair!' Was that her voice? It sounded more of a low, husky, uncontrolled moan.

'I don't like playing fair. I like getting what I want. And what I want is *you*.'

He teased her a little more, letting his long, exploratory fingers drift across her stomach and circle her belly button, then he turned away so that he could start re-packing the picnic things, indiscriminately tipping them into the generous-sized basket before covering the lot with one of the linen tea cloths and heading, with his towel, to the boat.

'Come on.' He glanced over his shoulder to where she was standing, staring at him with a small frown. 'We should get going, Alex. It'll be dark very soon and when it gets dark on the water, it gets pretty disorienting.'

Giving her time to think about what he had just said, he helped her into the boat and got the motor going, sitting down to steer it away from the island.

'I've never seen a sunset to compare with the ones you find here,' Gabriel mused, thinking that he hadn't exactly been sitting around looking at sunsets any time in the recent past. 'I'd quite like to carry on sharing the experience with you.'

The lights of his house glittered like tiny stars in the distance as the glowing orange sun began its steady descent.

'I don't see how that's going to be possible.' Alex saw exactly how he might imagine that it would be possible.

'Don't you?' He swerved the boat towards the mooring on the island. 'I asked you once to marry me and I'm asking you again. This time I think you'll find my reasons more persuasive. Okay, I will concede that you may have had doubts the first time I asked, but we have spent time together now and you have to agree that we've been getting on famously.'

Alex saw the white of his teeth as he grinned, looking away from her and out towards the jetty by his house.

'That's just sex,' she mumbled and he shot her a look of censure.

'Don't denigrate what we have, Alex. You satisfy me and I'm pretty happy with that. Throw into the mix the fact that we have a child, a child who is now accustomed to having both his parents on tap, and what further reasons could you look for?'

Just love, Alex thought in confusion. That one little emotion that had not once been allowed to break through the surface of his lust. And wouldn't lust fade, anyway? Didn't it always? Unless there was something more fundamental to tether it down?

'How do you think Luke will feel if I disappear the second you return to England?'

'He's just a kid…'

'And kids are not entitled to be hurt? Upset? Confused?'

'I'm not saying *that*…'

'No? Then I don't understand what you're saying.' There was no way that Gabriel was going to let the sun go down on an argument. Not when he was stuck with having to return to London before the break of dawn the following morning. He spun her round to face him, his face hard and uncompromising.

'Let's get the facts down on the table,' he said, grimly steamrollering her objections before she could open her mouth to voice them. He also slowed the boat because a captive Alex would be infinitely easier to handle. 'I am a man of honour. I was prepared to marry you and you turned me down. I respected that. However, the situation has changed. You are now no longer just the mother of my child and someone I had a brief fling with years ago. We are lovers and I, for one, find that a very satisfying situation.' An understatement if ever there was one. She had managed to eclipse the memory of every other woman he had slept with, which was no mean feat. Considering she was now bound to him with bonds that were stronger than steel, that was nothing short of being an eminently desirable bonus. What if the years and the responsibility of single motherhood had turned her into a hag? Of course, he would still have proposed, but how much more tedious the situation would have been. As it stood, he was filled with a sense of well-being at how things had turned out.

'You can't deny that the past few weeks have been good. I've made substantial progress with my son and I don't relish the thought of having that come to an end and don't even think of giving me a patronising lecture on the richly rewarding relationship a father can have with his son with arranged visits twice a week with the occasional weekend thrown in. What we have is a good thing and marriage will make it better.

Stability for Luke and goodbye to all stress and strain for you. No longer will you have to do things on your own. This was meant to be.'

Alex was silent. She felt manoeuvred although every word he had spoken had been the truth. What they had had been good. Was there such a thing as *too good*? Because the fly in the ointment, for her, was that, like a fool, she had hurtled back into his arms and allowed him back into her heart. The sentiment was not reciprocated. For him, their rekindled sex life was proof positive that the traditional outcome he wanted was for the taking. By *meant to be*, he really was saying *the way I intended it to be*.

'Did you plan all this?' she asked in a small voice, willing back foolish tears.

Gabriel frowned. *Plan*, he considered, had never had a more inhumane sound and he didn't like that. He had lavished her with attention and had recaptured her sexy body with an enthusiasm that even he had not foreseen. He had made gigantic strides with Luke and had kept a watchful and protective eye on her when she had met his parents, sensitive to her insecurities. To try and imply that his consideration had been grounded in an ulterior motive was unacceptable.

'How could I plan that you would willingly come to me?' he questioned with silky assurance. 'How could I plan that the sex between us would be so hot?' He angrily raced the boat towards its mooring, slowing it into a sweeping curve only when the jetty was within spitting distance. 'I have done everything to please you and yet you treat my good intentions as a crime.'

'I don't mean to...'

Gabriel secured the boat with an expertise born of experience and grasped her hand to help her out. It was so dark now that she was little more than a shadowy figure but he could feel the very slight tremor in her slender arms and her quiver of hesitancy. It seemed very important that she didn't escape him and he didn't stop to analyse why this was.

'If we go our separate ways,' he told her in a driven undertone, 'consider the consequences.' As she fell into step beside him, he resolved to stop being Mr Nice Guy, waiting while she made her mind up. Only a fool played the waiting game indefinitely. He had given her the space she had needed. The time for politely standing back while she dithered and possibly made the wrong choices was over. 'Removing Luke from the situation for a minute, there's *us*...' he ground out. 'You can't sit on the fence for ever. That's not fair to Luke and it damn well isn't fair on *me*. It's make your mind up time, Alex.' He stopped and turned to her, wishing heartily that he could see her expressive face. 'I can't see you without wanting to take you to bed,' he admitted roughly. 'And I can't think of Luke without wanting to seal our relationship. But I won't wait for ever while you go through the pros and cons for the millioneth time. If you don't want to legalise what we have, then I walk.'

'What do you mean *you walk*?' Alex felt the colour drain out of her face.

'I *mean*,' Gabriel asserted, 'I won't wait around for ever. Would you mind the thought of my bedding another woman? Getting serious about her? Do you want to see me arrive on your doorstep for my two hour stint with Luke with a woman on my arm?'

Alex felt as though the ground had suddenly been swept from under her feet. While she had been trying to sort herself out, she hadn't paused to consider that Gabriel might have been doing his own thinking. He was a man of action. He always had been. How could she imagine that he would have sat around twiddling his thumbs while she wrestled with her own fragile emotional state? The thought of another woman sharing his bed sickened her.

Gabriel responded to the lengthening silence with something close to panic. He could feel it surging through his system like poison, bringing him out in a sweat. It was like nothing he had ever felt before and he was rocked with relief when she said, with a catch in her voice, 'I…I don't like thinking of you with anyone else…'

Not even her afterthought, *'Let me think about it,'* could shake the rush of satisfaction that slammed into him. Didn't he always get what he wanted?

CHAPTER EIGHT

ALEX had the following day to really consider the development between them. Gabriel had left the island very early in the morning and she had wakened to a note on the pillow next to her telling her that he would be in touch later, to enjoy what remained of her stay, with a telling postscript that they would *discuss their situation* once she was back in London.

She had stared helplessly at that note, with its bold black writing, for a long time. Her determination to stick to her guns, to be a fully fledged twenty-first century woman who wouldn't barter her freedom for the sake of a mistake that happened years ago, seemed to have vanished in a puff of smoke. She was now having to face the fact that she had ditched all her good intentions for a man who might or might not have waged a deliberate war on her senses to get what he had wanted from the start, who had stripped her to the bare essentials and then offered her an ultimatum which he must have known she couldn't have refused. Did he know that she had fallen in love with him all over again? Probably. She had as good as admitted that when she had confessed to him that she didn't like the thought of him sharing a bed with another woman. The thought of that made her feel sick.

Not even the distraction of Luke and his endless excited kite-flying could distract her from the confused, hopeless train of her thoughts. So she married him because she was in love with him, because marriage would ensure stability for their son. Then what? She hadn't heard even the remotest admission from him that the union he wanted was anything more than a business arrangement at the end of the day, albeit one with the bonus of good sex. So what would happen when the good sex tapered off? Would she be left clinging to him? Hopeful that her love might spread to him like some sort of contagious virus?

By the end of the day she was exhausted from dashing around outside and was nursing a slight headache from her relentless analysing of everything. She wished that her brain had a switch, something she could conveniently turn off when it got too bothersome.

The house felt unbearably empty without Gabriel around and it depressed her to think how quickly she had become accustomed to his presence. She put Luke to bed and was further confronted with the reality of what Gabriel had told her because Luke was only marginally interested in having a story read to him. He was much more interested in trying to find out where Gabriel was and when he would be seeing him. She was beginning to realise that she and Luke were no longer a team of two. How would Luke react if Gabriel was no longer a constant in his life when they returned to England? He was only young now, but would he come to blame her in later years for depriving him of his father?

The magic of the island seemed to have disappeared now that Gabriel was no longer in the house and when she finally sat down to the simple crab salad which had been earlier prepared for her the food tasted like sawdust.

It was a relief when she heard the sound of the doorbell. For one glorious moment she wondered whether it was Gabriel. A cancelled meeting or, even more unbelievable, he was returning because he just couldn't be out of her company. That second thought she squashed with ruthless speed as she headed for the front door.

Both housekeepers had already left for the evening and far more likely it was one of them who had forgotten something. It was not that unusual an occurrence. They both had quarters at the house and Ana, particularly, was prone to forgetting some item of clothing or book or personal possession which she had left in her room.

But the interruption was a blessed relief from her thoughts and she was smiling as she pulled open the door halfway, looking forward to enticing whichever of the housekeepers it happened to be into some conversation. She had enjoyed practising her Spanish with both of them and was interested in their lives outside the splendid house.

In her head, there was no room for the unexpected and her shock at seeing Cristobel on her doorstep made her stumble backwards.

'You!'

'I know. I don't suppose you were expecting me.' She placed one hand on the door and Alex noticed that her nails were beautifully manicured and painted a vibrant shade of red. It was an insignificant detail but it distracted her momentarily from the nervous banging of her heart against her ribcage.

'What do you want?'

'To have a girlie chat, of course. What else?'

'I really don't think that Gabriel…'

'But Gabriel's not here, is he? He is in London.'

'How do you know that?'

'I don't *do* doorstep conversations.' Cristobel flashed her a cool smile and pushed against the door.

Of course Alex could have slammed the door in her face. She was, after all, a good six inches taller than the diminutive blonde. Taller, stronger but, unfortunately, she afterwards thought, lacking in the necessary aggression. Would Bambi have come out on top against a pit bull intent on destruction?

Okay, so she wasn't, an hour an a half later, having to apply plaster to open wounds, but her head was reeling.

She was surprised that she had managed to shove the thought of Gabriel's ex-fiancée to the back of her mind with such single-minded efficiency. She had no idea how she had been represented in the gossip columns. Newspapers had been non-existent for the past few weeks. She had cocooned herself in a bubble and, except for the occasional vague notion that *reality* was waiting *back home*, she had successfully managed to stifle anything too demanding.

Cristobel's appearance, she now thought, had brought all that up to the surface.

She had no idea where the other woman had gone after she had left the house and she didn't care. She had just wanted to be rid of the venomous blonde's presence, the blonde who had flicked her hair and looked at her with hard, bright eyes and told her that Gabriel had only hooked up with her through a misguided sense of duty, that his heart would always belong to *her*, that she would get him back and would have him in her bed just as soon as the whole *duty thing* wore off, because wear off it inevitably would.

'You may think that you've won,' she had said with a cool smile, while those diamond-hard eyes had given her the once-over and found her lacking in all the important departments, 'but you haven't. You haven't got the class or the looks to keep him and the fact that you haven't got an engagement ring on your finger is proof enough of that. A man like Gabriel might like tradition but playing happy families with a woman he doesn't give a damn about isn't his style. You might speak a little Spanish but you have a lot to learn about how a Spaniard thinks, especially a Spaniard like Gabriel.'

Replaying the conversation in her head, Alex groaned aloud and stuck buried her face in a pillow.

She wondered if it had been that final dig that had prompted her to say, with a calmness she hadn't imagined possible, 'Gabriel has already proposed. In fact, Gabriel has proposed more than once and, not that it's any of your business, we'll be getting married as soon as I return to England.' Well, it had been worth it to see that flash of anger that contorted Cristobel's beautiful face. She had almost been tempted to spin a fairy story about Gabriel being madly in love with her, but not even she could fashion a lie that was so outrageous.

Now, of course, she was left with the residue from that brief moment of retaliation but she began to wonder whether the thought of accepting his proposal hadn't been there, playing away at the back of her mind, since he had left, like the familiar strains of background music, just discernible but not jarring enough to require attention.

She rolled over onto her side, eyes wide open. With pernicious determination, she felt a little seed of hope bury itself inside her and take root.

Yes, she could think pessimistically about Gabriel's proposal. Yes, she could work herself up into a lather predicting worst case scenarios.

But she loved him and wasn't it possible that he might come to feel the same about her? He was attracted to her, there was no doubt about that, and if she continued to make herself exciting to him, then was it really inevitable that he would stray? Hadn't she read somewhere that men were creatures of habit? Or something like that?

She hurriedly closed her mind to the unlikely thought of Gabriel being a *creature of habit*.

In the morning, she would leave and head back to London with her mind made up.

Decision made, Alex found it difficult to sleep. Memories of Cristobel's attack on her were replaced by hungry curiosity as to how Gabriel would react to her acceptance of his proposal. Would he be relieved that he had finally won, got his own way? Or surprised that she had given up the fight at long last? Or would he be ecstatic and declare his undying love for her? That last improbable scenario kept her smiling for the remainder of the following day.

'I wish we weren't going back to London,' Luke complained as she tugged him through airport security. No private jet this time. She was leaving ahead of schedule so that she could surprise Gabriel and what kind of surprise would it be if she had to call him to sort out his jet?

'You'll be seeing your dad, though. Aren't you looking forward to that?'

Leading questions about Gabriel were always a sure fire way of captivating Luke's attention. He had developed an inexhaustible thirst to find out everything he could about his father, although this usually filtered down to awestruck eulogies about the guy who had already succeeded in filling the role of the strongest, fastest, cleverest dad, at least compared to the other dads he pulled out of the hat from his kindergarten class. Alex had met a couple of those particular dads in question and it was easy to understand why. How could the average man, hair thinning and stomach thickening, ever compare to Gabriel? The fact was that Gabriel towered above the average *human being*. He would always be the one outrunning the other dads in the fathers' race on sports days and grabbing the attention of every teacher at parents evenings.

Not too long ago, she would have found it impossible to associate Gabriel with stuff as tedious as school sports days and parents' evenings, but she had see him throw himself into the role of winning his son over. Whatever he did, he did with the full weight of his conviction. She guessed that would include everything that got thrown at him in terms of his duties as far as Luke was concerned.

Like the irrepressible force of a powerful undertow, this brought her thoughts right back to square one: how far would Gabriel go to complete the perfect husband role? He would move mountains for his son…but for *her*?

She would have to lay down one or two ground rules. Capitulation wouldn't be solely on his terms.

Arriving back in London was like suddenly finding herself flung head first into a prison cell from which she had temporarily been released. Even Luke appeared to have gone into a slump as he tightly clutched her hand through airport security. His interminable chatter had petered out to the occasional doleful and nostalgic remark about the beach or his precious kite, which he had been persuaded to leave behind due to lack of suitcase space, or the glorious big house belonging to his grandparents. Bracing talk about school the following Monday and his favourite, fish and chips, for dinner was greeted with lukewarm enthusiasm. Only the promise of phoning Gabriel met with a positive response, and since that was precisely what Alex was itching to do, she dialled Gabriel's number pretty much as soon as she had settled Luke in the sitting room with his favourite cartoon and a snack.

About to leave for a meeting, Gabriel recognised Alex's telephone number. Without skipping a beat, he told his secretary to cancel his meeting and, with experience born from long service, his secretary reached for her phone, also without skipping a beat.

Gabriel had been surprised to discover how much he enjoyed hearing her voice at the end of a line. He relaxed back into his leather chair and swivelled it round so that he was staring at the fairly boring panorama of grey sky, scudding clouds and tips of buildings.

'Am I interrupting you?'

'Wall to wall meetings,' Gabriel said, loosening his tie. 'But no big deal.' He wasn't going to be drawn into letting her think that she could do as she pleased. Work had always been the foundation of his life and, even if he had taken a break, a much needed break, for a short while, it was *still* the foundation of his life. It was what made him the success story he was today.

Women had never been allowed to overstep those boundaries and the fact that he had just cancelled his high level meeting for a phone call was testament to the fact that she occupied a special place. She was the mother of his son. He was quite pleased that, in a roundabout way, this seemed to elevate him to a flattering level.

'How is Luke? Is he missing me?' Then, before she could answer that, he continued in a roughened voice, 'Are *you* missing me? Would you be insulted if I told you that I had to take a very cold shower last night because I couldn't get you out of my head?'

How was it that the sound of his voice could do foolish things to her body? Her cheeks reddened and the telltale signs of that craving of hers spread through her body, leaving her damp and hot and flustered.

But she didn't intend to let that reduce her to a weak, stammering mess. She thought back to Cristobel and that hideous attack on her. Had she been telling the truth? Did Gabriel's heart really belong to the blonde? He had been drawn enough to her to propose marriage so that said *something*. And now here she was, on the brink of accepting his marriage proposal and, when she stripped away all the lust and sex, she was left with a business arrangement. Her return to London had been salutary in helping her remember that. As had Cristobel.

'I'm back in London, actually.'

Gabriel smiled slowly. Her return could only mean that she was lonely without him around and, despite the fact that he had never cared for the dependent, clingy type, he realised and accepted with stunning alacrity that Alex somehow didn't fall into this category.

'Where in London?'

'Where do you think, Gabriel? My house, of course.'

'We'll have to do something about that,' he murmured, half to himself.

'I'd like to talk to you, but not on the phone. Face to face. Would you be able to get away some time later this evening?'

'I can get away right now.'

'What about those wall to wall meetings?'

'You'd be surprised how flexible they could be.'

'No…' *Right now* seemed a little too sudden. 'I need to settle in for a bit. There's stuff to do around here.'

'Stuff to do? What stuff?' Gabriel frowned because *stuff* had never been offered up as an excuse not to see him by any woman.

'I need to get Luke changed and fed and I need to unpack and have a shower and wash my hair… Why don't you come around six-thirty? You can have some time with Luke and then we can…chat. I'll fix something to eat. Although I'm not sure what I've got in the fridge. Actually, I haven't got anything in the fridge. Maybe I could pop out and buy one or two things…'

'*I'll* bring something over!'

'You don't know what I need.'

'You need food. I'll bring food.'

'Okay.' She resisted the temptation to ask whether he knew where his local supermarket was and then concluded that he would probably send someone out to buy a few items on his behalf.

Would this be their life together? Extreme wealth and privilege that would inevitably remove Luke, and her, from the realms of the ordinary? Did she want that for her son? She realised that she didn't. She had had a richly, rewarding and very grounded upbringing and that was something she intended to confer upon her son.

'And I don't want to be fussy here,' she said, as gently as she could, predicting a blank wall of incomprehension that would greet her conditions, 'but Luke's had a pretty rich diet for the past few weeks. It would do him good to have simple home-cooked fare.'

'Okay. You're losing me here.' Gabriel raked his fingers through his hair and fought off a feeling of having suddenly been dumped in quicksand. He had no idea what she was talking about but, strangely enough, he would still have had the conversation, given the choice between that and his meeting. 'He's had the finest food money could buy in Spain. Pretty healthy too.' He frowned. 'I'm sure there was lots of fish.'

'Maybe you could just pick up some bread and butter and other essentials and some baked beans. Oh, and something simple for us to eat.'

'Simple like what?'

'I'll leave it up to you. Anyway, I think I hear Luke. I've left him in the sitting room watching a cartoon. He's missed that a bit, watching cartoons, I think… See you later.'

Gabriel gazed at the phone in stupefaction as he heard the distinctive sound of a disconnected line.

However, instead of fully appreciating the rest of his day and proceeding with the important business of running his empire, he managed to find himself wandering around a supermarket two hours later with a trolley and not much of an idea as to what to put in it.

At six-thirty, Alex opened the door to a dishevelled-looking Gabriel, still in his suit and holding three carrier bags with a couple more on the ground by his feet.

'I come complete with shopping. I can't overestimate that achievement, considering I had to battle with a trolley that seemed to have a mind of its own.' She looked fresh and clean and sexy-as-hell in a pair of old jogging bottoms and a T-shirt that barely skimmed her flat, tanned stomach.

'So I see. Come on in. Luke's been clamouring for you.'

She opened the door, feeling very ordinary next to him, and Luke bounded out behind her like an eager puppy hearing the sound of its master's footsteps. Several drawings were thrust at Gabriel, who looked at them with a gravity that thrilled Luke to death and made Alex smile because representational art was not exactly Luke's forte. Objects were pointed out with engaging earnestness and all adult conversation was lost in the deluge of excitable childish chatter.

'You bought the baked beans.' She held up a four pack and turned it around with an expression of mock wonder. 'I didn't think you'd remember.'

So it was baked beans on toast with cheese for Luke and only when he had finally been settled into bed did she and Gabriel reconvene in the kitchen.

Having felt calm and controlled amidst the chaos of having Luke around as the centre of attention, she was now very much aware of Gabriel's *presence*, that certain something he possessed that allowed him to own the space around him, and unfortunately her with it.

'You never answered my question…' His dark-as-night eyes roamed over her until she turned pink under the scrutiny.

'What question?'

'Did you miss me?'

Stupid question, Alex thought. *Did a fish miss water when it was removed from it?* He hadn't come any closer to her.

In fact, he had adopted a seat at the table while she remained standing, leaning against the kitchen counter, but she still felt as though she was being touched.

'Is sex all you think about?'

'It's definitely been on my mind pretty much since I returned to London.'

Alex wondered whether she should now be expected to simper with pleasure. She folded her arms and delivered a long, cool look which was like water off a duck's back, apparently, because Gabriel matched her look with an amused gleam in his eyes.

'Is the Ice Queen back in residence?'

'There's more to life than sex.'

'Really?' He threw her a wolfish grin. 'I wish you'd run those alternatives by me. I'm all ears.'

'For goodness' sake, Gabriel! You are *so* childish sometimes.'

'It's so refreshing being with a woman who feels free to criticise me,' he said with infuriating good humour. 'I didn't know what you wanted to eat, by the way, so I bought a variety of things.'

'So I saw.' She turned to glance at the improbable stack of items residing on her kitchen counter. Fresh tiger prawns and fillet steak nudged shoulders with lots of attractive jars and bottles containing interesting-sounding sauces whilst essentials such as eggs, milk and cheese had obviously not found favour, due to their lack of immediate sex appeal. She sighed. Even when it came to food, Gabriel would always make a beeline for whatever was easiest on the eye.

She began scrutinising the products and finally did the best she could with the prawns and whatever sauces seemed the least flamboyant.

'I've given a lot of thought to what you said about the benefits of getting married,' she said casually with her back to him, even though she could feel his eyes boring into her, making her clumsy with the knife.

'And...?' Gabriel found that he was holding his breath. Ridiculous.

'And I've decided that you're right.' *Keep it on a business level*, Alex reminded herself. *Use the language he understands.* She flicked on the stove, busying herself with heating the sauces, while her heart continued to pound like a jack hammer inside her.

Eventually, when she could no longer hide behind the business of stirring a sauce and watching a pot of pasta boil, she turned round to look at him.

God, why did he have to be so *beautiful*? He would object to that description, but he really was *beautiful* and that sheer overwhelming, masculine beauty made it doubly difficult to talk to him with the detachment she needed. She drew in a shaky breath and moved to sit opposite him.

'Good. I knew you would come to your senses sooner or later.'

'You've become an important part of Luke's life and it would be wrong to yank him away when he's become accustomed to you. In retrospect, it may have been a mistake to take that prolonged holiday in Spain. It might have been better for you to get to know him over here, on his own territory, where he could have maintained some kind of a distance...'

Gabriel's mouth tightened. 'Is it your mission,' he asked softly, 'to find things to say that enrage me?'

'Of course not!' And nor had she been fair. Didn't she *want* what was best for Luke? Those snatched weeks in Spain had been the happiest in her son's life. But somewhere inside her was the voice of self-protection telling her that she needed to make sure that Gabriel didn't think that he had scored a home run, that it was essential to maintain *some* distance between them, even if that distance was a front.

'I'm saying that I feel I've been put in the position where I haven't got much of a choice…'

'And I should feel better? Wrong choice of wording.'

'Sorry, but it's the truth.' She remembered Cristobel, the spurned ex-fiancée. She remembered his threats that he would find someone else if she walked away from him. Both were significant markers in indicating the direction she should choose to go and a complete cave-in wasn't on the signpost.

Gabriel raked his fingers through his hair and gave her a dark, fulminating look. 'I don't want to have an argument with you,' he told her with what he considered considerable self-restraint. 'You have made me very happy in agreeing to be my wife. We should be celebrating.' He stood up and fetched them both glasses. He had bought three bottles of wine. He opened the Chablis now and poured them both a glass, while she set the plates on the table in silence, thinking about phase two of what she needed to say.

'Okay,' Alex cleared her throat and gazed down at the food, which looked unappetising, despite the *no expense spared* approach to food shopping Gabriel had clearly taken. She sipped some of the wine, which was delicious. 'There are just a few ground rules I think we need to get straight before we go ahead with this…um…plan…'

Gabriel frowned. He didn't care for the word *plan*, even though he would have been the first to admit that marriage as a sensible merger had always been his way forward. He had become engaged to Cristobel because it had made sense at the time, and he had proposed to Alex because of the situation in which he had found himself. He was programmed into the ways of tradition. It would have been unthinkable to have continued his relationship with Cristobel, given the circumstances. On every front, he would readily have admitted that marrying Alex was the most logical, indeed inevitable, course of action. But, somehow, he didn't like to think that she was beginning to see it his way. It was a thought that confused him.

'*Ground rules?* What *ground rules*? We're not planning a military campaign.'

'I used to think that marriage was all about romance but now I realise that it's all about a sensible outcome. I realised that in Spain when I saw how happy Luke was, having both parents on tap. He's only young now, but that will become more and more important the older he gets. I never thought I'd agree with you when you first asked me to marry you because it made sense. I couldn't think of marriage to anyone in terms of a balance sheet but…' she shrugged and looked away '…you were right and I was wrong.'

Gabriel wondered how it was that being right sounded so pointless. Hadn't he got what he had wanted? Yes, he had! He focused on that and shook off his feelings of dissatisfaction.

This didn't seem to be the right conclusion to good news. Shouldn't they be making love right about now?

'What,' Alex asked with genuine curiosity, 'turned you off the concept of marrying for love? I mean, your parents are so happy and so in love with one another…'

'…That it should have washed off on me somehow?' Gabriel flushed darkly. He had always felt the weight of expectation on his shoulders. That he would fall madly in love, get married and live in perfect bliss with a litter of kids until the day he died. 'I left home at sixteen to board and then university here and, except for a few breaks in between…' one of them being the very break that had landed him in this situation '…I was destined to carry the weight of my father's legacy on my shoulders. At the time, it was going through some financial troubles. Appalling management in some of its branches.

Trouble with unions in other parts. I buried myself deep in my work. There was a lot to do and I was surrounded by other people who were similarly committed to long hours and one hundred per cent dedicated service to the various companies. You'd be surprised how many marriages fall by the wayside when there's no husband in evidence for little Johnny's prize-giving. You can say that that was more of a learning curve for me than my parents' blissful contentment.'

'That's terrible,' Alex murmured, truly shocked. 'What's the point in working twenty-four hours a day when you haven't got the time to enjoy the fruits of your labours?'

'Spare me the philosophizing.' Gabriel shifted uncomfortably and shot her a veiled, brooding look because he had heard that refrain a thousand times from his mother until she had eventually given up.

'So what's the point in getting married if you're never going to be around for Luke anyway?'

'Look, shall we go and discuss this somewhere a little more comfortable? These chairs aren't meant for a guy as big as me.'

Which had the immediate effect of distracting Alex in mid-flow as her gaze travelled over him, taking in his drop dead good looks and the spread of his muscular thighs on the small chair.

When she raised her flustered eyes to him, he was grinning at her. 'So,' he drawled, 'where does the good sex feature in this business deal you've agreed to?'

'I...I know what you're trying to do...' Alex licked her lips nervously and wondered at the speed with which she had been derailed.

'What's that?'

'You're trying to distract me.'

'By telling you that I'm not very comfortable in this Goldilocks chair?' To emphasise his point, he shifted and then stood up to flex his muscles. He had rolled up the sleeves of his white work shirt and Alex stared weakly and compulsively at the dark hair on his forearms.

'I was saying…'

'I heard you. You think I'll stick a wedding band on your finger and then disappear back off to work, only to resurface when my son's due to graduate from university.' He took the two steps needed to get to where she was sitting with an expression of rigid intent that Gabriel found strangely cute and endearing, and he bent over to support himself on the arms of her chair.

'You underestimate your pulling power, my darling,' he murmured, stroking her with his voice until her face was red-hot.

'What…what do you mean?'

'You know exactly what I mean. You just want to hear me say it. Shall I tell you, my darling, so that you're in no doubt? Or I could just…' he lowered himself so that he was kneeling in front of her '…show you…hmm…? Do you like me like this…? On my knees in front of you…?'

Alex bit down on the whimper that threatened to escape and tried to give him a stern look, but he was already insinuating himself between her legs and playing with the soft cotton of her T-shirt. When his fingers brushed against the bare skin of her breast, she gasped and half closed her eyes.

'You remembered…' He shoved up the T-shirt and felt the swift kick of hungry craving.

'Remembered what…?'

'How much I like it when you don't wear a bra. I love your breasts. Have I told you that before? But I think I might have forgotten what they taste like…'

'Gabriel!' Alex said in a desperate voice. 'I'm trying to *talk*…'

'And I'm listening. Really. I'm all ears. Don't mind me.' He delicately tickled the erect bud of her nipple with the tip of his tongue and when she squirmed and moaned softly, he had to struggle to contain himself.

'The door…'

'I'll close it.' He quietly shut the kitchen door and then stood for a few seconds, just looking at her sprawled in the chair, with her rucked T-shirt and the glistening disc of her nipple where he had been licking it. Her eyes were half closed and she was breathing softly.

Talk or no talk, she had agreed to be his wife and he savoured the taste of sweet elation as he strolled lazily to continue what he had started.

CHAPTER NINE

'WE STILL need to talk.' Alex felt that she had let the side down by falling at the first hurdle and making love with him. How could she have the serious talk she had intended on having when his legs were wrapped around hers and the covers were half off their bodies and she could only vaguely remember making her way up the stairs with him to her bedroom?

One minute she was busily trying to get a grip on the situation and the very next minute she had sabotaged her own good intentions and fallen back into bed with him when he'd crooked his finger and given her that smile of his that could unravel every thought in her head. The devastating effect he had had on her senses the first time round was nothing compared to the effect he was capable of having on her now. She closed her eyes in resigned despair as he pushed back her hair and deposited a kiss on her forehead.

'So we do. You can't accuse me of not being willing to listen.'

'How could I have a conversation when you were… were…?'

'Having fun with you?' Gabriel laughed throatily, his good humour fully restored after an hour and a half of very satisfying lovemaking. He slipped his hand under the bed cover and idly toyed with her breast, liking the way it responded to his teasing fingers, even though they were both too spent at the moment to take that teasing touch any further.

'There are a few conditions to my marrying you, Gabriel.' Somehow it didn't feel right to be having this kind of conversation when she was lying naked next to him, nor did she want to spoil the atmosphere of contentment between them but she knew the sort of man he was, the sort who would take her acquiescence for granted and expect her to do as she was told the minute that wedding ring was on her finger. Right now, she had a certain power over him because he fancied her but that power had a time limit and it was important for her to speak her mind now. Or forever, she thought with ironic humour, hold her peace.

'*Conditions?* What are you talking about? What kind of *conditions*?' He propped himself up on his elbow and looked at her with a perplexed frown.

'I don't want to live in London. I gave it a try because I felt that I had to escape and do something for myself after I had Luke and was back on my feet, but I prefer living in the country. I'm not saying that I want to move back to Ireland or anything like that, but I'd like to have some greenery around. Maybe somewhere just outside London so that it wouldn't be too much of a headache for you to commute in.'

'Agreed.'

'You agree? Just like that?'

'Do you think it might be more fun if I argued? Granted, make up sex can be good but it's not worth the effort in this instance.' Gabriel lay back, hands folded behind his head and stared up at the ceiling. Being the dispenser of someone else's wishes felt good and, whilst he had never, not even for a passing second, considered living anywhere but in the thick of it, the prospect of a slightly less frenetic pace of life was not necessarily a bad thing. Train links into central London were quick and Luke would benefit from country living. What kid wouldn't? Fresh air, open spaces…all that corny stuff countryphiles were ever eager to mouth on about now seemed a good idea.

'What sort of house did you have in mind? Country manor? Thatched cottage? No, maybe not that. Converted chapel? Georgian splendour? Give me some details and I can get my people working on it.'

Alex was torn between amusement and annoyance. In Gabriel's world, where having exactly what you wanted was only the snap of a finger away, choosing a house would really not even constitute a minor inconvenience. People to source the right one in the right place, whatever the cost and just maybe one viewing so that the box could be ticked and the green light given.

'Which brings me to my next condition,' Alex said carefully, which earned her another frowning glance.

'What is this?' Gabriel asked, controlling his irritation with difficulty. 'A lesson for me on how to jump through hoops? I should tell you that that particular form of exercise isn't something I plan on getting used to.'

'Marriage is about compromise. I happen to be compromising a lot to marry you because I think it would be right for Luke.' That sounded a great deal more noble than it felt because she couldn't think of a single thing she wouldn't toss to the four winds for the man lying next to her. 'And I want him to be brought up with the values I grew up with,' she continued hurriedly. 'Respect for other people and determination to work hard. I don't want him thinking that he's better than anyone else because his father happens to have a bit of money.'

'I have more than a bit.'

'Having a house appear out of nowhere, like magic, isn't the right way for him to start learning those life lessons.'

'You are the most difficult woman in the world to please! You want to move to the country. I agree. But that's not enough.' He leapt out of bed and Alex sat up in consternation.

'Where are you going?'

'To take a shower.'

'But I'm talking to you!'

'You're not talking to me!' Gabriel headed towards the connecting door to her en suite bathroom, the single most important luxury Alex had looked for when she had bought the house. 'You're laying down rules and regulations.'

'That's what people do with business arrangements!'

'Since when does sex enter a business arrangement?' Gabriel threw over his shoulder and she glared at him because, even when she was mad at him, she still found him so sinfully sexy that she could barely take her eyes off him.

'It's called fringe benefits.'

Gabriel would have slammed the bathroom door behind him but Luke would probably come flying into the bedroom from the sound of it reverberating through the tiny house and there was no way that he wanted his son to see him in this mood. *Business arrangement! Fringe benefits!* He found both descriptions outrageously offensive, even though he was pretty sure he had used those terms himself in the past.

'That's not the language I expect any woman of mine to use,' he informed her coldly, before shutting the bathroom door behind him.

It took a few seconds before Alex was galvanised into action and she scrambled off the bed, hastily flinging on underwear, her T-shirt and a pair of stretchy drawstring shorts from a drawer before pushing open the bathroom door and being greeted by a wall of condensation.

'I'm sorry you don't like the language I use—' her voice was trembling and her knuckles were white as she gripped the sides of the toilet seat, which was the only place to sit in the small bathroom '—but I'm trying really hard to get a perspective on this.' Did he think that, because she fell into his arms, her principles would also obey the same laws and collapse without putting up a fight? 'I don't want something as big as a house purchase to be without our involvement. Luke should have a say in the kind of home we're going to provide for him and so should I. Money might be a convenience but time is priceless and that's what I want you to put into this marriage. I know it's going to be difficult for you because you're accustomed to doing exactly what you want but…' Her voice was suddenly very loud as the shower was switched off and Gabriel stepped out of the cubicle, which he dwarfed.

He took his time drying and then slung the towel around his waist. 'I have taken more time off in the past few weeks than I ever have in my whole life.' Except when he had first met her. He had behaved out of character then as well. 'And, if it means so much to you, then we can look for a house together.'

Alex smiled with relief and followed him out of the room. 'That's great. So…'

'*So…*?' Having brought no clothes with him, he contented himself with a baggy old bathrobe of hers which was hanging on a hook behind the door, then he took a seat at her dressing table and folded his arms. If getting her on board meant listening to everything she had to say, then so be it, but he didn't intend to be a pushover.

'There's just one more thing.'

'Just the *one more*? I'm shocked. I thought we were here for the rest of the night with your list of provisos and conditions.'

Alex flushed. 'It concerns other women.'

'Other women?' Gabriel couldn't believe what he was hearing. He realised that the thought of another woman hadn't actually crossed his mind since he had met Alex again after all this time.

'Yes. Other women. You have to promise me that there won't be any.'

'What kind of a promise is that?' Gabriel threw his hands up in the air in a gesture of frustration. He had had a lifetime of doing exactly what he wanted when it came to the opposite sex. He had power, money, good looks and status and that had all been enough to ensure compliance in the female sex. Even Cristobel had recognised his boundaries and had steered clear of them. He felt his hackles rise at the thought of someone dictating what he could or couldn't do. The question of whether he wanted to or not didn't come into it.

What sort of loser tolerated a woman dictating his every movement? Certainly not him!

'I think if we're to take this whole thing seriously, then...'

'This is getting more ridiculous by the minute. Who knows what's going to happen in the future? Do you think I have a crystal ball stashed away somewhere?'

Alex shook her head mutely. It had been a stupid request but his refusal to give it house room was telling. This wasn't a guy who loved her and would be overjoyed to forswear all other women. Duty to his son might run bone-deep but he had no responsibilities to *her*.

Could she marry someone who would be a hero, but only when on show?

She thought back to Cristobel, to her smug, sly, knowing smile when she had explained to Alex that Gabriel was a Spaniard, that sooner or later he would find his eyes straying, that that was to be expected.

She thought back to what he had told her, that if she didn't marry him then he would inevitably take his attentions elsewhere. She remembered all too well the sick, cloying feeling that had generated in her. Right now, Gabriel wanted her physically. It was a bonus to a marriage which, in his eyes, was the inevitable consequence of their situation.

But Gabriel was a man accustomed to variety. He lived life in the fast lane and the past few weeks spent with her and his son were probably the most normal he had ever had. He had made a huge effort to spend time with them, had set aside his compulsion to work and had condensed his essential business conversations to those times when she was either asleep or else involved with Luke. It would have constituted a big sacrifice and yet, here she was, like an unwelcome drill sergeant, dishing out orders and expecting obedience.

In her desperation to build up her defences and set some rules that might erect walls around her vulnerable core, she had overlooked one very important thing. Gabriel didn't take orders and certainly not from a woman to whom he had no bone-deep emotional connection. They were bound together by Luke but a child could only provide so much glue to a relationship.

And didn't she want this marriage to work? Wasn't that why she had raced back to London so that she could accept his proposal?

From her muddled train of thought there slowly emerged the clarity of her options. She could either love Gabriel in silence and wait hopelessly for the day when he got bored of her or she could do her damnedest to *make* him love her. She could be a passive victim or she could fight for her man.

Yes, it was galling to think that all those sweet dreams of a guy who would fly to the moon and back for her were no longer on the cards, but whoever said that love was a walk in the park? She had loved Gabriel years ago and it had got her nowhere and here she was again, loving him even more, and, unless she did her own groundwork, it would get her nowhere in the end again.

She drew in a deep shaky breath and eventually gave him a rueful, conciliatory smile.

'You're right. It was crazy of me to ask the impossible of you.'

'Are you saying that you don't think me capable of fidelity?' Gabriel growled aggressively and Alex bit back the temptation to tell him what a *difficult* man he could be. His personality was one of extremes. It was why she loved him. He made her feel alive.

'I wish you wouldn't put words in my mouth, Gabriel. I never said that.'

Gabriel ignored that interruption. 'No. But you imply that I am the sort of man who would marry a woman and then proceed to bring a harem of mistresses into the marital home. In front of my son!'

'You look really silly in that bathrobe,' Alex said, to defuse the tension.

'You're trying to change the subject.'

'I'm trying to tell you that it was a stupid condition and I shouldn't have said anything.'

Never one to dwell on imaginary scenarios, Gabriel's mind did a swift detour and began to rocket down an altogether different road. 'Is this whole fidelity issue your way of looking for some kind of excuse to have outside relationships?'

'What?'

'You heard me. I'm not going to repeat myself.'

'Of course that wasn't what I was implying! I'm not that devious!' Alex tried and failed to get her head round the concept of having another guy share her bed. 'But if I *did*,' she couldn't resist adding, 'would you be jealous?'

It was one of those rare instances when Gabriel felt put on the spot and he instinctively shied away from committing himself to any kind of answer.

'I am not a jealous man. I never have been.'

But you would be if you loved me, Alex thought sadly, pinning a brave smile to her face.

'Okay.'

'Which isn't to say that I'm not possessive.' He thought it better to clear up that little issue, once and for all. 'If I thought that you had even looked at another guy when you were wearing my ring on your finger, I would beat him to a pulp.' A red mist descended on him when he thought of her with someone else and he expertly fielded that uncomfortable thought by shoving it to the back of his mind.

That was something, she thought, with a definite lift of her spirits.

'I'm glad we cleared the air,' she confessed, walking towards him. She reached out and clasped her hands behind his neck. 'It's good to talk.'

Gabriel grunted and she perched on his lap and slipped her hand under the fold of the bathrobe.

'You should keep some clothes here.'

'Why? You won't be here much longer.' The feel of her fingers splayed on his chest was doing decidedly pleasant things to other parts of his body.

On this front, at least, Alex was assured of her power over him, temporary though it might be. Just so long as he desired her, he would not have eyes for anyone else. Gabriel, if nothing else, was a one woman man.

'True,' she conceded. 'I'll break the news to my folks tomorrow.'

'And we can make this legal by the end of next week.'

'Why so soon?'

Good question, Gabriel thought. She wasn't the blushing bride with his baby inside her, rushing down the aisle to seal the deal before the baby was born.

'Why not?' he answered smoothly. 'I'm not someone who enjoys delay once I'm committed in a certain direction. Besides, the faster you leave this dump, the better for all concerned.'

'We could just move in with you and take it slowly until we find our feet.'

'No can do.' Gabriel was a little disconcerted at just how much he really *didn't* want that outcome.

'Oh. Forgot. Demands of tradition.'

'That's right. *Demands of tradition.* Not that you won't be moving in with me as soon as possible. In fact, I can arrange for everything to be completed by tomorrow evening.'

'There you go. Not consulting me again.'

'Do you ever agree to anything without putting up a fight?' He shifted her, settling her comfortably on his hard body, letting her know how much he wanted her.

'Would you prefer me to be grateful and submissive?'

'Is that a serious question?'

Alex realised that it was and she was strangely relieved when he said, with an amused smile, 'If you were grateful and submissive, I wouldn't know what had hit me. I would have to take you to a doctor to get you checked over.'

'I find gratitude and submission hard to do,' she conceded truthfully. 'I bet Cristobel was grateful and submissive.' She could have kicked herself for bringing that contentious subject to the table.

'She was...obedient. I've since discovered that obedience is not all that it's made out to be when it comes to women. Not enough of a challenge.'

Alex was busily wondering whether being described as *challenging* was a good thing or a bad thing when Gabriel interrupted her furious musings.

'And, while we're on the subject of rules and conditions, I have a few of my own…'

'Am I going to like them?' she asked cautiously. She gasped as his hand found her breast and he played with it, rolling his finger over her erect nipple and sending shivers of excitement through her.

'First of all, you're going to have to dress the part of my wife.'

'You can't be serious.'

'Deadly serious.'

Alex envisaged smart designer wear and diamonds the size of eggs on her fingers and shuddered. She had seen Cristobel in action. An advert for everything money could possibly buy. The woman had dripped jewellery and screamed *designer*. Every inch of her had been polished, buffed and preened to expensive perfection.

'I can't.'

'What's that supposed to mean? Can I remind you of the compromise conversation you insisted on having earlier?'

'I can't turn into a decorative Christmas bauble for your benefit, Gabriel.'

'What the hell are you talking about?'

'Bejewelled up to the eyeballs…long red talons for nails… big coiffured hair, lacquered to within an inch of its miserable life…'

Gabriel threw back his head and laughed and he laughed even harder when he saw her frowning, disdainful expression. Of one thing he was in no doubt—Alex was not impressed by his vast wealth. In fact, he would have wagered his soul that if she had met him all those years ago and had known the vast legacy that was his birthright, she would have turned on her rubber-soled trainers and stomped off.

'I haven't got sufficient imagination to picture you… What was it…? *Bejewelled up to the eyeballs*…? With long red nails and big hair…?'

'I've seen your ex-fiancée in action,' Alex retorted tartly. 'And I'm not going blonde either. I never held with the myth that they have more fun.'

'I'd never ask you to go blonde. And, before you launch into another wild interpretation of what I want, all I'm saying is that when you're my wife…no, let's just say from the second you set foot out of the house tomorrow…no revealing clothes. No tight dresses, no handkerchiefs for skirts…' He wasn't sure when it had hit him that he didn't want other men ogling her, but hit him it had and, since she felt free and easy to lay down her laws, then two could play at that game.

'I don't own any tight dresses.'

'Good! Then no change there would work for me.'

'I can't remember Cristobel dressing like a frump.' Alex frowned, bewildered by this proviso. 'In fact, when I went shopping with her that time, I seem to recall that she was dressed in a very, very revealing outfit. Right down to the killer heels.'

'Not sure where you're going with this…'

'How come there's one rule for her and another rule for me?'

'Like I said…I'm possessive when it comes to you. Learn to live with it.'

Never having had a devious bone in her body, Alex blushed as she entered a large tick in the column in her head that was dedicated to winning Gabriel over. He might not love her in the same way that she loved him, but possessiveness was a far cry from indifference. Plus, he hadn't been possessive when it came to Cristobel. That had to say something.

'Okay,' she said airily. 'I'm not into all that girlie dressing for men stuff, anyway…'

'Oh, I wouldn't take it too far,' Gabriel murmured. 'You can dress in anything you want, but for my eyes only. Or,' he continued, shoving up her top and losing himself in the sight of her fabulous breasts, 'you can dress in nothing at all.' He could no longer resist and an arrow of pure burning white heat shot through her as he took one nipple into his mouth and proceeded to suckle it with lazy, concentrated intensity. As if suckling that nipple was the only thing in the world he wanted to do at that precise moment in time.

Except it wasn't, as he laid down his number two condition. Which was her duty as his wife to make sure that he was satisfied at all times.

With any other man, this would have been a breathtakingly chauvinistic statement and one which would have had Alex's hackles rising but she was ashamed of the flood of warmth that invaded her body at his boldly assertive declaration.

It might seem crude to wage war on a man's defences through sex but Gabriel was a highly sexual man and the longer she kept him entertained in that department, the more time she had to win him over in the department that really mattered. And entertaining him in that department, she sheepishly acknowledged to herself, was never going to be a sacrifice, was it? One touch from him and she melted like tinder in an inferno.

She would learn how to cook as well. Wasn't that other route to a man's heart through his stomach? They did an awful lot of eating out and she couldn't picture Gabriel as the sort of man who had ever spent time encouraging his women to read recipe books so that they could whip him up some paella like his mother used to make. The opposite, in fact. But, as his wife, surely that wouldn't be a bad idea? Surely domesticity could creep up on him and stage an invasion before he knew what was happening to him?

If nothing worked, if lust turned out to be a passing pleasure and Luke was really and truly the only reason he would stay with her, then he would eventually stray but she didn't want to think about that. She made love with the passion of sheer optimism and, afterwards, enjoyed the contentment of just lying in his arms and hearing the soft beating of his heart.

'What are your thoughts on home-cooked food?' she asked dreamily.

'I can't say I have any,' Gabriel replied with lazy amusement.

'Why do you think that is?' She shifted on to one elbow and tried very hard not to look at him with puppy dog eyes. The irony of knowing just how thorough her U-turn had been didn't escape her. Not only had she descended from her unassailable position of wanting to stand firm and maintain a healthy distance from the guy who had lied to her and subsequently dumped her, she had positively burnt the map so that she could never, ever find her way back to that safe place again.

'Why cook meals when someone else can cook them better in a restaurant? I know where this is going,' he added dryly, and Alex feigned bewilderment. 'Don't worry. You don't want Luke to have a precious upbringing. I get it. I agree with you. I'll hire a cook. No problem.'

Alex smiled, unwilling to become embroiled in a circuitous argument about what constituted a *precious upbringing* and what didn't. She was amused that Gabriel's solution to the dilemma of eating out wasn't a loyalty card to a supermarket but hiring a chef. He inhabited a different world to the one she knew but, bit by bit, she would make inroads into his world and change him.

His mobile gave its sharp intrusive buzz and he picked up the call, turning away from her and speaking in rapid Spanish. Business. She half listened to the conversation, bored by talk of share options and cost projections. She let her mind wander pleasantly and tried not to run her hands along his back in a nauseatingly loving manner. Thinking of herself as controlling the situation did her no end of good but she was still bitterly disappointed when he ended his call and turned to her with a regretful expression.

'Crisis at work, *cara*. I know you'd rather I was around twenty-four seven but…' he shrugged and smiled ruefully '…I'm going to have to fly to New York for a few days. Might even be as long as a week.'

Alex laughed and raked her fingers through her short dark hair, ruffling it so that it stood up in boyish spikes.

'What makes you think that I want you around twenty-four seven?'

Gabriel frowned. 'Your little speech about wanting me to spend time with you?'

'Time with *Luke*.' She beamed at him. However rosy her plans were for capturing him, she still didn't intend for him to think that she was on her hands and knees begging for scraps of his attention. 'So you can put that gigantic ego of yours away. Actually, I'm perfectly happy in your absence. I can start doing a little packing, just books and ornaments and stuff. I won't look for a job yet if we might be moving further out of London. Hmm. Maybe,' she mused aloud, 'I'll go visit my family in Ireland. Mum's been complaining that she misses Luke and I can tell them about the wedding plans first-hand.'

Gabriel was disconcerted to feel a twinge of annoyance at this sudden, cheerfully independent plan of action. Of course it made perfect sense for her to talk to her family face to face! She was very close to them.

'You'll have to give me your landline there.' He squashed the ridiculous notion that he wanted her to be there at his beck and call and certainly not grinning when he told her that he was going to be out of the country.

'Why? I'll take my mobile.'

'No can do. You're not good at remembering to charge it. What if I need to get in touch with you?'

Alex shrugged and rattled off her parents' telephone number although, at the end of it, went on to say that she might change her mind.

'Woman's prerogative. I might just get Mum and Dad to come down to London. They haven't been in ages. So I'm not sure. I'll let you know.' Another broad smile.

Gabriel grunted. His timescale for the wedding was shortening by the second. He didn't like this house. He didn't like the fact that he had to trek halfway across London to see his son, particularly as he had become accustomed to having him around. And he didn't like Alex thinking that she could skip around wherever and whenever she wanted like a single girl. Which she wasn't. Who knew if there was some guy lurking back in her home town? Naturally, he wasn't going to express any concern in that area but, if she was married, there would be none of this nonsense. He decided that he would cut short his trip to New York by a day or two. There was no need for him to sit in on every single meeting and hold Edwards's hand. Time the man stepped up to the mark.

Alex surreptitiously looked at him, proud that she had put on such a good show of not looking deflated at the thought of him leaving the country. The less dependent she was, the more he would respect her and the more he respected her, the more her value would rise. She was sure of it.

And, when he returned, she would welcome him with open arms. And Luke would be there with his floppy dark hair and his winning smile. And she would cook something, although she would take care not to make a great big deal of it. Just something hot and homely and heartwarming.

And she really would have, but something was slipped under her door two days later that would blow all her plans to smithereens…

CHAPTER TEN

THE neatly clipped newspaper page was accompanied by a saccharine note that read: *I thought you should see this*. Alex had just dropped Luke off to his playgroup and done some shopping; the envelope lying on the mat inside the door must have been hand-delivered. She stared at the picture for ages, during which time life seemed to slow to a standstill.

Gabriel was, as always, distinctive, his proud, arrogant head inclined down towards Cristobel's uplifted face. Had Cristobel delivered the clipping? Of course she had! Who else? It was from an American tabloid. What had she been doing in New York? Suddenly a host of sickening doubts and misgivings rushed through Alex like a swarm of locusts, devouring everything in its path. She dumped the shopping bags on the floor and sat down so that she could give the picture one hundred per cent of her attention.

Gabriel had spoken to her on the telephone twice since he had left the country and she had spent ages talking to him, chatting about nothing in particular, content to enjoy the rich, lazy drawl of his voice and to hear about what he had been doing. Now she wondered whether Cristobel had been in the hotel room whilst he had made those calls. Maybe she had been tapping her long scarlet nails and looking at her diamond watch as she had impatiently waited for him to wrap it up.

In complete turmoil, Alex found that she couldn't concentrate at all for the remainder of the day. She had intended to start packing away some of her possessions, boxing up the ones she would take with her to her new house. Her new life! Now, it all seemed pointless. She would have fought tooth and nail to turn her charade of a marriage into something meaningful, but seeing that picture of Cristobel with Gabriel had shown her that there was nothing to fight over and to carry on kidding herself otherwise would have reduced her to the level of a joke.

She wondered if she should just pack her bags and return to Ireland. Should she? What would be the point of that? Gabriel would find her and he wouldn't be pleased.

It was all too easy to project a scenario in which Gabriel hunted her down and used his mighty power and influence to take Luke away from her. Would he do that? Previously she would have sworn with one hand on the Bible that he would never have been capable of any such thing, but just how well did she know him? Hadn't her very first meeting with him been based on a lie? Hadn't he manipulated a situation years ago because it had suited him at the time? He had pretended to be someone he wasn't and he had told her that it was because anonymity had given him a taste of freedom for a while but couldn't it equally have been true that he had sussed her within seconds and realised that she wasn't the kind of girl who found rich, spoiled men attractive? And so he had cleverly *dropped the trappings and adopted a different cover?*

Alex hated thinking like that, but she couldn't deny the grainy photo of Gabriel and Cristobel together. The bags of shopping, lots of food items in preparation for the Domestic Goddess she was to become, lay on the floor cruelly mocking her fanciful, pie-in-the-sky dreams.

By seven that evening she was ready for bed and was so spent from her troubled thoughts that she failed to stir when the phone rang at ten. And rang. And rang.

Frustrated, Gabriel raked his fingers through his hair and stared at his mobile. No reply from the landline and her cell-phone was switched off. He had never met a woman who was so disorganised when it came to her mobile phone. It was seldom charged and, when it was, it was continually programmed on silent so that phone calls were routinely missed because she couldn't hear it ring and, when she did hear it, locating the thing in her oversized bag was an accomplishment based solely on luck.

He would have to phone her in the morning. He would never have credited it, but whereas women had always run a poor second to work, Alex seemed to fly in the face of this immutable truth. He thought about her way too much when she wasn't around and especially now, when Cristobel had appeared on the scene because she *just happened to be doing some shopping in New York and had heard that he was around from his secretary*. Out of a misplaced sense of good manners and residual guilt, he had taken her to dinner and had had a first hand opportunity to see for himself just how inconsequential Cristobel had been to him. It astounded him that he had ever found himself drifting into an engagement to her. For someone who prided himself on his astute judgement and razor-sharp acumen, he realised that he had very nearly sleep-walked himself into the worst situation of his life.

He had been struck by a strong sense of gratitude that he now had Alex and Luke in his life. Frankly, he found it difficult to remember a time when he didn't, which was weirdly comforting and confusing at the same time.

When, the following day, he tried calling again, this time at six in the morning, when she surely could be nowhere else but in the house, and received no answer, a sense of foreboding edged its way past his initial concern.

He had a series of meetings lined up and he did his best to concentrate on the business of sealing this deal, but his thoughts were elsewhere.

Had she decided to go and visit her parents in Ireland? On the spur of the moment, he dialled the landline number she had given him and the phone was answered by a woman who confirmed that her parents were away and wouldn't be back for another week. He had to cut short a rambling description of where they had gone and how long overdue the holiday had been.

Never again would Gabriel underestimate the power of his imagination. Unable to get through to her, he could only think that a disaster had occurred. His palms grew clammy and he began to feel sick as he thought of various scenarios involving hospitals and emergency rooms. Had Luke been taken ill? Surely Alex would have called him immediately if that had been the case? The answer to that was yes. With lightning speed, his thoughts veered off that train of thought to a more likely one: Alex had had an accident of some sort and had been unable to get through to him.

Once planted in his head, he was unable to shake the feeling that something was disastrously wrong.

Gabriel was not of the temperament to sit around twiddling his thumbs and stressing and he was honest enough to admit that no amount of high level meetings had the power to distract. He was a man of action and, in a move that would have shocked anyone who knew him well, he delegated the remainder of what needed doing to the members of the board who had accompanied him on the trip to New York. He had always been pivotal in any talks of strategic importance but he had to concede that if the deal fell through, then the deal fell through. No amount of success in this matter was worth the way his mind was going off the rails.

Not for the first time, he missed the availability of *Concorde* for transatlantic speed. However, his name carried sufficient weight to ensure that he was sitting in the next available first class cabin leaving New York.

He would have had a very hard time admitting it to anyone, but he felt out of control and he breathed a sigh of relief when the plane finally landed at Heathrow.

In possession of hand luggage only, he was out of the airport in record time and heading for her house without bothering to detour past his apartment.

Three loud bangs on the door had Alex almost spilling the cup of coffee she had made, her first for the day. In an effort to conceal her terrible frame of mind, she had spent the past day and a half over-compensating with Luke and had had a hellish time trying to settle him in bed after two bowls of ice cream and a chocolate bar. She knew that Gabriel had been trying to get hold of her and she had taken care to ignore his persistent ringing because she just didn't trust herself not to lash out at him. He had also tried her mobile. She had seen the missed calls and had erased them, furious with herself for having got herself all tangled up again, just like she had before, hopelessly loving a guy who was so bad for her.

Her whole body tensed with shock as she pulled open the door to find Gabriel standing in front of her, the lines of his strong face tense.

'Gabriel! What are you doing here? You're not due back for a couple of days…' Her voice trailed off as he strode past her into the small hallway, turning at the bottom of the stairs to look at her with a dark, shuttered expression.

Alex quietly shut the door and leaned against it. She hadn't had time to brace herself to face him. Now, she was all over the place. Her heart was hammering inside her and she had broken out in a fine film of nervous perspiration. Why had he returned early? Surely it had something to do with Cristobel. The coincidence was just too uncanny otherwise.

'I've been trying to get through to you,' Gabriel said tightly. He stared at her across the width of the hall, his keen dark eyes taking in her nerves and wondering what the hell was going on.

'Yes, I know.'

'You knew but you chose not to take my calls?'

'Have you come straight from the airport? Why?'

Relief that she was all right, as was Luke, or she would have said something, mingled now with anger and a certain amount of confusion.

'I…was worried about you both,' Gabriel said heavily. 'Can you blame me? I was thousands of miles away, with no idea what was going on over here.'

'Sorry,' Alex mumbled, looking down at her silly bedroom slippers. Even with her mind doing crazy loops in her head and her heart splintering into a thousand pieces, she was still aware of the fact that she would have changed into something a little more attractive had she known that he was going to descend on her. Instead, she was wearing her oldest track pants and a T-shirt with a comical motif that had faded to the point of obscurity after a million washes.

'So?' he prompted harshly, because she appeared to have frozen into immobility. 'Care to tell me what's going on? I dropped everything to get over here.'

Alex thought of him abandoning his meetings and his conferences so that he could fly back to London and fought against that desperate treacherous tendency to read something significant into his behaviour.

'Maybe we should go into the sitting room,' she mumbled, edging away from the front door with her arms firmly folded in front of her.

'Not until you tell me what's going on. I worked out it couldn't be Luke or you would have picked up my calls. Which led me to think that something might have happened to you.'

'Something like what?'

'Oh, for God's sake! What do you think? Some kind of… of accident…'

'And don't pretend you would have cared one jot!' Alex blurted out, tears springing to her eyes so that she had to stare back down at the ground again and gather herself.

The silence bristled between them. Gabriel had the strangest *now or never* feeling. What was he supposed to do with that?

'There's something you need to see,' Alex continued in a shaky, driven voice and she walked quickly past him, towards the sitting room and her handbag, where that wretched newspaper clipping had taken up residence in her wallet and had been steadily burning a hole in it for the past few interminable days.

Gabriel watched, mystified and irrationally panic stricken as she rummaged in her oversized sack and finally withdrew a piece of paper which she handed silently over to him.

It took him a few seconds to recognise Cristobel, staring up at him for all the world as though they were lovers. He hadn't even been aware of any paparazzi around at the time. He could just remember feeling impatient and keen to see the back of her. Unfortunately, that had not been transmitted in the shot, artfully snapped to fabricate a story out of nothing.

'She came to see me after you had left the island. I didn't tell you. She said that she would have you back, but I didn't want to believe her…'

Gabriel tore his eyes away from the newspaper clipping and then he quietly scrunched it between his fingers and tossed it on to the table between them. He shoved his hands in his pockets and reluctantly raised his eyes to hers.

'You wanted me to marry you because of Luke and the second I accepted, you resumed your...your...' Her head ached with the effort of not crying but her voice was unsteady and, since she couldn't look at him, she looked instead at the crumpled piece of evidence on the table. 'Would you ever have told me that you'd met Cristobel in New York if she hadn't been kind enough to provide proof of it?'

'There was nothing to tell.'

'Nothing to *you*, maybe.'

'I'm not...in the habit of explaining my actions to anyone. Well...I never was...'

'I can't be married to a man who doesn't think that he's accountable at all to his wife. I know that appearances for you are everything, but how do you think it makes me feel to realise that you're happy to take up where you left off with your ex-fiancée? Cristobel would have no problem sneaking around with you behind my back. Apparently that's *the Spanish way*. Whatever *that's* supposed to mean. I guess she just meant that that's *your way*. Marry because you have an overdeveloped sense of obligation but then just carry on doing exactly what you want!'

'She must have set the whole thing up...'

'Is that *all* you have to say, Gabriel? That *she must have set the whole thing up?*' Alex clenched her fists tightly and tears of bitter disappointment and frustration pricked the backs of her eyes. The cold, sickening realisation that this would be the soundtrack of her marriage, were she to marry him, swept over her with torrential force. Building crazy fantasies in her head and nursing girlish dreams of getting him to love her were frankly delusional. She would be entering into a contract, one that would see her financially secure for life, but that was it. No more, no less.

'No.'

'No *what*? Why can't you at least be honest with me?'

'Talking about feelings doesn't come easy for me. I've never been one of those touchy-feely kind of guys…'

'Okay.' Alex turned away, defeated, and walked towards the window, away from him.

'No, it's not okay.' Gabriel raked his fingers through his hair and was gripped with sudden indecision. She wasn't looking at him. She was staring through the window at nothing in particular and he couldn't blame her. If Cristobel had sat and plotted for a thousand years, she couldn't have come up with a better way of getting her own back on him for her ruined marriage plans. And how had he reacted when that horrendous picture had been thrust at him? With virtual silence. Was it any wonder that she couldn't bear to set eyes on him?

'I…' he began hesitantly. He shook his head, impatient with himself, and strode towards her, ignoring the way she shied back as she spun around and watched him descending on her.

'I had no idea that Cristobel was going to be in New York,' he said slowly. 'She got me on my mobile, claimed that she just wanted to talk to me, that I owed her that much at least, so I reluctantly agreed to take her out to dinner.'

'Yes, well, I could see reluctance brimming over in that snapshot of the two of you.'

This close to her, he could breathe in her clean soapy scent and the elusive apple and honey fragrance of her recently washed hair.

'Whatever you see in that photo,' he murmured, 'you're way off target. The dinner was only successful in so far as it made me see what a damn fool I had been to have ever became engaged to Cristobel. Not only is she a vain, shallow person, but there was a spitefulness there that repelled me.'

'You're just saying that,' Alex whispered.

'She must have planned the whole thing, right down to making sure that someone would be there to capture us on camera. She knows that there's no hope in hell that I'll ever have anything more to do with her, but a woman scorned is still a woman scorned.'

Alex folded her arms and stared at the right sleeve of his shirt.

'You...you do things to me, Alex...'

'Oh, *really*.'

'Yes, *really*.' He tilted her head so that she could look at him and she jerked back. Her eyes were glazed and damp and he felt his heart constrict. 'You do the same things to me that I do to you.'

'What's that?' Alex flung at him, rubbing her leaking eyes with the back of her hand. 'Turn you on?'

'Make me cry.'

At that, Alex looked up at him. Her mouth was parted, ready for attack, but her brain had seized up. She made a soft choking sound and blinked.

'I was an arrogant sod the first time you met me. Too young to realise that you were the best thing to ever happen in my life. You showed up again and I was still an arrogant sod but it didn't take me long to grow accustomed to you. To have you in my head every minute of the day. I can't focus when you're not around. You complete me.'

Alex's eyes were like saucers. For someone who didn't do the touchy-feely stuff, he seemed pretty spectacular right now and she didn't want the moment to end.

'You're gaping.' He gave her a crooked smile. He risked touching her, just a feathery brush of his finger along her cheek. 'I love you, Alex, and if you still want to walk away from marrying me then I won't try to stop you.'

'You *love* me? Why didn't you ever *say*?'

'I didn't recognise it, my darling. How was I to know that love was something that could ram into you when you weren't looking with the force of a freight train? How was I to spot that the first sign would be when your sense of complete control starts unravelling?'

Alex smiled, then she beamed and then she reached up and stroked his face. 'And I love you too. I never stopped, Gabriel. Even when I was as mad as hell with you, I still loved you. That's why I agreed to marry you. After Cristobel came and spouted all that stuff about you being the sort of Spaniard who would lose interest in me, I knew that I had to do whatever I could to turn what you felt for me into something strong enough to see us through.'

She closed her eyes and reached up, her mouth searching for his, her lips parting as he kissed her with fierce, burning hunger. She whimpered when he eventually pulled back to look down at her with such loving eyes that her heart skipped a beat.

'So you'll marry me…' he murmured huskily.

'You wouldn't be able to stop me.'

'You wait and see,' Gabriel promised solemnly. 'I will be the best father, the best husband, the best lover and the best friend you will ever have.'

A sigh of pure contentment escaped her lips. She curled her arms around his neck and sighed again when his hand cupped her breast with possessive intimacy.

'Right back at you,' she whispered.

EPILOGUE

THOSE missed years could never be replaced but Alex was good at not allowing Gabriel to beat himself up over that. The present was all that mattered and the present was a pretty wonderful place to be, he had to concede.

Luke was now seven and the apple of his father's eye. Indeed, Gabriel could hardly remember that time when he had lived and breathed work. His life had been one-dimensional, he now realised, although if someone had said so to him at the time he wouldn't have had a clue where they were coming from.

'I blame you,' he mused aloud, as Alex slid into the chair opposite him.

They had returned to the island to celebrate their third wedding anniversary, having left Luke with his grandparents in Spain. The housekeepers had been dispatched and here was his beloved wife now, dressed in a floaty cream creation which he would enjoy removing very, very slowly in a couple of hours' time.

Food had been prepared by Ana, who was still their loyal retainer at the house, and Alex was doing the honours. *I may not be a brilliant cook*, she had laughed, *but I'm good at heating things up.*

'Blame me for what?' She grinned because, over time, she was discovering just how complex this man of hers was.

'I've been domesticated.'

Alex sipped her champagne and smiled, leaning across the table and cupping her face in her hand. 'It's inevitable, I'm afraid.'

'So your mother told me the last time we visited them. Your married brothers have become pussycats.'

What he had anticipated as being a difficult relationship had been surprisingly easy. Alex's parents had accepted him without fuss and, although her brothers had initially given him a few filthy looks, they had grudgingly allowed him into their hallowed circle when he had proved himself knowledgeable on most things Irish. After some consolidated help from the Internet on his part. Now he had fun outsmarting them on their own turf, although they had wised up to his tactics and were always polishing up new ways to catch him out.

'Nice dress, by the way,' he murmured, angling his body so that he could nudge his thigh against her leg under the table. 'I'm going to enjoy taking it off. All those little buttons at the front. Could be an interesting challenge.'

Their eyes met and Alex felt that wonderful whoosh in her stomach that always happened when he was with her.

'You have a one track mind,' she teased, laughing.

'And you're always the woman at the end of that track.'

'Quite right!'

'The past three years have been the best of my life,' Gabriel told her seriously. 'I always thought that I was a pretty relaxed kind of guy. I was wrong. You taught me how to kick back. You and Luke…' he cleared his throat, just in case his voice did something stupid like sound unsteady '…you mean everything to me.'

'Which is terrific…' Alex stroked the side of his face with her hand and smiled tenderly at this brilliant man who was her own breath of life '…just so long as there's room in there for a little more love because I'm pregnant.'

Gabriel stood up and tugged her to her feet, his smile warm and loving. His hand moved to curve over her still flat stomach and he thought, with pleasure and with a sense of utter peace and contentment, that this was what it was to be home.

SURRENDER TO HER SPANISH HUSBAND

BY
MAGGIE COX

The day **Maggie Cox** saw the film version of *Wuthering Heights,* with a beautiful Merle Oberon and a very handsome Laurence Olivier, was the day she became hooked on romance. From that day onwards she spent a lot of time dreaming up her own romances, secretly hoping that one day she might become published and get paid for doing what she loved most! Now that her dream is being realised, she wakes up every morning and counts her blessings. She is married to a gorgeous man, and is the mother of two wonderful sons. Her two other great passions in life—besides her family and reading/writing—are music and films.

With grateful thanks to my lovely editor
Sally Williamson.
Her gentle guidance and support help
make my part of the deal a joy!

CHAPTER ONE

AN EAR-SPLITTING bolt of lightning shrieked through the air, lighting up the interior of the house's cosy hallway and outlining in threatening shadow the figure that loomed up behind the door's decorative stained glass panels. Her foot on the first tread of the stairs, on her way up to the hot scented bath that promised to be the perfect antidote to the day's accumulated stresses and strains, Jenny came to a sudden shocked standstill.

It was almost ten in the evening. There had been no phone call to tell her of the imminent arrival of a guest, and there were no other occupants in the entire place but her. Bearing in mind Raven Cottage's remote, some might say wild location—miles from anywhere—she had to quickly rid herself of the nightmarish scenario that her mind unhelpfully and frighteningly presented her with. But deepening dread paralysed her for long seconds before she could shake it off.

Installed as temporary caretaker of the charming thatched-roof guesthouse for nearly three full months now, courtesy of her friend Lily, who had gone to visit her parents in Australia, in all that time Jenny had not once chafed against her isolated surroundings at all. If anything, its lonely proximity to the Atlantic Ocean had given her a chance to properly take stock of all that had happened. Bit by bit she'd been rebuilding her esteem.

Divorce was never easy, but hers had been reluctant and sorrowful. She still ached for what might have been if her ex-husband hadn't rent her heart in two by deciding he could no longer continue with the marriage. Even though that had been years ago, from time to time Jenny still reeled from it. Standing out at the water's edge sometimes, she'd stare at the colossal waves sweeping into the shore and they seemed to symbolise the emotional battering she had taken. And If the divorce hadn't been traumatic enough fate had then delivered another blow—one that that had been particularly cruel.

But maybe it was because it was such a stormy 'end of the world' kind of night that her imagination seemed intent on putting her centre stage into a scene straight out of a horror movie…the kind that made her wonder if the people who watched them were altogether sane.

The shadowy figure outside lifted the brass knocker, banging it loudly. The discordant sound was like nerve-jangling rifle-shot, intent on drilling a hole through her skull. Biting her lip, Jenny breathed in deeply.

'Just a minute. I'm coming!' Having raised her voice above the din of a growling roll of thunder she fleetingly wished she'd pretended she wasn't home. Her caller would hopefully have just gone away and she could have enjoyed her longed-for bath in peace. But, knowing Lily needed the business, she plastered on a smile then opened the door.

'*Dios mio!* Could there be a more remote inhospitable place in the world?'

The darkly clothed male figure who, even after only the short sprint from his car, looked as if he'd been swimming in a roiling wild river, immediately vented his frustration.

Eyes the colour of silken jet pierced Jenny like dangerously sharpened dagger-points. Her determinedly upbeat smile vanished. It had been on the tip of her tongue to burst out *Well, if it's so inhospitable, and you'd rather be somewhere else, why have you bothered to knock on my door?* But the words died in her throat—because her visitor was shockingly familiar.

Eyes widening, she pressed her hand to her chest. 'Rodrigo. What are you doing here?' Her body shivered hard from the blast of freezing air that the opened door brought with it.

Her ex-husband stepped inside, causing Jenny to back up nervously. Shaking his mane of sleekly dark hair, then staring at her with a gaze that deluged her with a sea of haunting memories, he wiped the back of his hand across his damply glistening face. 'I might ask you the same question.'

'I'm looking after the place for Lily while she's away in Australia.' Clearly Jenny's presence was as much a surprise to him as his was to her. The ridiculous hope that he'd sought her out because he wanted to reconcile was cruelly and devastatingly snatched away. Despite her sorrow, she forced herself to carry on speaking. 'Now it's your turn. What brings you to the wilds of Cornwall? I wouldn't have thought it could hold much appeal—especially in the winter. The Mediterranean is much more your style.'

He sighed, as though it pained him to even consider some suitably witty repartee. 'I'm in the area because I have a meeting tomorrow. Have you a room? For pity's sake don't turn me out into that—that violent monsoon again!'

'I'd take pity on anyone who was in danger of being swept away by such wild weather…even *you*, Rodrigo. It's pretty grim out there tonight. Anyway… you're in luck. We're not fully booked. We're actually very quiet at the moment.'

Best not tell him he's the only guest just the same… Unconsciously grimacing, Jenny skirted round her formidably built ex-husband to hastily shut the door against the raging storm.

'Thanks.' Reaching out a hand, he squeezed her shoulder as his well-cut lips formed a lopsided smile. 'It is gratifying to know that you don't hate me enough to leave me to my fate.'

Parrying the nervous heat that flooded her, she backed up again.

'I expect you'd like to go straight to your room? You must be dying to get out of those soaking wet clothes.'

Another inconvenient wave of heat suffused Jenny at the remark she'd made. But she'd been referring to the imminent shedding of Rodrigo's clothes, so it hardly came as a surprise.

'I am. But first I will have to make a dash back to the car to collect my luggage.'

No sooner was this said than done, and once again Jenny was treated to a perfectly icy blast of arctic cold as she waited for Rodrigo to return with his suitcase, and an expensive calf leather shoulder bag that she knew contained a laptop.

'You'd better give me your coat,' she said, making herself wait patiently as he removed his damp trench-coat and then held it out to her. She desperately wanted to present an appearance of composure, even though inside her feelings easily mirrored the violent chaos of the storm.

A fleeting rueful smile touched Rodrigo's lips. 'I don't want to ruin Lily's polished wooden floor-boards,' he remarked.

Hanging the garment on a peg at the back of the door, she saw droplets of icy water from the hem drip rhythmically onto the raffia doormat. 'I'll hang it in the utility room in a little while,' she told him.

The spicy cologne that clung to the material of his

coat made a direct assay into her already besieged senses, causing another disturbing skirmish low in her belly. She frowned, hugging her arms over the lilac wool sweater that she'd teamed with well-worn faded blue jeans. 'So…where's this meeting you've got tomorrow?'

'Penzance. I was booked into a hotel there, but the roads were treacherous in this storm, and my sat nav stopped working. As I was driving I remembered that Lily had a guesthouse somewhere close by. I didn't even have to look for it—that was the crazy thing. Believe it or not somehow the place just loomed up before me… It's a total surprise to find *you* here.'

He hesitated, as if he was going to add something, and Jenny deliberately smothered the persistent ridiculous hope that doggedly had hold of her heart with a pincer grip.

'So you only need a room for the one night?'

'That's right. And what you said earlier was right too…the Mediterranean *is* more to my taste.'

'Then God forbid that you should suffer more than you have to!' she answered waspishly, turning away. Her insides went crazy when Rodrigo caught hold of her hand.

'Do you want to make me suffer, Jenny?' His dark eyes glittered.

Pulling her hand free from his icy cold palm, she dismissively tossed her head. 'I can assure you that I've got far more important things to do with my time. The room's this way.'

She led him upstairs to the luxurious accommodation at the front of the house, knowing that it was the best room in the building. No matter what had transpired between them as a couple, she knew he had faultless good taste—and she didn't want him to find flaws in her friend's much loved business. In the morning he would be treated to something pretty spectacular. When the landscape wasn't shrouded in mist and dark, or sheeted with blinding incessant rain, he'd find a view that couldn't fail to stir the senses and feed the soul. Again—despite her personal feelings—Jenny hoped Rodrigo would appreciate it.

Artists, writers, honeymooning couples and folk recovering from illness, divorce or bereavement—they had all stayed in that room, Lily had told her. With its unparalleled vista reflecting the Atlantic Ocean's dramatically beautiful unpredictability, it was a firm favourite with everyone. And, going by the comments in the visitors' book, they all swore that the bewitching and haunting wild scenery had definitely worked its magic, making them devotees for life by the time it came for them to leave.

Now, surveying the exotically handsome looks of the man who had once been her husband as he deposited his stylish suitcase and bag on top of the lovingly created silk patchwork quilt on the bed, Jenny saw him glance round the room with little evidence of pleasure or satisfaction on his face. Didn't he like it? There was a brooding, disenchanted air about him that reminded her that he had seen and done it all, more or less, and since there wasn't much that could impress him it was probably a waste of time even trying.

On her friend's behalf, Jenny was affronted. The beautifully presented room, with its plush velvet curtains and matching swags, tasteful designer wallpaper that had cost an arm and a leg, immaculate antique Davenport and sumptuous king-sized bed, complete with bespoke iron bedstead, had taken a large chunk of her friend's savings to perfect. It was a luxurious and relaxing atmosphere, yet at the same time Lily had managed to retain the old-fashioned English charm that the tourists expected and loved. And, being in the business of interior design, Jenny had been happy to advise her.

After the devastating death of Lily's sister and her husband in a car crash, Lily had found herself sole owner of Raven Cottage, and she had become absolutely determined to rise above the terrible tragedy she'd suffered and make the guesthouse a resounding success in their memory.

Like Jenny, Lily was no stranger to the bitter and jolting twists of fate that could cut a person off at the knees. That was why the bond between them that had begun all those years ago at school had deepened even more over the last couple of years.

Just before they had entered the room Jenny had flicked a switch to turn on two small antique table lamps either side of the bed, bathing the room in a softly inviting amber glow. As the rain whipped at the old-fashioned windows, and the crashing thunder overhead literally shook the rafters, she thought it would be hard to find a cosier place to shelter from such primitive violent weather. But again she found herself wondering if her jaded ex-husband even had the capacity to appreciate it.

'So...how come you've got a meeting in Cornwall?' Summoning a determinedly neutral tone, Jenny focused her apprehensive gaze on Rodrigo Martinez—billionaire owner of a chain of spa/hotels that were some of the most exclusive in the world. His carved handsome face, with its deep-set black eyes and spiked ebony lashes still damp from the rain, gave her his full attention. In return, her hungry glance moved helplessly over his arrestingly fit body. A body that suggested a disturbing physicality for which the outer garb of black sweater and jeans was only a thin shield. Rodrigo's simmering sexuality had fascinated and thrilled Jenny right from the beginning.

'I'm opening one of my hotels in Penzance,' he replied, his accent underlined by the husky gravel of his voice. 'Research tells me it's a popular area.'

'So naturally you want to capitalise on it?'

Unoffended, he shrugged. 'I'm a businessman in the hotel trade...what did you expect?'

Jenny's mouth dried with hurt. 'Nothing. I expect nothing of you, Rodrigo. Except maybe for you to act like you've always acted. I learned that lesson a long time ago, remember?'

'And you still bear a grudge towards me for it, by the sound of things.' Sighing, he drove his fingers irritably though his rain-damp hair. 'I need to get out of these wet things and take a hot shower. Unless you're feeling reckless and want to join me, I suggest it's time you vacated my room.'

'Go to hell!' Jenny reacted instantly, her heart suffused with indignant anger as well as painful regret.

'You think I haven't been there before, *querida*?' Shaking his head, his voice low, Rodrigo ruefully dropped his hands to his hips.

'When was that? When you failed to secure some million-dollar deal to make you even richer? That must have been a real low point!'

'What a flattering not to mention *damning* opinion you have of me, Jenny. You think all I'm interested in in life is making money?'

'I don't think that at all.' Her hand curved round the doorknob, Jenny met his disturbing gaze with unflinching steadiness. 'I *know* it.' She would have slammed out through the door there and then if her innate good nature hadn't got the better of her. 'I'll make you some coffee and get you a bite to eat. I expect you're hungry after your long drive. It'll be in the kitchen when you're ready.'

'Jenny?'

'Yes?'

'Nothing...it will keep. We can talk later.'

Bereft of a handy reply, and hardly trusting herself

to speak without becoming emotional, Jenny left the room. In the corridor her footsteps slowed. It had been over two years since she'd seen Rodrigo. She'd foolishly kept hoping he'd ring or get in touch, but he never had. In her mind she'd imagined him saying he'd made a mistake—he'd only asked her for a divorce because he was stressed—he'd been working too hard and hadn't been thinking straight. *No such event had occurred.* When she'd returned to the UK from Barcelona, where they had lived together, Jenny's friends had advised her not to waste any more precious time thinking about him. If he couldn't see the gift he had so easily let go then he just wasn't worth it. Why didn't she just spend the money he'd insisted she take as a divorce settlement, have a good time, and forget him?

As if she was going to wake up one morning and forget how to breathe. Day and night Rodrigo's memory haunted her. Her thoughts seemed incapable of dwelling on much else. But she wasn't happy that he still had the power to affect her so profoundly. She wanted to show him that she'd moved on…made a new and satisfying life without him. But after the pain and mayhem her brother Tim had caused when Jenny had returned to the family home 'new and satisfying' would have been a lie.

Her teeth clamping painfully down on her lip, Jenny headed back downstairs to the kitchen. A violent shudder rolled through her as a flash of lightning eerily illuminated the house's interior. The hall lights flickered wildly. To add to the sticky, uncomfortable tension in the air that shrouded her like a fine cloying mist—despite the arctic temperature outside—she nearly jumped out of her skin when a slightly overweight, well-fed tabby weaved her way awkwardly round her legs and almost sent her sprawling.

'Cozette, you naughty girl!' Jenny scolded, scooping the purring feline up from the floor and then holding the generous bundle of warm soft fur close into her chest.

She didn't mind admitting that Lily's pet cat had become a very welcome companion during her sojourn in the wilds of Cornwall.

'How many times have I told you not to do that? Never mind, are you scared of the storm? Is that what's bothering you? Poor little kitty…don't worry. I'll take you into the kitchen and find you a nice tasty bite to eat to help take your mind off this terrible racket!'

Upstairs in his room, in the act of retrieving his laptop from its leather holdall and wondering if this Cornish wilderness had even *heard* of the internet, Rodrigo paused. The voice that drifted up to him from downstairs riveted him. *It always had.* Now he stood perfectly still, listening. The lady had a voice as alluringly velvet as a warm midsummer's night, and it wrapped itself round his senses like a soft Andalucian breeze, full of the scents of jasmine, orange and honeysuckle and other exotic flowers that could render one hypnotised by their scent alone.

Hearing Jenny's voice again after being denied the sound for over two years… The effect it had always had on him ricocheted hotly through Rodrigo's brain. *Not to mention other sensitive parts of his body.* As he listened to her croon now, to what he quickly deduced must be Lily's pet cat, the napped velvet tones and cultured British accent were enough to raise goosebumps up and down his forearms and unquestioningly to arouse him. He blew out a breath. *Steady, Rodrigo…*he ruefully warned himself. She was still pretty mad at him, and had every right to be.

They'd been married for just over a year when he'd declared that they must part. Even now he could hardly believe he'd said the words—never mind seen them through. He should definitely rein in the almost instantaneous lust that had all but exploded through him at the sight of her tonight. Those luminous cornflower-blue eyes in a stunning oval face framed by a gilded curtain of shoulder-length blonde hair had always hit him where it hurt. He had never set out to wound her so badly. But—that aside—he had travelled to this spectacularly haunting part of the country for the purposes of business, *not* pleasure. And of all the startling scenarios he might have envisaged on this trip, having his beautiful ex-wife open the door to him on arrival at her friend's guesthouse was not one of them—though he had to admit his spur-of-the-moment plan had been influenced by the hope of hearing news of her.

His heavy sigh was laden with equal parts of frustration and tension. He kicked off his Italian-made shoes and tore off his socks, allowing his long tanned feet to sink gratefully into the luxurious carpet, before stripping off his clothes and heading for the shower…

'Do you have access to the internet here?'

'What? Oh, yes…but the signal's a bit dodgy. I mean, it comes and goes…especially in a storm like this.'

'I feared as much.'

'We'll probably get connected again tomorrow, when things have calmed down a bit. You may as well resign yourself to a night of not working. Think you can cope?'

'Very funny. Is this my coffee?'

'Yes. Sit down and help yourself. I presume you still take sugar? At any rate I've added two.'

'It's still the one pleasure I cannot give up,' Rodrigo joked. Seeing the glimpse of hurt that flitted across Jenny's face, he could have bitten out his tongue. The truth was that *she* had been the hardest pleasure of all to give up. Going by the ache in his ribs and low down in his belly, she still was.

As he arranged himself at the table, a generous mug of coffee steaming invitingly before him alongside a neat round plate piled high with sandwiches fashioned out of thick-cut wholemeal bread, Rodrigo tried to smother the swift stab of longing that filled him as he stared at Jenny.

Pulling his gaze reluctantly away, he made a leisurely inventory of the homely, country-style kitchen that surrounded him. With its mismatched stand-alone oak and pine furniture, old-fashioned cooking range and long wooden shelves lined with quaint but fashionable china it was a million miles from the state-of-the-art bespoke modern interiors that his exclusive holiday resorts prided themselves on featuring. But its homespun charm was seductive and inviting all the same. In fact it reminded Rodrigo very much of the simple Andalucian farmhouse high in the Serrania de Ronda hills he had grown up in. He experienced a fierce pang of longing as the not very often explored memory unexpectedly gripped him.

'This looks very good,' he muttered, taking a swig of the burning coffee and a hungry bite of a ham and English mustard sandwich.

'If you'd arrived earlier you could have had dinner…I cooked a cottage pie, but I've put what was left of it in the freezer now. Will this snack be enough for you? I've some fruitcake you can have afterwards with your coffee, if you like.'

As she talked, Jenny brought a decorative round tin to the table and opened it. Inside nestled a clearly homemade fruitcake that smelled mouthwateringly of cloves, cinnamon and nutmeg.

Rodrigo nodded approvingly. 'I might have to take you up on that offer. You know how fond I am of homemade cake.' His well-cut lips curved in a smile. '*Is* it one of yours?'

'I made it, yes.'

'Still the little home-maker, I see, Jenny Wren.' The nickname he had settled on from the very first time they were together came out before he could halt it. The flawless alabaster skin bloomed hotly with what he guessed must be embarrassed heat. Checking his apology, he lazily watched to see what she would do next.

Outside, a flurry of stormy wind crashed against the windows, bringing with it a sleeting rush of hammering rain. Jenny's clearly affected gaze locked with his.

'Don't call me that,' she said brokenly, the volume of her voice descending almost to a whisper.

Beneath his black cashmere sweater, Rodrigo sensed tension grip his spine. 'Why not?'

'You forfeited the right when you told me our marriage was over…that's why.'

'Then I won't use it again.'

'Thank you. Besides…I told you it's the name my father always called me, and he really loved me. Eat your food, Rodrigo, you must be hungry.'

Miserable with regret, he knew that any comment he made would likely pour petrol on an already simmering fire, and automatically crammed another bite of bread and ham into his mouth. It might as well have been sawdust for all the enjoyment he received from it.

Jenny moved away across the unadorned warm brick floor to one of the many immaculately clean pine worktops that filled the room. Presenting her back to him, she started slicing up more bread from the generous-sized loaf on the breadboard, her hurried, quick movements telling him that mentioning her father had definitely made her even more upset than she was already.

'I know how much you loved him too. He raised you and your brother single-handedly after your mother died,' he remarked. 'I would have liked to have met him. I too lost my parents when I was young… remember? My father first, and then my mother.' Carrying his mug of coffee with him, Rodrigo went to join her at the counter.

Clearly startled, Jenny glanced up, her hands stilling on the knife and bread. 'Yes, I remember.'

'Their deaths spurred me on to make my own way in life…so although it was tough for a while without them I am grateful.'

'Would you—do you need that coffee topped up? The water in the kettle should still be hot,' Jenny said, anxious to move the conversation away from the dangerously personal direction it had taken.

'No, thanks. It is fine just as it is.'

'Are you sure? It's no trouble.'

Warmth spread through Rodrigo's entire being as he stared down into the lovely face before him. How he resisted the almost overwhelming urge to pull Jenny into his arms, he didn't know. Except that—as she'd told him earlier about using the pet name he had for her—he had *forfeited the right.* But the warmth that had invaded him remained, making him he realise it had been a long time since a woman had taken care of him so thoughtfully. *Not since Jenny had left, in fact.*

For the past two years he had been travelling and working abroad almost continually, and it shocked him to learn that a part of him missed that treatment. From the very first time he'd met her Rodrigo had received the impression that it was Jenny's nature to be helpful, kind and thoughtful of others. All this was coupled with an extraordinary beauty—and she had been a blessing he had hardly been able to believe had come his way.

CHAPTER TWO

'WHY don't you make yourself a drink and come and talk to me while I eat?' Rodrigo suggested, his steady dark gaze making Jenny feel as though he was putting her under a powerful microscope.

For a little while she was utterly hypnotised by his compelling examination. He was staring at her as if he honestly craved her company, and she couldn't help but feel all at sea about that. What were his motives? she wondered. It was natural to be suspicious after two years without a word. And if she was honest she was also afraid of hearing the other reasons why he'd let her go, besides the fact that he couldn't properly commit to their union because of his dedication to work. More than once at the back of her mind she'd entertained the possibility that he'd been having an affair. If that was the case then she definitely didn't want to hear about it. Rodrigo had already broken her heart, and she had no desire to have it shattered again.

'I don't have time to talk to you now,' Jenny answered nervously, tucking some corn-gold strands behind her ear. 'Besides…you've had ample time to contact me if you wanted to talk, and the mere fact that you haven't clearly illustrates what I've always known to be true: your work is much more important than any relationship. What's to be gained by digging over old ground? I picked up the pieces after our farcical marriage and made a new life, and you just returned to the one you liked best as a bachelor.'

A muscle jerked visibly in Rodrigo's high-angled cheekbone. 'What a pretty picture you paint of my conduct.'

'I'm only telling the truth. Our marriage *was* a mistake, was it not?' Her breath was so tight Jenny felt dizzy. 'I'm as much at fault as you. I had no business accepting your proposal when we'd only known each other for three short months, but I quickly learned that your work was priority number one and always would be.'

Returning to the table, Rodrigo dropped down into the chair he had vacated. Linking his hands, he lifted his dark eyes to observe Jenny. 'Why have you never spent any of the settlement I made on you?' he asked.

'Because I didn't want your damn money in the first place!' Her heart pounding fit to burst, she willed the threatening tears that were backed up behind her lids to freeze over. 'I thought I was marrying the man I loved…not entering into a lucrative business deal.'

'You have every right to the money.' Shaking his head wearily, Rodrigo surprised Jenny with a lost look that made her insides turn over. 'I let you down—made you a promise I couldn't keep. It was only fair that I compensated you for that.'

'I didn't want compensation. After the divorce I just wanted to rebuild my life and start over. I wanted to forget about you, Rodrigo.'

'And did you?'

The question hung in the air between them like a detonated grenade. Not trusting him enough to voice the truth, Jenny moved away from the pine counter and assumed a businesslike air. 'There are a few things I have to do before I turn in for the night, and I have to get on.'

'Conscientious as ever, I see. Lily has a good friend in you, Jenny.'

'She's been a good friend to me too…a real support the past two years especially.'

'She must despise me for what I did to you.' Rodrigo's mouth twisted wryly.

'On the contrary. The truth is you rarely even come into our conversation. Now, I've got to empty the rubbish and check over the house before I lock up for the night.'

'How long is Lily away?'

'She's been gone nearly three months now. She's due back in a fortnight.'

'I see. And what about the interior design consultancy that you intended to resurrect when you returned to the UK? Are you not involved with that any more?'

'I'm still running it, though business has been a bit slow throughout the summer months. That's why I was able to come here and help Lily out.'

'And how are things with your brother Tim? Are you still paying the mortgage on the family home you shared with him? I remember he had a particular talent for avoiding work and paying his own share.'

Rodrigo's question, along with his sardonic remark, made Jenny feel queasy. Of course Rodrigo had no idea what had happened when she'd returned…how sour things had turned between her and Tim—culminating in a most shocking event that she would never forget…

'Tim met somebody and moved to Scotland after I bought out his share of the house.'

'So you're still living there?'

Feeling her face throb with uncomfortable heat beneath Rodrigo's razor-sharp scrutiny, Jenny glanced away. 'I'd better go and see to those bins.'

She was still wary of further probing questions as she lifted out the recycling bag from its plastic container beneath the double butler sink that Lily had excitedly sourced from a local reclamation yard, and prayed Rodrigo would cease quizzing her.

Heading for the door opening into the utility room, she threw over her shoulder, 'Why don't you just relax and enjoy your refreshments in peace?'

'Jenny?'

Turning, she found to her astonishment that he was right behind her, his half-drunk mug of coffee left on the table. Her heart foolishly hammered at his unexpected nearness. 'What is it?'

'Let me do that for you…it sounds like a war zone out there and I don't like the idea of you coming under fire on your own.'

Even as he uttered the words a thunderous crash resounded above them, its threatening echoes rumbling like some disgruntled giant disturbed from his sleep. Once again all the lights buzzed precariously on and off, as though the whole place might be plunged into darkness at any second.

Clutching the recycling bag tightly between her fingers, Jenny shook her head. 'I'm not afraid of the storm. I'll only be gone a couple of minutes.'

Not hanging around to see if he would try to persuade her, she rushed out through the door into the utility room. Once there, she opened the back door to the part of the garden where a paved pathway led towards a sturdy iron gate, beyond which was the road. *Or where she knew there should be a road.* Switching on the night light, all she could see through the grey shroud of misty, heavily falling rain was an uprooted tree lying drunkenly across the path. The ferocious wind was tossing everything around as though it were the flimsy furniture in a child's dolls' house. Lily's beloved greenhouse was ominously shaking and shuddering. It was definitely under threat of losing its moorings as the rain viciously pelted the thin glass panes, Jenny saw. Dangerously, just a few feet away a slim-stemmed birch was being all but battered to kingdom come. If it came crashing down on top of Lily's beloved greenhouse the several almost ripened tomato plants that she'd been tending like a broody mother hen would certainly be demolished—as would every other plant and vegetable in there.

The idea of being the one who was responsible for losing them galvanised Jenny into action. Determinedly she headed for the shed at the bottom of the garden, the wind's eerie elemental power making her stumble more than once as she negotiated her way round the fallen tree that lay across the path. A while ago, whilst searching for a particular garden tool, she'd spotted what looked like a fairly robust rolled up tarpaulin inside the shed, which could now be put to good use.

The large tarpaulin clutched against her sodden chest, along with some tent pegs she'd found, Jenny shook her drenched hair from her eyes and then steeled herself to walk back to the other side of the garden where the greenhouse stood. Grimacing as another bolt of silver lightning lit up the sky, she uncurled the tarp, shaking it out as best as she could.

It didn't take long for her to realise she was fighting a losing battle. Every time she managed to get one corner straightened out the wind all but ripped it out of her now freezing hands and she had to fight to uncurl it again. The rain was like a grey blindfold over her eyes as she worked, making her curse out loud because she hadn't thought about the implications of such a storm earlier, when she'd first seen the darkening clouds appear in the sky.

'What are you trying to do?'

A voice to the side of her lifted to make itself heard above the storm. Already drenched to the skin from his dash from the back door to reach Jenny's side, Rodrigo was staring at her as though she was quite mad.

'The greenhouse!' she shouted, pointing. 'I need to secure it so it won't get flattened by the storm. I was going to throw the tarp over it and then fasten it to the ground to hold it.'

Comprehending, Rodrigo unceremoniously relieved her of the wildly blowing tarpaulin and then shoved one corner back into her hands. 'Move back and we will shake it out together,' he instructed. 'Do you have anything to secure it?'

'Yes.' She quickly stooped to retrieve the long tent pegs she'd left by her feet. 'These.' She handed them over.

'We need a hammer to bang them into the ground.' Momentarily he shifted his gaze down to her feet, as if expecting to see the necessary tool lying there.

'Oh, God.' Biting her lip, Jenny stared back at Rodrigo with an apologetic shrug. 'I forgot to bring the mallet with me. It's still in the shed.'

'I'll get it. Stay here.'

'It's at the other end of the garden. Can you see it?'

'Yes, I see it.' Before he left, Rodrigo furnished her

with a wry look. 'And do your best not to get blown away by the wind while I am gone…I am looking forward to my full English breakfast in the morning, and that's not going to happen without a cook!'

No sooner had he left than he was back again, a large wooden mallet clutched tightly in his hand, as if the storm and the fallen tree had been but mere annoying trifles that had not even vaguely threatened his mission. Taking charge with reassuring confidence, he yelled instructions to Jenny, helping them both negotiate the best way of working in the increasingly untamed weather.

By the time they had the tarp over the greenhouse roof and the sides rolled down securely over the glass walls—Rodrigo having deftly banged in the tent pegs through the loops to fasten it to the ground—Jenny felt as if she'd been packed in ice and left to freeze. *Thank God her ex had been around to help her.* That was all she could think as she took one last glance through the drowning rain at the secured tarp covering Lily's treasured greenhouse. She'd never have managed it on her own, she realised.

Gratefully dashing into the house again, she knew she must look half-drowned, with her sodden clothing and dripping hair. Next to the efficient DIY expert, who still managed to look nothing less than gorgeous even though he was also wet through, Jenny felt like something the cat had dragged in. It wasn't a picture she wanted to project to anyone…least of all the man that had broken her heart. But her hands were so chilled that she could barely even make a fist, and she had no choice but to leave the locking of the door behind them to Rodrigo too.

Dark hair was plastered to his well-shaped head, and Jenny watched an icy rivulet of water streak down his face over high-sculpted cheekbones and a clean-cut jaw that didn't have so much as a smidgeon of spare flesh detracting from its perfect symmetry. On its way, the pearl of moisture flirted briefly with a corner of his mouth, making her dangerously aware of how full and sensual his upper lip was—just like one of those Italian sculptures that art-lovers gasped at because they were so beautiful.

'Tomorrow morning I'm going to cook you the best breakfast you've ever had.' She took a nervous swallow. 'I owe you big-time for what you just did. Lily has worked so hard to grow her own vegetables, and—'

The lips that had so riveted her attention were suddenly laid over hers as gently as a butterfly wing. Shocked rigid, Jenny was nonetheless *compos mentis* enough to register the erotic warmth of the breath that came with it, as well as the burning heat hovering beguilingly beneath the rough velvet skin that had been rendered arctic cold from his rescue mission outside.

As soon as Rodrigo lifted his mouth away from hers her body throbbed with insistent hunger for a second helping of that incredibly arousing fleeting contact. The idea of having a properly passionate kiss from her one-time husband again made her feel dizzy with want…quite primitively crazy with it.

Fearing her gaze must easily reflect her torrid feelings, Jenny stepped away, her hands fiddling with the drenched ends of her shoulder-length hair, praying he wouldn't guess how violently his brief kiss had affected her. 'What was that for?' she breathed.

He shrugged, as though amused. 'Regard it as a thank-you from the absent Lily. No doubt she would be quite moved to learn that you care so much about her greenhouse that you were willing to venture outside in a violent storm to protect it.' Rodrigo smiled. 'Now…I think we both need to rid ourselves of these wet clothes before we succumb to pneumonia, don't you?'

The suggestion sounded like something X-rated articulated in that sexy Spanish voice. So much so that Jenny felt as if a fire had been lit beneath her blood. But, with his hands on his hips, Rodrigo's next words quickly brought her disturbing fantasies to an abrupt if regretful end.

'We'd better not stand here talking all night. We need to get back to our rooms, change into dry clothing and then return downstairs for a hot drink to warm us up…*sí*?'

'Good idea,' Jenny muttered, wrenching her gaze determinedly away from his. Ascending the staircase, she hurried as though being chased by some dogged pursuer up to no good. But in her heart of hearts she knew it was her own tumultuous feelings that she was really hoping to distance herself from…

In the shower, as he stood beneath the needle-sharp scalding spray, Rodrigo stared through the curtain of water, filled with disbelief at what had just happened between him and his pretty ex-wife.

Recalling the incident with more intent, he remembered that her sweet-lipped cupid's bow pink mouth had suddenly become like the most sensuous narcotic. A longing to still the tantalising little quiver he had glimpsed, to taste the heat as well as the rain-cold damp he knew he would find there, had spontaneously driven him to press his mouth against hers. What Rodrigo had not been expecting was that kissing Jenny's soft little mouth would feel so instantly essential to him the moment he made contact.

Reliving the experience made his insides dance wildly. How could he have forgotten that she could make him feel like that? His mind moved on to a far more disturbing thought. How many lovers had she taken to her bed since they had parted? She was young and beautiful, and these dark cold nights stuck out here on her own would undoubtedly get lonely. He had no right to feel so jealous and angrily affronted by the idea. Jenny was free to do as she liked. They were divorced. But if she had *not* taken a lover was it because she still thought of him?

The idea sent a burning arrow of explosive heat

straight to Rodrigo's loins and he murmured an expletive in Spanish. How long since he had had a woman? He traced the outline of a circle in the collected steam on the shower stall's glass, added a downturned mouth and scowled. *Clearly long enough for it to seriously start to bother him.*

It wasn't that there was ever a lack of opportunity. Females of all ages had taken a profound interest in him ever since he'd started to hit puberty at around thirteen. But he had done nothing about more recent opportunities because he had allowed work to gobble up his free time like an insatiable termite instead. Before he'd realised it the days and weeks in his diary had suddenly revealed that a whole year had gone by—a year during which he could practically equal a Franciscan monk for lack of sexual activity. Not to mention the complete dearth of a social life or even anything remotely related to relaxation.

He was beginning to feel a little like an automated machine—going here, going there, and hardly even noticing his surroundings. It scarcely mattered whether it was some sensual eastern paradise or one of the glamorous foreign playgrounds of the rich and famous—private playgrounds to which gradually, through his single-minded dedication to his goal, Rodrigo had at last gained membership. But the successful business he'd been so focused on achieving from such a young age had gradually turned into a monster, intent on gorging every ounce of energy and life force he possessed in return for the rewards he'd once deemed so essential to his self-esteem and his life.

Frighteningly, he had experienced periods of late when his body had threatened to barely get him through the day at all. More frightening still was the fact that very little in his life—either some achievement or something material—managed to give him pleasure any more. It appeared as though he was numb to the sensation. Even this new project, installing one of his exclusive resorts in this scenic, wild and—as research informed him—*desirable* corner of south-west England was quickly starting to lose the excitement and appeal it had initially held. But the last thing his shareholders wanted to hear was that he had lost that lucrative, moneymaking killer instinct that had helped so spectacularly to line their pockets too.

Sighing, Rodrigo stepped out of the shower onto the aquamarine tiled floor. Reaching for a voluminous white towel that had been left warming on the radiator, he dried himself vigorously, dressed in clean jeans and a sweatshirt, combed his fingers through his still damp hair and then turned to view his scowling reflection in the steamy mirror.

He didn't like what he saw. The confirmation of his thoughts about the lack of relaxation in any form was written clear in the dullness of his eyes, in the new lines he spied round his mouth and gouged into his forehead. Even through the steam they mercilessly confronted him.

A picture came into his mind of his angelic-looking ex-wife. Would a hot night of unconstrained lust in her bed, with soft sighs, mutually hungry needs passionately met, cure him of the dullness in his eyes? Would it help him regain some of the strength and vitality that lately he sensed he had lost?

Grimacing as another wave of erotic heat seized his body, Rodrigo didn't doubt it would. But after the way he had treated her would Jenny even consider it?

As he turned to leave the room he silently acknowledged that it wasn't just the promise of a warming nighttime drink he was hoping for…

She was standing by the stove, watching over a simmering pan of milk. Somehow knowing he was there, she turned towards him and, surprisingly, gifted him with a smile. Her lovely face was scrubbed clean as a child's and her huge china-blue eyes set up such a violent longing in Rodrigo that he barely knew how to handle it. It wasn't just the natural healthy longing of a sexually aroused male at the sight of an attractive woman either. It was the totally contradictory yearning for an impossible dream that he usually dismissed as viciously as swatting an annoying fly—a dream that he had had within his grasp but had incredibly let go. But sometimes—like now—it broke through his insatiable need for success and acceptance by the world and almost throttled those desires by the throat. *Yet its tantalising promise could never be for him.* He was a pragmatist, a realist...a man a million miles away from ever putting his faith in such an impossibly unattainable idea. *No doubt his lovely ex-wife would back him up on that.*

Wearing a full-length cream dressing gown, its lapels patterned with tiny sprigged red roses, little Jenny Wren radiated the kind of innocence and purity that made Rodrigo briefly mourn for the hopefulness and joy of his early youth. *Before* he had discovered that in his ardent pursuit of success the world would extract every ounce of that hopefulness and joy and pay him back with constant growing tension and a vague unease that all was not right.

Rubbing his hand over his chest in a bid to ease the sudden clutch of discomfort that had collected there, he appreciatively registered that Jenny's golden hair had been left to dry naturally, in almost too tempting to touch blonde ringlets. Finding himself in a trance, he paused in the doorway just to gaze at her...enjoying the stirring sight she made as if paying homage to an exquisite work of art in a gallery.

'I'm making hot chocolate. Is that okay?'

'It is more than just okay. I could not think of a more perfect ending to a night like this.'

Liar, his silent inner voice mocked as he easily thought of a far more exciting and alluring alternative. But, as if to illustrate his comment, a violent blast of furious thunder overhead made the whole house feel as though the very walls were about to disintegrate into a pile of rubble.

'Sit down. I'll bring it over to you when it's ready.'

'I get the feeling that there's no one around tonight but us. Am I right in thinking I'm the only guest staying here?'

'You are. Like I said…' she whipped up the milk in the pan with a tiny whisk as if she was no stranger to the task '…we're pretty quiet at the moment. The summer holidays are long over, and it probably won't get busy again until nearly Christmas.'

'And will you still be here then, helping Lily out?'

Jenny's slender shoulders visibly stilled. 'No. I won't. I told you…she's due back in a couple of weeks and I'll be returning to London.'

'To the house you grew up in as a child.'

'Yes.'

'Yet you seem more at home here than anywhere I've seen you before.'

'What makes you say that?'

'Because this rural environment suits you… In fact, it wouldn't require a great stretch of the imagination to see you as a country girl, Jenny. Yes, I can visualise you sitting in your cosy little stone cottage each evening as the sun goes down, the tantalising smell of the day's fruitful baking lingering in the air.'

'And in this tantalising little scenario am I on my own?' The catch in her voice had Rodrigo frowning deeply.

'I don't know.' He shrugged. 'You tell *me*.' Even though his voice was calm, it felt as if an icy boulder had taken up residence inside his belly.

'You know I've always wanted a family.'

'Yes.' He shifted uncomfortably in his chair. 'I do know that.'

'But you never wanted children, did you?'

'No. I didn't.'

'Then it was just as well you decided our marriage wouldn't work, wasn't it?'

Lifting the pan off the stove, Jenny poured the steaming milk into two waiting ceramic mugs, then gave the contents a brief stir. Bringing their drinks to the table, where Rodrigo sat silently and broodingly waiting, she lowered herself into the chair opposite him. Straight away he scented the soap she'd used to wash herself with. It smelled like newly laundered linen. Once again it lit a fire in his blood that made him feel more alive and intensely aware than he had in ages.

Sighing softly, she focused her shimmering cornflower-blue eyes on his. 'One day you might meet someone you really care for, Rodrigo, and change your mind about having children.'

'I don't think so.'

'How can you be so sure?'

'Because I know exactly what I want and what I don't want. There's no confusion about that.' His mouth set uncompromisingly.

'It must be marvellous to be so certain of things… to be so sure that you're right.'

Jenny turned her face away. When she glanced back Rodrigo couldn't pretend he didn't see the avalanche of hurt in her eyes. It all but sliced him in two, knowing he was the cause of it.

'It doesn't feel so marvellous when you put it like that,' he replied drolly.

'Then let's change the subject. Let's not talk about us—what we want or don't want—let's stick to safer topics. Your shower…was the water hot enough?'

Shrugging, Rodrigo warmed his still chilled hands round his mug of hot chocolate. 'It was fine.'

'Good.'

'You worry too much about others, Jenny.'

'I suppose I do. At least I worry that Lily's guests have everything that they need and are comfortable. It's a big responsibility, taking care of someone else's house and business, and I want to do a good job for her while I'm here.'

'Trust me…you do such a good job of taking care of your guests that you would put a top hotel to shame.'

'I suppose you'd know about that, wouldn't you?'

'I suppose I would.' Regarding her from beneath the sweeping black lashes that any female would envy, Rodrigo edged a corner of his mouth towards a smile. 'Anyway, I've always believed in acknowledging effort and good work where I see it.'

'Your staff must love you for that. As well as being paid well, everyone wants to feel valued.'

He raised an eyebrow. 'I agree. Sometimes employers can forget that.'

In his mind Rodrigo made a quick inventory of some of the people who worked for him… Were they happy? Did they consider him a good employer? Certainly his management team seemed to think so. After all, in fifteen years he had had very few complaints. From that he had to deduce that all must be well. For their loyalty and hard work he rewarded his staff with regular bonuses and luxury breaks at different foreign resorts from the ones they worked in, as well as seeing to it that they all had good pensions and private healthcare. He also knew that despite his strict adherence to high standards, he was well liked.

'So, you still enjoy your work?' Jenny enquired, dark blonde brows lifting a little.

'Yes, I do,' Rodrigo replied.

Now it was *his* turn to guard and protect his feelings. The stormy night, this warm cosy house and its unexpected pretty and familiar hostess might have lulled him into relaxing far more than he had in ages, but he was not about to confess to Jenny that lately he had fallen a little bit out of love with his chosen career.

'I suppose that was a bit of a stupid question.'

'It wasn't.'

'I mean...your work is your life, right? Of course you must still enjoy it.'

Taking a brief sip of her drink, Jenny licked the chocolate-coloured froth from her lips with the tip of her elegant pink tongue. Already feeling the disturbingly sensual effects of her alluring sweet company, Rodrigo felt the taut muscles in his belly constrict even more.

'My dad was only a plumber, but he really enjoyed his work too.' Her gaze roamed from Rodrigo's features down to his Ralph Lauren sweatshirt. 'Of course he didn't dress nearly as stylishly or expensively as you. Truth is he never made a lot of money, even though he worked hard. If he thought a customer would struggle to pay his bill he'd only charge them half the price. He wasn't a natural businessman, I'm afraid. But he was the very best father you could wish for.'

'You clearly admired and loved him very much.'

'I did. After all, what could be more important than being a good parent, and supporting, loving and adoring your children so that they don't ever doubt they mean everything to you? Being good at business is nothing in comparison to that.'

CHAPTER THREE

RODRIGO'S expression suggested an iron portcullis had slammed down over his emotions—as if everything in him, every feeling and sense, had been incontrovertibly closed and shielded against anything Jenny cared to throw at him.

She hadn't deliberately intended to make a jibe about his preference for work as opposed to having children, but she supposed it was inevitable it should come out like that. The fact was she had loved being married to him. Had prayed he would change his mind about them having a family together, and hoped his love affair with work would one day dim when it was replaced by the joys of fatherhood… But her prayers and hopes had been cruelly shattered the day he'd come home and announced their marriage was over.

It had been like listening to an icily aloof stranger, Jenny remembered with a shudder. Here in the kitchen, where the heat from the cooking range lent an air of cosiness and security as the storm rampaged outside, she wished the sense of safety and warmth she felt went beyond creature comforts. *She wished it were created by mutual love between her and Rodrigo.*

The force of her yearning made her want to weep. But she was wasting her time, dwelling on such futile things. Better that she remembered that her handsome ex-husband was just a visiting guest in the house, staying for one night only because circumstances dictated it…*not* because he'd intended them to meet and be alone together.

As soon as Lily had asked her to stand in for her for three months Jenny had vowed she'd be utterly professional and considerate at all times, and that was how she meant to proceed for the remainder of the time Rodrigo was there. She would treat him just like any other guest. She could manage that for twenty-four hours, couldn't she?

Her head swam for a moment.

'I'm going to check the house, then go to bed,' she announced, rising to her feet.

'Why do I get the distinct feeling that you're running away?' Rodrigo asked lazily.

'I'm not running away! If anyone knows how to do that it's *you*, not me.'

'You sound as though you've missed me, *querida*. Could that be the truth behind this petulant temper of yours?'

'I'm not petulant. And I haven't missed you. I'm merely getting on with my life without you and relieved that I'm not sitting up late every night waiting for a phone call to tell me you'll be home late or have to fly off somewhere for two weeks without me.'

'Then I've done you a favour.'

'If the idea helps you to believe what you did was right, then go ahead and think that. At any rate, I'm too tired to stand here and argue with you about it. By the way, what time do you want breakfast in the morning?'

'I'm an early riser, as you know. Seven-thirty okay with you?'

Jenny briefly met his mocking glance and forced herself not to react to it.

'Seven-thirty's fine.'

'Then I'll bid you goodnight, Jenny,' he said, taking her hint that the evening was at a close and he was most certainly going to bed alone. 'Sleep well. I hope the storm doesn't disturb you too much.'

'Goodnight,' she muttered, determinedly heading for the door.

The storm contributed to a practically sleepless night for Rodrigo. Yet he couldn't blame the turbulent display of thunder and lightning for his wakefulness entirely. The truth was he was tortured by how callously he'd ended his marriage, even though he'd genuinely believed at the time that he was doing it for the right reasons. For two years he'd held his disturbing feelings at bay, but now, being with Jenny again, they were uncomfortably surfacing.

Her words about sitting up late every night waiting

for a call to say he was coming home or flying off somewhere played over and over in his mind, driving him almost to madness. Several times he got up and walked the floor, wondering if she too was awake, like him, remembering that painful final scene between them when Rodrigo had sounded the death knell on their marriage.

At some point during the early hours, with no lessening of the fury of the storm, he crawled back into bed. A splitting headache knifing through his head, he determinedly closed his eyes, willing sleep to free him from the disturbing litany of guilt-ridden thoughts that plagued him.

When Rodrigo didn't show for breakfast at seven-thirty, Jenny put the generous plate of bacon and eggs she'd cooked in the oven, to keep them warm, then made a second fresh pot of coffee. Grimacing at the arc of furious lightning splintering overhead in the distance as she glanced out of the window, she shivered, pulling the edges of her cardigan closer over her chest to keep warm.

What was keeping Rodrigo? He was, as he'd said, an early riser.

As she continued to stare out the window through the driving rain at the reluctant dawn appearing on the horizon, she wondered if he could risk travelling anywhere in weather like this. A horrible vision of the tyres of his car skidding uncontrollably in the wet, causing the vehicle to crash violently into a tree and injure him, insinuated its way into her mind and wouldn't go away. Before she'd realised her intentions Jenny found herself apprehensively making her way upstairs. Gingerly, she knocked on Rodrigo's door.

'Rodrigo?' she called. 'Are you up yet? It's almost a quarter to eight.'

No reply. Again she rapped her knuckles against the door, her heart thudding hard under her ribs.

'Rodrigo, are you all right?'

From inside the room came a sound like a heavy book crashing to the floor. It was followed by some indecipherable low-voiced muttering. The door swung open before she had the chance to step back and Rodrigo stood there, rubbing at his eyes, his black hair more unruly than she'd ever seen it, his body encased in nothing but navy-blue silk pyjama bottoms clinging sexily low round his arrow-straight hips. The provocative sight made Jenny's mouth go dry.

Quickly pulling herself together, she folded her arms over her chest. 'Overslept, did you? That must be a first.'

'Who the hell could sleep with that din going on all night?' he retorted irritably, 'It sounded like a bombing raid!'

'It's just as wild this morning,' Jenny replied, serious-voiced, 'I don't think you should attempt to drive anywhere for a while yet…at least until things calm down.'

'Scared I might get swept off the road and end up in a ditch somewhere, *querida*?'

'That's not funny. I know male pride might convince you that you're invincible, but you'd be crazy not to listen to what I say. I've been here nearly three months now, and even in the summer the weather can get pretty scary.'

'Well, I'm neither crazy nor ignorant, and I thank you for your concern. Perhaps I'll put my meeting off for one more day and go tomorrow instead.'

Feeling a little stunned that he would even consider such an option, Jenny widened her blue eyes. 'Anyway…' she started to retreat '…your breakfast's keeping warm in the oven and I've made a fresh pot of coffee because the first one went cold. I've been up since six-thirty myself. Maybe some hot food and something to drink will revive you after your sleepless night?'

Rodrigo's suddenly amused gaze swept disturbingly up and down Jenny's figure. 'Maybe it will. Or maybe the fact that you look so wide awake and beautiful this morning will revive me even more? But that coffee sounds good too. Give me a few minutes and I'll come downstairs and join you.'

'Okay.'

Even though he'd ostensibly taken the day off, to Jenny's utmost surprise Rodrigo insisted on making himself useful, and she couldn't find it in her heart to refuse his help. At least if he was undertaking a couple of necessary DIY jobs around the house they wouldn't be at loggerheads, she reasoned. But it was disconcerting to see how impressively practical and handy he was.

Who would guess he was one of the wealthiest hoteliers in the world, much more at home in Armani tailoring and working behind a king-sized desk than getting his hands dirty in jeans and a plain black T-shirt, as he rolled up rain-damaged linoleum in the utility room and repaired some no longer properly functioning blinds in a bedroom?

The rain was still thundering against the roof when Jenny called to him upstairs to come and eat lunch. Was this relentlessly stormy weather never going to end?

Rodrigo witnessed her shiver as he came through the door into the kitchen. Immediately he frowned. 'Are you okay?'

'I'm fine. Somebody just walked over my grave, that's all.'

'What do you mean?' He was studying her with alarm.

'It's just an expression.' She smiled awkwardly. 'Nothing to worry about. Sit down—you must be starving. It's only chilli con carne on a baked potato, but it's hot and nourishing.'

'Trust me...it's very welcome'

'I never realised you had such talent for DIY.'

'I spent a lot of time with my uncle when I was young. He was a carpenter. He taught me that there is honour in a man being able to put his hands to work.' He pulled out a chair at the table and sat down.

'But your father wanted you to go into business?' Jenny remembered.

'Sí he did.'

'And you never yearned to be a carpenter instead?'

A forkful of food on its way to his lips, Rodrigo paused to answer her. 'Maybe I did for a while… But then I got more realistic—in terms of earning a living, at least.'

Sitting down opposite him, Jenny made a start on her own meal. Every now and then her gaze flicked to the tight bronzed biceps displayed by his T-shirt and her stomach rolled over.

They ate in an oddly companionable silence for a while, until he glanced across at her and asked, 'Do you miss your brother since he moved to Scotland?'

'No, I don't. You remember how difficult he could be sometimes? Well, things got worse when I returned to the house. He felt I should just sign it over to him completely…give him everything. He was badly in debt because of one thing and another and he blamed me.'

'That sounds about right—but why did he blame you?'

'Because I'd looked out for him ever since our parents died and he was jealous that I was getting on well with my career and he couldn't seem to stick at anything for long without getting into trouble. Anyway…in the end I bought him out and he moved to Scotland to live with some besotted girl he met.'

'You haven't heard from him?'

'No.' She didn't particularly *want* to hear from him either. Truth to tell, she needed more time to get over the hell he'd put her through.

His disturbing dark eyes roaming her face, Rodrigo put down his fork and stopped eating. 'You could have bought a place of your own with the settlement I made you. Then you could have just let him have the house and forgotten about him.'

Her heart racing, Jenny stared. 'I didn't want to touch a penny of that money. In fact now that we've met up again you must take it back. Do you think you're the only one who has any pride? I didn't want anything of yours after you heartlessly told me our marriage was finished. Don't you understand that? I told that solicitor of yours when he rang me about the settlement. If you wanted to cut the ties between us then we should have cut them completely! I want to make my own way in the world—just like I did before I met you.'

Could she make it any more clear how little she wanted to do with him? Each word flayed him.

Taking a long draught of the water she had poured him, Rodrigo returned the glass to the table, wiped his napkin over his lips and got up, before quietly saying. 'I should get back to what I was doing. There's still quite a bit to do. Thanks for the meal.'

She ached to say something to make him linger, but sheer hurt at the fact they were no longer together overwhelmed Jenny and she sat in silence as he walked across the floor and went out.

That evening, as they sat across the table from each other finishing their evening meal, Jenny began to realise how unwell she was feeling. Not just a tad on the warm side either. Her skin was fever-hot.

Resisting the urge to touch her hand to her head to gauge her temperature, she tugged the sides of the dressing gown she'd donned after her bath more securely over her chest. 'If this rain continues to fall we'll have to build an ark.' She smiled. 'Your carpentry skills will certainly come in handy.'

The timbre of her own voice took her aback. It sounded as if she regularly smoked cigarettes and downed whisky. *Damn!* She hoped she wasn't developing a cold. That was the *last* thing she needed when she was in a position of responsibility while her friend was away.

'Are you all right?' Rodrigo enquired, black eyes sweeping what she now knew must be her fever-bright reflection.

'I'm sorry…' Jenny mumbled. The drugging fatigue that washed over her was making her suddenly long for her bed. She pushed to her feet. 'I'm afraid I'm not feeling too good all of a sudden. I'll have to go to bed. Take your time finishing your food. There's no hurry. I mean of course it's up to you when you want to call it a day, it's just that...well...can I ask you a favour?'

'Ask away.' His dark gaze continuing to mirror concern, Rodrigo also stood up.

'Do you think you could turn off the lights for me and make sure that Cozette is in her basket before you go up to your room? She's probably hiding somewhere again because of the storm. The thunder and lightning really spook her.'

'I'll do everything you ask, but will you be okay? Studying you now, I can see that you look quite feverish. Shall I call a doctor?'

'Heavens, no. I'm just getting a bit of a cold after being in and out of the rain, that's all. I'm sure it won't hang around long.' But all the same Jenny put her hand up to her head. Her fingers almost sizzled at the burning heat that emanated from her skin. 'I'll—I'll get a good night's sleep and I'm sure I'll be feeling back to my normal self in the morning. What time do you think you'd like your breakfast?'

'Any time that you—Jenny? Are you sure you are all right?'

'I'm fine. I just need to—' To accompany her sky-high temperature, a wave of sickness arose inside her stomach. Her sight was going worryingly hazy, and Jenny sensed the strength in her legs frighteningly desert her. In the next surreal moment her knees crumpled like paper and the warm bricked floor rushed towards her.

The last thing she remembered before she blacked

out was Rodrigo catching her as she fell. His arms were strong as iron bars as he swept her up close to his chest. There was a faint scent of some arrestingly exotic cologne on the air just before darkness closed in on her and she surrendered to unconsciousness with impunity…

Having found Jenny's bedroom by glimpsing some feminine clothing thrown over a chair beside a bed through a slightly ajar door on the same landing as his, Rodrigo kicked the door further open and carried her limp body across to it.

Bending a little to yank down the freshly laundered covers, he carefully lowered his charge onto smoothly ironed white sheets. As soon as he had done so she turned onto her side, clearly shivering despite the warm woollen dressing gown she wore. His heart all but missed a beat at the sound of her softly ragged breath.

Muttering a soft, 'Gracias a Dios,' that she had regained consciousness, he drew the embroidered covers carefully over her shoulders, then sat on the edge of the bed to touch the flat of his hand against her forehead. 'Maldita sea!' She was burning fiercer than the hotplate on the stove downstairs. It did not bode well. He had to act fast to help bring that temperature down, but first he had to find the telephone number for an emergency doctor.

After murmuring some consoling words in Jenny's ear, Rodrigo leapt to his feet and ran downstairs. The telephone was on the small chestnut bureau in the hallway. Picking up the receiver, he rifled through an alphabetised leather-bound address book, managing to quickly locate the number of her friend's GP. Greeted by an answer-machine message that gave him a number for emergencies only, he hissed out his frustration. Seconds later he spoke to a weary sounding male voice in person.

Explaining the reason for his call, Rodrigo was taken aback when the doctor swiftly pronounced that he couldn't possibly come out to Raven Cottage on a 'filthy night such as this'. He already had several patients to visit in the local vicinity, and unless it was a case of life or death Rodrigo would just have to take the medical advice he was about to dispense and look after Ms Renfrew himself. If her temperature did not go down within the next twenty-four hours then he should by all means ring again.

Accustomed to only having to snap his fingers and get what he needed, Rodrigo was appalled at the doctor's seemingly cavalier attitude. Wrestling the strongest urge to call the man an uncaring imbecile, he corralled his temper and quickly scribbled down the ensuing medical instructions. In any case, he had already made up his mind to ring his own personal physician in Barcelona for help should the advice he'd been given take too long to effect a change.

Back upstairs in Jenny's bedroom, he touched his hand to her forehead again. Her skin still felt hotter than a radiator with the dial turned to maximum. As if to echo the fear that bolted through him, a deafening explosion of thunder burst violently overhead. Refusing to believe that her condition would worsen, Rodrigo urgently tugged down the quilt that covered her. The warm woollen dressing gown would have to go too.

Half lifting Jenny's limp slender form towards him, he tried to be as quick and as deft as he could. But his heartbeat accelerated as he observed her unnaturally rose-tinted cheeks and fluttering lashes, her body jerking now and then as if in acute pain. Out of the blue a partially remembered Spanish lullaby came to him. Softly, beneath his breath, he began to sing. *'Duerme, niña Chiquita sleep my little babe Duerme, mi alma sleep my precious soul.'*

Lifting his hand, he smoothed some delicate golden tendrils back from the pale fevered brow before him. Then, with the dressing-gown cast aside, he gently lowered Jenny back down into the bed. The nightdress she wore underneath was a sleeveless cotton affair in white, with a chain of tiny pink rosebuds dancing across the demure round-necked bodice. In the innocent gown she looked like some fairy tale princess waiting to be woken from a dream with a kiss from a handsome enraptured hero.

Grimacing ruefully, Rodrigo levered himself to his feet. First the lullaby he had not heard since his grandmother had crooned it to him as a child, then an observation that was too whimsical for words! Ever since he had stepped over the threshold of

Raven Cottage he'd been feeling as if he was under some kind of enchantment. But there was no time to waste reflecting on the strangeness of his reactions. Not when he had to urgently bring down that temperature.

Hurriedly seeking out the adjoining bathroom, he filled a decorative ceramic bowl with tepid water, grabbed a washcloth off the towel-rail and returned to his patient's bedside. Steeping the washcloth in the water, he carefully squeezed it out again. Pressing it against Jenny's forehead, then at the sides of her neck, he murmured, 'You will be better very soon sweetheart…I promise.'

Where did he get such confidence in his healing powers? he wondered. Especially when the tight little knot of anxiety that had taken up residence inside his chest had to be a far truer indication of how he was feeling.

'So…so hot…' she murmured, moving her head from side to side. 'Need some…water…'

'Here.' Sliding his arm round Jenny's shoulders, Rodrigo helped raise her head, then reached for the carafe of water on the nightstand. Pouring some into the matching glass, he touched the cup to her lips. She sipped thirstily, some of the liquid escaping to streak down her chin onto her gown.

'Please…let me lie down again.' Her sky-blue eyes opened wide to stare up at him. 'You—you shouldn't be doing this.'

'Why?' Rodrigo smiled, lifting an eyebrow at the

flash of lightning outside the window that for electrifying moments dwarfed the dim glow of the lamp. 'What else should I be doing on a night like this? You are ill, Jenny, and I am the only one around to take care of you.'

'But you—you're not responsible for me any more.' As she bit down anxiously on her quivering lower lip her feverishly bright blue gaze was shrouded in tears.

'Do not talk further...you will only distress yourself. Rest. That is what you must do now. It's all you *can* do.'

Moving back to the bathroom, Rodrigo searched through the mahogany cabinet for some of the regular medication that was recommended for flu and fever. The doctor had advised him to give some to Jenny just as soon as he could. It would settle her and help her have a more comfortable night. Discovering an unopened packet near the back of the cabinet, he scooped it up in triumph and not a little gratitude.

It wasn't the easiest task to get her to take the two capsules he placed in her hand. She was trembling so violently with fever. Fear slashed through Rodrigo's insides that she might take a turn for the worst after all. If she did then that singularly unhelpful doctor would rue the day he had refused to come out to her, he vowed passionately.

Biting back his apprehension and doubt, he persuaded Jenny to swallow the pills with a slurp of water. With her eyes closed again, she turned onto her side. A couple of minutes later she displayed all the signs of sleeping deeply.

Freeing a relieved sigh, Rodrigo scraped a hand round his stubbled jaw, studying her closely, with microscopic thoroughness. *It was no hardship to watch her...not when she resembled some slumbering angel lying there.*

Downstairs in the kitchen, a gratingly anxious *meow* greeted him. Smiling, he dropped to his haunches to gather up the softly striped ball of fur that had instantly pressed against his ankles, as though desperate for reassurance. The feline was clearly jittery about the storm, and he took a few moments to pet and make a fuss of her before popping the animal back onto the woolly plaid blanket in her basket beside the range.

Making a swift inspection of his surroundings and spying the uncovered cake of which he'd enjoyed a slice earlier, he replaced the lid on the tin so it wouldn't dry out. Satisfied that all was as it should be, he flicked off the lights and headed back upstairs. Dropping by his bedroom first, Rodrigo grabbed some paperwork relating to the meeting rearranged for the following day, dragged the satin quilt off the bed and returned to Jenny, unable to suppress the concern that had been building inside him ever since she'd fainted into his arms earlier. He was anxious to ascertain how she was doing.

He saw at once that she was still asleep, but even so he laid his cheek briefly against her chest to reassure himself that the soft rise and fall of her breathing was progressing normally. The action sent a spasm of volcanic need jackknifing through his body that almost tore his breath from his lungs. The sweetly intoxicating scent of her flesh combined with the touch of her soft breast beneath his cheekbone almost made him forget she was ill and made him long to be able to lie down beside her instead.

He glanced ruefully across at the rattan-cushioned chair he planned to spend the night in to watch over her, and his sigh was stoic. He didn't suppose he would get much sleep at all tonight, no matter *where* he slept. Not when he needed to keep his wits sharply about him to take care of Jenny. In four hours' time he would get her to take another dose of flu medication. Before that he would be sponging her down with tepid water again, to cool her temperature.

Moving across to the chair, Rodrigo stared down at the sheaf of papers in his hand. His reluctance to give the words on the page the proper attention hardly surprised him. Not when every sense and faculty he possessed was completely given over to the welfare of the lovely young woman sleeping fitfully in the bed before him. His unexpectedly dedicated commitment to his former wife left him with little desire for anything else right now.

If Jenny were well, no doubt she'd find it quite ironic. She firmly believed he had no inclination to care for anyone but himself. Many times during the brief year they'd been together she'd bemoaned the fact that he was too wrapped up in his work to spend proper time with her. Eventually Rodrigo had had to face up to the fact that he was poor husband material because it was true…he *was* married more to his work than Jenny. And that was ironic too, really, when he considered the simplicity of his mother's long-ago hope for him. Her heartfelt desire had been that her only son would find a warm, loving partner for life, father a healthy brood of children and then settle down somewhere he could be happy—preferably somewhere in Andalucia—and be content for the rest of his existence.

It was his *father* who had conditioned and programmed him from an early age to seek the lucrative rewards of a successful career in business. Benito Martinez had all but banged the idea into Rodrigo's head with a sledgehammer, giving him no choice to explore the alternatives. As a young man Benito had tried and failed to make his fortune from a house-building business. He had made some poor financial decisions and—to his shame—had lost everything. If Rodrigo achieved success in business then he, Benito, would truly be able to hold his head up in their village at last, and show them that the Martinez name meant something.

The implication had been that until such a time he would remain disappointed. And in pursuing an idea that hadn't even originated from him Rodrigo had learned that sometimes children were expected to fulfil the frustrated dreams of their parents instead of following their own…

The most disturbing images and feelings had been running through Jenny's brain. Nearly all of them involved a man who looked as if he'd stepped out of a Renaissance painting. Such endlessly dark soulful eyes he had, such glossy black hair and a heavenly shaped mouth. *His beautiful face haunted her.* His warm accented voice took her to a land of hot sun, cool Mediterranean waters and the echo of an ancient drumbeat that had been the heart of its people for centuries. Her Renaissance man also had powerful muscular arms that could carry her anywhere he wanted if Jenny allowed it, and those arms seemed to represent security and safety and something else—something essential that she'd longed for. It didn't matter right then that her fevered mind struggled to put a name to it.

A choking cough suddenly seized her. Each breathless convulsion was like a scythe slicing through her brain, it hurt so much. The arms she had dreamed of were suddenly holding her up, lifting a glass of water to her parched lips, patiently supporting and encouraging her as she gulped thirstily. Sensing her hand tremble where it circled the glass, Jenny gripped it a bit too tightly to still the tremors and accidentally tipped half the contents over her nightgown. The icy water that connected with her heated skin was akin to the touch of the coldest steel blade, and she gasped in shock.

'Oh, how stupid! What have I done?'

'It's nothing to be anxious about, *querida*, and nothing that cannot be put right in a moment. Here...I will help you remove this, then get you a towel and a clean gown.'

Before Jenny could find the strength even to protest, Rodrigo was lifting up her nightgown, bunching it into a ball, and heading off into the bathroom. Too sick to mind that he'd just seen her naked, she crossed her arms over her chest, shivering violently from a combination of fever, cold, and pure distress that she was too weak to help herself. He returned quickly, to drape a large bathtowel round her shoulders. The floral smell of lavender-scented washing detergent as well as the disturbingly sensual whiff of her ex-husband's aftershave permeated her fogged brain to cause a faint skirmish of acute awareness deep in her belly.

'Thanks.' She couldn't bring herself to raise her eyes to look at him.

'Where do you keep your clean nightgowns? In that chest of drawers over there?'

'The second one down.'

As deftly as he'd removed the wet nightgown, Rodrigo slid a fresh one down over Jenny's head and shoulders, with the same pragmatic ease. Outside the bedroom window another starburst of vivid white lightning followed by another rumble of thunder reminded her that the persistent storm had not yet exorcised its rage.

A sense of feeling safely cocooned here inside, whilst the elements caused mayhem around them, rippled beguilingly through her. It was no good feeling resentful or embarrassed about needing Rodrigo's help tonight, she concluded wearily. All she could do was surrender to the deep malaise that dragged at her limbs and made her head feel as though it was stuffed with cloth and pray and hope that when the morning came she would be over the worst and finally able to care for herself. Till then, she had no choice but to leave Rodrigo in charge.

Lowering her head resignedly against the pillows once more, Jenny shut her eyes to the surprising and hypnotic sound of his husky velvet tones softly singing what sounded very much like a lullaby in Spanish.

CHAPTER FOUR

IN THE space of a heartbeat a lovely consoling dream—a dream about a man who had a healing touch and a honeyed voice to match—turned into a nightmare of a passage in darkness, with flames licking under the only door. Jenny's pulses were wild with terror. Suddenly it was impossible to breathe. Consumed with fear that she would die there, she let words tumble from her lips incoherent and terrified as she pleaded to be rescued—pleaded for her very life.

Strong hands imprisoned her wrists and implored her to calm down in case she hurt herself. It was all right, the disembodied voice soothingly promised. Nothing was going to harm her—he would make sure of that.

As awareness of her true surroundings returned, Jenny stared frantically at the lean, high-cheek-boned face that stared back at her with rock-like steadiness in his depthless black eyes, as if whatever troubled her—however big or small—he would handle it. Her heart continued to thump crazily beneath her ribs until bit by agonising bit she recognised Rodrigo.

'It's all right,' he soothed again and the kindness mirrored back to her from his glance and his voice was like being in receipt of a warm woollen blanket on a raw winter's night. Slowly her terror started to recede. 'You were having a nightmare, baby…but you were here all the time, safe in your bed. You're burning up with fever. You're going to have to let me do what I can to help make you more comfortable.'

'A nightmare…' she mumbled through the tousled skeins of spun-gold hair that in her urgency to be free had spilled across her face.

'Don't move,' Rodrigo told her firmly. 'I'll be straight back.'

True to his word, he was, bringing with him the ceramic bowl refilled with fresh tepid water and a newly rinsed washcloth. Without words he began to apply the cloth to Jenny's face, neck and shoulders, tugging down the thin straps of her nightgown to do so, smiling directly into her eyes when her gaze dazedly fell into his.

After a while he said, 'You were screaming, "Fire!"' Neither his expression nor the tone of his voice changed as he stated this. Calmly and methodically he continued to cool her heated skin with the gently wrung-out cloth.

'I haven't had that nightmare in ages.' A violent shiver bounced up Jenny's spine like tumbleweed tossed around by strong winds. Desperately she tried to push away the cloying dark remnants of the stark cold horror that had visited her. She felt so weak and ill. But even more than the longing to be free of her sickness she craved the comfort and reassurance of someone who cared about her.

What did it say about her life that in her time of need she had to depend on the man who had left her? Was she destined to pay the price of the poor choices she had made for the rest of her days? She was so tired of being afraid, so weary of waiting for some new disaster to yet again destroy everything she'd once depended upon, leaving her with the sense that she was nervously walking a precipice that at any second she might plunge off.

'So…what makes you have such disturbing nightmares? Do you know?'

As Rodrigo touched the cool washcloth to the area just below her throat, Jenny shivered again. 'The house burned down. I—I lost everything… my parents' photos, the mementoes of mine and Tim's childhood, all our furniture and belongings… everything.'

'You were not there at the time? You didn't get hurt?'

'No. I was away when it happened, thank God. But every time I dream about it somehow I'm there in the middle of it all and I can't get out.'

'Why did you not let me know about this?' Her ex-husband's voice sounded fierce for a moment.

'We'd parted. We were no longer together and it was up to me to handle it.'

Rodrigo breathed in deeply. 'So what caused this fire?'

'The police investigation concluded it was an electrical fault.'

'That was the most incredible bad luck. But we won't talk about such distressing matters right now. It won't help. I'm going to give you some more medication to help lower your temperature and then you will sleep again.'

Letting the cloth drop back into the bowl, Rodrigo moved the items onto the nightstand then turned back to Jenny to lightly curl his hand round her delicately made wrist. Adjusting his palm, he thoughtfully stroked the pad of his thumb across the finer skin at the base of her fingers.

'And this time it will be a healing, dreamless sleep, I am certain…no more nightmares.'

'You sound so sure.'

'I *am* sure.'

'Why?'

'Because my intuition tells me so.'

'You believe in that?'

'I do.'

After swallowing down the two capsules that Rodrigo gave her with a few sips of water, Jenny smiled shakily. 'You should have been a doctor.'

'What? And deprive the hotel business of my incredible flair and superb know-how?'

'You'd be superb at whatever career you chose, Rodrigo. You would have made the best carpenter too.'

Unable to ignore the weariness that was like a powerful warm wave taking her under, Jenny slid back down into the bed, her eyelids closing even before her head touched the pillow. She'd happily accept the idea of a dreamless sleep, she silently admitted. But she'd equally welcome another dream of a man with sable eyes deep enough to swim in and a gentle sure touch that was far more healing than any medicine…

For a long time after Jenny had returned to the land of sleep Rodrigo sat in the rattan chair, listening to the rain lash furiously against the windows, soberly mulling over what she'd told him about her family home burning down and losing everything.

He had been drifting off himself when her anguished cry had rent the air and sent him bolting out of his seat as if an explosion had just ripped through the room. But even though his heartbeat had thundered in alarm, he'd still had the presence of mind to stay calm, so that when she emerged more fully from whatever nighttime horrors had visited her he could reassure her that it was only a dream. Those incandescent blue eyes of hers definitely didn't lack courage, but he'd sensed early on in their acquaintance that there was some fragility in her make-up too.

It had made it all the harder for him to end a

marriage that should never have happened in the first place. But Rodrigo had been so head over heels in love with Jenny from the instant he'd seen her chatting to a friend, one of the receptionists at the hotel he'd been staying at in London, that for a while he hadn't been thinking straight.

Now, after witnessing the distress caused by her nightmare, Rodrigo willingly resigned himself to the fact that he would be getting no sleep for the rest of the night. How could he risk even dozing if that fever of hers got worse? It was vital to stay alert in case he had to make an emergency dash in his car to the nearest hospital. But even the idea of negotiating a safe path through this hostile storm in the pitch-dark, in an area he wasn't even familiar with, keeping one eye on his possibly dangerously ill passenger as he drove, filled him with dread. Yet there was no question that he would do what had to be done and deliver Jenny safely into the competent medical hands she deserved…

Grimly firming his mouth, he beat his fingers in a soft, restless tattoo on the arms of his chair. It was best not to concentrate on the worst-case scenario, he decided. If Jenny woke suddenly he would not want her to sense that he was rattled by the situation in any way.

Needing a distraction, he reached for the sheaf of papers he had brought from his room, resolving to concentrate.

Two hours later the thunder and lightning was at

last a spent force, the storm having subsided to the ghostly sound of the wind rushing pell-mell through the trees and faintly rattling the windows. Judging by the hushed rhythmic breaths that had softly accompanied the reading of his documents Jenny was still sleeping peacefully, and a welcome atmosphere of calm had descended on the room.

His eyes feeling as if he'd rinsed them out with gravel, Rodrigo laid down his papers and stood up. Yawning and stretching, he moved barefoot to Jenny's bedside. Glancing down at her angelic profile—at the curling dark blonde lashes brushing the tip of her velvet cheekbone, the slim, elegant nose and lips as serene as those of the blessed Madonna herself—he felt a rush of forceful commanding need rock him to his soul.

After helping her change her gown during the night and seeing her naked once again it was hard to get the arresting image of her bewitching perfection to leave his mind. *She was so lovely that Rodrigo had to force away the idea of her being with someone else.* It made him feel jealous and suddenly possessive. If he had a second chance with her then he would definitely *not* spend all his time at work. Even *he* must learn from the lessons of the past.

Suddenly realizing the road his hypnotized thoughts were taking him down, Rodrigo shook his head. For heaven's sake, was he going mad? His marriage to Jenny was finished—over. He'd made his choice and he was destined to live by it. Dedication and hard work had helped him become the owner and head of one of the most successful luxury spa hotel empires in the world, and he wasn't about to ease off the gas for anything—least of all a precarious rekindling of a relationship that he'd really known from the first could never work. The only real solace and satisfaction to be had in life was in his work. No woman, no matter how soft, feminine and lovely, could bring him more happiness and fulfilment than that. He might indulge his need for sex and companionship from time to time, but that was all.

Moving away from where Jenny lay peacefully sleeping, in case he was tempted to meander into the realms of such pointless fantasy again, he rubbed his palm round his unshaven jaw with a scowl. Reaching the window, he swept the curtain aside to see the faint pink and gold light of dawn edging the horizon. Hovering over the smooth glass of the sea, it was a sublime sight. *A sight surely worth missing out on a night's sleep for...* It didn't happen very often that he did that. The strict routine he adhered to didn't factor in long, soulful glances at charming scenery.

'Rodrigo?'

'Sí?'

He spun round with a jolt to find Jenny throwing back the covers and lifting her legs out of the bed.

'What time is it?'

'Just after seven a.m. Where do you think you're going?'

Reaching her side, Rodrigo frowned deeply. To

his surprise she kept her head bowed and he sensed she was embarrassed.

'I—I need the bathroom.'

'Let me help you.'

'I can manage.'

But even as she strove to rise to her feet he saw that she was trembling like some fragile birch leaf in the wind. It was clear she was still feverish, and far from recovered.

'I disagree.' His tone strongly disapproving, Rodrigo had no hesitation in scooping her up into his arms and marching into the bathroom. Through the paper-thin cotton of her nightgown her body heat all but scorched him. There was no way on earth that she'd be fit enough to run her friend's guesethouse for a good few days yet. He also knew he wouldn't or *couldn't* leave her stranded. His scheduled business meeting would just have to be postponed again. No doubt his contractors would be relieved to have the extra time to get things ready for the boss's inspection.

Switching on the light, Rodrigo carefully stood Jenny down in the middle of the floor. And, because he couldn't resist, he gently moved a few tousled strands of corn-gold silk back from her face. 'I will be waiting right outside the door to help you back to bed,' he told her. The unsullied crystal of her huge blue eyes reminded him of an Andalucian mountain lake, caressed by sunlight. His stomach rolled over at the sight.

'Okay…'

When she emerged from the room a few minutes later Rodrigo once again swept her up into his arms to carry her back to bed. As she settled back under the covers Jenny's expression was forlorn. 'I'm so embarrassed that I've let you do all this for me that I almost don't know what to say to you.'

'Were you well last night?'

'No, but—'

'Are you feeling any better today?'

'No… But I still—'

'Is there someone—some friend, family member or even a neighbour I can ring—who will come and take care of you for the next few days?'

Rodrigo didn't miss the flash of despair in her eyes. 'Not that I can think of…no…'

'Then there is nothing else for you to do but go back to sleep. I am here, and will remain so until such time as you are able to get back on your feet and go about your business as normal. If anyone rings to make a reservation then I'll simply tell them we are closed until you are better.'

'But what about your work? You came down here for a meeting, didn't you?'

'It is easy enough to delay for another day or two.'

'You would do that for me?'

'I know you find that hard to believe but, yes, Jenny…I *would*.'

'Even so, I can't let you, Rodrigo.'

'You have no say in the matter. It's my own decision. No one is forcing me to do anything I don't want to do—least of all you.'

'I feel so useless.' Her pretty mouth struggling with emotion, she looked as if she might cry.

Still feeling appalled that there was no one Jenny could ask to help but him—his own past neglect of her not withstanding—Rodrigo gave her a gentle shove so that her spun-gold head fell back onto the creamy white pillows.

'Since I have already complimented you on your ability to make guests feel more than at home here, and have seen how dedicated you are to running things for Lily in her absence, that's clearly not true. Go back to sleep. When you wake I'll make you a cup of tea, if that's your preference. But I warn you that my tea-making skills would hardly earn me a job working here.'

Chuckling, he reached out to lay his palm flat against Jenny's forehead. She was still unnaturally warm, but thankfully not as dangerously hot as last night. Cautiously, he prayed that meant her fever had broken and she was over the worst.

'You're a long way from recovered, *querida*, but hopefully you are on the mend. Right now I need a shower and a shave—then I'll see what has to be done downstairs. Do as I say and get some more rest… I'll return in a while to make sure everything is okay.'

Settling back against the bank of pillows she'd just about mustered the strength to arrange behind her,

Jenny swept her gaze round the sunlit bedroom with frustrated resignation and felt a little jab of fear piercing her. It was perfectly true that she felt weaker than a newborn foal, and twice as vulnerable, but to have allowed Rodrigo, her work-obsessed ex-husband, to postpone his business meeting to help take care of her… Well, it hadn't featured in even her *wildest* dreams. *And why had she trusted him so easily when his past record of considering her needs was so abysmal?* It was inexplicable.

She'd had similar issues with Tim. Jenny knew her brother wasn't the type of man who could take care of anything much. He certainly wouldn't have been able to even look after their home if she should have fallen ill. In truth, he would have simply gone out and left her. His attitude to any sort of responsibility was casual, to say the least. When she'd returned to live in her old home after she and Rodrigo had split up, the beautiful Victorian semi she'd grown up in had been an absolute *tip*. It had taken several weeks of diligent home-making application on Jenny's part to restore it to anywhere near its former beauty and comfort.

Then, after months of growing suspicion of her brother's irresponsible behaviour, she'd discovered the real reason he was inclined to let things slide—and that included work. It was because he despised any demands that came between him and his increasing dependence on drugs.

A flutter of pain tightened her chest. *Dark times…*

Not the kind of thing Jenny wanted to recall when she was feeling so poorly.

In stark contrast, the vibrant and charismatic Rodrigo had taken on the mantle of carer so gallantly and effortlessly that she was already half bewitched by him all over again. *Dangerous.* Her temperature had soared even higher when he'd swept her up into his arms to take her to the bathroom and back to bed when she came out. There was no disputing the man's strength, or the beguiling warmth of his body at close quarters, or the fine and expensive way he smelled. But the situation couldn't continue for much longer, Jenny vowed. Somehow she had to get better quickly to resume her stewardship of Lily's guesthouse. It was kind of Rodrigo to say he would tell people they were closed until she was recovered, but it was her friend's precious income she was denying if she allowed that.

'How are you feeling?'

The man himself stood in the doorway, carrying a tray with a cup of tea on it. The sight of him had the same effect as a shot of dizzying adrenaline in the arm. He was wearing a fitted coal-black T-shirt and faded light blue denims that hugged his muscular thighs like a glove. The deceptively ordinary clothing must *love* being so close to his smooth bronzed skin, Jenny thought wildly, because the things they did for that mouthwateringly fit body surely shouldn't be allowed in a defenceless woman's bedroom.

Flustered, she sat up a bit straighter against her

pillows. 'I thought about lying to you and telling you that I felt much better, but if I got up and fell flat on my face I realised you'd pretty soon get the picture that perhaps I should have made a will…just in case.'

'At least you've got your sense of humour back. That's got to be a good sign. And you're not going to die…not on *my* watch.'

Moving towards the bed, Rodrigo deposited her cup of tea on the nightstand.

'Room service as well?' Jenny quipped, wishing it wasn't so hard to breathe whenever he came near. 'Did you master that when you were starting out in the hotel business too?'

CHAPTER FIVE

'IF YOU want to learn how a business works from the ground up then you have to familiarise yourself with everything.'

'I agree. When I first started doing interior design I found there were so many dimensions to it that I hadn't realised. It made the work even more interesting, though.'

'And how's business these days?' Rodrigo asked.

'It's been a bit up and down, which is why I could come here and help Lily out. But I've got a couple of good commissions coming up.'

Her plump lower lip was receiving some unfair treatment from her teeth as she chewed on it, he observed.

'Anyway...from what you say about the way you approach things it's obvious that you've become a success because you're so...thorough.'

The corners of his mouth edged into a sardonic smile. 'I am, as you say thorough. That applies to whatever I might be engaged in, if you recall.'

Jenny lapsed into a self-conscious and pink-cheeked silence. Had the same stimulating scenario gone through *her* mind as had just flashed through his? *Rodrigo certainly hoped so.*

'Thanks for the tea. You've made it exactly the way I like it.'

'Muchas gracias, señorita.' He made a mock bow. 'I aim to please. Here.' Carefully he passed her the cup and saucer, noting immediately that her hands shook a little as she accepted it. 'And after you drink it you are to stay put for the rest of the day. I'll see to everything else that needs to be done.'

'I'll have to pay you for your help, Rodrigo.'

'What?'

'It's only right. If you're working for me I'll have to pay you…especially as I'm delaying your return to your own job.'

'That's crazy talk. You need do no such thing.' A spasm of anger shot through him that she would think for even a second that he expected to be paid for helping take care of her when she was ill. 'Now that the rain's stopped I'm going into the garden to check on the greenhouse. I'll remove the tarpaulin we put up the other night and look over any damage that the storm might have caused. For lunch I'll make us a simple soup—my cooking skills do actually exceed my tea-making ones, though I confess I didn't demonstrate them when we were together. You were clearly a bit rundown for this fever to have occurred and no doubt your immune system needs building up again with good food.'

'Right now I couldn't contemplate eating anything—not when my sense of taste is probably non-existent.' Taking the tiniest sip of the hot tea he'd made, Jenny passed him back the delicate blue and white cup with its matching saucer almost immediately. 'I don't mean to sound ungrateful, but I feel so stupidly weak that I—' Touching her hand to her head, she grimaced.

'Does something hurt?' Rodrigo demanded, examining her flushed pretty face with renewed concern.

'My head feels like a re-enactment of the Battle of Waterloo is going on inside it,' she answered. 'I really need to shut my eyes again. Do you mind?'

'Of course not… It's clear that you are nowhere near recovered.' After returning her cup and saucer to the nightstand, when next Rodrigo looked she'd slid back down into the bed and buried herself beneath the plump feather duvet like a small animal going into hibernation.

'Rest, then, *querida*,' he said with a smile, and although he would have been quite happy to stand and gaze at her for a while longer, he wrestled the desire to the ground and headed back downstairs.

During the following three days it honestly went through Jenny's mind more than once that if she slipped away into the afterlife one fever-racked night it might be a blessing. Never before had her constitution been under such miserable threat. But she held onto the vehement assurance that Rodrigo had given her— 'You're not going to die…not on *my* watch.'

Had she ever slept this much in the whole of her twenty-seven years? Her dad had told her once that even as an infant she had only slept six hours out of every twenty-four. *Not much rest to be had then for her long-suffering parents.*

But during those memorable three days while she was ill Jenny heard Rodrigo moving reassuringly round the house, doing this and that, and at one point forced opened her heavy lids to see a smart-suited stranger urging her to 'just relax' whilst he placed a cold thermometer under her arm to take her temperature. Whatever the doctor concluded it had caused Rodrigo to move into her bedroom permanently, it seemed—because whenever Jenny did manage to open her eyes he was there in the rattan chair next to her bed, either scribbling away on a notepad with his pen or tapping away at the keys on his laptop. A couple of times she registered him speaking on the phone too…once in mellifluous Spanish.

But, as much as his continued presence reassured her, Jenny had mixed emotions about it. Her tired brain could hardly credit why he would stay with her for so long and not simply leave… It was nothing like his old behaviour, when work had always come first.

On the fourth day of her illness she woke up

feeling less likely to die and longing for a bath. Her teeth were also in dire need of the brushing of a lifetime, because frankly her mouth tasted as though some small creature had crept inside and died in it. It was after eight in the morning, and the rattan chair beside her was empty of her handsome dark-haired guard. With a little jolt of unease in her stomach at the fresh realisation of just how much she had been relying on Rodrigo she swung her legs over the side of the bed and stood up.

Wrong move, Jenny... The room spun alarmingly, as though she'd just stepped off a manically twirling carousel

'What are you doing?'

'I need a bath. If I don't have one soon you'll have to report me to the health and safety department.'

Moving away from the doorway, his face unsmiling, Rodrigo walked right up to her. Recently showered and shaved, and wearing a fresh white T-shirt and black corded jeans, the man smelled *gorgeous*. It made Jenny all the more flustered and aware of her own less than scented condition after lying ill in bed for three days.

'Are you up to having a bath, *querida*? Perhaps I could bring a basin of warm water and you could have a bed-bath instead?'

'With you playing nurse?' Her eyebrows flew up to her scalp. 'I don't think so!'

'This is hardly the time for false modesty, Jenny Wren. Besides...' a teasing spark of heat ignited in his soulful dark eyes '…I've seen you naked, remember? And not just when I helped you change into a fresh nightgown.'

She'd been praying she'd dreamt that. Learning that wasn't the case, she felt her heart skip an embarrassed beat. 'It's hardly gentlemanly of you to remind me about that.'

He chuckled—a husky, compelling sound that made her legs feel weaker than water. 'Sometimes I am a gentleman and others *not.* I don't have to leave it to your imagination to wonder about the times I am not…do I?'

Clutching the front of her nightgown a little desperately, Jenny tipped up her chin. 'I have to have a bath. In fact I insist. Just leave me alone for a while, would you? I'm quite capable of sorting it out for myself.'

But he'd already stalked into the bathroom and turned on the taps. Stepping back into the bedroom, he dropped his hands to his hips, grinning with a distinct air of amused defiance at her disbelieving look. 'Which bubble bath shall I pour in? You have several.'

'I—I…' Flustered, she bit heavily down on her lip again. It might appear ridiculous to Rodrigo to quibble about such an innocuous thing, but somehow pouring in her bath fragrance seemed like the ultimate in intimate acts when she was already feeling disconcertingly fragile. 'I'll do that.'

Moving into the already steam-filled bathroom on

legs that felt like cotton-wool, Jenny shouldn't have been a bit surprised to find Rodrigo right behind her, but she was.

'This is no time to be petulant,' he told her, stern-voiced. He stepped in front of her, his black eyes roving her face as if he would know the secrets of her very soul. 'Which fragrance shall I use? If you won't tell me then I will put in the rose...especially since you reminded me of one from the moment I saw you in the reception area of the Savoy Hotel.'

Stoically resisting a huge urge to cry, Jenny scanned the array of prettily shaped bottles on the shelf above the bath and sniffed. 'That's the most ridiculous thing I've ever heard.'

Rodrigo took hold of her elbows and impelled her towards him, so that she had no choice but to make him the sole focus of her attention. 'You didn't always throw my compliments back in my face, Jenny... No,' he added lazily, 'sometimes they could make you blush, and other times make you extremely affectionate as I recall.'

Now, as heat cascaded through her like a rampaging river, Jenny's legs really *did* feel as if they might not hold her up for very much longer. There was a heaviness and a heat between her thighs she couldn't deny.

'That was when I trusted and loved you,' she burst out irritably, pulling free of Rodrigo's loose hold on her—suddenly terrified of the need that made her want to surrender to his arms and give him everything. 'And I don't any more. Now I'm much more careful about who I give my affection to.'

'Is that your way of telling me you've found someone else?'

'Are you joking?' she answered scathingly. 'After the way my brother behaved as well, I don't think I'll ever trust another man again.'

'Not now, perhaps… But when enough time has passed you might learn that not all men are so despicable.' Tenderly Rodrigo smoothed back her hair, standing his ground as Jenny's body stiffened with tension

'If I ever make the mistake of trusting a man again, then I deserve everything I get!'

'Yet you *did* trust me again.' His tone was gentle but firm. 'You trusted me to take care of you while you were ill.'

'I didn't have much choice, did I?'

'Do you want to vent your anger at me Jenny? Is that it?'

'All I want is my bath,' she said weakly. Frighteningly, she sensed that the full flood of grief and pain over what had happened between them hovered dangerously close now that she'd opened the lid on it again. It must be because she was sick she reasoned. Usually she managed to contain her hurt and rage much better.

'Then that's exactly what you shall have.' Reaching up to the shelf for the crystal bottle labelled 'English Rose,' Rodrigo gave her an unperturbed smile. After liberally applying it to the splashing hot water, he returned the bottle to the shelf. 'I'll leave you to get into the tub by yourself, but if you need me I'll be just outside the door,' he told her.

'Thanks,' she murmured. And as soon as the closed door was a barrier between them she dropped down onto the loo seat and allowed herself to listen to the sound of her heart breaking again…

That was when I trusted and loved you, she'd said. He could drive himself mad with regret and pain because she'd never say she loved and trusted him again. And it wasn't easy for Rodrigo to leave Jenny to cry. He'd sensed the hurt she normally held in strict check had just catapulted to the surface and spilled over. Every heaving sob was like a knife slicing through his heart, and it disturbed him to discover that he could be so affected by this woman's tears.

Why had it not been that way before? The more she had cried, the more he had been furious with what he saw as typically female behaviour employed to manipulate his emotions. He sat in the rattan chair and dropped his head in his hands. Listening to Jenny's distress was nothing less than pure torture.

A few moments later, the sound of her crying ceased. Resisting the strongest urge to knock on the door and ask if she felt better, he heard the relieved groan she released as she settled herself back into the hot water. About five minutes later, lost in his own thoughts, Rodrigo jolted when he heard her call out his name. He was at the door in a second.

'What is it? Are you okay?'

'Can you—can you come in?'

Surprised, he didn't hesitate. Such a picture she made, lying there amidst the fragrant pink bubbles, her big blue eyes staring back at him like a crestfallen child's, that Rodrigo's heart slammed hard against his ribs.

'Do you want me to scrub your back?' he joked, although the idea of sliding his hands over that gleaming wet satin skin was definitely no cause for amusement. Even as he stood looking down at her his body throbbed with equal measures of pleasure and pain.

'Could you help me wash my hair?' Jenny asked softly, her expression clearly nervous in case he should refuse.

'Of course… Where is your shampoo?'

'Here.' She handed him a tube-shaped bottle.

Dropping to his knees behind her, Rodrigo breathed her in, stealing a vital couple of moments to contain the lava-flow of desire that rocked through him and stay clear-headed enough to do the job in hand. But every sense he had was already saturated with her essence, even before he touched her.

Applying some shampoo to her already dampened hair, he could hardly attest to breathing as he began to move his palms slowly over her scalp. Nobody had ever told him that washing a woman's hair could be so immensely satisfying and erotic. Over one satiny-smooth shoulder he glimpsed the delicate swell of her breast, disappearing provocatively down into a sea of pink foam.

'Rodrigo?'

'Yes?' His voice sounded as if it scraped over gravel, he was so aroused.

'I'm sorry I acted like such an idiot just now. Perhaps we can call a truce?'

'I'm not at war with you, Jenny. I never was.'

'What do you mean?'

Jenny turned her head to glance at him, and he painfully observed the tiny collection of moisture bubbles clinging to the delicate furrow above her top lip. He yearned to lick away every one.

'I've never thought of you as my enemy…that's all.'

'So you want us to be friends? Is that what you're saying?'

'*Dios!* I know you are ill, but I don't want you to delude yourself that it's friendship I'm interested in! Pass me that jug so I can rinse your hair, would you?' He clicked his fingers, scarcely able to contain his impatience and—it had to be admitted—his *annoyance.* Suddenly he was in no mood for playing games. Not when it was all but killing him to wash her hair.

'Are you mad at me for asking you to do this?' When Rodrigo had finished rinsing, Jenny hurriedly scraped her fingers through her damp shoulder-length locks to move them out of her face, her gaze anxiously tracking him as he stood up and moved round the tub to survey her.

'No. I'm not mad at you at all. But don't fool yourself that all I want to do is take care of you while you're ill. Trust me…I'm not as selfless or gallant as you may imagine. Neither am I made of stone.'

'Oh.'

'Is that all you can say?'

'Rodrigo, I didn't ask you to stay and take care of me. Are you saying that I should sleep with you as some kind of thank-you?'

'Dios!'

His handsome face looked so thunderous that Jenny shrank back as far as she could in the tub, her heart beating hard.

'That you even *dare* make such a crass remark is beyond belief. Admitting that I desire you does not mean I'm suggesting you give me your body for services rendered! I know perfectly well that you're not immune or unaware of the attraction flaring between us again. I was merely being honest about my intention.'

'And that is?'

He curled his lip in a sardonic smile, then folded his arms across his chest. His action drew Jenny's heated gaze to the ripple of toned hard muscle in his bronzed biceps and taut torso, and she felt the hot sting of arousal burning in the tips of her breasts.

'I am definitely going to make love to you very

soon, Jenny,' he drawled. 'I will, of course, wait until you are fully recovered, but make no mistake that it will happen. Now… Do you need my help getting out of that tub?'

'No!' she answered quickly, disconcerted to see him nod with a little mocking smile.

'Okay, then. If you think you can manage on your own then I'll go downstairs and prepare some breakfast for us. You are hungry this morning, yes?'

Hungry? Suddenly the word had all kinds of dangerous connotations for Jenny.

CHAPTER SIX

CURLED up on the living room couch with a cosy woollen blanket, Jenny watched Rodrigo rise from where he'd been stoking the burning logs in the woodstove, then smooth his long artistic hands down his jeans. Although she was still feeling frustratingly tired and achy, it was impossible not to notice how strong, well made and fit he was. He might work in the hotel trade on the business side of things, but he wasn't a man who shied away from hard physical work either.

Earlier, she'd glanced out of the kitchen window to see just how hard he'd been working in the storm-tossed garden. It looked as if it had been given a serious face-lift. Even the fallen tree had been moved to lie safely against the fence, and without its temporary tarpaulin Lily's beloved greenhouse appeared intact and sturdy as ever.

'You'll be wanting to head off soon, now that I'm feeling better.' Suddenly, the thoughts that had been buzzing round inside Jenny's head were out in the open.

Remaining quiet, Rodrigo strode across to lay his palm against her forehead. A hot current of awareness hummed right down to the very edges of her toes.

'You are still a little warm.' He frowned, his ebony gaze sweeping over her like an arresting searchlight.

'Yes, but I really am feeling so much better.'

'But hardly well enough to get back to work and run Lily's business efficiently. Today is Friday…I'll stay until Monday at least, to make sure you are well on your way back to being fighting fit before I go.'

'You don't have to.'

In answer to that comment, he merely raised an eyebrow.

'By the way, I've been meaning to ask you… Have we had any enquiries about bookings over the last few days?'

'*Sí*…we have.'

'And?' Jenny's hands twisted anxiously in the folds of the woollen blanket.

'And I made the required reservations, of course. They were both for the end of the month, when your friend returns from Australia. A married couple from Jersey and a single woman from Edinburgh. All the details are in the reservations book.'

'She'll be pleased about that. Thanks for seeing to things. You've been working hard in the garden too, I noticed. I can't let you do all this for nothing.'

'We have already put that subject to bed, have we not?'

'Okay…I'll drop it. But as soon as I feel able I'll cook you something nice.'

Cozette chose that particular moment to stroll into the room and make a beeline for Jenny's lap.

She grinned in delight as she stroked her hand over the deliciously soft striped fur. 'Cozette, my angel! How have you been, baby? Have you missed me?' The cat rubbed its face against Jenny's arm, then settled into the blanket against her middle to purr contentedly.

'Little traitor.' Rodrigo grinned, dropping easily down to his haunches to fondly pet the animal.

'A traitor… Why?'

'Because since you've been ill she's behaved like I am the sun, moon and stars—playing up to me, wanting me to pamper and pet her whenever she gets the chance…just as if she lives for nobody's attention but mine. Now she's with you I see that she was merely toying with my affections, like the typically mercenary little female she is!'

'All females aren't mercenary, Rodrigo.' Imbuing her tone with a teacher-like scold, Jenny bravely met his mocking glance. Almost instantly the humour in his eyes vanished, leaving her with the strangest sensation that she was falling through space—plummeting at frightening speed—with no sense or idea of when or *if* she would land safely on earth again. A gasp caught and died in her throat as he reached for her hand to place it firmly against his rough-velvet cheek.

'I find myself intensely jealous of the attention that you're paying Cozette, *querida*...I'm wondering if you have any left to spare for me.' Moving her palm to his lips, he pressed a warm kiss into the centre.

'I expect you've been missing the routine and demands of your work.' Keeping her voice deliberately light, so that he wouldn't see how affected she was, Jenny retrieved her hand to lay it over Cozette again. She prayed Rodrigo wouldn't see that it was trembling. 'Your friends are probably missing you too. I feel slightly guilty that I've monopolised your time because of this stupid illness.'

'So you expect never to get ill? You are infallible?'

'I didn't mean that. All I meant was that it was inconvenient.'

'You know my lifestyle. I travel too much to be concerned with friends.'

Shrugging, Rodrigo rose to his feet, briefly rubbing his hands together.

'You don't always have to isolate yourself from people, Rodrigo.'

'I am perfectly happy with the way things are.'

'Really?' It hurt Jenny to hear that.

'I find it works better for me if I keep a little distance.'

'But still...don't you get a bit lonely, doing all that travelling and never really being close to anyone?'

'My work is my life. You of all people know that.

Now, I've got some phone calls to make that have been backing up. Are you okay by yourself for a while?'

'Yes, I'm fine.' Her heart thudding heavily, because Rodrigo suddenly seemed to be clearly illustrating his preference for a little distance, Jenny sighed.

'At least you have Cozette for company, no?'

'I told you—I'm fine. I don't need a babysitter… Just go and make your phone calls and forget about me.'

'I'll make my phone calls…but I won't forget about you, Jenny Wren.'

Because he'd taken the wind out of her sails, Jenny glared at him. 'Just go!'

'Okay, okay, I'm going.' Having the audacity to chuckle at her petulant tone, he held up his hands in a gesture of surrender and backed slowly out of the room.

As soon as he was gone, Jenny was appalled to find hot tears boiling up behind her eyes. Suddenly the prospect of him leaving made her stomach lurch with sadness. What was the matter with her, for goodness' sake? She was over him, wasn't she? What on earth was she doing, attaching herself to the idea that somewhere deep inside he perhaps still held a torch for her? They'd parted a long time ago now. Why couldn't she just accept that and get on with her life as she'd been doing before he'd shown up?

Lifting her hand up to her face, she stared at the

spot that his lips had so spine-tinglingly caressed. It throbbed like a brand. Did he still not need anyone at all…ever?

In the afternoon, after the light lunch he'd prepared for them both, Rodrigo absented himself again, leaving Jenny with a stack of DVDs to choose from to keep her entertained. It appeared she was in no mood for conversation.

Seeing definite signs of her recovery, even though her complexion was still marble-pale, he took the opportunity to return to his room to work. Yet from time to time, as he studied his paperwork and made his phone calls, he couldn't help remembering how they'd been captured by each other's gazes just before he'd kissed her palm. It caused a flutter of mayhem in his stomach to recall it. Irritable, but not wanting to explore why, he diverted his attention to his most pressing phone call.

It had been just as he'd thought at the site in Penzance—the building schedule had indeed fallen behind, and even more so with all the rain. Although Rodrigo had had to delay the meeting because of Jenny, he now wanted to get to the root of the hold-up. There were several things he wanted the manager to keep him up to speed with, in fact, which meant that the afternoon flew by in a long, detailed discussion until Rodrigo had thoroughly satisfied himself that all was now proceeding as it should be.

Rising from behind the antique desk in his room,

he rolled his shoulders to unlock the cramps in his muscles. Sighing, he strolled across to the window. In the far distance the sun-kissed silver Atlantic lapped the sand-covered shore, the white foam rolling in and out again as it had done since time immemorial but no-less mesmerising. Narrowing his gaze, he observed the seagulls cutting cleanly across the winter blue sky that would soon turn to dusk, dipping gracefully every now and then into the ocean in avid search of their supper. An urgent need suddenly arose inside him to breathe in some of that wild sea air.

Jenny was dozing on the couch when he looked in on her and so, deciding to follow his impulse, Rodrigo drove down to the beach.

She was definitely over the worst, he assured himself, so he could risk leaving her to sleep for a while. He tucked his rich burgundy cashmere scarf deep into the neckline of his leather jacket and strode across the sand, wincing but enjoying the bracing air. On Monday, when he left this place, his usual routine would be quickly reinstated, he reflected. Jenny would no longer need his help, so work would once again take precedence.

A sharp twist low down in his belly protested at the idea with a painful jolt. It was merely frustration, Rodrigo thought impatiently—frustration at not being able to satisfy his lustful desire for his pretty ex-wife. He knew he'd sworn that he would make love to her soon, but the more he thought about it, the more he guessed that wouldn't be wise. Jenny still had dreams in her eyes, he realized, and if he got involved with her even briefly and then left again it would no doubt reinforce her angry belief that cruelty was indeed inherent in his character.

No… He just had to put any further thoughts of bedding her right out of his mind. Instead, as soon as his business meeting was over, he would return to London where he could hook up with a Spanish actress he knew. He occasionally took her to dinner—and more often than not to bed. She was a real Latin firecracker, and knew all kinds of stimulating ways to entertain and relax a hard-working man.

But the thought of the red-lipped fiery *señorita* left Rodrigo cold when he compared her charms to the warm and beguiling Jenny.

Biting back a ripe curse, he saluted an old man who was walking a terrier, then—with his head down against the strong gusting wind—retraced his steps back to the car.

'Where did you go?'

'I took a walk on the beach. You were sleeping when I left.'

'I sensed you weren't in the house when I woke up.'

'So you missed me, then?'

'I didn't say that. I just didn't want you to leave without saying goodbye.'

'I would not have left without telling you I intended to go…nor would I have absconded without paying my bill.'

Her mouth dropping open, Jenny stared at Rodrigo in amazement. 'You don't think I'm going to charge you for your stay when all you've done since you walked in here is look after me?'

'That was hardly your fault. Besides…' his hand scraped through his windblown black hair, then down over his jacket '…it's a business your friend is running here, *querida*—not a charity.'

At the apt reminder Jenny's heart sank. *Some helpful caretaker she'd turned out to be!* Her own business was struggling, and she had an inkling it was because her heart wasn't really in it. When she returned to London she would throw herself into things a bit more determinedly, but what if she just wasn't cut out to run a business at all? Ostensibly her talents lay in her creativity, not making money.

Thinking back over what she'd had to deal with in the past as far as her relationships were concerned, she wished she could have been stronger. But her trust had been shattered both by her brother and Rodrigo, and she'd defy anyone to cope with that and be full of confidence.

Glancing across at the flickering television screen, Rodrigo slipped off his jacket and threw it onto a cream pin-tucked armchair. Even at a distance Jenny scented the tang of the sea that clung to him from his walk. She wished she'd been well enough to accompany him.

'What are you watching?' he asked interestedly.

'Pride and Prejudice.' She swallowed down the regret that washed over her. All she'd ever really desired was a kind, loving husband, children of her own and a lovely home. A wistful sigh escaped her at the story unfolding on the screen, where she knew the heroine Lizzie *would* get the man and the house she dreamed of. 'I love period dramas…the clothes, the beauty of the architecture, the manners…and the simmering unspoken passions underneath all that buttoned-up corsetry and politeness.'

The phrase 'buttoned-up corsetry' made Rodrigo wince. He was having trouble enough trying to keep his desire for Jenny under tight control without being taunted by images of her in an old-fashioned virginal white corset—that he, of course, would be only too eager to divest her of…

'And is Mr Darcy your idea of the perfect man, Jenny?'

Her blue eyes looked dreamy for a moment, but then she shook her head. 'Not really.' Her fingers plucked restlessly at the plaid wool blanket. 'After all, he's just a character in a book. If you really lived with a man like that I'd bet it wouldn't be long before his true colours emerged. He'd probably prove to be exactly what she originally thinks him to be—an egomaniac who believes it is his God-given right to have exactly what he wants including a wife who reflects his pompous vision of himself! It's been my experience that men are selfish creatures, on the whole. They only really want what *they* want…no matter how much it may hurt the women who care for them.'

Rodrigo winced. He knew instantly this wasn't just about the fictional Mr Darcy. 'I'm sorry your experience of men has been so negative,' he murmured.

Tugging the blanket up around her chest, she visibly shivered. 'I'm not just referring to you. My brother Tim was an addict… You didn't know that, did you? You name it, he was hooked on it. Pot, cocaine, heroin, alcohol, gambling—everything. And when his own money wasn't enough to pay for it all, he thought it his right to demand mine. Especially after you and I parted and he thought I was rich.'

'I had my reservations about your brother, but I had no idea he was as you say. I wish you could have shared that with me when we were together.'

'Why? You couldn't have changed him. If you'd got to know him he'd only have ended up using you for what he could get…just like he did with me. It didn't matter that we were brother and sister.'

'What happened before he went to Scotland, Jenny? I want to know.'

She stared at him with a haunted look. 'He put me through hell, trying to get our family house from me.' She dropped her head onto her raised knees. Glancing up again, she pushed back her hair. 'When I finally agreed to buy him out, that and the legal costs almost bankrupted me. The court case was horrendous. He persuaded a besotted rich girlfriend to pay for some whiz-bang lawyer, and the lies he told about me to plead his case were vile…such vindictive, terrible lies that I wanted to die. Anyway, when I was worn out with fighting I agreed to a settlement. I only did it because I knew if he won the case everything my parents had worked so hard for would have been sold for a song to pay for his out-of-control lifestyle. Ironic that not long after he'd been paid out the house caught fire and burned down and it all went anyway.'

'My God! If I had had any idea that that was the situation you were returning to when we broke up I would have—'

'You would have what, Rodrigo? Taken me back?' Her eyes glittering, Jenny shook her head. 'I don't think so. Besides…I can fight my own battles.'

'You are strong, that is true… But it grieves me to hear you went through that alone.'

Switching off the television, Rodrigo lowered himself onto the end of the couch. His glance alighted on Jenny's lovely face as fervently as a ship looked for the lodestar—and he saw that her gaze shimmered with tears.

'The truth is I don't know if I have the heart to continue with my business' she confessed. 'I worked so hard at it—and for what? The thing I wanted most in the world was a family and a home of my own. You and I only lasted a year, my parents are gone, and my relationship with my brother is non-existent because of what happened. I never envisaged spending the rest of my life alone.'

'And neither will you be alone for ever, Jenny. It simply is not possible. One day everything will change for the better and you will have your dream.'

'Does your famous intuition tell you that Rodrigo?'

Fielding the swathe of pain that cut through him at the despondency in her voice, Rodrigo struggled to find the words to convince her life would improve. It didn't help that he had played a big part in making her mistrust her future.

'It's no surprise that you got ill. There is too much hurt and unhappiness weighing down your heart, and I honestly regret that.'

Jenny stared at him. 'I think you do. But, like me, you can't help how you're made. Your past has shaped you too, and you've grown to believe that work is the most important thing. I don't like the idea of you being alone for the rest of your life either.'

'Maybe I deserve to? Anyway, I will just have to live with my mistakes, if that's what they are.'

'Sometimes you're far too hard on yourself—do you know that?'

When she leaned over and squeezed his arm, Rodrigo sensed such a tide of heat and longing sweep over him that all he could do was stare down at that small perfect palm circling his wrist without any words at all. Then his brain engaged properly.

'I'm a man who goes for what he wants and gets it, Jenny. To get on in this life you have to cultivate some steel. To this day I've never allowed sentiment to get in the way of making the decisions that suit *me* best—whether that's in my private life or my work. You know that to your cost. So please don't waste your time thinking I need kindness and forgiveness.'

CHAPTER SEVEN

RODRIGO was on his feet before Jenny had a chance to respond. 'It's getting late, and I should see to our meal. Finish watching your DVD…relax and enjoy it.'

Without glancing back to gauge her expression, he strode out through the door into the hallway. The cat followed him. In the kitchen, he automatically located the ingredients he needed for their meal from the fridge and the larder, pausing briefly to fill a dish of food for Cozette when her pitiful mewing became too loud to ignore. Straightening, he leant his hip against the counter, pressing his fingers deeply into his brow.

It was about time Jenny fully realised that he couldn't pursue a relationship with her for a second time. Even if that meant that next time he met her eyes they would be even more wary and sad around him.

If he hadn't been married to her before would he have stayed and played nursemaid as he had done? It was an uncomfortable thought, but a truthful one at least. He'd stayed purely because it was Jenny. On Monday he was leaving, all being well, and right now he needed to employ some of that distance he spoke about. God knew it should be second nature to him when it came to relationships—especially when someone threatened to get too close. But twice now Jenny had almost made him forget that. If he employed his usual strategy it would make it less hard for him to go and easier for Jenny to let him.

A long time ago his father had warned him not to let his focus stray from his ambition. 'Play by all means,' he had advised his son. 'But do not allow yourself to become too involved.' Having made the error once before of thinking he could have it all—marriage *and* a successful business—Rodrigo intended to steer well clear of such a dangerous and misleading temptation again.

In the charmingly decorated living room, with its gently ticking French antique clock, Jenny was asleep. About to shake her, Rodrigo saw that she slumbered as deeply and peacefully as an untroubled child—just as if she'd laid all her worries and cares aside. Her angelic features were slightly flushed, and her glorious hair tumbled round her shoulders in shining ringlets the hue of golden summer sunshine.

It seemed heartless to wake her to tell her that a meal was ready. Instead he divested her of the blanket tucked round her, then lifted her carefully into his arms. She barely even stirred. Just disconcertingly rested her head against his chest and gently sighed.

Clenching his jaw, because her soft, pliant body was exquisitely, painfully arousing him, Rodrigo carried her upstairs to bed. Leaving the door slightly ajar, to let the light flood in from the landing, he didn't bother to switch on the lamp. The rose scent from her skin sneaked captivatingly under his radar. It stormed his senses as he laid her down under the covers. With great care he removed her already opened dressing gown, then dropped it onto a nearby chair.

As he leaned over to tuck the covers up round her shoulders, Jenny's stunning blue eyes fluttered open. 'Mmm…' she breathed, coiling her arms round his neck. 'You smell so nice.'

He froze. She must be dreaming he thought. But then she laid her hand across his cheek, tenderly stroking it.

'You're such a good man, really…and sometimes… sometimes so hard to resist.'

'Do you know what you are saying?' he demanded huskily.

'Yes, I do. I'm wide awake, Rodrigo.'

'This is a dangerous game you're playing, Jenny Wren.'

'Don't you want to kiss me?' she whispered, her hand moving gracefully from his cheek into his hair.

His blood heating violently, Rodrigo gripped her shoulder. Self-control was suddenly frighteningly thin. 'I want much more than just a sweet, drowsy little kiss, my angel. Unless you are prepared for that, then we will stop this right here, right now.'

In answer, Jenny gazed up at him with her bewitching light eyes full of longing. Then, with a fleeting bold smile, she slanted her petal-soft lips against his.

Kissing her back fully on the mouth was like coming home at last. His fantasy of tasting her like this again was like a pastel watercolour compared to vividly sensuous passionate reality. With a rough groan, Rodrigo let his hard, sensually aching body fall against the inviting feminine curves beneath him. His lips clashed urgently with Jenny's for a short-lived second before his tongue hungrily invaded the hot purse of the sweetest silken mouth he'd ever tasted. He devoured it like a pauper at a banquet.

Arching her body to get closer, she feathered soft little gasps of pleasure over him, and as he pressed her deep down into the mattress she matched every groan and feverish demand he was meting out with equal ardour. Her small hands urgently pushed at his sweater, in search of the warm hard flesh underneath, and she tangled her long bare legs with his still jean-clad ones.

Rodrigo was left in no doubt that they were of a single mind. Sweeping the counterpane aside so he could join her in bed, he shucked off his expensive Italian loafers, jettisoned his sweater, and repositioned himself on top of her. Then he feverishly manoeuvred Jenny's simple white nightgown up over her pale thighs until his palms located her firmly defined satin hipbones. Stilling for just a moment, he unzipped his fly.

It was as if he'd left his mind at the door. Pure, undiluted primal desire was what was driving him—desire sharpened into dizzying focus by Jenny's seductive hot mouth brushing against his over and over. Her hands were moulding themselves to his jean-clad rear as she impelled him urgently towards her.

'You have bewitched me without even trying,' he breathed against her ear, and then, freeing himself, he inserted his hard aching shaft deeply between her slender thighs in a long shattering thrust. Secluded by the semi-dark, they stared back at each other in mutual wonderment.

If this was a dream then Jenny wanted it to go on for ever… It was true she *had* been lost in the most delicious sensual fantasy about Rodrigo when she'd sensed him lift her up from the couch. The warm, woody scent of him along with the colossal strength in his arms had made that fantasy blossom into the most vividly detailed erotic sequence she could have imagined.

Then she had opened her eyes, felt his warm breath on her face, and been so transfixed by the most tempting magnetic sea of ebony silk that she hadn't had a prayer of resisting.

She could fool herself by pretending she was

delirious because of her illness, or that as a result of her fever she wasn't yet in her right mind—but both would be a lie. Jenny knew *exactly* what she was doing—and why. She wanted Rodrigo more than she'd ever wanted him. Two years apart hadn't quelled that desire.

The Spaniard had intoxicated her senses from the moment he'd stepped up to her at the Savoy and so charmingly asked to know her name and if she'd like to have dinner with him. And when he'd stepped into Lily's guesthouse from out of the rain and then come to her rescue when she'd fallen ill—well…she was so *drunk* on whatever magic he'd conjured up that she could barely think straight. Even in the throes of raging fever she'd ached to be loved by him once more. *Now she had her wish.*

Although Rodrigo's kisses were greedily burning, he gulped at her as if he was drinking from the rejuvenating crystal waters of a life-giving well—as if every taste of her was too precious to spill even a drop. Moving deeply inside her, his magnificently taut male body rocked Jenny to the furthest reaches of her soul. He'd helped take care of her when illness had struck her down, even postponing his meeting. *He had never done that before.* Now, incredibly, he was meeting another great need. A need to be held and loved by him once again—a need that she'd feared would never be met again.

Rodrigo had talked about maintaining distance as friends… Surely he couldn't want to put distance between them a second time after a union as profoundly magnetic and unforgettable as this?

Cupping her hands round his arrow-straight hips, Jenny took him even deeper, locking her legs round his hard-muscled back. 'Is this good for you?' she breathed, catching a glimmer of surprise in his eyes.

'Is this *good*? You underestimate your powers of seduction, my angel. Right now my body, my heart, my soul—they are all lost to you.'

Although his words touched Jenny deeply, his smile was as sinfully delicious as a taste of decadent chocolate ice cream in the middle of a strict diet. *The kind a girl would willingly put on a couple of pounds for...*

He began to thrust harder and deeper, making Jenny cry out as he bent his head to nip the hotly tingling tips of her breasts with the edges of his teeth, then soothed them with the heat from his hot damp mouth. The dammed up feelings building inside her burst violently free. Surely the barrier restraining them had been guarded only by the slimmest of gossamer threads? As soon as she had wound her arms round Rodrigo's neck she had started to come undone...the incredibly seductive scent of his body was enough to do that alone.

A ragged cry left her throat as wave after wave of rapturous sensation bombarded her. Her heart hammering, Rodrigo's name was suddenly a heartfelt mantra of unimagined joy on her lips. Shockingly, twin rivulets of tears seeped from the corners of her eyes, mingling with the joy and pleasure. The sheer magnitude of her emotions overwhelmed her—as if every deep wound and fear she'd stored away inside her heart had suddenly surfaced at once. But Jenny scarcely had time to dwell on that as Rodrigo shivered in her arms and convulsed. Holding onto the broad, magnificent slopes of his hard male shoulders, she registered the scalding spurt of his vigorous male seed seeking its home inside her.

What have you done, Jenny? It simply wasn't like her not to think about something as vital as protection. But right then, with her body feeling so loved and languorous and her head still a little woozy from her bout of sickness, she somehow didn't care.

Resting his head on her shoulder, Rodrigo murmured something vehement in Spanish. Judging by the tone, it sounded pretty much as if he was berating himself for the same thing.

He propped himself up on an elbow, his dark gaze serious. 'I would be lying if I said I didn't know what got into me to make love with you without taking precautions, Jenny… But I want you to know I'm profoundly sorry for compromising you like this.'

'Is that all you have to say about what we just shared, Rodrigo?' Lightly, Jenny wove her fingers through the glossy sable strands of his hair.

'No.' He caught her hand, then brushed his lips across her knuckles, his expression intense. 'It is not all I have to say at all. What we just shared was incredible, wonderful...*beyond* wonderful. You are a lovely, generous, sexy woman, Jenny. Already you've made sure that I'll never forget you.'

Her heartbeat jumped in dismay. 'If you're talking about leaving then please don't. What I want right now is just to savour these precious moments we've got together without thinking about anything that makes me sad.'

'You were crying. I saw tears in your eyes.' Tracing the outline of her mouth with his forefinger, he dragged her plump lower lip downwards for a moment.

'It was overwhelming...the way you loved me. You touched feelings that I'd suppressed for a long time. Something inside me broke open, Rodrigo...something that I've held back for far too long. I feel—' Suddenly self-conscious, Jenny turned away from his intense ebony glance. 'I feel cleansed, somehow.'

'So you will sleep much better tonight. No bad dreams will come to visit you again, hmm?' Rolling over onto his side he laid his bare arm protectively across her middle.

'You'll keep them away for me,' she agreed.

Just hearing him say that the bad dreams wouldn't come made Jenny feel safe. But with her head still feeling achy and hot she sensed her body succumbing to another helpless wave of tiredness. Sighing, she snuggled down deeper into the bed. Under the covers, Rodrigo's hand moved possessively over her bare hip.

Registering the sensuous tug in her solar plexus, along with the surge of heat in her breasts, Jenny smiled. 'That's nice.'

'I have even more nice things to show you if you want.'

'You do?' *Just the anticipation made her feel boneless.*

'But there is something I need to do first.'

'What's that?'

'Sit up for me a minute.'

'Why?'

'So many questions… Have you never heard that sometimes you just need to go with the flow?'

Jenny obediently scooted up, and without preamble found her nightdress expertly pulled up over her head and flung to the side. Her skin prickled with goosebumps at the hot appreciative glance Rodrigo shamelessly submitted her to. His slow burning gaze all but devoured her.

'You are like an exquisite painting of a fairy queen come to life,' he said huskily. 'Perhaps I have dreamed you up?'

'I'm no dream, Rodrigo. I'm fallible flesh and blood, just like you. If I was a dream then I couldn't be hurt, could I?' She heard the catch in her voice.

Unperturbed by her comment, Rodrigo shrugged his shoulders and smiled. 'I don't care what you say. You'll always be my favourite fantasy…the one I'll summon when I'm alone in my bed at night after a hard day and need reminding of something beautiful.'

Not liking his reference to being alone, and the scene it conjured up of him being back in Barcelona without her, Jenny shivered. Desolate, she folded her arms over her chest. 'I'm cold, Rodrigo.'

'Then lie down with me, *querida*, and let me put the heat back into your blood to keep you warm…'

'Maldita sea!' He could hardly credit his clumsiness. That was the second mug he'd managed to break that morning. Sweeping the broken remnants into a dustpan, Rodrigo impatiently deposited them into the bin. Then he reached up to the overhead pine cupboard with its meticulously arranged shelves of bright painted crockery for another one.

He groaned as a tight muscle in his back stretched a little too abruptly. Strenuous exercise never fazed him. When all was said and done he was a man in the peak of fitness—even if lately his body *had* sometimes felt fustratingly fatigued. But last night he'd been making love to Jenny until the early hours of the morning. *And the more he'd demanded of her body, the more he'd craved.* It seemed as if his impossible desire was never sated.

His hand stilled on the coffee percolator's handle. It pricked his conscience that he might have selfishly taken advantage of her when she was not totally well, but she had more than matched his passion, he recalled. The memory of her soft inner thighs clamped round his middle instantly hardened him. He hissed out a ragged breath. The sooner he returned to work the better. He was quickly realising that the longer he stayed, the more this white-hot lust and longing for Jenny would consume him…no doubt to the detriment of his ability to think straight, concentrate on his work and all he had set out to uphold and achieve. *Just as his father had warned him it would.*

'Is there any of that coffee going begging? I can't tell you how good it smells.'

Rodrigo spun round. Jenny stood in the doorway, dressed in light blue denims and a sweatshirt that was just a shade darker than her eyes. The picture she made was stunning and fragile at the same time.

Rodrigo's heart lurched. 'What are you doing up? I told you to rest.'

'I'm sick of resting. I need to be up and about again or I'll go mad. Let me pour the coffee. I can do that much at least.'

Seeing her hand tremble as she reached for the coffee jug, he tutted. 'You are your own worst enemy—you know that? I'd almost forgotten how impatient you are.'

'I've lots of faults, that's true.'

'Come here.'

'Why?' She blinked owlishly at him.

He let her finish pouring the coffee, then pulled her into his arms. Everything about her delighted him…her slim compact body, sunshine gold hair, flawless blue eyes and pale satin skin.

Outside, a light rain fell onto the greenhouse roof and the neat flowerbeds alongside it. The air had a real crisp, cold bite to it. In an attempt to cool his ardour—as well as help distract a mind that seemed intent on dwelling on one thing and one thing only—Rodrigo had already been out walking, and the icy temperature had made him glad to return inside. It had also made him ache momentarily for the sunshine of Barcelona. But standing here with his arms wrapped round a sweetly scented Jenny he felt warm as toast and—not surprisingly—*aroused.*

'I want to kiss you good morning,' he murmured, lowering his face to hers.

Jenny ducked her head out of the way. 'You've already kissed me a hundred times this morning.' She grinned, her cheeks turning charmingly pink. 'I just hope you don't catch what I've had—then you'll be sorry!'

'Never.' He feigned a disapproving look. 'I would never be sorry for kissing you. It would be worth being struck down for a few days just to have had the chance to sample your irresistible charms again, my angel.'

'But then you wouldn't be able to go to your meeting and I'd have to look after you.'

'How tedious for you.' Rodrigo tried to hide his automatic resistance to the idea but failed.

'Why do you think that would be tedious for me?' A tiny concerned crease appeared between Jenny's neatly arched brows, 'I would relish every minute of it, Rodrigo.'

'And you would do it just because you have a naturally caring instinct, and not for any gain?'

'What gain? What are you talking about?'

'Wanting more of me than I can give.'

Unable to hide her alarm, Jenny stiffened in his arms.

CHAPTER EIGHT

'IF I TOOK care of you while you were ill it wouldn't be for any ulterior motive, Rodrigo. It would merely be because I care about you. Do you have a problem with that?'

All desire for coffee had fled. Jenny felt as if her stomach had a dead weight inside it at the suspicion and pain mirrored in her ex-husband's silky dark eyes.

Abruptly removing his arms from round her waist, he moved away, leaving her feeling as if she'd gone from summer to winter in one fell swoop.

'I don't want you to care about me.' A muscle flinched at the side of his jaw. 'I'd like us to part as friends, of course, but—'

'What?'

'When I leave it's best if you just forget about me. The commitment I have to my work is heavy. As I explained, that's why our marriage couldn't work. At least I was honest with you. A man like me hasn't the right to pursue a serious relationship when he knows that because of his dedication to business there's a high probability it will fail.'

'You must have been hurt very badly somewhere along the line to make you believe that—to believe that any attempt at a committed relationship would fail.'

'No!'

His denial was fierce. Jenny stepped back in alarm.

'Just because I happen to prefer concentrating my time and energy on making a success of my work doesn't mean that someone hurt me. The reality is that I'm aware of the false promises a relationship can breed…the false hope. Look around you—how many relationships do you see that even survive? I prefer to focus on something with a higher rate of success… something that does deliver on its promise.'

'And work can fulfil every hope, every dream of happiness, can it?'

'For me, right now, it gives me exactly what I want.'

'That sounds to me like somebody *did* hurt you, Rodrigo—or at least poisoned your mind about what can be possible as far as relationships go.'

'*Dios mio!* How have we got onto this tedious subject?'

Moving restlessly, as if his skin was suddenly too tight to contain whatever emotions were flooding him, the handsome Spaniard fixed her with a cold glare. Jenny held her ground.

'I know that we broke up and things didn't work out, but it wasn't because I didn't at least *try* to make it a success! But you- you decided not to try at all. What we had was really beautiful…have you forgotten that? And you just threw it away as if it meant nothing at all. I've thought about things a lot, lying ill in bed, and I know that for me life would be pretty meaningless if there was never anyone else to share it with.'

'To look after, you mean?'

'To take care of your husband and family isn't something to be ashamed of.' Inside her chest, Jenny's heart thudded hard. 'You talk as if it is.'

'You are right.' His expression surprisingly softening, Rodrigo nodded. 'Just because I have some issues about relationships, it doesn't mean that I think *you* shouldn't go for what you want, Jenny. A woman like you was not created to be alone. I know that instinctively.'

Stepping closer, he reached out to circle her waist again. Then, dipping his head, he gently brushed his mouth against hers. More than any of the passionate kisses she had received from him, that tender little kiss made Jenny's heart ache as if it had been cut in two…all the more because she tasted *goodbye* in it.

'How could I not wish anything but that all your dreams come true? I'm already envious of the man you'll eventually marry. When he gets a taste of your love and care he'll know what an angel he's fallen in love with.'

'And you, Rodrigo?' Tenderly laying her palm against his bronzed sculpted cheek, Jenny felt the pain in her heart constrict her voice to barely above a whisper. 'You're absolutely sure that you don't want my love and care?'

'I don't deserve it. And that's not because I'm feeling sorry for myself. I'm purely being realistic. And at the end of the day I'm too selfish to put someone else's welfare before myself, as you do. I tried to make our relationship work, but something in my make-up just wouldn't let me make it the priority it should have been. I've hurt you once already, Jenny… don't let me hurt you again.'

Sensing his stubbornness in clinging to such a damaging conviction, she swallowed hard. 'I can hardly equate what you're saying with how you've been towards me since you've been here. Now that we've been able to spend some proper time together without your work getting in the way, I can't imagine a man more thoughtful and caring…and, yes, unselfish. You could have left at any time, but you didn't. It's just not true that you're too self-obsessed to put someone else before yourself. I've seen a different side to you these past few days, Rodrigo…a side that really makes me hopeful.'

'Well, you should guard against that, because you'll only end up disappointed again.'

Fielding the huge swell of distress that welled up inside her, Jenny broke free of Rodrigo's hold. Reaching for her mug of coffee, she carried it across to the table. As she sat down she immediately sensed Cozette brush up against her ankles. Because she was so upset, she didn't gather the purring cat onto her lap as usual. Instead her glance alighted earnestly on Rodrigo's handsome yet troubled face, and it struck her hard that there were more shadows etched into those sublime angles and features than happiness.

'You claim the man I've spent the past few days with is too selfish to care for others? We're talking about the man who postponed an important business meeting to take care of his ex-wife—a man who sat beside her sickbed all night in a hard chair in preference to going to his own comfortable bed—a man who cooked for her and washed her hair. The same man who's so convinced only his work can bring him the happiness he craves. I think I need enlightening here, Rodrigo, because I'm honestly confused.'

Even before he opened his mouth Rodrigo despised himself for what he was about to say. Behind his hammering heart a small voice mocked: *You know what you're about to throw away again don't you?*

'To start with, I think you're deluding yourself about what I could potentially be like. This is a unique situation. We were brought together by the storm and by your sudden illness. In normal circumstances I *would* have put the demands of my business first. I'm not going to lie to you about that. I run a multi-million-pound international hotel chain that demands my input to ensure its continued success. I've worked extremely hard to get where I am—to enjoy the rewards it brings—and my aim is to continue to work hard. And, secondly, do you think I would have stayed on to take care of you if that old attraction between us hadn't flared up again? I'm only human, Jenny…even *I* can't resist the potent allure of sex.'

With her hands folded on the table, Jenny raised her stunned blue gaze to his. 'Is that all this meant to you…? A convenient opportunity to assuage your lust? I can hardly believe you could be so cruel.'

'I just want you to know the truth.'

'The truth… Yes, I realise that must be a real priority with you—especially when you stood beside me in front of the registrar and repeated your marriage vows as if they meant something. Clearly now I know they meant nothing to you at all. You should have told me from the beginning you were only here under duress. It would have been better if you'd just braved the roads and driven away to find another place to stay. It certainly would have been better for *me*!'

Feeling as if his words had hammered nails into his own coffin, Rodrigo grimaced. 'When I said my marriage vows I meant them. But sadly time and a large dose of reality proved me wrong,' he murmured. 'I should never have asked you to marry me in the first place. That *was* selfish of me.'

'Yes, it was, Rodrigo. It was selfish and cruel when probably all you wanted to do was have a brief sexual liaison without any inconvenient emotional strings attached.' Rising to her feet, Jenny hugged herself, as though fending off any more potentially hurtful blows. 'Well…in the light of all you've just told me I think it would be best if you just packed your things and left. You're probably itching to get back to work anyway. There's no need for you to stay here until Monday. I certainly don't want you staying out of any sense of obligation. In any case, I'm feeling more or less back to my normal self now, and I can't stay in bed indefinitely…not when I've a million and one things to do to get this place shipshape before Lily comes home.'

'Jenny—'

'What?'

She was withdrawing…shutting herself off from him with devastating intention, Rodrigo saw. The realisation put him in turmoil, even though he knew he was the cause.

'I promised I'd stay until Monday, and you are not right yet—I can see that. To reassure you, I'm not staying out of a sense of obligation or duty. It makes sense for you to take the next couple of days to fully get your strength back before you throw yourself into work again.'

'And you're suggesting that out of the goodness of your heart, are you? Forgive me if I can't quite believe that.'

At the door, her glance was scathing. Yet within the bitterness of her tone Rodrigo thought he heard sorrow, and regret too. His chest was so tight that he unconsciously rubbed his palm across it.

'You should just go on your way, Rodrigo, and do whatever's best for you. Put this whole inconvenient episode behind you and get back to the world you're clearly much more comfortable with. That's my advice to you.'

With her head held high, Jenny left him alone with his own morose thoughts…

Throwing herself back into taking care of things was what she had decided to do. If her body ached, or her head suddenly swam with heat, Jenny determinedly ignored it. She couldn't afford to be ill any longer.

Rodrigo had wounded her with his cruel words and the candid admission that the only reason he'd stayed to take care of her was because of the sexual attraction that had brought them together in the first place and his hope of having his lust fulfilled. Well, she had definitely contributed to helping him achieve *that* ambition. But—even though she was disappointed in him, as well as mad at herself for falling so hard for him again—Jenny found she couldn't regret the making love part. *It had been the realisation of a dream she had long held to hold him in her arms again.*

Now that he was leaving it would be all she had to console her over the harsh winter months back in London. Winter months during which she would try hard to keep her spirits up even as she worked at a career she'd lost heart in pursuing with any conviction, living in a small, cheerless rented flat because she'd lost the home she'd taken such pride in to a malevolent fire.

Seeking to drown out her despairing thoughts, she switched on the vacuum cleaner, running the machine up and down the hall carpet as if her life depended on it. Poor Cozette ran for cover at the frenetic, noisy activity, disappearing upstairs as swiftly as a bullet from a gun.

A short while later Rodrigo passed her in the hallway while she was working. But he barely glanced at her before he too ascended the staircase, presumably going up to his room to pack. Biting her lip, Jenny blinked back the scalding tears that surged into her eyes.

She was busy dusting the heavy oak sideboard in the living room when he appeared again. Sensing the aloof air that cloaked him, Jenny shivered. She saw that he was wearing his expensive raincoat—the one that had dripped onto the raffia mat that end-of-the-world stormy night—and knew with a heavy heart that nothing but sorrow lay ahead of her.

'So you're leaving, then?'

Pursing his well-cut lips, he nodded. 'It's not the way I would have liked to say goodbye, Jenny... whether you believe me or not. But it seems I have no choice, seeing as you've more or less told me to go. Can I settle my bill?'

You could say you refuse to leave me this way! You could say you've changed your mind. Do you think I wouldn't forgive you?

'Of course.' She made herself walk across the carpet and out through the door ahead of him. But she felt like an automaton because her senses were so numbed by grief.

Pausing by the chestnut bureau in the hall that accommodated the telephone and the reservations book, she glanced up at Rodrigo with a frown.

'What am I doing? I said I wouldn't charge you. You don't have to pay anything.'

'And I told you how I felt about that.' He proffered a gold Mastercard.

Staring at it dumbly for a few seconds, she registered the reminder that he owned a multi-million-pound business.

'Just because you've got money it doesn't mean you should always pay. You looked after me when I was sick and I'm very grateful. This is my way of saying thank you.'

'I've had shelter here too, as well as eaten your food!' His velvet-dark gaze flashed unrestrained impatience.

Distress welling up inside her at his antagonistic tone, Jenny smoothed a shaky hand across her ponytail. 'I don't want to argue about this. Please… just accept your stay here as a gift. I'm sure you're impatient to be on your way and get back to work. Here's a map of the area in case you need it.' She returned the credit card, along with a slim folded map. 'Where will you go after your meeting here?'

'Back to Barcelona.'

After shoving both items she'd given him carelessly into his coat pocket, to Jenny's surprise he captured her hand. Her heart began to race wildly.

'It's been incredible, seeing you again. I'll never forget it. Looking after you…being in this peaceful place… It provided a rest I badly needed—even though there were a couple of nights when I must have aged about a hundred years because your fever was bad. I know I said that I only stayed because of my attraction for you, Jenny, but I promise you…there was not one second when I wished I was somewhere else.'

Her long-lashed summer-blue eyes regarded him gravely. 'At one point you told me your body, heart and soul were lost to me. I know you only said it in the throes of passion, so was that a lie too?'

It took Rodrigo a couple of moments to field the anguish that deluged him and regain his composure. 'It was no lie. When I said it, I meant it. I've never said such things to any other woman before or since you. I also meant our wedding vows when I made them, and truly regret that I couldn't keep them.'

'And yet now you can leave so easily? Without even the merest suggestion that we might see each other again?'

'I would willingly see you again, but whether it would be a good idea or not is debatable. My schedule is so crazy, and you know how much I have to travel. I wouldn't want to make you any promises I couldn't keep. I wouldn't want to let you down a second time.'

'Don't worry about it. It's okay. We had a nice time together, even though I was ill, and we'll part as friends… Is that what you want to hear?'

In answer, Rodrigo pressed a light kiss to her scented cheek and let go of her hand. He stooped to pick up his laptop case and slipped the leather strap over his shoulder. 'I hope you won't stay angry with me for ever. I hope one day you can forgive me. Don't overdo things. Please take my advice and get some more rest. *Adios*, my beautiful Jenny Wren.'

He hardly knew where he was driving—just followed the instructions to take him to Penzance from the now functioning satellite navigation system which had gone askew in the storm. It was as if he was on automatic pilot.

Verdant fields, hills, quaint Cornish villages and breathtaking beaches that were a Mecca for devoted surfers passed him by in a barely registered blur. In his mind all Rodrigo saw was Jenny's dazzling tear-washed blue gaze and the slight rosy flush to her cheeks that her illness had left behind. She was the most incredible woman…*too* incredible for a lost cause like him to even imagine having a meaningful relationship with. He could see her again, yes, and for a few short weeks, months—even a year—things might go well. But sooner or later Rodrigo's addiction to his work plus his insatiable desire for greater and greater success would bear down on him *and* Jenny, and then she would despair of him, start to mistrust him, and finally declare she had had enough and leave.

Slamming the heel of his hand against the steering wheel, he spared himself nothing with his vehement curse. Then, blinking dazedly at the map flashing on the sat nav, he saw that it showed he was now entering Penzance.

CHAPTER NINE

JENNY bade an affectionate goodbye to her rejuvenated friend Lily, then returned to London and unexpected good news. There was a cheque in the post from the insurers in answer to her claim for her house.

Having waited a long time for the situation to be resolved, she now found the amount exceeded all her hopes. It meant she had a real chance to start again—to maybe buy another property, expand her business, or do whatever she wanted for a while without stressing about income.

However, nothing could make up for Rodrigo walking away. She knew that. Not when every morning she woke to the stark possibility that she might never see him again. Just the thought was like a dagger in her breast. Her senses had been in a state of frozen animation since he'd left. Before when she'd been with him she'd felt everything so *intensely.* Now she felt nothing.

The one small light on the horizon was that the money she'd received would give her some much-needed options to help improve her future. She still refused to consider spending any of the settlement Rodrigo had given her, and one day if she had the chance she would see that he got back every penny. But now that she was home again her three months in Cornwall seemed like a distant dream…especially the part where on a stormy October night Rodrigo had appeared.

Suddenly her small rented flat, with its impersonal air and lack of love, seemed too small to contain her increasing restlessness, and it was in this agitated state of mind that one dismal rainy evening she did a pregnancy test because her period was overdue. When the result showed positive Jenny dropped down onto the edge of the bath in stupefied shock. Staring down at the test, she finally registered the enormity of what she was seeing. *She was carrying Rodrigo's baby inside her.* The one event she'd believed would never happen had astoundingly occurred. But what was she going to do about it? Of course he would have to know—even if he decided absolutely he wanted nothing further to do with her *or* the child. She prayed that wouldn't be so. Hadn't he more than amply demonstrated that he wasn't exactly immune to her when they were together in Cornwall?

The following afternoon she took a break from work to visit a travel agent's. With thumping heart and a dry mouth she booked flights and hotel accommodation for Barcelona. What was to stop her? she argued silently as she handed over her credit card.

Thanks to her claim, she had the funds. Only yesterday she'd wrapped up the job she'd been working on so she was perfectly free to go. And her reasons were perfectly legitimate. Not only would she benefit from the warmer climate, but she would be able to see Rodrigo again and break the news that she scarcely believed was true herself.

He was going to be a father. Their re-ignited passion in Cornwall had made a baby…

'*Buenos dias, sennorita…* What can I get you?'

'Just a glass of orange juice please…*gràciis*.'

When the smiling young waiter disappeared back inside the busy café, with its hypnotic salsa music drifting out onto the Moorish-style terrace, Jenny leaned back in her chair and flipped through her Catalan phrasebook, vowing to familiarise herself with the language she had started to learn when she was last there. But then a trickle of perspiration slid down her back inside her cotton sleeveless shirt and she shut her eyes to bask in the idyllic aromatic sunshine as the ebb and flow of other diners' conversations sounded on the air around her.

'Excuse me…but aren't you staying at our hotel?'

Jenny's eyes opened with a start at the sound of the unfamiliar American voice. A beaming masculine face with a row of impossibly white teeth beneath a neatly trimmed greying moustache loomed back at her. An enthusiastic hand was stuck out to shake hers.

'I'm Dean Lovitch and this is my wife Margaret. We arrived three days ago, same as you. We saw you at Reception but you looked a little distracted, if you don't mind me saying, and it didn't seem right to bother you just then. We've just been to visit the Sagrada Familia. Have you seen it yet?'

'You mean the unfinished cathedral? I visited it once two years ago, when I was last here, but I fully intend to go again. I've been mainly taking it easy for the past few days rather than visit the tourist spots, to tell you the truth. I was rather under the weather before I came out here.'

'I'm real sorry to hear that. But it seems like a good place to come to if you're in need of a pick-me-up, don't you think? Mind if we join you? All the other tables seem to be taken.'

'Go ahead. I'm Jenny Renfrew, by the way.'

'It's good to meet you, Jenny.'

The couple sat themselves down opposite her—the tall, spaghetti-thin husband and his plump, diminutive sandy-haired wife. Straightening in her chair, Jenny vowed to be sociable. She was here for a fortnight, after all. No doubt there would be plenty of other warm sunny afternoons in which to ponder her life over a cool drink on a terrace somewhere. Besides… Dean and Margaret had the kind of faces that immediately instilled trust, she decided. Their manner was warmly considerate, and she wasn't surprised to learn that they had three grown-up children who had all 'fled the nest'—which was why they'd decided a long overdue holiday in Europe was called for to help them adjust.

'Are you here all by yourself, Jenny?' Margaret softly enquired as the waiter placed the glass of juice she'd ordered in front of her.

'I am.'

'You seem so young. Isn't there someone special who could have come with you?'

'You mean like a boyfriend?' Fielding the arresting vision of Rodrigo that swarmed into her mind, making her tummy flip over, Jenny wrapped her hands tightly round her glass. 'There's no one special in my life, I'm afraid.'

'Well, there seems to be no shortage of good-looking boys around, that's for sure.' Dean grinned. 'It's a wonder a pretty English Rose like you hasn't got at least a dozen of them lining up to ask you for a date. Perhaps you do, but you're just not telling? I'm sure your parents told you that you gotta be careful. I'm glad that I've got sons, quite frankly. I would have been prematurely grey if I'd had a daughter! Especially one that looked like you.'

'Dean, you're embarrassing Jenny.'

'Sorry, sweetheart.' He instantly apologized. 'Hey, I've just had a great idea. We were going to check out this supposedly incredible spa hotel this afternoon. Margaret thought she might book herself a massage, and I hear the grounds are spectacular. Want to come with us?'

'A spa hotel you said?' Inside her chest, Jenny's heart seemed to ricochet against her ribs.

'Yeah… It's owned by some local billionaire, so we hear, and just a few streets over. How do you feel about seeing how the other half lives for a while, Jenny?'

In the end she couldn't resist accompanying the sociable Americans. Despite choosing her accommodation because of its proximity to his star hotel, she'd put off confronting Rodrigo with her news for three days now, while she nervously rehearsed how to tell him about it in her head, but sooner or later she would have to see him.

But as soon as Jenny stepped out of the sultry heat into the air-conditioned foyer of the dazzling chrome and glass hotel and onto the sleek marble floor, with its chic contemporary furniture and coolly stylish décor, her heart started to thump and her legs turned to marshmallow.

Rodrigo was the owner of all this, she reminded herself.

Faced with the reality of his wealth again after two long years, she found it was almost too much to take in. The man who had sat by her sickbed on a hard rattan chair without so much as even one small complaint, the man who had made himself so at home in Lily's humble, quaint guesthouse was the owner of this incredibly chic, ultra-modern luxurious hotel and several others like it. It was indeed a sobering thought.

'Shall we have the grand tour?' Dean smiled, already walking towards a formidably smart receptionist who looked more like a catwalk model for some elite designer label than a hotel employee.

'You're very quiet, Jenny,' the diminutive Margaret whispered to the younger woman as they followed another stylishly uniformed receptionist up the sweeping marble staircase to the first floor, the soothing sound of water spilling gently into an indoor fountain accompanying them. 'I think I can guess how you feel… The scent of money is practically oozing out of the walls. It's a little bit overwhelming, isn't it?'

Her gaze on the modern sculpture and eye-catching art, Jenny was still struggling to articulate something conversational when she noticed twin doors opening at the end of the walkway they were travelling down. A tall, dark-haired, designer-suited male figure emerged ahead of a group of similarly attired people. *Rodrigo!* She would recognise him in a veritable *sea* of strangers.

Suddenly there was no audible sound at all apart from the loud roaring of blood rushing at a hundred miles an hour through Jenny's head. *Oh, God…don't let him see me… Please don't let him see me.* What was he going to think if he should catch sight of her? That she'd deliberately tracked him down, expecting something from him? She'd *die* if he thought that—even though she was expecting his baby.

He was holding open the door for his board members, or whoever they were. She saw that now. Seeing him glance casually towards their little group, she momentarily froze. In the same instant a sickening sense of nausea gripped her insides. What a moment for morning sickness to hit! Her intention had been to walk swiftly back down the marble staircase, hopefully unseen, and try to meet Rodrigo at some later date. But now, disconcerted by the nausea, she turned on her heel too quickly and a searing pain shot through her ankle. It made her stumble awkwardly and, unable to right herself, she completely lost her balance.

'Oh, God.' Suddenly she was in a humiliating heap on the floor, with every pair of eyes in the vicinity on *her.*

'Are you okay, honey? Are you hurt?' Margaret's American husband dropped to his haunches, his avuncular features genuinely concerned as he put a comforting arm round Jenny's shoulders.

'I think I've twisted my ankle. I turned on it too suddenly… That's just typical of me, I'm afraid.'

On the periphery of her consciousness she saw a striking-looking dark-suited male issue an urgent command and, glancing up, watched an almost choreographed seam appear down the middle of the small group of people that had quickly gathered round her, allowing the man to step to the front.

He stared down at Jenny with utter disbelief in his ebony dark gaze. 'Is it really you?' he husked.

'Yes, Rodrigo.' She sighed heavily, pushing a swathe of tumbling blonde hair out of her eyes, her humiliation and embarrassment total. 'It's me.'

'What have you done to yourself?'

'It's unbelievable, I know, but I think I've twisted my ankle.'

'Does it hurt?' He crouched to gently circle the slim joint with his hand.

Jenny immediately flinched at the dizzying sensation of pain, though she was not unaware of the intoxicating warmth emanating from his large smooth palm either.

'Yes, it hurts.' She despaired of the quaver in her voice—was terrified Rodrigo might judge her as feeble and clumsy. To be frank, she'd have quite liked a handy magic spell to make her disappear.

But now the handsome Spaniard was at ground level too, and Dean Lovitch was assessing him with definite suspicion in his eyes.

'Do you know this lady?' he demanded.

'Yes, I do. And you are?'

As if sensing the other man's authority, Dean slowly withdrew his arm from round Jenny's shoulders. 'I'm Dean Lovitch. My wife and I are staying at the same hotel as Jenny and we all came here together.'

'She will be all right now, Señor Lovitch. *I* will take care of her.'

'And your name is?'

'Rodrigo Martinez. This is my hotel.'

'Oh.' Getting swiftly to his feet, his face a little red, Dean placed his arm round his wife's shoulders, as if needing to bolster himself after the shock of learning Rodrigo's identity.

'Please…' Jenny whispered, her blue eyes imploring as she glanced into the hypnotic beam of Rodrigo's. 'Don't be concerned about me. I'll be okay in a minute. My friends will help me… As Mr Lovitch told you, I'm staying at the same hotel as them. Go back to your meeting, or whatever it is you were doing, Rodrigo. I'll catch up with you at a more convenient time.'

'You're in no position to tell me to do anything, Jenny. Not when you have been injured in my own hotel and I don't even know what you are doing here. I have a personal suite in the building. I'll take you there and then call our resident doctor to take a look at your ankle.'

Just as he'd done at Lily's, Rodrigo slid his arm beneath Jenny to lift her bodily against him. Registering a mixture of surprise and respect in the interested glances watching them so avidly, she tried to rouse herself to protest. But it wasn't easy when the sensation of being held once more in front of Rodrigo's wonderful chest, along with the warmth of his hard body, was besieging her without mercy.

'You shouldn't be taking me anywhere! Put me down, Rodrigo…please.'

'Not on your life, *querida.* Stop fighting me and just relax.'

'Want us to wait for you, Jenny?' Dean asked anxiously.

Jenny shook her head, attempting a reassuring smile in her new friends' direction. 'Don't let this spoil your visit, you two. I—I expect I'll see you later, back at the hotel.'

What would the couple make of Rodrigo's possessive 'take charge' stance when she'd categorically told them there was no one special in her life? she fretted.

Issuing some crisp instructions to a well-dressed hovering male colleague, Rodrigo swept past the gathered throng of curious onlookers with a purposeful stride towards the elevator, his strong arms supporting Jenny as though she weighed no more than the smallest child…

Lying Jenny down on the plush leather couch in the suite's sitting room, Rodrigo propped her injured ankle carefully up on some satin cushions. Carrying her from the hall downstairs to the elevator, then up to the suite, had been like an exquisite form of masochism. He had felt every sweet contour of her body beneath her simple summer clothes, breathed in her heat and rose-tinted scent a thousand times magnified, and whenever she'd gazed up at him with those crystalline blue eyes all he'd been able to do was fall into silence. He had missed her more than he had dreamed possible, but it wasn't something that reassured him.

What was she doing in Barcelona? Had she come to look for him? The idea all but stalled his heart, even though he knew such an undertaking was fruitless. Hadn't he made it clear enough back in Cornwall that there could be no future for them? Jenny's unexpected enchanting presence definitely raised the spectre of a familiar old fear he hardly felt equipped to deal with again.

'I'll get you a glass of water. The doctor should be with us any minute now.'

'You're always coming to my rescue.'

'Did you think I would leave you lying there in the middle of the floor? Perhaps you were hoping that some other man would come to your rescue instead?'

'What are you talking about?'

Rodrigo shrugged, not liking the dizzying surge of jealousy that gripped his guts in a vice at the idea she might even *look* at another man, let alone hope for one to rescue her. 'Did you come to Barcelona on your own, or do you have a companion? And how is it that you are here?'

She glanced at him with a distressed look. 'Yes, I came to Barcelona on my own, and no, I don't have a companion. And I'm here because I—I...'

'Yes?'

'I'm here because something has happened that I need to tell you about.'

'Did your brother come back from Scotland? Has he been bothering you again?'

'No.' Jenny sighed. 'It's not that.'

'Why did you come to the hotel instead of my apartment?'

'I didn't intentionally come here today to find you. The American couple I was with downstairs wanted to visit the hotel because they'd heard it was something special. Margaret wanted a massage, and they asked me to join them to have a look round. Now I wish I hadn't.'

'Why? Because you didn't want to see me again?'

'I didn't even know you were here! How could I know when you haven't even been in touch?' In her agitation, Jenny restlessly moved her leg off the satin cushion, grimacing as the pain in her ankle obviously registered with a vengeance.

'*Maldita`sea!* Where is that doctor?'

'I don't want to see your doctor, Rodrigo. I'd much rather you rang me a taxi so I can go back to my own hotel. I probably just need to pack some ice round my ankle and it'll be fine.'

'Don't be ridiculous.'

'I'm not being ridiculous,' she protested, huffing and folding her arms over her candy-pink shirt. 'I'm being sensible. You don't want me here—I know that. You're clearly embarrassed that I've shown up, and to top it all off in such a stupidly dramatic way too. I'm not trying to compromise you, Rodrigo, whatever you may privately think. Our meeting up again like this at your hotel is pure coincidence. Now I just want to go.'

Profoundly disturbed by the idea that Jenny would refuse any further help from him, as well as leave on bad terms, Rodrigo dropped down onto the couch beside her. Before he knew what he intended, he'd reached for her hand and brought it up to his lips. Once again the subtle but lethal rose-tinted fragrance that clung to her invaded him. Heady desire infiltrated his blood with a vengeance, searing him hotter than any desert wind might. Inside, a quiet desperation clamored to have that desire once again fulfilled. 'I didn't realise until now that I've been suffering from a faulty memory, Jenny Wren.' The smile he delivered to her widened blue eyes was unapologetically provocative.

'Meaning?'

'I thought my recollection of your beauty was unimpeachable. But now I see it was not. You're far lovelier than even *I,* who has examined you closely, could recall. When I saw you standing there with your friends I honestly believed I must be dreaming.'

Someone rapped loudly on the outer door. Biting back his intense frustration, Rodrigo rose swiftly to go and greet the resident hotel doctor.

CHAPTER TEN

THE doctor's verdict was that Jenny had suffered only a slight sprain. During the whole time that she was being examined by the smart-suited professional her mind was racing.

The startling evidence of Rodrigo's wealth and status was all around her. From the chic contemporary furniture in the fabulously designed flower-filled air-conditioned suite to the stunning art on the walls and even the timelessly elegant way he was dressed. Every tanned, whipcord-lean, hard-muscled inch of him screamed success beyond the wildest of dreams.

Even though making her mark in business had never been her main priority Jenny still felt a little insecure that she hadn't made a better go of her own venture. But the reality was that her brother's addiction and sometimes cruel conduct had sapped her energy and her emotions down to the marrow—especially when he'd instigated the court case to try and take the family home away from her. All that had been coupled with her distress at her marriage ending, and Jenny was amazed she'd been able to continue working and functioning normally at all.

As Rodrigo politely thanked the urbane doctor and then showed him out, she determinedly swung her legs to the floor. Her injured ankle had a very neat professional bandage applied round it now, but it still throbbed like merry hell. Gingerly she slid her bare foot into her flat, brown-strapped leather sandal. It didn't exactly help her confidence to feel so physically vulnerable in front of Rodrigo once more. Especially knowing she still had to tell him about her pregnancy.

'What do you think you're doing?'

The rich-accented voice at the door made her jump.

'I'm putting my sandal back on. Thanks very much for getting the doctor to see me, but I'm not intending on taking up much more of your time.'

'You said earlier that you had something to tell me?'

'I do.'

'And that is?'

As he stood there in front of Jenny, with his arms folded across the front of that elegant suit, Rodrigo's sable eyes were admonishing and yet somehow wickedly teasing too. His black hair had a burnished shine on it fierce enough to dazzle an Alps skier. Frankly, he looked like the drop-dead gorgeous cover model of an *haute couture* fashion magazine for men, and just as intimidating. When he'd helped her throw the tarpaulin over Lily's storm-threatened greenhouse he had somehow seemed far more approachable and a little less out of her league.

'I'm pregnant.'

'What?'

Jenny was glad she was sitting down. Rodrigo's stunned expression was already making her anxious. 'I did a pregnancy test when my period was late and it was positive.'

'My God.' He crossed the room to the couch where she sat. 'Why didn't you ring me straight away?'

'It's not really the kind of news you should convey over the phone, is it?' It was hard to hear herself across the sound of her galloping heart. 'I thought it was best if I came out here to see you and tell you to your face. I know you never wanted children, and the fact is we're no longer married either…but I hoped that when you heard you were going to be a father you might—you might consider the possibility of us trying again.'

Did she really have the temerity to risk suggesting such a thing? Jenny thought in disbelief. And suddenly she found herself more vulnerable in front of Rodrigo than any illness or injury could ever render her.

When he dropped down onto the end of the couch she longed to know what thoughts were dwelling behind that serious dark gaze, but she feared hearing them revealed too.

'Jenny, *querida*, I—'

She laid her hand across his. 'Don't say no straight away… Please just think about it for a while. Do you think you could do that?'

To her surprise, he moved her hand and tucked it possessively inside his.

'*Sí*… I can do that. But you have to understand what a great shock this news is to me.'

Hearing doubt and apprehension in his voice, instead of the elation she imagined most soon-to-be fathers might express, Jenny felt the hurt ebb through her, making her want to tug her hand free. However, sheer hope made her keep it where it was, resting in the delicious warmth of Rodrigo's palm.

'But not a terrible one, I hope? To have a child is the most wonderful thing, Rodrigo… I know you've always resisted the idea, but given time you might come round to seeing that it can be the most amazing blessing.'

'One thing I do know is that we cannot have you remaining at your hotel. Clearly you should stay at the apartment. I'll drive you back there myself. You can stay there with me at least until you need to go back home. That will give us plenty of time to discuss things. We can pick up your luggage on the way.'

Now she did tug her hand free. He was talking about her going home, and that wasn't what she wanted to hear at all. Telling herself that he needed time to fully absorb her news before he reached a decision about renewing their relationship, Jenny realised she had no choice but to be patient. As much as her heart ached to have Rodrigo genuinely care for her, just as she cared for him, as well as yearning for him to embrace the idea of them having a child, she would simply have to bide her time.

But it was hard when she was so in love that the depth of her feelings was like a gnawing physical ache inside her.

Her breathing hitched. Staring back into Rodrigo's sculpted handsome face, it was as though she was looking at him for the very first time. The echo of her thudding heart reverberated round her brain. 'Do you really want me to come back with you now to the apartment?' she questioned quietly. 'What about your work?'

'Did you hear me say that work was my priority today, *querida*?' His lips formed a surprisingly tender smile, the charismatic gesture charging the space and making it thrillingly intimate. Looping his arm round her shoulders, he tipped up Jenny's chin so that she was forced to meet his disturbing gaze head-on. 'Whatever else is going on, Jenny Wren…it is good to have you here.'

His warm lips brushed gently and beguilingly against hers. Jenny heard her last defence crash to the ground in a pile of rubble and smoke. Her senses were so intoxicated by him, her heart so full, how could it do anything else?

But a kiss that had started out as an affectionate caress quickly flared into something more urgent and primal as his tongue dived commandingly inside her mouth and his strong arms circled her waist to crush her to him. His hand palmed her breast. The exquisite pressure against the already throbbing sensitive tip made Jenny emit a softly ragged sigh.

Tensing, Rodrigo immediately removed his lips to stare down at her with a rueful smile. 'My apologies for taking advantage of you yet again, *querida*… especially when you're injured and hurting. But it's clear I have a tendency to temporarily lose my mind whenever I'm around you.'

She wanted to tell him it didn't matter…that he could lose his mind around her whenever he liked. But the nausea that had gripped her downstairs suddenly returned in a debilitating wave.

'Jenny?' There was definitely alarm in Rodrigo's examining ebony gaze. 'What's the matter?'

When she didn't immediately answer, because she was concentrating all her attention on not disgracing herself, he jumped to his feet and swore.

'*Maldita sea!* Clearly you are in shock after your accident. The doctor should have foreseen this… How could he have been so remiss? What was he thinking of? Let me get you some water.'

He was back in a trice, proffering a tall crystal glass. Jenny gulped down the cool, clear mineral water it contained as though it were a lifeline. A few seconds later the sickness that had so uncomfortably invaded her thankfully abated.

'It's all right. It's not shock, Rodrigo. It's just a touch of morning sickness. I'm getting used to it.'

'Oh.' He appeared to mull this over. 'The sooner I get you back to the apartment in La Ribera the better,' he announced decisively. 'Then you can rest as much as you like until you feel better.' Delving into his inside jacket pocket for his mobile, he reeled off some urgent-sounding instructions in Spanish to the person he'd called. 'My car will be at the front entrance in five minutes,' he informed her.

He'd left Jenny relaxing on the terrace beneath an umbrella, her injured ankle elevated on a chair, a fresh glass of juice and a light snack at her elbow, and returned to work. Rodrigo's plan was to finish as early as he could to rejoin her. She'd been worryingly quiet when they'd left the hotel to drive to the apartment in La Ribera—the apartment they'd once shared. Something told him it was because he hadn't acted as if he welcomed her surprising and unexpected news about the baby.

He truly regretted that, but truth to tell he'd been knocked sideways by it—as well as by Jenny showing up at his hotel as she had. The idea of becoming a father still reverberated through him like the aftershocks of a quake. Understandably, he was feeling a little dazed. Yet after their passionate night together in Cornwall he *had* worried about the possibility of such an event happening after so thoughtlessly making love to Jenny without protection. There was no question he wouldn't do the right thing by her. Their child would have everything an infant could need and more. But the impact of a child on his up-until-now independent lifestyle certainly gave him pause.

And if he'd been a bit heavy-handed about insisting Jenny stay with him at the apartment while they thrashed things out he made no apology for it. *How else could he keep an eye on her and make sure all was well?* Her complexion was still far too pale for his total peace of mind. Was the pregnancy already taking its toll on her?

Not for the first time Rodrigo found himself regretting that he'd left her that day, when she'd only just started to recover from the fever that had afflicted her. Thoughts and memories of their time together had relentlessly assailed him ever since. And sometimes during business meetings at work Rodrigo had found his attention wandering from the agenda with worrying frequency. *His father would roll over in his grave!*

Each time it had happened it had been without a doubt because he was thinking about Jenny... He was usually recalling her enchanting blonde looks, the way she always smelled so good, the way she moved her hands so gracefully to illustrate what she was saying, and most of all the way her enticingly beautiful body had felt under his again...*sublime.*

That particular stirring memory had disrupted many a good night's sleep. And the next day Rodrigo was inevitably grouchy and ill-tempered due to lack of rest.

* * *

The Barcelona apartment was situated in an impressive eighteenth century building in an area that had formerly been the preserve of the traditional fishing industry. Now it was an ultra-modern destination, packed with boutiques, chic restaurants and bars. Rodrigo himself had had a large say in the innovative interiors that occupied the building, and a couple of prestigious awards had come his way because of it. *But right now all that seemed irrelevant somehow.* The only thing that really concerned him was Jenny.

She wasn't out on the terrace where he'd left her. Cursing his inability to leave work when he'd said he would in order to be with her, he quickened his stride, thinking maybe she'd got fed up with waiting and phoned for a cab to go back to her hotel.

As he flung open all the doors in the apartment his anxiety grew. But when at last he peered into the stylish contemporary living room it was to discover Jenny, dozing lightly on one of the sumptuous white couches.

'You're back,' she said huskily, opening her eyes.

The strangest sensation seized Rodrigo… It was a heartfelt impulse to know what it might be like to come home to Jenny *every* day when he finished work…to have her say 'You're back' and not be able to hide her pleasure or joy. For a second his throat was too dry to speak.

'Did you see the sunset?' she added softly, when

he remained mute. She briefly glanced out through the opened French windows that led onto another pretty balcony. 'It's so beautiful. I can even see the spires of Gaudi's cathedral. I'd forgotten just how incredible it is.'

The dazzling amber and gold rays that flooded onto the room's burnished wood floor were *nothing* compared to the incandescent loveliness of the girl in front of him, Rodrigo thought hungrily.

Before he could stop himself he promised to take her to see the work that had been done on the cathedral since she'd last been there, before adding, 'How's your ankle?'

'A lot less painful since I took one of the painkillers your doctor left.'

'Perhaps you shouldn't take any more. You're pregnant, remember?'

'I did check with the doctor when you briefly left the room to answer the phone.' Jenny frowned. 'But of course I would be sensible about things like that.'

'I'm glad to hear it. And it's good to see that you have some colour back in your cheeks too,' he observed, unbuttoning his jacket as he moved towards her.

'Did you have another long meeting?' Drawing her legs up to the side, Jenny curved her mouth into a sympathetic smile as he sat down beside her.

'There are *always* long meetings and equally long unsocial hours when you run a business. I'm sure you remember that, since it was one of the reasons I knew it wasn't fair to you to carry on with our marriage.' He shrugged, impatiently tugging his royal blue silk tie free from his shirt collar. 'But just the same I'm sorry I didn't get back as early as I promised.'

'There's no need to apologise...I do understand.'

'You do?'

Rodrigo couldn't quite believe she meant that. He'd always been acutely aware of just how much time he spent away from home when he was working, and had been uneasy about it when he'd been married to Jenny.

'Yes, I do. You must be hungry,' she commented lightly, her summer-blue gaze dipping for a moment when he glanced steadily back at her.

'I am, but I've got into the habit of eating out most evenings when I'm here. You must also be hungry, *querida*. Shall we go out to dinner? Are you up to it?'

'I'll be fine. I've got to start putting my weight on my ankle again if I want it to get better.'

'I wasn't particularly meaning your injured ankle. I was referring to the fact that you're with child.'

Their eyes met and locked. Jenny gave Rodrigo a slow smile. 'It's not some illness, you know. I'm not going to suddenly retire from the world just because I'm pregnant!'

CHAPTER ELEVEN

'I CAN still hardly believe it.'

In one fluid, easy motion, Rodrigo got to his feet. A little anxious, Jenny watched him move to the centre of the room and then turn to face her. The last spectacular amber gold rays of the sunset turned to fiery orange before dying away completely. In its wake the room became dim and silent. Uncurling her legs, she gingerly put both feet to the floor, trying not to wince as she experimentally put some of her weight onto her bandaged ankle.

But the pain of her injury was nothing compared to the sense of desolation that was rapidly growing inside her at the idea of Rodrigo rejecting her pregnancy or thinking she was trying to manipulate him back into marriage.

'I want this baby,' Jenny said dully, folding her arms protectively across her stomach. 'I want to keep it and I will. No matter what you decide to do.'

Her throat was suddenly so tight and painful that tears were a scant breath away. But any weeping she did she resolved to do in private. It was already humiliating enough to have the father of her expected child look at her as though he'd just heard the worst news he'd ever received, without humiliating herself further by breaking her heart in front of him.

'To raise a child…' levelling his gaze, Rodrigo wiped his hand over his cheekbone '…it's best that the parents are in a stable relationship…no?'

'Ideally, I think, yes. But I know we don't live in a perfect world. People make mistakes, and sometimes it's just not possible to have a stable relationship. In that case one might decide to raise a child on one's own. I'm willing to do that, Rodrigo. If you really can't contemplate us being together any more, don't worry that I'm going to demand you support me.'

'Is this how you were with your feckless brother?'

'What do you mean?'

'I mean he demands money to feed his addictions and you simply give it to him without a fight…without standing up for yourself?'

Jenny's stomach plummeted to the ground, as though she were travelling in an out-of-control elevator. 'I didn't just *give* him the money! You have no idea how he could be. He was manipulative and cruel, and he had ways of getting what he wanted no matter how much I resisted his demands or said what I thought.' Shuddering at the memories that mercilessly flooded back, Jenny felt her eyes burn as she stared at Rodrigo. 'He used to taunt me that I wasn't a "real woman" because my marriage had failed. The fault obviously must lie with me. When insults illustrating how useless I was both as your wife and a businesswoman didn't work he used fits of pure rage to intimidate me. When that kind of thing happens more times than you care to remember your confidence in your ability to do anything can very quickly desert you, and for a while my business got into trouble because I felt so overwhelmed. I'm not proud of that. But I *am* proud of the fact that one day I woke up and took steps to end the misery—despite the horrible threats that came my way. I fought to keep the house in court, then gave Tim a more than generous price for his share of it when I won so that he could move on somewhere else. You may not know this about me, Rodrigo, but I *am* strong. Strong enough to face whatever challenges might lie ahead and not be defeated…even challenges like raising a child on my own.'

'Your worthless brother shouted at you repeatedly?'

'Yes.'

'*Cabrón!* You are well rid of him. If I had known you were returning to such a situation I would have stepped in and dealt with it once and for all.'

'I know,' Jenny sighed. 'That's why I never told you the truth about how Tim could be.'

'In any case…understand that you will *not* be raising our child on your own.'

Immediately Jenny sensed the steely resolve in his voice.

'Do you really think I would stand aside and let you do that? I may not have planned on starting a family, but that doesn't mean that I won't face up to my responsibilities. I most definitely *will*.'

A single hard-to-contain tear slid down Jenny's cheek. 'Is that the only way you view this, Rodrigo? As a kind of duty you have to fulfil?'

'My head is spinning at what you've just told me about the situation with your brother—the fact that I unknowingly let you return to such abuse. It makes me furious. But I'm sorry…I don't mean to sound so cold.' The tension in his shoulders visibly relaxing, he sat down beside her and cupped her chilled hands between his palms. 'We will reach the best solution for both the child and us—of that I am certain. Will you just allow me a little time to think things through?'

'Take as long as you want.' Too distressed to want to notice how emphatically his touch warmed her, Jenny sniffed, tugging back her hands. 'I'll give you my home phone number in England before I leave. When you've had enough time to think things over you can ring me.'

It was almost *unbearable* to be so close to the man she loved and yet feel a distance wider than the most yawning chasm. Intent on escaping to deal with her tormenting emotions in private, Jenny surged to her feet. The pain that jackknifed through her ankle almost made her cry out, but she stoically ignored it.

Before she had the chance to move away, Rodrigo

stood up beside her. Firmly turning her round to face him, he settled his hands either side of her waist. 'You are not running back to England. We'll work things out together, Jenny. Don't turn away from me…please. I don't think I could bear it.'

The desolation she saw etched in the sublime angles and planes of his beautiful face almost made Jenny catch her breath. Somewhere inside her hope leapt like a rekindled flame in a burned-low candle. 'Oh, Rodrigo…' Touching her hand to his hollowed cheek, she suddenly couldn't prevent the steady flow of scalding tears that seeped from her eyes.

Murmuring something low, Rodrigo lifted her high in his arms against his chest and stalked with her into his bedroom. In the dim half-light of the balmy evening he urgently covered Jenny with his body on the king-sized bed as though the world might end if he didn't. Then he claimed her lips again and again with hot, open-mouthed kisses as passion-driven hands tore at her clothes—removing hers, then his own, before holding her arms high above her head and linking their fingers.

As their gazes locked in the subdued evening light, with the sensual, drugging scent of late-in-the-season exotic blooms drifting up to them from the lovely gardens below, he drove himself hard into her body, his soulful dark eyes burning like the sparks of fiery embers into the walls of her heart and capturing it.

His highly charged possession registered right down to the very corners of Jenny's soul. Meeting her lover's kisses with equal mindless hunger, she felt Rodrigo's fingers press deep into her buttocks to make their bodies fit even more closely. Her senses were already drowning in the musky heat of his slick, hard-muscled male form when they were seized by her violent climax. She barely knew where the feral cry that left her lips came from, but the sea of powerful sensual release was so profoundly intense and shocking that it rocked through her like an earthquake.

Glancing up, she looked, stunned, into Rodrigo's scorching gaze. As he rose above her she recognised blazing intent as he bucked, renting the sultry air with a primeval shout of his own. And as the echoes of that heart-jolting shout died away to mere shadows he laid his dark head between Jenny's breasts, the ragged deep breaths that left his lips gradually slowing.

Letting her lids flutter closed, Jenny played softly with his hair. The dark strands were incredibly soft and silky in her hand and cried out to be touched. *If only he loved me*, she thought fervently. If only he loved our baby and me with no holds barred, as if we were the most important things in the whole world to him. Then how perfect these stunning moments would be.

But he had asked her to give him time, she recalled. And she would...she *would*.

Stirring, Rodrigo lifted his head to contemplate her with a wicked lascivious grin, before pressing his lips to her still flat, smooth-skinned stomach, deliberately letting them linger so that his heat felt like a brand. Then he glanced back at her again, and the expression in his long-lashed sable eyes made Jenny's insides cartwheel.

'It is incredible that you carry the fruit of our loving deep inside you,' he murmured, and his rich voice had a definite catch in it. 'And now you have intoxicated me like a drug, and I am indeed… addicted.'

Moving upwards again, he bent his head to suckle her rose-tipped breasts in turn, and Jenny realised that the fire which had blazed between them had embers that were all too ready to be stoked again. As he smiled into her eyes, Rodrigo's gaze was again hungry and hot.

'I'm not trying to trap you, Rodrigo…with the baby, I mean' she said softly.

'Angel, you trapped me the first moment I saw you. I have never had such a violent reaction to the mere sight of a beautiful woman before. And when I found Lily's place, on that cold and rainy night, I could hardly believe that the storm had steered me back into your presence again. But let's not talk right now…I'm too impatient for words when all I really want to do is enjoy you. Come, sit astride me, so that I can savour every beautiful inch of you.'

His big hands were careful to help her avoid hurting her ankle as they swapped positions. Then it was Jenny's turn to feast her eyes on the taut, bronzed-skinned body beneath her, with a gentle riot of curling black hair dusting his nipples, disappearing in a slim, sensual column down to his narrow-hipped pelvis. Adjusting her thighs over his, she hungrily accepted him inside her. His penetration was deep and smooth, and she moaned low and tossed her head back with the sheer wild pleasure of it. Then she started to rock a little…

'I'd like us to take a shower together before we go out to dinner,' Rodrigo told her huskily.

'What about my bandaged ankle?'

He lifted a shoulder. 'What about it? There are infinite ways we can accommodate whatever is needed, my angel.' His expression glazed with passion, he cupped Jenny's hips to rock her even harder against him. 'You can lean against me the whole time…' His breath was ragged again as he watched her move over him, her blonde hair an enticing tousled mass of corn-gold against her pale slim shoulders. 'And I can wash your hair for you, just like I did once before. I'm an expert now, remember? Then you can wash mine. Afterwards, I will redo the dressing for you.'

'Rodrigo?'

'What is it, beautiful?'

'Didn't you—?' Another helpless moan left Jenny's lips as he pushed upwards and high inside her. 'Didn't you say something about not talking?'

'*Sí.* I did. I guess you'll just have to kiss me passionately to make me stop.'

* * *

His black silk pyjama bottoms riding low on his hips, his chest bare, Rodrigo returned to the bedroom with the two cups of coffee he'd made. Last night they had agreed to give going out to dinner a miss. Instead he had ordered some food from a favourite local restaurant to be delivered, and they'd enjoyed it sitting in their robes at the huge glass table in the dining room.

Now, the sun-kissed morning light was drifting in through the large plate-glass windows, and the undrawn coffee-coloured silk curtains were moving gently either side of the frames in the breeze.

The delicate light outlined Jenny's still sleeping form. Her slim pale arms were down by her sides as she slept on her stomach in the middle of the huge canopied bed, her golden hair a riot of silk over her shoulders and her exquisitely shaped back bare to the waist.

Leaving the coffee on a bedside cabinet, Rodrigo simply stood at the side of the bed to gaze at her. Just the sight of her made the blood pound hard in his veins. And last night…last night he had been so close to confessing that he loved and adored her. *What had held him back?* She was carrying his baby, for goodness' sake!

The thought was like a small explosion inside him. Prevalent in his emotions was pride, possessiveness and joy…ecstasy, even. It hardly made sense that he couldn't voice his feelings to Jenny. But unfortunately, given his past, it *did* make sense.

Even now Rodrigo sensed his father's austere ghost looming over him—his disapproving gaze and the countless warnings he'd drummed into him about the dangers of losing his focus making him shudder. Then he thought about how his dedication to the business and his long hours away from home had doubtless contributed the unhappiness he'd seen in Jenny when they were together. Could he risk hurting her a second time? He was crazy about her. It would hurt so much more this time if things between them didn't work out...all the more because they would have a child together.

In the bed, Jenny drew her knees up under the covers, rolling over onto her side, facing Rodrigo. Her dazzling eyes opened like precious sapphires winking back at him. His blood heated as if molten honey were being siphoned through his veins.

'*Buenos días*, beautiful...I've brought you some coffee.'

Grabbing the silk counterpane in front of her as she sat up against her pillow, she made a face. 'Not coffee. I can't stomach it at the moment, I'm afraid. But you go ahead.'

'This is because you are pregnant?' Again the immense enormity of the situation facing him hit Rodrigo.

'Yes. I haven't visited my doctor yet to confirm it, but when I return to the UK I will.'

'There's no need to wait until you return to the UK to do that. I can arrange an appointment for you to see a top obstetrician at any time, Jenny. In fact I'll get onto it as soon as we've had breakfast.'

'But don't get an appointment for today, will you?'

'Why not?' Rodrigo frowned. *Was she hiding the fact that something might be wrong?*

'Because you promised we'd visit the cathedral together today, remember? When I was here last I visited it on my own, but it wasn't the same without you.'

Her sweet dimpled smile eased his fears, and he climbed across the bed so he could join her. 'Then a promise is a promise, is it not? So we'll get ready soon and go to the cathedral. The earlier the better, as the lines of tourists form quickly. And afterwards we'll have lunch at a great restaurant I know that does fine dining.'

'We could have cheese sandwiches and a bottle of squash in the park…I really wouldn't care, Rodrigo. You don't have to impress me with fine dining.'

'I've never met another woman who was so easily satisfied.'

'Did I say anything about being easily satisfied, Señor Martinez?'

Rodrigo's stomach muscles clenched hard as iron when Jenny tugged at the drawstring on his pyjamas and then, with a warm, seductive glint in her summer-blue eyes, deliberately loosened them.

'So, you want me to show you how good I am in bed, Jenny Wren?'

She met his lowering mouth with a hungry little groan. 'Yes, please!'

CHAPTER TWELVE

It was like a fairytale castle, and quite wonderful to have the chance to see it again—even more so because Rodrigo accompanied her.

As she leaned on the walking stick he'd provided Jenny gazed up at the collection of imbedded seashells in the cathedral walls, squinting in the warm early-morning sunshine to marvel at the tapering spires and curved walls, as well as the astonishing un-cathedral-like mounds of fruit that looked as if they were fashioned out of wax.

Gaudi had been a lover of nature, Rodrigo explained to her—he'd wanted to incorporate as much of nature as he could into his cathedral. Everywhere Jenny glanced was a quirky little gem, like a waterspout coming out of the mouth of a salamander or frog, and delight and awe were prevalent as she looked avidly around her. Inside, the cavernous interior was like a huge carcass that had been abandoned. But as they gazed from the walkway down at the tall cranes that were still very much part of the construction they saw that work on the Cathedral was still undoubtedly in progress. Even though the building would not be finished until around 2030 Jenny could easily imagine it filled with tall flickering pillar candles and a stunning altarpiece that the great and the good could marvel at and pay their respects.

Beside her on the walkway, Rodrigo stayed protectively close. A warm little buzz of pleasure assailed her every time she realised it. He might have experienced the cathedral many times before, but he clearly didn't take its beauty and magnificence for granted, and Jenny was certain she spent just as much time stealing furtive glances at his wonderful strong-boned profile as she did examining the stunning construction.

Leaning towards her, he whispered, 'I think it's time you took the weight off that ankle for a while. Come…we'll go back down and find a seat somewhere.'

Eschewing Jenny's idea of a simple picnic in the park, Rodrigo took her to a fabulous restaurant for lunch, which had a fleet of gleaming and expensive cars parked outside. It seemed he knew the manager well, because he was enthusiastically greeted like a long-lost friend and attention was danced upon him from the moment he and Jenny walked through the door.

Awed by the elaborate crystal chandelier twinkling above them, and the generous-sized table laid immaculately with sparkling silver cutlery overlooking a stunning white terrace, Jenny glanced down at her simple white short-sleeved blouse and aubergine-coloured skirt, praying she wasn't underdressed.

If Rodrigo's teasing sensual smile was anything to go by, she needn't have worried. Every glance he sent her way touched her like an intimate caress—as if to remind her of the passionate loving they had shared and *would* share again. And, although there were several amazing-looking women close by, having lunch with their partners or friends, it seemed he had eyes only for Jenny.

Yet as she tackled her deliciously light starter she began to feel queasy again. *This time it wasn't due to her hormones.* Why did he seem to be deliberately avoiding the topic of her pregnancy? He had asked her to give him time, but was that fair? What if he decided that he still didn't want to be with her, despite the fact they were going to have a child together? Now she didn't know if she *could* wait to have his verdict. It seemed that she'd already waited a long time for what she wanted in life.

Somewhere outside, the sound of a child's distressed crying highlighted her apprehension about the fact that her own baby's father had still not made a decision about their future.

'Rodrigo?'

'Yes, *querida*?'

'I need to talk about our situation…about what's going to happen?'

His fingers twirled the stem of his wine glass.

With a brooding expression, he lifted his gaze. 'I asked you to give me some time, did I not?'

'We don't have to get married again, if that's what you're worried about. We can still raise a child together unwed.'

But even as the words left her lips Jenny's acute sense of distress pressed in on her, like a claustrophobic bubble about to swallow her up. More than anything she'd always yearned for a family of her own. She'd waited so long to have her dream come true—had endured enough disappointment and hurt to last a lifetime. From across the table she observed Rodrigo's shuttered expression, and she couldn't help wondering if she was about to endure *more*.

'This is not easy for me,' he breathed.

'I can see that.'

His mobile phone rang. Reaching into his jacket pocket, he didn't ignore it, as Jenny had hoped he might. He spoke entirely in Spanish to the caller. She was completely excluded from the animated conversation.

When it came to an end Rodrigo leaned towards her, his air definitely distracted. 'I apologise for interrupting our meal with that call, but something has come up at the hotel that needs my attention. In fact...' he glanced down at the solid gold diver's watch that so expensively circled his tanned wrist '...I'm going to have to leave you for a while, I'm afraid. Would you mind very much if I arranged for my driver to take you back to the apartment when you've finished eating? All your needs will be catered for—you only have to ask. It's vital that I get back to the hotel for a meeting as quickly as possible.'

'You mean you're not even going to have lunch with me?'

'I'm sorry, Jenny. But this is very important.'

'And what we were just discussing *isn't*?' Crushed that he was proposing to abandon her in the restaurant to finish her lunch alone, Jenny picked up her linen napkin and threw it onto her side-plate. Searing colour scorched her cheeks as she faced him.

'Of course it's important.' Scowling in frustration, Rodrigo drummed his fingers on the table. 'But I have responsibilities—'

'Don't we all? I understand you're committed and dedicated to your job, Rodrigo—you wouldn't be such a resounding success at it if you weren't. But sometimes we have to balance our priorities, don't you think? Sometimes there are other forms of success besides work. And if the fact that in a few months' time you're going to be a father isn't a priority, then I honestly don't know what is!'

She pushed to her feet, forgetting about her still bandaged ankle, and almost lost her footing. Immediately Rodrigo came round to her side. But when he circled Jenny's waist with his arm she angrily threw him off. Right then she didn't even care if they had an audience.

'If you're leaving to go back to the hotel then I'll leave now too,' she told him, mentally garnering every bit of resolve not to cry. 'To tell you the truth, Rodrigo, I don't think I'm so keen to stay with a man who'll always put work before his personal life anyway—especially when he has a child to consider. What if our baby was ill and I needed you with me as his father, to be supportive? Would you say *Sorry, but I've got to get back to work?* Don't bother with a reply... Going by past experience I think I already know your answer.'

The Black Mercedes drew up in the private car park of the spectacular glass and chrome hotel. In the elegant, luxurious confines that separated them from the driver, Rodrigo tugged Jenny's pale slim hand onto his lap. His expression was racked and conflicted, she saw.

'Do you know how bad I feel about leaving you like this?'

'If you feel so bad then you'll postpone your meeting...at least for a couple of hours...so we can talk,' Jenny returned reasonably.

Scraping his fingers through his ebony mane, Rodrigo emitted a long frustrated sigh. 'I'm afraid that's impossible.'

'Impossible meaning you can't postpone it, or you *won't*?'

'*Dios mio!* An extraordinary meeting has been urgently called, with half a dozen shareholders waiting on my decision about a considerable financial undertaking for the hotel, and I absolutely *cannot* postpone it. Initially I instructed my second-in-command to stand in for me, but when I spoke to him at lunch I realised he was not as fully informed about the deal as I am. I'm genuinely sorry about this, *querida*, but we will talk as long as you want when I return. I promise you.'

With a quick kiss on her cheek, and the drift of his tantalising cologne lingering in the space he'd left behind, Rodrigo knocked on the glass partition to give some instructions to his driver and in a flash… was gone.

Never before had he endured such hard-to-bear impatience. It was like torture. As his driver weaved the car through the converging traffic, with furious horns being honked loudly and drivers gesticulating wildly, Rodrigo almost…*almost* wanted to get out and walk back to the apartment.

For about the hundredth time he checked the time on his watch. Leaving his delighted shareholders toasting him with champagne after the mutually satisfying outcome of the meeting—as well as the extremely healthy financial report his accountant had given them—he'd all but knocked them over to get out of the boardroom.

Dragging his tie away from his shirt collar, he glanced out of the tinted car windows and gritted his teeth. *All he wanted to do now was get back to Jenny.* He should have postponed the meeting. His portfolio and kudos were such that he could have easily put it off until it was more convenient. Now, remembering Jenny's disbelieving face and angry declaration that she wasn't so keen any more to be with a man who put his work first, Rodrigo wished he *had*. Oh, why had he messed up again when he'd been given an incredible second chance to make things right?

A sight suddenly transfixed him. The car had purred to a stop to let a small family cross the road in front of them. There was an older woman, with a red tint in her hair, and a pretty young couple with a baby. All three of them were fussing and cooing over the infant, until Rodrigo's driver beeped on his horn to indicate to them that they could safely cross, and suddenly Rodrigo was deluged by his need to hold Jenny close and confess his adoration and love for her—to make her see how sorry he was for being such an idiot.

Why on earth had it taken him so long to realise what a precious jewel he had in his grasp? Had he been blind? What if after this new disappointment she completely gave up on him and left him for good? Although it was totally his own fault, he didn't think he could bear it. She was carrying his baby, and—given the chance—he *would* be the supportive father she yearned for him to be. Never again would he put some damn board meeting before *her*. Somewhere along the line he'd lost perspective. Being a success in business had become like a runaway train.

Rapping on the glass partition, he spoke rapidly to his driver, opened the passenger door and leapt out.

With his heart pounding and the sweat sticking his shirt like glue to his back in the sultry afternoon sun he sprinted hard all the way back to the apartment.

She was gone. With mounting shock Rodrigo found the bedroom empty of all her baggage and belongings. The luxurious apartment had never felt so lonely or so empty—apart from the first time Jenny had left, that was.

With a despairing oath he prowled the rooms, searching for clues that might tell him where she'd gone. There wasn't even a note. However, he did find a scrap of paper with her address and telephone number back in the UK written hastily on it, left poignantly on his pillow.

Hardly daring even to mentally articulate the conclusion that was rapidly forming in his mind, he rang the concierge to have his worst fears confirmed: Jenny had indeed ordered a cab to take her to the airport…

Thankfully the airport manager had been a fantastic help. He'd had to waive quite a few airport regulations to get Rodrigo as far as the passenger lounge where customers waited before boarding their flights. Now, with his impatient gaze scanning the sea of heads, he felt his heartbeat almost careen to a standstill when he spied Jenny on a seat at the back, in deep conversation with a young, curly-haired youth dressed very casually in baggy denims and an equally baggy sweatshirt.

Rodrigo straightened his silk tie and stole a couple of moments in which to compose himself. His heart was still pounding. Suddenly, as if she'd sensed his presence, Jenny glanced up, her gaze colliding in astonishment with his.

Moving to stand in front of her, he felt the words he so desperately wanted to say die on his lips as he glanced avidly into her stunning summer-blue eyes.

'Forgive me,' he finally breathed. 'I've been such an idiot! I should never have gone to that meeting instead of staying and talking to you.'

'What are you—what are you doing here, Rodrigo?'

He grimaced. 'More to the point, *mi angel*…what are *you* doing here?'

She dipped her head. 'I'm flying home. I would willingly walk through fire for you, Rodrigo, but I won't stay around where I'm not wanted. When I saw that you were quite willing to leave me alone at lunch and go to a meeting, I realised that it was no different from the first time we were together. It's your business that means the world to you…not me or our baby. I'm afraid that Barcelona suddenly lost its charm.' She swallowed hard. 'When I get home we can discuss things on the phone. I left my number on your pillow.'

'You would walk through fire for me, you said?'

'I love you. Didn't you know that?'

With a racing heart, Rodrigo dropped down into the shiny hard chair next to her. When the curly-haired young man Jenny had been talking to openly stared at him he pierced him with a steely gaze and said, 'Do you mind? I'm having a private conversation with my fiancée.'

Jenny gulped, pressing her hand against her heart. 'What did you say?'

'Wait a moment. I want to do this properly, Jenny Wren.'

To her utter amazement, Rodrigo dropped down onto his bended knee in front of her. Several heads in the lounge's vicinity swivelled interestedly. Reaching for her hand, he raised it to his lips. The warmth of his mouth made her insides dissolve as surely as ice cream beneath a blazing sun. 'Will you marry me Jenny—and this time for good? Marry me and make me happier than I'm sure I deserve.' Removing the solid gold signet ring from the little finger on his left hand, he slid it onto Jenny's wedding finger.

'Are you serious, Rodrigo?' She couldn't help the husky catch in her voice. The whole scenario was overwhelming...*surreal*, even.

'More serious than I've ever been about anything in my life,' he answered, grinning. 'The business has always meant a lot to me...I don't deny that. My father drummed it into me from a young age that I should strive to make a name for myself in business...

that I should work hard and not be distracted from my focus. Not even if I fell in love. But the dream of success he sold to me was *his*, not mine. My mother was the wise one, but it took me until today to realize just *how* wise. She wanted me to have a family, Jenny. She told me it was the most important thing and she was right. And even though her relationship with my father was not exactly made in heaven she believed in the legacy of a loving family with all her heart. Now my own feelings echo that. You and our baby mean the world to me and I will always endeavour to put you both first…I swear it.'

'Do you mean that?' As she bent down to whisper the question, Jenny found her lips captured eagerly and hungrily, and for long moments she forgot everything but the sensation of the delicious pressure of Rodrigo's passionate mouth on hers.

Drawing away from him after a while, she was shocked to hear the steady resounding echo of applause in her ears. Several people were on their feet in support, and when Rodrigo also got to his feet he winked at Jenny, then turned to give their audience a highly theatrical bow.

As he pulled her back into his arms she gazed up eagerly into his loving dark eyes and smiled. 'I reckon that wild storm *did* bring you to me that night, Rodrigo. It took me a while to believe that fate had brought you back…given us a second chance…but now I don't doubt it. I'm just so grateful, my love.'

'And I echo the words I told you then… My body, my heart and my soul are yours for ever, my bewitching Jenny Wren. I pray you never have cause to doubt it, but I swear I will spend the rest of my life showing you how ardent I am!'

There's a Mills & Boon® series that's perfect for you. We publish ten series and, with new titles every month, you never have to wait long for your favourite to come along.

Blaze®

Scorching hot, sexy reads
4 new stories every month

By Request

Relive the romance with the best of the best
9 new stories every month

Cherish™

Romance to melt the heart every time
12 new stories every month

Desire™

Passionate and dramatic love stories
8 new stories every month